SILENT MANIFEST

SEAN O'BRIEN

EDGE SCIENCE FICTION AND FANTASY PUBLISHING
An Imprint of HADES PUBLICATIONS, INC.
CALGARY

Silent Manifest

Copyright © 2019 by Sean O'Brien

This is a work of fiction. Names, characters, places, and incidents are the products of the author's imagination or are used fictitiously and are not to be construed as real. Any resemblance to actual events, locales, organizations, or persons, living or dead, is entirely coincidental.

EDGE SCIENCE FICTION AND FANTASY PUBLISHING
An Imprint of HADES PUBLICATIONS, INC.
P.O. Box 1714, Calgary, Alberta, T2P 2L7, Canada

The EDGE Team:
Producer: Brian Hades
Acquisitions Editor: Michelle Heumann
Edited by: Kathryn Shalley
Cover Design: 100 Covers
Book Design: Mark Steele

ISBN: 978-1-77053-192-5

EDGE Science Fiction and Fantasy Publishing and Hades Publications, Inc. acknowledges the ongoing support of the Alberta Foundation for the Arts and the Canada Council for the Arts for our publishing programme.

Library and Archives Canada Cataloguing in Publication
CIP Data on file with the National Library of Canada
ISBN: 978-1-77053-192-5
(e-Book ISBN: 978-1-77053-191-8)

FIRST EDITION
(20190730)
Printed in USA
www.edgewebsite.com

Publisher's Note:

Thank you for purchasing this book. It began as an idea, was shaped by the creativity of its talented author, and was subsequently molded into the book you have before you by a team of editors and designers.

Like all EDGE books, this book is the result of the creative talents of a dedicated team of individuals who all believe that books (whether in print or pixels) have the magical ability to take you on an adventure to new and wondrous places powered by the author's imagination.

As EDGE's publisher, I hope that you enjoy this book. It is a part of our ongoing quest to discover talented authors and to make their creative writing available to you.

We also hope that you will share your discovery and enjoyment of this novel on social media through Facebook, Twitter, Goodreads, Pinterest, etc., and by posting your opinions and/or reviews on Amazon and other review sites and blogs. By doing so, others will be able to share your discovery and passion for this book.

Brian Hades, publisher

Chapter One

"What's wrong, Blueberry? Don't like your potassium infusion?" Donn patted the glass canopy of pod 8-Delta-8. Although the tiny occupant of the pod was not in life-threatening danger, Donn nevertheless was concerned. He was about to speak more gentle words of encouragement when he was interrupted.

"Caretakers and crew, good morning," OSIRIS' calm computer voice greeted him. "Please rise and repeat with me our prayerpledge."

Donn stood at attention and awaited the recitation. His mind was on the upcoming full assessment he had planned — Blueberry had been less responsive to her potassium therapy than he had expected. If she didn't show significant signs of improvement today, he would have to upgrade her status to Serious. He hadn't put any of his swimmers on that footing in three months.

At the computer voice's command, Donn stiffened and spoke in low and reverent tones, even while he committed the barest of thoughts to the words. "I promise to ensure the health and well-being of those within my care, and through them, ensure the continued vitality and dominion of the human race. I will put nothing ahead of the mission to secure humanity's future in the stars. Amen."

Donn relaxed as he spoke the final word, and looked towards the master board that dominated the interior bulkhead back near the bay's entrance. All 1,728 lights shone a steady pale green. No one was in crisis, of course — he would have known long before the master board lights changed. He regarded the perfect symmetry of the board, arcing above the control saddle in an impressive panorama.

Even from his vantage point deep into the bay, he had an unobstructed view of the board.

There was something at once satisfying and unnerving about the uniformity of the pattern — twelve banks of twelve-by-twelve grids, all shining back at him. All the panel told him was that no one was in biochemical crisis. It did not tell him what he truly wanted to know.

He resisted the faint impulse to simply trust the lights and forgo the assessment. He knew Blueberry was hovering close to danger, and although her numbers were within the preset tolerances, Donn knew that she was only a few percentage points off amber.

"All right, OSIRIS, I'd like to have Agnes now," Donn said to the air. He turned away from the master board and headed to the wide, deep, and tall arrangement of pods in his bay. He smiled without thinking. The indicator lights did not do justice to the majesty of the sight before him. Over seventeen hundred glass-canopied pseudowombs, each one the size of a small oven, lay in the dim, blue-tinged light of the bay.

"Agnes, you ready?" Donn said, standing before pod 1-Alpha-1.

A new voice — a facet of OSIRIS' complex computing power — greeted him. "I am. I should remind you, Donn, that full assessments are only required once per trimester. This will be your twenty-fourth full assessment."

"I know, Agnes. I'm off my goal of one per week," Donn smirked.

"That was not what I meant," Agnes said, and Donn thought he could hear a prim frown. Despite her total lack of a corporeal body, this part of the ship's computer was almost as real to him as the preborns under his care.

She continued, "You are not following procedure with these frequent assessments."

Donn paused, his hand resting lightly on the smooth, curved surface of pod 1-Alpha-1's glass canopy. Agnes had nagged him before about his schedule (he knew he was to blame for that, since he had helped choose her personality from OSIRIS' bank almost nine months ago when the voyage had started) but she had never before sounded menacing.

"Well then, all I'd say is for you to check the description of a caretaker's duties. What does it say about regular assessments of pods?" He had stopped smirking.

"Caretakers will assess each pod at least once per trimester. More frequent assessments will be held at the caretaker's discretion when the need arises." Agnes voice was flat.

"There you are. I'm determining the need has arisen. Now, can we get on with this?"

Agnes did not answer immediately, and Donn was about to call her name again when her voice came through. "Yes. Pod One-Alpha-One. Standing by."

Donn hesitated a moment before selecting the peepers from his multitool. Detaching from the heavy mutitool, the peepers allowed him to see through the opaque glass of the pseudowomb and observe the tiny preborn within. The master control board had indicated this preborn, whom Donn had long ago nicknamed "Prima Donna" due to her position as 1-Alpha-1, as healthy. Had he wished, he could have pulled up her numbers from the master control saddle, or looked in on her from there. But it was something far more visceral to be here, physically close to the developing baby. To press his hands against the warm glass, as he might caress a mother's belly. In the calculating part of his brain, he knew he was getting very little additional information from a visual inspection, but he didn't heed that. It was important.

"Lookin' good, Donna," he said, and spoke to Agnes. "All good. Advance, please."

The pod slowly swung up on its track while another took its place and snapped into the receiving house, ready for inspection. The faint hum of the conveyor track stopped as 2-Alpha-1 waited patiently for Donn to pass it along.

"Hey, Tootsie," Donn said, patting the glass canopy and peering inside. All looked normal. Donn bade Agnes advance the pod again.

The procedure continued for dozens and dozens of pods: Donn greeting each preborn with their own special nickname, checking the physical development, patting or smoothing the canopy, and asking Agnes to move along. If he did not need to make any adjustments, it took him perhaps twenty seconds per pod. But there were frequent disruptions in his routine.

"Okay, let's see how Lunchpail is doing." Ninety minutes later, Donn was watching pod 11-Beta-2 click into place. "Agnes, didn't Lunchpail have a pH problem last check?"

"Negative."

Donn caressed the canopy. "I was pretty sure he did," he said, punching up the readout on the pod casing and scrolling through biochemistry tests. "Yeah, here we go. He was seven point three seven last check, and he's at seven point three six now. So we need to nudge that up."

"That number is within tolerances," Agnes said.

Donn sighed. "Not this again. How many times are we going to have this discussion? Yes, I'm aware. The range is seven point four five to seven point three five. I know. But I don't want Lunchpail to be hovering near the acidosis side of the number, okay? So please adjust the umbilical feed towards the alkaline by point zero four over the next twenty-four hours."

"I need your express order to override the—"

Donn lost his patience. "Authorized! Override the protocols and change the damn fluid balance!"

Agnes met his frustration with prim calm. "Override accepted. Change log updated."

Donn smoothed his coveralls and attempted to calm himself as well. "Agnes, please place a monitor tag on Lunchpail's pod."

"I don't understand the designation 'Lunchpail.'"

Donn tapped the canopy. "This one. Eleven-Beta-Two."

"Acknowledged. Monitor tag set." Agnes' voice dropped a half octave. "You really shouldn't refer to the pod by these names you've invented, Donn."

"Advance, please. Why not?"

Lunchpail's pod swung upwards and Mighty Mite's pod slid into place in the viewing platform.

"Because, for one, you know they won't keep those names when we make planetfall. So you'll have to learn whole new ones then when the parents are assigned."

Donn peered into Mighty Mite's pod, noting that his growth had accelerated nicely. "Mighty Mite's name already doesn't fit him. Or maybe it does — he's gone from undersized to on the high end of normal. So he's gone from mite to mighty. Done with this column," he said, patting the canopy of 12-Beta-2.

The hidden machinery hummed as a new column of pseudowomb pods loaded into the feeder system. "And anyway, who says I will have to abandon their nicknames? I think it'll be neat for each of them to have something like that. Makes 'em special."

He grinned at the ceiling where the electronic entity of OSIRIS, and therefore Agnes, existed — if the computer could be said to exist anywhere. He knew he was in violation of standards and practices with his nicknames, but he enjoyed the feeling.

"Donn, you must realize that it will be a serious violation of procedure to maintain your caretaker relationship once the preborns have exited their pseudowombs and placed with their assigned parental units."

Donn laughed as 1-Gamma-2 locked into place. "Shit, Agnes. Could you say that any more coldly? You mean, when the babies are born and given to their parents, don't you?"

"I am observing proper nomenclature. As you would do well to do."

"Oh, is that so? And if not? What are you going to do? Replace me?" Donn chuckled. "Almost twelve light years from Earth. I think my job's pretty secure." He looked into the pod. "Well, Kikiboots, let's take a look at you."

Agnes said, "You have fourteen separate formal violations on your record, and more than twice that many admonishments. You must conform to standard practices. It is for the good of the future colony, Donn."

Donn patted Kiki's canopy and nodded. Coming along very nicely. "Advance, Agnes. And let me get something clear to you. I take the colony's future very seriously. You think naming these embryos," he said, placing both his hands on 2-Gamma-2 as it slid into place, "is subverting the stability of the colony? Or performing multiple assessments? Or making minor adjustments to help them thrive? Shit, Agnes, I want each one of my swimmers to be healthy, productive, and happy members of the colony."

"And the nicknames help?"

Donn glanced at Garnet's body, folded in on itself in fetal sleep, and checked the synthetic placenta filter. It had been running a little inefficient last time, but now was registering as perfect. "Advance. They do, yes."

"How?"

"Because I also want them to be individuals. Look at this, Agnes," he said, sweeping his hand at the huge bay where his hundreds and hundreds of preborns waited. "This isn't how this was meant to be. I understand why it needs to be this way, but this isn't natural. So if I can counter this, just a little, with a stupid nickname, then by Jezeus, I'm going to."

The echo of his words rebounded through the cavernous bay. When the reverberations had died down, Agnes spoke. "Regardless. Your flouting of protocol and procedure must be noted. In accordance with Standards and Practices section six, subsection two, I am placing an admonishment in your file once again for improper—"

"OSIRIS, shut down Agnes. I'll do the rest of this manually."

The computer voice changed to the soft, androgynous tones of OSIRIS. "Agnes personality facet muted. Manual control established."

Donn nodded and checked on 3-Gamma-2. "Sorry about that, Peanut. Mommy and Daddy were having a discussion. Though I guess I shouldn't call myself that. And definitely not Agnes." He patted the canopy then reached for the manual advance button on the side of the feed apparatus.

Disabling Agnes slowed him down significantly, and he knew the act had been a petulant one: he had not prevented the official admonishment by shutting her up. Indeed, he may have earned another violation, if Agnes decided to take computerized umbrage at her silencing.

"There are definite disadvantages to artificial personalities, Wonder Girl," he said to 4-Gamma-2.

Ten hours later, Donn was significantly behind. He had stubbornly refused to recall Agnes, even though the manual interfaces required more time. He pushed the peepers up to his forehead and rubbed his eyes as 4-Theta-8 snapped into place. He summoned up some cheer for the preborn, knowing full well the developing human could in no way perceive him. "Hey, it's Daisy! Hey, Daisy. Let's take a look at you."

He grabbed the peepers and prepared to settle them back on his eyes when OSIRIS' voice suddenly sounded in the bay. "Alert. Catastrophic pod malfunction in bay K-seven. Repeat, catastrophic pod malfunction in bay K-seven."

Donn looked up from Daisy's pod and said, "K-seven? Where's Thom?"

"Caretaker Agee is in bay K-seven."

Donn dropped his peepers and ran to the exit hatch of his own bay, slapping the "open" control on the hatch. As it cycled open, he said, "What's happened? What kind of malfunction?"

OSIRIS said calmly, "Unknown. Pod One-Mu-Twelve biomedical sensor failure. Correction: second pod malfunction. Two-Mu-Twelve also unresponsive."

Donn's training reasserted itself and fought off panic. "Is there an environmental problem? Breach in the hull, venting atmosphere?" Even as he suggested the idea, he knew it was wrong. The pods were sealed against such a hazard, and were secure in their holding areas. A hull breach would not affect them unless it was enormous, and then, it would not affect them one at a time.

"I'm reading normal environment in bay K-seven. Now reading a third malfunction. Pod Three-Mu-Twelve inoperative."

The exit hatch finally opened and Donn stepped through. He turned left and hurried towards K-7. The corridor curved upward slightly, but because of the ship's spin, the floor was always down to him. Even as he ran, OSIRIS added, "Fourth malfunction. Pod Four-Mu-Twelve inoperative."

He sprinted the length of the corridor to K-7's entrance hatch, shouting as he ran. "What's going on in there? Tell me what you see."

"Internal cameras offline. Fifth malfunction. Pod Five-Mu-Twelve inoperative."

Donn saw the closed corridor hatch ahead of him. "OSIRIS, open hatch K-seven-eight junction."

"Acknowledged. Cycle begun. Sixth malfunction. Pod Six-Mu-Twelve inoperative."

Donn slowed to allow the junction hatch to open, then stepped through and continued his run. He was now in Thom's corridor. The difference in decor was striking, and in the past, Donn had marveled at the painstaking detail Thom showed in the artwork.

Mythological creatures of every description festooned the walls in a long, unbroken mural. There was no consistency to the mythos — Chinese dragons cavorted freely alongside leprechauns while a djinn took tea with Paul Bunyan.

Donn had always admired the effort Thom had put into the decoration, but was faintly disturbed by it. Now, though, he did not give the creatures a second glance, instead focusing on the entry lock. Above the lock, Thom had written in stylized old English script, "Here There Be Dragons."

Squinting briefly at the environmental condition display — all green lights — Donn hit the "open" button. The hatch began to cycle open. OSIRIS chimed in again, "Seventh malfunction. Pod Seven-Mu-Twelve inoperative."

He didn't know what he expected to find, but feared some conduit had exploded or an electrical system had gone berserk and that Thom was doing his best to cope with the disaster.

Then why hadn't Thom himself called for help?

As the entrance hatch cycled open with agonizing slowness, Donn swore in frustrated impotence as OSIRIS announced the failure of an eighth pod.

Donn angled his body through the hatchway as it began to iris open. The bay was structurally identical to his own, though Thom had continued his fanciful decorations into the bay itself. The bay was brightly lit, and the ranks of pods trailed off into the distance. Donn headed deep into the bay, towards Rack 12, the farthest from the entrance.

He could hear the retrieval system in use. Pods were traveling in a steady progression from their spots in the bay to where Thom stood, perhaps fifty meters away.

Before his conscious mind could accurately analyze all the elements before him, Donn knew the situation was horribly wrong. Details added up swiftly: the pod retrieval system was moving too quickly for Thom to do any kind of accurate check on each pod. There was also something shiny and moist on the deck where Thom was standing.

And the air had a sticky, sweet odor.

All this Donn noticed in a scant few moments as he dashed deep into the bay, passing rows and columns of pods. He opened his mouth to call to Thom.

The caretaker of K-7 calmly raised the heavy wrench-like multitool he was holding and brought it down with shattering force on the glass canopy of the approaching pod.

OSIRIS intoned, "Ninth malfunction. Pod Nine-Mu-Twelve inoperative."

Donn yelped incoherently, his mind temporarily unable to understand what he saw. For an instant, he saw in his memory the battlefield in low earth orbit, three years ago, when the Starfish fleet had appeared out of nowhere and begun their attack. In his LEO fighter, climbing with jets straining, he saw his fellow pilots blasted into oblivion with astonishing speed and efficiency. He could not then immediately understand the enormity of what he was witnessing — Earth's defense fleet, and his friends and comrades, smashed to uselessness in a matter of minutes by the star-shaped alien fighters.

And now, he saw a caretaker calmly murdering the blameless lives he had pledged to protect.

Like he had three years ago in orbit, he did not stop to think. He launched ahead, heedless of the consequences. Donn closed the distance with wide strides and then left his feet, sailing through the air in a perfect open-field tackle against the caretaker.

Thom had manually advanced to Pod Ten-Mu-Twelve and had raised his multitool again when Donn's shoulder smashed into his midsection. Both men went sprawling to the deck. Donn felt the soft flesh of Thom's abdomen give with the impact, and felt the heavy multitool glance off his own leg as Thom dropped it. Thom's body jackknifed in half and landed a few feet away, while Donn himself landed heavily on the deck, his momentum arrested by the sticky substance that coated it.

The left side of his face was on the deck, and he tasted the warm, salty-sweet fluid. He knew with sick horror that this was synthetic amniotic fluid — wine-colored fluid that had gushed off of the pods when Thom had smashed them. His eyes focused after the tackle, and he saw a glistening figure, dark brown and curled in a helpless pose, a few meters away on the deck.

One of the preborns had fallen out of its pod.

The umbilical was still attached to the preborn, extending eight or nine centimeters before terminating in a gruesome ragged end. It was no longer connected to the pod.

Thom groaned and the sound brought Donn back to the situation. He pushed up from the deck, his skin sticking slightly to the amniotic fluid, and scrambled towards the caretaker.

"What the fuck are you doing?" he shouted, climbing up Thom's body until he reached the man's bearded face. Thom's legs were coated in amniotic fluid, and his eyes, two pools of white in a craggy, hair-covered face, were wild.

"Save them! Save the children!" Thom screamed.

Donn stared at him for a moment, lost. "Save them? You were killing them!"

"Help me save them! It's better this way!"

Despite the insanity of Thom's utterance, the words reminded Donn that the preborns might still be rescued. "OSIRIS! Alert all K-Deck caretakers to get to K-seven. Tell them to bring all the portable ELS units they can."

OSIRIS acknowledged the command. Donn glared at Thom once more, then pushed off him and turned to the preborn he had spied on the ground. He crawled to it, hoping. It was only one month before its scheduled birth — maybe it had survived and was breathing on its own.

When he reached the baby, he knew it was dead. Its skull had been partially beaten in, and multiple lacerations across its head and face told the rest of the gruesome story. Thom's attack with the heavy multitool must have staved in the pod canopy, and the force of the blow had hit the preborn along with glass shards from the canopy.

At least it had most likely died quickly. Donn swallowed and patted the baby once before scanning the ground for the others.

He felt his gorge rising as he realized he was standing in a graveyard. Nine infant bodies lay all around him, moist and unmoving.

No, one was stirring. He walked to it, his deck shoes making obscene sticking noises in the pseudoamniotic fluid, and gingerly examined it. The baby was alive, though badly hurt. He could see the wounds on its shoulders and chest, blood mixing with the clear fluid of the pseudowomb. The baby's eyes were open, and they looked about in wonder at this new, deadly world into which it had been thrust.

"Shh, shh ... it's okay ... you're gonna be okay," Donn said, his hands moving hesitantly towards the infant. He was loathe to move it, in case it had a spinal or head injury, but he needed to stop the bleeding and assess it. If he could get it to one of K-7's emergency life support units, maybe this baby had a chance.

He took a deep breath and reached to lift the baby from the deck when he saw movement out of the corner of his eye.

Thom had risen and hefted the multitool.

"No! Don't save it ... this is the best for them," Thom said, advancing on Donn and the baby.

Donn had no choice. He lay the baby back down and raised his arm in time to deflect the downward smash from Thom's makeshift weapon. He felt the heavy metal of the multitool on his forearm and winced in pain even as he redirected the blow. The force of the impact sent Thom off-balance, and he stepped forward in an ungainly stride, the multitool deflecting to Thom's left.

Donn, still on the deck, aimed with military precision a kick at Thom's right knee. He connected and saw the joint bend at an unnatural angle. Thom howled in pain and fell to the ground, crashing to the deck.

Donn did not hesitate, but aimed an uppercut through the V of Thom's legs, punching forcefully into his groin. He remembered his close fighting instructor's words: "You can fight fair, or you can fight to win."

Thom's groans turned into screams of pain as he released his hold on the multitool and reached too late for his testicles, rolling over into a fetal position amid the other nine babies.

Donn, satisfied that Thom was at least temporarily incapacitated, turned back to the baby. He reached for it, his forearm throbbing, and gently scooped it up. He carefully rose and trotted towards the bulkhead where the nearest ELS unit was.

"OSIRIS! Activate ELS unit six," he called, and as he approached the bulkhead, he saw the ELS panel light up green. Thom's artwork covered the surface of the bulkhead, a fairy ring of dancers cavorting amid the ELS panel's indicators. Donn opened the drawer and carefully placed the infant inside. He tore open the sterile lead package and attached the sensors swiftly but delicately to the baby's chest, noting the open wounds. He completed the biomed sensor attachments and glanced at the small readout screen on the ELS.

The EEG and EKG indicators were flatlines, as was the respiration indicator, but that could be because the hookups either hadn't registered yet, or that Donn had placed them incorrectly. He watched, his chest heaving, as both indicators remained flat. The baby's temperature was slightly below normal, but that was immaterial.

"Come on, Champ, come on," Donn said, his eyes never leaving the readout.

The lines remained flat.

Donn cursed and reached for the IV needle, tearing the package open and holding the syringe sideways in his mouth as he took the baby's arm. He felt the slick yet sticky surface of the baby's skin and hunted for a vein.

Before he could insert the needle, he heard a scraping sound of metal on metal behind him. He whirled and saw Thom had regained his feet and had taken the multitool from the deck once again. He was partially doubled over, obviously still in pain from Donn's attack, but was making for the pod racks again.

"Thom!" Donn shouted, the syringe falling from his mouth. He released the baby and charged the caretaker. Thom turned, and for a moment, Donn wondered if the bearded madman would use the multitool on him first. He slowed his advance, wary of Thom and his makeshift weapon.

But Thom's voice and face were drowned in sorrow. "You don't understand. This is better. Better than what they have coming to—"

Donn caught movement from the entrance to K-7, and he saw Thom turn fully towards it. Donn lunged forward and seized Thom's weapon hand with both of his own, grimacing at the pain in his own forearm, then hooked his left heel behind Thom's right and tipped the man heavily to the deck.

Thom landed with a sickening thud, the back of his skull cracking loudly against the deckplate. He did not move.

"What the hell's happening in here?" Donn recognized the voice of Paul Yune, the Caretaker for K-6.

"Paul! We've got multiple embryos out of their pods! Get them into the ELS units as fast as you can!" Donn did not look to confirm that his order was being obeyed — he instead regarded the moist, motionless babies littered all around the deck. Thom's body, too, lay unmoving among them. Donn glanced at the man, and stepped over his body to recover another baby just beyond him.

The tiny body was bleeding from multiple lacerations, as the one Donn had placed into the ELS unit had been. Worse, its eyes were open but did not move. Donn raised the baby's chest to his ear, the drying amniotic fluid still tacky.

Even with the sounds of Yune moving about the bay, Donn was certain he heard nothing. This baby was also dead.

He rose from his kneeling position, still cradling the dead infant in his arms, and looked at the carnage. Again came the flashback to the battle three years ago. LEO fighters, welding seams still visible from their hurried construction, flew like arrows launched by ancient longbowmen towards the enemy Starfish. Donn remembered the feeling of awesome power that settled in his loins when he regarded the sheer numbers of fighters on all sides. He was one of many, a wing commander no less, in the fight to repel the enigmatic alien invaders from Earth.

He watched helplessly as squadron members burst into flame and debris, the Starfish direct-energy weapons brutal and efficient in their destructive force. For an instant, the destroyed fighter's inertia had kept it aloft before it began its curving descent back to the planet. For a split second, before he had sealed his escape cocoon and ejected, he had flown in an airborne graveyard.

And now he stood, almost ten light years distant in space and three years distant in time from those grotesque memories, on a deckplate littered with the bodies of murdered infants.

He didn't understand how either slaughter could have happened.

"Donn," Paul said from behind him.

Donn turned, still holding the dead baby.

"None of them … they're all dead," Paul said, his characteristically gentle voice almost inaudible.

Donn nodded slightly and looked at the walls for an explanation.

Fairyland creatures danced in innocent joy.

Chapter Two

He was still looking at the walls when a half-dozen care-takers and Linna Margulies, the liaison officer for the deck, entered the bay.

Fan out," said Margulies. "Make sure there aren't any other preborns where we can't see them." Without hesitation, the others spread themselves out amid the dozen columns of pods, leaving Donn and Paul near Thom's still-motionless body.

"Linna, over here," Donn called, putting aside his personal distaste for the woman. Margulies walked heavily towards the two men, nodding curtly at them both when she got there.

"Shit," she said, glancing down at Thom's body. "What happened here?"

Donn did not wait for his meek companion to speak. "I heard OSIRIS sound the alert, and came over. When I got here, Thom was smashing the pods with a multitool." Donn indicated the destroyed pods to his left. "So I stopped him."

Margulies spoke flatly while looking at the carnage. "How many did he get?"

"I think nine."

"Oh, my God," Paul whispered next to him.

Margulies shut her eyes momentarily, her eyelids pressed so hard against one another that wrinkles appeared in the outer corners of her eyes. When she reopened her eyes, they were steel.

"And him?" She knelt down next to Thom and felt for a pulse.

Donn swallowed. "I haven't checked. So much was happening—"

"He's alive," Marguiles announced.

"Alive?" Donn said. Until that moment, it had not occurred to him that he might have killed Thom.

"Yeah," Margulies said. "Did you call for medical help for him?"

"For him? No, I just called for help for the babies."

Margulies looked at him, the skin on the bridge of her nose crinkling. She had a way of expressing, in a single look, instant and total disdain — as if she were speaking with the most incompetent person she had ever encountered in her professional life.

She was giving Donn that look, and it took a supreme effort of will on his part to refrain from snapping at her.

Margulies spoke to the air. "OSIRIS, alert medical personnel. One adult caretaker, male, injured. Possible head trauma."

"Acknowledged. Medical personnel responding."

Donn cleared his throat. "Listen, Linna—"

"So you said you stopped him. How?"

"I tackled him, and we had a scuffle. Got me with the multitool," Donn indicated his forearm. "I guess in there somewhere he landed on his head."

"You guess."

Paul glanced at both Donn and Margulies, then said quietly, "I'm going to ... help the others look." He padded away, his deck shoes making a tearing sound as he walked through the drying psuedoamniotic fluid.

Neither Donn nor Margulies watched him go.

"Did anyone else see Thom smashing the pods?" she said, her eyes never leaving Donn's.

Donn shook his head, and the heat of their shared enmity cooled in him somewhat as he remembered. "Actually, that's another thing. OSIRIS reported that the bay cams were out. I thought that was odd."

Linna snorted, then said to the air, "OSIRIS, what's the camera status for K-seven?"

"Internal cameras offline in bay K-seven."

"Why?"

"Unscheduled maintenance cycle."

Linna and Donn exchanged glances. She asked, "Who authorized the cycle?"

"Unknown."

Donn grunted. "How's that possible? An unscheduled maintenance cycle, which no one—"

Linna held up a preemptive hand. "OSIRIS, is this an emergency maintenance cycle that you started?"

"No. This came from outside."

"Search your records. Find me the source for the command."

"Working on it," OSIRIS said, and fell silent.

Linna murmured, "Who could have authorized a maintenance cycle, and what's more, who would want to?"

Donn shrugged. "What does it matter? Nine preborns dead … Jezeus." He swallowed and looked at the other K-Deck caretakers moving about the bay. He saw Hunsaker cradling a tiny, motionless body; Baskny kneeling down beside two others, her palm hard against her forehead; Vern standing silent and bewildered.

"We can't help them," Margulies said. "But if there's something wrong with OSIRIS, we need to know."

Donn looked away from the grisly cleanup. He knew if he thought too much on it, he'd lose himself in grief. "How could someone order a maintenance cycle?"

Linna shook her head once. "I don't know. That's why I'm asking OSIRIS."

As the two waited for an answer, the K-7 bay doors opened again and admitted three green-smocked medics. They pushed a gurney through the bay, slowing when they hit the amniotic fluid. Donn could see their faces grow pale as they saw the caretakers holding preborns out of their pods. He waved them over, recognizing all three vaguely. He'd not had any reason to visit the infirmary during the trip, but had of course seen them from time to time.

Two of the medics set up their equipment while the third squatted near Thom. "What happened?"

"He was knocked to the deck. Head smashed into the deckplates, and he lost consciousness," Donn reported.

The medic nodded faintly, reaching around to the back of Thom's head. Her eyes looked away as she examined the wound by touch.

Donn frowned as he saw her grimace suddenly. "Bad?"

"Yeah. Skull fracture. Pretty nasty one." She withdrew her gloved hand, which was smeared with blood. She barked instructions to the rest of her team. Donn glanced one more time at Thom's figure and backed away, putting some distance between himself and the body.

"Search complete," OSIRIS said. "I can find no authorization source for the command. It appears I have a new command sub-pathway."

"What?" Margulies said. "How could that have happened?"

"I have been reprogrammed." OSIRIS was matter-of-fact about it.

"How? When did this happen?" Donn asked.

Margulies glared at Donn, though at his impertinence in asking a question of the computer or at the evidence itself, he could not say.

"Sixteen fifty-four today."

Margulies blurted, "About half an hour ago?"

"Correct. Twenty-six minutes ago, to be more precise."

"OSIRIS, how would—" Donn began, but Margulies cut him off.

"I'll handle this," she said, stepping closer to him, as if to interpose her body between him and the all-present shipboard computer.

"Jezeus, Linna, I was just going to ask him—"

"I'll take over the questioning."

"—how that could have happened!" He ended his comment louder, trying to speak over her.

"I'm crew. You're a caretaker. This is my job, not yours," Margulies said, her nostrils flaring.

"A caretaker went berserk, Linna. This is for all of us to figure out." He saw the medics glance in their direction as they worked on Thom. Donn scanned the bay, and saw the rest of the caretakers had frozen in their positions and were watching the exchange.

"No, it's not. You have your own preborns to take care of. Now shut up and let me continue."

"And what about Thom's embryos? Who's going to watch over them?"

Margulies looked shocked. "What?"

"All these." Donn waved at the pods. "Seventeen hundred of 'em. How're we gonna watch them now?"

"I'll put OSIRIS on it. We'll have to go to computer monitoring. It's only a month now. Less."

Donn could hear her voice beginning to falter. He softened his approach. "Linna, I'm just saying I want to help out, that's all."

His gentle words did not have a calming effect on her. If anything, she became more strident. "If you want to help out, then go back to your bay and take care of your pods." She turned to the others. "All of you caretakers. Go back to your bays or quarters. Resume your normal work schedules. Let the crew handle this."

Donn saw the caretakers look to him, their eyes searching for guidance. He nodded gently. "Do as she says, guys. Use the ELS units here and in your own bays to..." he paused, searching for the proper words in this unprecedented catastrophe, "hold the deceased until we can perform a service for them, okay?"

The six caretakers all looked at each other, waiting for one of them to move first. Finally, Hunsaker started toward the exit, now cradling two bloody figures. The others followed.

"We're not holding a service," Margulies said, though she waited for the six to leave before speaking. Her voice was gentler, smaller that it had been.

"Why not?"

"Because it sends the wrong message. We can't be focused on that right now," Linna said grimly.

"Are you out of your mind? Nine babies died today." Donn could feel his face growing redder.

Margulies' mouth was a line. "We're less than a month from planetfall. You know how much we have to do in that time. Sleepers to wake, colonization supplies to unship, all kinds of pod conversions to plan. It's already an impossible time for us. We can't be thinking about what happened here."

"Nine babies, Linna." Donn's voice was an accusing whisper.

"Don't you think I know that? But a memorial would only remind people that they died. We have to think of the future now, not the past."

"You can't stop us, Linna. If we want to hold a memorial, what are you going to do about it?"

"Please, Donn. Don't fight me on this. Not now."

"We're holding a memorial." Donn looked at her evenly.

Margulies sighed, then said in careful tones, "I'm hereby ordering you to return to a normal work schedule. If you incite the caretakers to shirk their work responsibilities, you'll be disciplined."

"How? You gonna fire me, here? Send back to Earth for a replacement caretaker?"

"I would rather not go into it now."

"Then you do what you have to do."

"There's no reason for us to have a confrontation on this," Margulies said, but the gentleness in her voice was giving way to irritation.

Donn looked at her for a moment. The run-ins he'd had with her were numerous — if he were honest with himself, he'd admit that there were largely because of his pigheaded insistence to do things his way instead of hers. She was supposed to be enforcing shipwide policy on a whole battery of procedures, and Donn knew he wasn't making her job easy. But this was not just a simple disagreement on nomenclature or protocol. "You're right. Because there's nothing you can do to stop me."

Margulies' jaw twitched. "Colony assignments can be changed. You like the one you have, don't you?"

Donn furrowed his brow. "You can't be serious. You would put the colony in jeopardy by reassigning me, just out of spite? To prove some point about who's in charge?"

"I think we can get by with one less recon pilot once we hit planetfall. Satellites will do your job. I've thought so from the first, anyway."

Donn snorted. "I can get my job done."

"You didn't get it done in the war."

The comment exploded in the air between them. For a moment, Donn was back three years again, back on Earth, reading the names of the dead pilots, the besieged cities, the notes of defeat and loss in news broadcasts on the web, feeling condemning eyes on him when he moved through the community, his midnight black uniform of the High Guard a mourning shroud. He had failed his squadron, his unit, and his planet.

Not for the first time, Donn had thought it would have been so much better to have died, blown to pieces above the Earth, and then for those pieces to burn away in the purgatory of the atmosphere as they descended, leaving nothing behind — no shame, no regret — and not being witness to the near-end of humanity at the hands of the enigmatic Starfish.

But he had survived. Survived through the war, and through the peace that had followed. And he had found a new purpose here. Margulies wasn't wrong. Men like him had indeed let the planet down, had failed all of humanity. No soldier had ever carried that burden, and save for a brokered peace made in the eleventh hour, the final chapter of humankind might have been written in the blood of their failure.

Strangely, he found himself respecting Margulies for her boldness, her tactlessness.

"All the more reason for me to want to get things done now, Linna."

She blinked, and Donn saw the apology in her eyes before she spoke it. "Sorry. That was low of me." She took a deep breath and continued in more measured tones, "But I'm going to stand on my original order. Don't do a memorial. It's the wrong message, Donn. We need to move forward, not look back," she grimaced as she said the final words.

It was in him at that moment to point out the hypocrisy of her statement, on the heels of her war reference. But he still felt the odd sense of respect for her. And, he noted cynically, it'd make him look like a petulant child. She'd said it, and there was no taking it back. At least, though, he knew what was in her thoughts. That counted for something.

He nodded and looked around the bay. The scenes of pixies and benign dragons stared back at him, forever frozen in attitudes of carefree frivolity.

Chapter Three

"She said what?" Kearney said, hands on her hips, eyes flashing.

"No memorial," Donn repeated. He was sitting on the edge of her bed, knees wide apart, hands dangling between them. He looked up at her. The bed was low to the ground, perhaps half a meter high. This gave Kearney the appearance of height, though she was a clear forty centimeters shorter than he.

That, and her attitude. She thrust her face forward, as if sniffing the air between them. "I can't believe it. What gives her the right to say that?"

Donn shrugged.

Kearney looked down at him for a beat, her lined face intent. "Well? What are you going to do about it?" There was more than a little challenge in her voice — one of the many qualities Donn had found himself attracted to in her, despite the age difference. Nothing she cared about floated by her unmolested. If he had wished to be insulting, he would call her meddlesome, arrogant, stubborn.

"Hold the service, of course," Donn grumbled to the deckplates.

Kearney snickered. "Fuckin-A right, we are."

"We?" Donn snapped his head back up.

"Of course. All of us. And not just K-Deck. The whole goddam ship." She scowled and looked at the bulkhead, decorated in a violet-red valance. She'd long ago shown him the commission she'd given one of the artists from B-Deck upon the beginning of the voyage: a faux-window, through which could be seen a garden and verdant hillside. Over the course of the trip, she'd managed to procure fabric and had hung a decorative window treatment around it. Like most everything else in her highly bedecked and thoroughly non-standard quarters, the color scheme trended heavily towards the violets. Donn once had joked that coming into her quarters — which she called her "parlor," "boudoir," or "salon," but never her "quarters" — was like stepping into a Bohemian brothel.

Kearney had laughed that rich laugh of hers, tipping her head back and giving full throat to her pleasure, and had remarked that he was a perspicacious man.

"I don't necessarily want to cause trouble. I just want to remember the dead,"

"We can do both," Kearney said, turning away from him and tapping her dresser open. A panel slid sideways to reveal a shallow but wide closet. She rummaged through her clothes, sliding her duty uniforms aside to reveal her collection of private attire.

Donn watched her. He was mildly transfixed on her movements. He could have turned away, but it would have required an effort of will to do so. In moments of idleness with her, he found himself watching. She was so very different from the military world in which he had until recently been immersed. In many other ways, she was comfortably similar: the same hard-edged certainty of things she had no idea about, the same aggressive approach to life, the same vague sense of belligerence to any and all comers, even her lovers.

But in six months, he didn't really know her. She was still a collection of gestures and postures to him, a catalog of sensations. In her own way, she lived in a pod.

He'd come to her immediately after the confrontation with Margulies in K-7. Kearney hadn't heard the alarm from OSIRIS, having been asleep during the crisis.

Donn placed his hands on his knees and pushed off, grunting slightly as he rose from the low bed. He padded to her and placed his hands delicately on her shoulders.

She responded with a subtle shifting of her weight, leaning back slightly as she continued to search for a garment.

She smelled impossibly of lavender and spice. Donn leaned in and kissed her neck, just above the high collar of her duty coverall. Some maverick strands of her vermillion hair caught his lips and contrasted with the soft, slightly grainy surface of her skin.

"Wait, Donn. Lemme get out of this," she said, her voice husky with promise.

Donn stepped back and watched her reach for the zipper at the top of her neck. She glanced over her shoulder and grinned, then pulled the zipper down with a businesslike motion.

She wore undergarments when it suited her, and evidently, this work cycle it had not suited her. Her naked flesh pimpled slightly in the cool air. Donn watched the muscles of her shoulder and upper back scamper like mice under a sheet as she tugged the coverall down and off. The dimples in her still-firm buttocks winked at him as she lifted one leg, then the other, and was nude before him.

Donn kissed her neck again, his hands reaching gently around her body to massage her small breasts. Her soft flesh rested in his palms. There was desire in him, and need, but he had enough self-awareness to know that he was using the moment for his own purposes. Escape, certainly. Validation. Affirmation of life itself.

As he caressed her, he knew suddenly that she, too, knew what was happening. He ceased his movements and withdrew his lips from her.

Kearney turned her head to half-face him, her bright eyes finding his. "Aren't you going to get your clothes off?" It wasn't a question. Her eyes understood and accepted.

Donn backed up and unzipped his own coveralls and wriggled his upper body out of them. He sat down on the low bed to remove them from his legs and feet. Kearney turned, nude and unashamed, and regarded him with a slight smile.

Donn looked up at her while he was still in the process of disrobing and chuckled suddenly. "Looks good, K," he said, nodding at her lower body.

Kearney looked down at herself and laughed. "Oh, I almost forgot. Yeah. Guy who works food prep and maintenance got me some blueberry paste. Mixed it with some vinegar, and, well, there you go. Do you like it?"

Donn finished disrobing but remained on the low bed, his eyes level with her dark violet pubic hair. He grinned at it. "Yeah. Never seen anything like it before."

"I'm glad. Doesn't even wash out, so it's there to stay for a while." She reached out to him with both her hands, and he took them and rose from the bed.

He gathered her in his arms, pulling her forcefully to him.

She grunted a little but smiled. "Hi there," she said, and stood on her toes to kiss him.

He leaned down and returned the kiss, and felt her hand slide down his abdomen and grasp his partially erect penis. He sighed into her mouth and let her minister to him, feeling her hand deftly stroke him to fullness.

She pivoted so that her back was to the bed, her hand never leaving his organ, and deftly lowered herself down onto her back, her eyes shining into his, speaking to him an unmistakable invitation.

He looked again at her violet mound of hair and knelt at her feet on the deck, the thin Persian rug Kearney had somehow managed to procure warm on his knees.

"What're you doing?" Kearney asked.

He answered by kissing her inner thigh, his cheek brushing against her labia. Kearney gasped softly.

She did indeed smell of blueberries.

Despite her moans of pleasure, he could tell she was not approaching orgasm. They had long ago agreed to be truthful to each other in the sexual realm. He had been adamant on that point months ago when they had first engaged in sex. He had asked her not to fake an orgasm for his sake, and she had cheekily replied, "I won't if you won't."

Now, though she was enjoying the sensation, he knew climax would not come easily. He also knew that this time, he was being selfish. He had not wanted her to orgasm purely because he wanted her to feel pleasure — that was partly true, but was not all. He needed to be successful in something.

He withdrew from her labia with shame mixed with determination, then almost angrily climbed on top of her, pressing his partly erect organ against her. When he entered her, she moaned gently and wrapped her arms around his neck.

Then he saw them.

The murdered babies in K-7. Lying in the thin pools of pseudoamniotic fluid, motionless.

Their eyes were open, and they were looking at him. Accusing him.

"Donn ... what's wrong?"

Her voice brought him back, and he felt himself slip out of her.

"Fuck. God dammit," he muttered in shame.

"It's all right," she said, and unclasped her hands from his neck. She slid her right hand under him, dipping her shoulder to reach further. Donn again found her hand clasped around him, massaging his softening genitals entirely. She squeezed and cajoled him back to firmness, then met his eyes again. "There. All better. Come on, Donn. Again."

Donn entered her again, desperately. He felt his brain fighting to maintain arousal, but in the corners of his mind's eye he saw the LEO fighters exploding, the dead embryos unblinking.

He saw his many failures.

Again, he slipped out of her, and this time, she didn't bother to try to stimulate him.

"Don't say anything," he snapped.

"All right," she said on the edge of curtness.

He looked down at her. She looked back up at him, her expression neutral.

"Sorry," he said.

"For what?"

"Everything." He pushed his arms against the mattress and rolled off her, his body in the narrow wedge of space between her and the edge of the mattress. He felt her hands on his muscular back.

"Shit, Donn, don't feel sorry for yourself. This happens."

Donn rose in one swift motion, his anger rising. He knew that he was again being unfair to her — but he also felt that whatever words came out of her just now would make the situation worse. In a perverted way, he wanted her to point at his soft organ and laugh, or to tell him he was an utter failure here, too. At least then, he would have reason to be angry with her.

He heard her sigh, and almost turned to her to shout. Instead, he walked away from her, finding the print of *Guernica* she had on the electronic wall display.

"You always liked that," Kearney said.

Donn turned his head and looked at her. She had turned to her side, her head propped up by one hand, her elbow denting the mattress.

Vague stirrings in his groin mocked him.

He ignored them and turned back to the display. "Not really," he said. He heard Kearney rise from the bed, and felt the heat of her body a moment before she pressed softly into him, the gentle curves of her small frame finding the hard edges of his large one.

"You keep looking at it every time you're here."

"Yeah. I don't get it. I don't understand it," he said, his eyes roaming from the bull to the horse to the dismembered soldier.

He felt her shrug. "Picasso said there's nothing to get. More like, 'whatever you get out of this is your doing, not mine.' Something like that."

Donn snorted. "Sounds like art-house crap to me."

Donn felt her body stiffen. "You're calling Picasso crap?"

He sighed and half turned. "No. I'm just saying I don't like mysteries. Whether it's this painting, or…"

"Or tonight?"

Donn swallowed and shook his head. "I know what happened tonight. I saw things again. The babies, the pilots." He finished his turn, facing Kearney, his back to Picasso's work. "It wasn't you, K. It really wasn't."

Kearney's eyebrow cocked slightly. "I didn't think it was," she said wryly.

Donn didn't rise to the bait. "I just had all sorts of stuff in my head. I probably shouldn't have tried to start anything."

Her shoulders moved up and down. "It's okay. Did you want to talk about anything?" She had the tone she adopted when she was trying hard to accommodate his needs when they did not mesh with her own. He always appreciated that.

"There were so many of them, K," he said, looking back at *Guernica*. "All around me. Death. Touching everything."

He felt Kearney's hand rest on his upper back and knew what that gesture had cost her. She had her own needs, and he was not fulfilling them. He knew this even as he could not find it in himself to care.

"Why not me, Kearney?"

Her hand froze. "What do you mean? Why didn't you go crazy and kill—"

"No, no — not today. Then. The war."

"Oh."

"We had even thought to come out of the sun. Make it behind us, hopefully that would mean something. Tried to time our intercept with where the sun was. Didn't make a difference. Starfish fighters didn't care. They just appeared, like demons, in front of us, then they were behind us, then on top of us. Missiles couldn't lock properly. How could they, when the Starfish can just pop in and out of space? Some of our own boys were hit by friendly fire in the chaos. Guns didn't do anything either. I know they got the reports that each Starfish fighter had some kind of distortion field around it, and it made anything physical we threw at them just vanish."

"Donn, you're scaring me," Kearney said gently. "Look around you, look at me. You're here, with me, on the *Chiron*. It's now, not then." She took one of his hands and pressed it against her chest. "Feel that? That's me. Here. Now."

Donn looked down at her. "I know, K. I know."

"You talked about reports they got. What did you mean?"

Donn sighed. "Sorry. I was thinking of the Tribunal." He removed his hand from her chest. "After we lost most of our LEO force and the Starfish had taken over the nine cities. The few of us who survived were called to answer why Earth's finest failed so badly." He remembered the peripheral details about the ordeal: the motel room off the Florida Keys where he and the other survivors had been interred, awaiting questioning; the way the military police looked away when the delivered his meals; the way the sunsets looked in the perpetual haze of the atmosphere.

"No one blamed you."

He snorted. "You know that's wrong. Everyone blamed us. And why not? Fifty-five nations, thirteen thousand some-odd low-Earth-orbit fighters, plus thirty thousand drone support craft — and as everyone kept pointing out, the best of the best up there to pilot them. And we had a hundred years of movies and books and stuff telling us how Earth always wins, how the aliens have a weakness, that good ol' American pluck and Yankee know-how can get the job done—"

"Donn, please—"

His voice continued to rise in bitterness. "—so when we didn't bring down a single Starfish craft, and lost over ten thousand of us, everyone pointed fingers. Didn't matter that every fucking drone we sent up got taken over and fought against us. We still didn't get the job done. The dead never had to answer questions. Only the few of us who were left did." He snorted again. "You'd have thought that, in the middle of an alien invasion — one which we were fucking *losing* — people would be less interested in making sure we had someone to blame. But I guess you can't underestimate the human capacity to miss what's important."

"But we found a peace, Donn. Maybe you had something to do with that."

"How? Our military was smashed, and the Starfish had shown that we couldn't touch them. They just came and went as they pleased. One hundred eighty million dead in two months. Nothing we did made a damn difference."

"But it did. The treaty. They left us alone. It was horrible, Donn. Of course it was. But it's over."

"Why? Why did they stop? They had us — there was no reason to stop. If they wanted us all dead, why did they suddenly stop?"

Kearney's moist eyes looked into his. "Our diplomats and ambassadors, that's why. We talked to them. Everyone says it was the greatest diplomatic victory in the history of humanity. We failed at war, but we succeeded at peace. Why can't you believe that?"

He stared at her, then looked back at *Guernica*. The painting seemed to mock him in its incomprehensibility. "Why did they come? Why did Thom break and kill those babies?" He stared at the bull, horse, and soldier. "What does all this mean, Kearney?"

She sighed. "I don't know, Donn. Maybe it means nothing." Her voice was half sympathy, half annoyance.

"Nothing?" He whirled on her, his deferred anger finding an outlet. "That's just what we say when we can't handle reality. That nothing means anything. That's the coward's way out — nihilism."

Her eyes narrowed slightly. "Maybe it'd be best if you were alone with your thoughts." She glanced at her door, then began pulling on her clothes as she spoke. "I'm certainly not helping you. Try to get some sleep if you can. Things will look a little bit clearer in the morning."

He snorted. "You believe that?" He took his own clothes and began dressing.

She shrugged. "I dunno." Once they were both dressed, she walked the four steps to her door control and opened it, waiting.

He looked at the now-open doorway, then back at her. "I get it. No need to make it fuckin' clear," he said, then exited.

As soon as he was clear of the doorway, he stopped. He knew he had been unfair. Kearney hadn't deserved his ire, not when she was simply trying to help. His problems were his own, and while she did have some measure of sympathy for him, she wasn't his personal therapist. She had other people in her life aboard ship: people who came to her for comfort, counseling, companionship. She was just that way. She had tried to help, but he had refused.

He turned and put his hand on the irising door to halt it. It reversed its motion and returned back into its recess, and he opened his mouth to speak to her.

She had already turned to her computer console and had activated the internal communications system. Her back was to him, but she turned to look at the door.

"Donn—" she said, her voice guilt-tinged.

"K, I'm sorry, I shouldn't have—"

The communications screen lit up as her call was completed, and Donn could see the handsome and young face of Jason Collins, one of the B-Deck caretakers, on the monitor. "Hello? Kearney?" he said.

Kearney had the grace to speak softly, though she was not embarrassed. "Sorry, Donn. I thought you'd left."

Donn swallowed and nodded silently. He knew that his relationship with Kearney was not exclusive, at least not on her side. That had been the arrangement from the first — she had been firm that they not get "tied down" to each other. Donn had agreed, thinking he would be able to contain his emotions at the thought of sharing her bed with others. They had not spoken openly of the arrangement since — that was his suggestion — and having never been confronted with the others, he had been able to put the thought away.

Now, though, as Collins' chiseled face peered out from her monitor, he could no longer pretend.

"It's okay," he said. "I was just gonna say I'm sorry." His bitterness and confusion would not let him leave it at that, though. "But it looks like you got another one lined up, so I'll leave you to it."

He saw the hurt in her eyes, but it was fleeting. She clamped down on her pain and her face was once again smirking and arrogant. "Yeah. Taking care of business, you know. See you, Donn." She looked pointedly at his hand, still blocking the door from closing.

He removed his hand, and the door closed on Kearney and on Picasso's *Guernica*.

Chapter Four

"Let's see how you're doing today, Cappucino," Donn said with a sigh as he watched Pod 9-Kappa-4 snap into place in its receiving cradle. He had arrived in his bay four hours ago, far ahead of his assigned work hours. He had slept little. Nothing made sense, except what he did here, among his preborns. He knew what this all meant. Looking at them, examining their biochemistry and development, giving them words of encouragement — this all made sense.

He slapped the "advance" button on the manual control, and the low whirr of the pod retrieval motors echoed in the bay.

Pod 10-Kappa-4 settled into the cradle, but before he could examine it, Agnes' voice said, "Donn, incoming call from Linna Margulies."

"Okay. Put her through. Audio only."

Linna's voice boomed in the bay. "Donn? Linna here. You've started early."

"Yeah. Got a head start on the day. Needed to make up some lost time. Agnes, turn down volume by ten percent."

Linna's response was quieter. "I suppose so. I wanted to know if you'd be available for questioning. We didn't get a chance to do a full debrief on what you say happened in K-seven."

Donn looked up at the ceiling at the speaker grille. "A full debrief? I thought we covered all that yesterday. I told you what happened."

"I still have a few questions. Some things to clear up with you."

"I'm already behind schedule, Linna. I was planning on a full sweep yesterday, and I'm—"

"Full sweep? It's not evaluation time again."

"I know, but I was doing one anyway."

"Why? The set evaluation times are more than enough to fully assess each and every preborn. Anything more frequent is redundant."

"I don't see it that way. I want to be thorough, and give these babies as great a head start as I can. Are you ordering me to cease my work, Linna?"

"Don't make this into more than what it is. I was just saying—"

Donn snapped, "I'll do all that's required of me and more. If you want to question me, go ahead, but I'm going to continue with my sweep."

"All right. I'll be down in a little bit."

Donn scowled at the grille. "You're coming here? Not over the comm?"

"No. I want to do this in person. I'll see you soon."

Donn looked at the grille for a few moments, thinking. Then he shook his head and examined 10-Kappa-4. "All right, Moose, let's see what we've got here. You had a teeny bit of trouble with your cord last time, so let's check on that real quick."

———— «» ————

He had advanced to 2-Lambda-4 when Margulies entered. Donn saw her silhouetted against the white light of the corridor outside.

"OSIRIS, increase lighting to standard," she said.

The bay brightened perceptibly, and Donn called out to her from his position deep in the bay. "Hey, hey … I keep it dim in here on purpose. Gets the right atmosphere for them. Agnes, return to my lighting preference."

The bay dimmed again, the blue-tinted running lights on the deck giving the vague impression of a sea.

"The glass is polarized, Donn. There's no way these preborns can be affected by the light outside. You know that." Margulies said, walking heavily toward him, her feet almost stomping the deck.

"Of course I do. But I'm trying to replicate the environment they're in. Even with polarization, some light gets through. You know that."

"Not enough for them to perceive," Margulies countered, approaching him.

Donn grunted. "Maybe, maybe not. I'm just trying to do what's best for them."

"We all are, Donn."

He turned from 2-Lambda-4 and regarded her in silence for a moment. "Then let me hold a memorial. That's what's best for them."

Donn thought he saw softness in her eyes for a moment. Then it was gone, and her steely resolve returned. "We've been through this. You can't bring those nine back. All a service would do is remind everyone that they are gone. What's the use of that?"

"You just said it. To remind everyone. That's why they call it a 'memorial,' Linna. To remember."

"To remember what? They were preborns. No one knew them, because they hadn't been born yet. They were a designation on a pod," she said, tapping Pod 2-Lambda-4 next to her. "Like this one. Two-Lambda-Four."

"The Admiral," Donn said.

"What?"

"The Admiral. This one is 'The Admiral.'"

Margulies sighed. "You and your nicknames. Nonstandard."

"Yep. And I keep doing it, don't I?"

She looked at him in silence for a long while. Donn turned to examine 2-Lambda-4 and pressed the "advance" key when he was done. 3-Lambda-4 arrived, and Donn said to it with more exuberance than usual, "Mermaid! How're you doing, honey?" He looked at Margulies, then back to the pod. "You're my little Mermaid, aren't you?"

Margulies sighed.

Donn turned to her.

"She's not yours. You have to stop doing this. It's unhealthy."

"That's not your call, Linna," Donn said. "I'm just doing my job as best I can."

"You know very well why we discourage this. It makes you attached to them in an inappropriate way."

"I don't find anything inappropriate about this."

She paused before speaking again. "I've tried to reason with you. I've tried to explain why we do things the way we do them. But you just…" Margulies lifted her chin and spoke to the air. "OSIRIS, place a formal reprimand in Caretaker Cardenio's file, dated today with the current time."

Donn smiled wolfishly at her. "You have to be joking."

Margulies did not heed him. "Reprimand as follows: that Caretaker Cardenio willfully and persistently used improper designations for the preborns under his care, thus risking mistreatment due to confusion."

"Dammit, Linna, that's bullshit and you know it!"

"Furthermore," Margulies continued, "he did show insubordinate behavior in refusing to conform to established procedure despite multiple warnings."

"This is fucked up," Donn murmured. He patted Mermaid's canopy. "Sorry, sweetheart, for my bad language."

"File it, OSIRIS."

"Acknowledged."

Margulies turned back to Donn. "Now, will you stop?"

"Nope."

Margulies scowled. "You think there's nothing we can do to you, don't you? Out here, nearing planetfall, you're indispensable. That these reprimands are just farts in the wind."

"Couldn't have said it better myself, Linna," he said, peering at Mermaid's numbers.

"There's always the Freezer."

Donn looked up from Mermaid's readout.

"It's not just the names. Don't make me do that."

"And who would you get to be caretaker of K-eight? You're not seriously considering promoting one of the Freezers, are you? They're not qualified."

"OSIRIS can take over for the last month. You've done more than enough sweeps to fulfill requirements. All that extra work you seem to like so much."

Donn swallowed. "You would, wouldn't you? Just to get your way and prove you're in command. You'd have me checking on corpsicles rather than be here, where I belong, doing what I do best. All because I didn't follow some silly-ass rule you invented yesterday. Or is there more to it, Linna? I know you've never liked me—"

Margulies rolled her eyes. "Don't be melodramatic. You more than anyone know the importance of discipline. I can't have you being a maverick. If the colony is to function we need every person doing what they are assigned to."

"You're goddam right. And I've been assigned all these kids to look after," he said, sweeping his arm to encompass the entire bay. "No one can do it better than I can, Linna. Sticking me with the corpsicles is a waste and you know it. You'd be putting my preborns at risk."

Margulies stared at him, her nostrils flaring. "I'm just giving you an official warning." Before he could object, she said, "Let me ask you the questions I had. You reported that you heard an alert from OSIRIS about an emergency in K-seven yesterday morning, right?"

Donn had thought to continue debating the memorial, but both she and he had already made up their minds. He answered, "Yeah, that's right. I got there as quick as I could. OSIRIS kept counting up." He felt the familiar dryness in his mouth again as he remembered.

"Right. And you entered the bay and say you saw Thom smashing the pods?"

"Yes."

"But no one else was with you?"

Donn narrowed his eyes. "No. Kearney was sleeping, and Yune wasn't in K-six. I wouldn't have been in the bay anyway, but I was doing one of those redundant sweeps you hate so much."

Margulies snorted but otherwise ignored the comment. "So no one can verify your version of events."

Donn's mouth opened in shock. "What the hell are you suggesting? That I'm lying about this?"

"I'm just pointing out that I have only your word to go on."

"And that's not good enough?"

Margulies merely shrugged.

Donn waited with mounting anger for her to elaborate. When he could no longer hold back, he blurted, "I can't believe what you're saying. You think I just went into K-seven and attacked him? What about the damaged pods? How did that happen?"

Margulies said evenly. "I only know what you tell me. You say Thom 'snapped' and smashed nine of them. Until you, heroically, stopped him." She stared unblinkingly at him.

Donn laughed — a quick, sharp, exhalation of breath. "You've got to be shitting me. So let me make sure I get what you're saying—"

"I'm not saying—"

Donn raised his voice and spoke over her, "You're saying that I decided to go into K-seven and start smashing pods. And when Thom tried to stop me, I clocked him. Am I close?"

"Donn, I'm not saying anything. I'm just pointing out that I haven't got a lot of independent evidence to corroborate your story."

"So you think I'm a murderer. Worse — a murderer of babies."

"You're the only ex-military on the ship."

Donn's eyes bulged. "What the hell does that mean?" he shouted. "You think I'm a baby-killer because I fought in the war? I went through eighteen weeks of training for this job, plus psych evaluations, simulation work, hypnosleep therapy, the works. Passed all of my qualifications with distinction. So don't you come at me saying because I was a LEO pilot I'm a baby-killer."

"You're putting words in my mouth. I'm just—"

"Then say what you mean, damn you!"

Margulies said evenly, "I can't verify your story. OSIRIS' cameras were out, so—"

"So I must have figured a way to do that, too? You've made me into a computer genius and a homicidal lunatic all in one go, Linna."

"Is it less implausible to say Thom was those things?"

Donn was almost shouting again. "I don't know about that. I know what I saw. Thom was smashing up the pods, saying stuff like, 'this is better for them' and other shit. I had to take him out. Yune came in about then. Why don't you ask him what he saw?"

"We have. He says he never saw which of you smashed the pods."

Donn pointed at her. "Hang on. You know when OSIRIS sent the alert message. Check the time index against the camera footage in my bay. You'll see that when the alert message was sent, I was in my bay doing my sweep. That proves that I wasn't the one to kill those babies."

"Don't you think we're checking all that now?"

Donn stared at her. "Let me ask you something. If you suspected me, why did you let me go back to my bay? If I might have been the baby-killer, why the fuck did you let me alone in here? I could have killed more!" He found his genuine anger rising — he was far more angry at the prospect that Margulies would have put his charges in danger than he was at the personal accusation.

Margulies stared at him. "I don't know what happened. Either you or Agee snapped."

"What the fuck is going on here?" He took a step towards Linna. "If you were worried, I should never have been let out of my quarters! I know I'm not the killer, but if you seriously thought I might be dangerous, you let me come back here, unattended? What's the matter with you?"

"Step back, Cardenio," Linna said, raising her hand.

Donn took three deep breaths and backed away. "This is seriously fucked up, Linna. But I know one thing. Thom killed those nine babies, not me. Check your video footage. You'll see that I was here when the alert sounded. You just try and assign me to the Freezer. You're gonna find me hard to move."

"A threat, Cardenio? Against a member of the crew?"

He snorted and turned away, back to Mermaid. "Take it however you want. Now get out. I got work to do."

Margulies turned to go, but stopped and turned back. "One more thing. Stay out of K-seven."

"Why?"

"We need to preserve the bay during the investigation."

Donn shrugged. "I have no reason to go in there."

Margulies glared at him, then left, and Donn waited for her to exit the bay before he exhaled. He realized that he had not done himself any favors with her, and despite his bluster, he really did not enjoy reprimands on his record. He knew they were largely meaningless here, almost ten light years from Earth, but his professional pride was hurt. And despite his own certainty that the video record would clear any suspicion off him, he was wounded that Linna would suspect him at all. Once again, she had managed to find a weak spot in his psyche.

He advanced the pod track without thought, and when it clicked into place, he spent a few more moments in thought before attending to Shortstop, in Pod 3-Lambda-4.

《 》

Hours later, he put Lassie back in her holding area and rolled his shoulders. All 1,728 tucked in and secure. In the early days and weeks, he'd struggled to remember even a few dozen of the nicknames he'd granted them. Now he could recall virtually all of them without glancing at the small physical notes he'd left on each pod housing. He rubbed the bridge of his nose where the peepers had irritated the flesh, and headed back to the control suite.

He put away his peepers and checked the board one last time. As he expected, the vast twelve-by-twelve-by-twelve grid of lights shone back unanimously green. He sighed and spoke aloud.

"All right, OSIRIS, bring Agnes back, please."

"Thank you, Donn," Agnes said primly.

"You're welcome. You still want to work with me, a rogue agent and maverick? Dangerously giving nicknames to my preborns in defiance of official policy?"

"I want to fulfill my function," Agnes said.

"That's all you have to say to me?"

"I don't have anything to say."

Donn shook his head in affected mock injury. "I'm hurt. After all we've been through. Not a word of apology?"

"Apology for what?"

"For not standing up for me against Margulies," Donn said, his voice teasing.

"That's not my place. And anyway, she told OSIRIS to do that, not me."

"But you are OSIRIS. You're just a computing facet of him."

Now Agnes sounded hurt. "I think that was uncalled for. I may be part of OSIRIS, but I'm my own entity."

"Nice try, OSIRIS," Donn said, suddenly irritated. "You're the result of a bunch of questions you asked me way back when we were first tailoring our individual logins. Agnes is just you trying to make a comfortable—" he stopped suddenly, the conversation was annoying him. After his encounters with Margulies and Kearney, he wondered if he wanted someone whom he could simply command. He shook his head at himself. That wasn't it. He wanted cause and effect to make sense.

He looked around the bay. Here, his problems were easy to identify, if difficult to solve. But he knew what he was up against, and it merely took effort and expertise to be successful.

"Say again, Donn? I didn't catch that," Agnes said.

"Never mind. Doesn't matter. I think I'll check in on Thom's preborns."

"What?"

Donn sighed in annoyance. "I'm going into bay K-seven to inspect the pods." He knew it was unnecessary — Margulies had been correct about their immediate safety. But he wanted to feel useful, to try and undo the psychic damage Thom had done to them.

And he felt like being defiant.

"I'm not allowed to let anyone in," the computer answered in OSIRIS' voice.

"What? Well, how the hell are we supposed to take care of them?"

"I'm monitoring all remaining pods and making the proper adjustments."

"What if something goes wrong? Something unexpected that isn't in your database?"

"That hasn't happened."

Donn raised his voice, "But what if it did? And you didn't know what to do?"

"I am instructed to call Crewmember Linna Margulies in case of an emergency."

Donn hesitated. At least that was an answer, but Margulies wasn't a caretaker. She would have even less ability than OSIRIS in an embryonic crisis. "And then what? She decides who to call in?"

"I don't know what happens next," OSIRIS said evenly. "I know that if a pod's numbers go outside parameters and I can't correct it, I am to notify her."

"Is anybody close?"

"Say again?"

"The pods! Are any of the pods close to being in danger?"

OSIRIS did not answer. Donn waited a few moments, then said, "OSIRIS, do you read me?"

"I read you. I am unsure if I am allowed to answer that question."

"What? Why not?"

"Liaison Officer Margulies ordered me not to let anyone into K-seven."

Donn pointed at the ceiling as he spoke, jabbing the air as he pressed home his point. "But I'm not asking you to let me in. I just want to know the pod numbers. Look, you want to keep all the pods safe and the preborns thriving, right? It's your main function?"

"I want to deliver the preborns to our destination in a healthy state."

"Yeah, I know you do. And Margulies wants the same thing. We all do. If you've been ordered not to let anyone into K-seven, I won't ask you to disobey that. But were you ordered not to reveal the K-seven pod status reports to anyone?"

"No."

"All right then." Donn settled into his control saddle. "Display on my monitors any K-seven pod numbers that are, let's say, twenty-five percent away from ideal results."

His monitor array changed immediately from his own near-perfect reports to a long list of pod designations with their biochemical abnormalities. When the monitors changed, he grinned at himself, pleased at this useless victory over Margulies. But as the list grew, he became alarmed.

"Holy shit! OSIRIS, how many pods are on this list?"

"Three hundred eight."

"There are three hundred and eight pods twenty-five percent out of true? Fuck me. What the hell has been going on in there?"

"Twenty-five percent out of true is within tolerances."

"The hell it is. Not in my bay, it's not." He rubbed his face. "Okay, just show me any pod that is thirty-three percent off."

"Tolerance level is forty percent, Donn."

"I know. But if you've got some at thirty-three percent, then they're knocking on the door. Once a preborn hits forty percent out of true, you need to do something drastic, and that can make things worse. I want to catch them as fast as I can. Gimme the thirty-three percent group." The list of pods shrunk to a more manageable twenty-three. "That's a little better. Okay, let's see what we've got here." He studied the first pod on the list. "All right, so this one here ... Eleven-Gamma-Four ... he's got a glucose deficiency, and a lactate surplus. You've decided to give the little guy more pyruvic acid?"

"Affirmative. Glucose deficiency results from a lack of pyr—"

"I know what the manual says. But I've seen this before. Up the oxygen content in the blood supply by five percent."

"That is not stand—"

"I know it's not. But he's got plenty of pyruvic acid. What he needs is more oxygen. Just do it."

"I will take an in vitro blood sample directly from his tissue to verify," OSIRIS said.

"No need for that. I hate to stick these guys unless I can't help it."

"Then I will use the blood laser diagnostic tool to—"

"Not yet. Look, OSIRIS, the numbers are right in front of you. It's clear. Up the oxygen by five percent"

"I am unsure of your authority here, Caretaker Cardenio."

Donn exhaled in exasperation. "You just called me a caretaker. I'm qualified to make these decisions. It's what I've been trained for." This was no longer merely a childish rebellion against authority — these preborns were in danger. "If you don't follow my instructions, this little guy in Eleven-Gamma-Four is not gonna thrive like he might."

OSIRIS answered, "I will take blood glucose levels with the laser sampler. If you are correct, I will increase oxygen supply by five percent."

Donn shrugged. The laser sampler wasn't a bad tool — he had used it many times himself. But when the problem and its solution were both crystal clear, as they were now, he disliked deploying diagnostic tools. Tools were only as good as the people wielding them, and even a laser sampler could give a false result. Still, he knew the dangers of relying on a single diagnostic method, so perhaps OSIRIS was right. The miniscule danger in the use of the laser sampler was well worth the certainty it would bring.

"Fine," Donn said. "While you're doing that, I'm going to look at the next one. Eight-Alpha-Five." Donn examined the numbers on his screen.

Two hours later, having argued with OSIRIS over the care of the twenty-three preborns one at a time (Donn won most of the arguments, but had been forced to abandon some of his more controversial and radical solutions on a small number of cases) he sat back in his control saddle.

"Are you certain you don't want to look at the twenty-five percenters, OSIRIS?" Donn said tiredly.

"I am already monitoring them. As I said, if their results deviate outside acceptable tolerances, I shall alert Liaison Officer Margulies."

Donn stifled a yawn. His enthusiasm for the task of fine-tuning care for another three hundred embryos was not enough to defeat his fatigue. "Okay. Any way I can get you to notify me if they go beyond thirty-three percent, like we did today?"

"No."

"Thought I'd ask. Hey, are your cameras operational again?"

"They are."

"Don't suppose you're allowed to show me the pickup, are you?"

"The way I interpret my orders, no."

"But you haven't been specifically ordered not to display the camera pickup?"

"No. But it is clear that Liaison Officer Margulies did not want you to enter the bay after the incident. My interpretation of her orders includes watching the bay under closed-circuit camera."

Donn mused, "That's probably a fair reading of your orders. 'Course, it makes me wonder why. And I still don't understand why your cameras were out at such a vital time. You told me that someone altered your programming to kill your cameras right when Thom went on his rampage. That just can't be a coincidence."

"I have no data to comment."

Donn looked thoughtfully at the screens before him, still displaying the biochemical data on the last pod from K-7 he had corrected. "OSIRIS, do you think you would be allowed to display the camera record from before the incident?"

There was a pause before OSIRIS responded. "My orders do not specify one way or another."

"Well, let me say this. If I could watch the footage you do have, it might show Thom doing something to the pods to mess them up biochemically. Hell, you saw the results. Over three hundred twenty-five percent or more out of true? That has to be alarming. Compare them to my numbers, or the numbers of anyone else on board. If I could see what he was up to, I might be better able to restore these swimmers to normal levels."

"Prior to the camera blackout, I was monitoring K-seven, as I do all bays. Caretaker Agee had not acted in a manner destructive to the pods."

"How do you know? Your programming was altered. How do you know your memory has not also been altered? Maybe Thom had been poisoning the embryos slowly, over time, and you never noticed." Donn found himself holding his breath. When he had begun this line of reasoning, he had been lying in an attempt to gain access to the footage. But now that he advanced his spurious argument, he found some merit in his own words. Could Thom have been embarking on a long-range project to kill every baby in his bay?

"I cannot, by the nature of the tampering, know if I have been altered. I cannot proceed on those grounds, for if one follows that logic, I cannot trust any of my inputs."

"No, that's not so. You know you've been altered. What could happen once could have happened twice. Show me the footage, and we can see if I am right."

OSIRIS' even voice did not betray a hint of indecision. "Acknowledged. When do you want the record to start?"

Donn blinked in surprise. He hadn't truly expected his chop-logic to work, but once OSIRIS had made up his mind, he was committed. "Uh, why don't you just run in backwards from right before you went dead. Let's say normal speed.

As soon as he finished, his monitors lit up with various camera angles from K-7. The display showed yesterday's date, the time several minutes prior to when Donn had heard the emergency call. Donn scanned his monitors until he saw Thom on one of them. "There, OSIRIS. Just give me the feeds that have Thom. I don't need to see the whole bay."

Several of his monitors went dead as OSIRIS ceased the feeds. Thom was working on a wall panel in his bay. The time index marker on the playback was running backwards at one second per second.

Donn leaned in and studied the various angles. None of them had a frontal view of his face, and Thom's body blocked most of the open panel's interior, but he was very clearly working on something. As Donn watched, it appeared that Thom was replacing wires and feeds in the bulkhead. His wirecuttters magically repaired two wires, and he worked deftly on others to untie connections and return wires to their original housings as the footage wound backwards. A strange device with exposed motherboards and leads was hooked into the wall panel, and as Donn watched Thom in retrograde action, the caretaker unhooked the makeshift device and placed it on his belt.

"What the hell is he doing? OSIRIS, what's back there?"

"My internal circuitry. I've identified the relevant circuits in the replay."

"What are they?"

"Closed-circuit camera control."

Donn watched as screws jumped from the ground to attach themselves to Thom's screwdriver as he screwed them back into place. The panel was reattached and Thom backpedaled away from it. The artwork of the dancing fairies and sylphs blended well with the access panel — a casual observer might have missed the panel altogether, so well did it fit in the scene.

"I'll be damned. He did it himself," Donn said. "OSIRIS, can you show me Thom's personnel file?"

"Of course not."

"I just wanted to see if he was skilled at computers, electrical engineering, stuff like that. What we saw … OSIRIS, he broke into your circuitry and shut off your cameras so you wouldn't know he was killing the babies. And made it look like an ordinary maintenance cycle so you wouldn't sound the alarm." Donn felt himself trembling. "This wasn't a guy who just snapped one day. He planned this. He planned the murders. But, for God's sake…why?"

Chapter Five

Donn was unable to convince OSIRIS to open bay K-7, or to reveal the contents of Thom's personnel file. The latter he understood — it was a classified document. No one had access to those except command crew. But why had Linna sealed the bay? Contamination of the crime scene? But what did she need to keep uncontaminated? Either she believed Donn's story or she didn't, and if she had checked the video footage of his own bay at the time the alarm had been sounded, she would know by now that Donn had been in K-8 when Thom was wrecking the pods. There was simply no reason to keep K-7 sealed: in fact, there was every reason not to deny entrance to the other caretakers. For a month, K-Deck could pull together and share responsibility for Thom's swimmers. It would be difficult, but certainly possible. Why had Margulies wanted no human involvement in the bay?

One thing was clear: OSIRIS was not budging. Thom's personnel file, and bay K-7, remained sealed. Donn rubbed his face and checked the time. Past four in the morning. He still had daily routine bay maintenance to do, and if he missed the prayerpledge in three hours, OSIRIS would notice.

"OSIRIS, I want to send a delayed message to all caretakers. Set for delivery at eight o'clock in the morning. No, make that nine o'clock. Message follows. 'Hello, Caretakers. As you know, we lost nine of our preborns recently. Please join me at noon for a brief memorial to honor the dead. The ceremony will take place in the Gem Diner. Thank you.' Message ends."

"Acknowledged. Message ready for delayed delivery."

"Thanks." He headed to bed. Three hours' sleep was better than nothing.

——— «» ———

When Donn entered the Gem Diner, more officially known as the G-M decks refectory, at half past eleven, it was nearly full. The Diner had been the site of a gradual, bloodless, playful mutiny over the course of a few months. The issue hadn't been the food: Donn was used to much plainer fare in the military. In addition, several members of the caretaker staff had brought their own regional spices and condiments to flavor the meals provided. Despite the young One Earth government, ethnic and cultural differences were still very much celebrated.

He was unused to the crowd: normally, the dining room wasn't crowded, as many caretakers had developed their own private schedules and did not conform to ordinary mealtimes. The crew had made a halfhearted attempt four months ago to enforce uniform mealtimes, but all that had resulted was a disgruntled crop of caretakers who took to writing on the once-white walls in open defiance. Now, virtually every surface of the refectory displayed writing or artwork, some witty, some purile. Donn himself had not contributed save for a smiley face here and there to mark his approval with an announcement of pairing (there were more than a few crossouts in those pairing announcements, but no one wrote comments to them). He saw Kearney's bohemian hand in places, either through vaguely sexual artwork or in naughty limericks hidden in alcoves and niches.

Those on the fringes of the crowd turned to him as he stood in the doorway, and began to shuffle out of his way with murmured greetings. He watched as the crowd parted before him, and the realization hit him.

They were expecting him to speak.

With everything that had gone on, he hadn't thought to prepare any remarks.

He gathered himself and walked towards the center of the refectory, nodding to caretakers as he met their eyes. Most were starting back at him with understanding, sorrow, or mild encouragement. He distracted himself by estimating the number of bodies in the diner, and came up with perhaps seventy. That would be roughly half of the Caretakers on board, not counting those who watched over the corpsicles in the Freezer. Even as he thought that, he saw a trio of people he only barely recognized, their steel-blue uniforms identifying them as Freezer staff.

Donn made his way to the far end of the refectory, near the food dispensing stations. He looked out at the crowd, but could only see the front edge. He grunted as he climbed up on a table near the dispensing stations.

Once he was on the table, the room became quiet. He looked out at everyone, and just before he spoke, he saw Kearney's bright eyes looking up at him from her niche. He hadn't seen her there before. She looked at him with smirking admiration.

It was exactly what he needed, and it was even sweeter to know that she was doing it on purpose. It required an act of will for her to admire him, and another one to show it — when she did, he knew what it meant. It was not a matter of being real, or authentic. That her emotions had to be manu-factured made them all the more valuable to him.

He smiled at her, but his soft joy at seeing her was muted when he saw the athletic and well-proportioned frame of Jason Collins shuffle into place behind her. He stood close enough to signify he was her companion, but not so close to actively insult Donn.

The hell of it was, Jason was a likeable man. Donn did not deal with him too often, as Jason was a B-Deck caretaker, but when he had, he had found the man impossible to hate. His calm, smooth confidence was inclusive rather than competitive — his demeanor had suggested that although he knew he was competent, he also assumed whomever he was interacting with was equally so.

Donn snorted. No wonder Kearney had chosen him, too.

He turned back to the crowd to find them waiting.

"Thank you all for coming," he said, "even though this is a sad occasion, I thought we ought to do something. I don't think it's right to let this terrible tragedy pass by without doing something."

He sensed rather than heard distinctly the approval of the audience, and he pressed on. "We lost nine of our preborns two days ago — no, not lost. Lost makes it sound like we misplaced them or something. We didn't lose them. One of our own killed them."

There was a collective gasp from the crowd, though whether they were alarmed at the event itself or at Donn's blunt talk, he could not tell.

"We're here to take care of these lives. We're Caretakers. We're supposed to deliver them alive and healthy to our destination on TC-Three. There's a reason we're here — because as good as OSIRIS is, and how good the automation is, the babies still need us. And we failed them."

Now the sounds from the crowd were indignant. He glanced at Kearney, who was looking through her eyelashes at him, her eyes bright and encouraging.

He raised his voice. "That's right. We failed them. When one of us fails, we all do. We have collective responsibility, even if we don't have collective blame. I'm sorry if that makes you mad, but it's the truth."

He took a breath, and spent the interval sweeping the crowd with his eyes. He knew almost everyone, but as he matched eyes with his fellow caretakers, he realized that he was merely familiar with them all. He didn't know any of them, not really. How could he claim to know any of them when the caretaker adjacent to him had committed such an atrocity? He knew only Kearney, and with a sudden, sad epiphany, he finally understood he didn't know her, either.

"But for now, let's bow our heads and remember the nine preborns who will never truly know life."

The room collectively looked down, some caretakers shuffling their feet. After a suitable moment had passed, Donn looked up and gasped.

Margulies stood in the doorway of the refectory, her slate-grey crew uniform standing out amid the multicolored and diverse dress of the caretakers.

Some of the assemblage, cued by his own stare, turned to look, and Donn could all but feel the conflicting emotions of awe and scorn emanating from the crowd.

Margulies held her ground, her blocky, imposing figure filling the hatchway. She held her head high and chin upward at a slight angle, and returned the unwelcome looks with her own assertion of authority.

"Are you here to shut this down, Linna? Tell us all to get back to work?" Donn's words echoed in the refectory, the only other sound a cackle of laughter from Kearney.

"No. I'm here to pay respects to the dead."

Donn chafed. "Oh."

Faces turned to him, then back to Margulies, uncertain.

"Please, go on," Margulies said, her voice even.

Donn hesitated. He had nothing else to say — he suspected Margulies knew that — but under her prompting, he had to come up with something. "Caretakers, crew," he nodded at Linna and continued, "this tragic event should make us all realize the fragile lives under our charge. How quickly and easily those lives can be lost." He saw the trio of Freezer staff in the far right corner and added, "Even in the Freezer. Everyone here is working for a better life for our preborns, our future parents, and those back home. On Earth," he added, remembering too late the shipboard prohibition of calling Earth "home."

"We know we'll face hardships on Tau Ceti Three, and we may lose some more lives there. But if we're to establish a foothold among the stars for humanity, we will..." he ran out of words. He truly did not know what would be needed upon planetfall. No one did.

Into the silence Margulies dropped her own words. "We will need to be as hardworking and vigilant as I know we all can be. Unselfish, communal, and willing to sacrifice for the greater good. Remember that — sacrifice."

Donn saw the heads in the crowd nod. She had found the words. A churlish part of him hated her for her eloquence. But he could not deny the wisdom of what she had said. Agenda or no, she was right. The future would be one of communal sacrifice for the well-being of the children, the colony, the future. A quotation exploded in his mind, and he cleared his throat before saying, "A society grows great when old men plant trees whose shade they know they shall never sit in."

A murmur of assent rippled through the crowd, and Donn glanced down at Kearney, who merely rolled her eyes, her lips pressed in a grim line.

"Well said, Donn," Margulies added.

"Thank you," Donn said, shaken by Kearney's unenthusiastic demeanor. Awkwardly to the assembled caretakers, he added, "That's all I had for you. Thank you all for coming." He found a clear space in front of the table and hopped down to the deck.

In a short time, the refectory was abuzz with muted and inconsequential conversations. Caretakers greeted one another and then stood awkwardly in small knots, unsure what to say or do. Some began to file out. Donn sought out Kearney and found her with Collins, his lean height towering over her. As he approached, a crewmember from the engineering staff reached out to shake Kearney's hand. "Thanks again for your nice letter to the captain about my, well, my situation," she was saying. "It really helped."

"I'm happy to do it," Kearney said, returning the handshake. The engineer moved off, and Donn waited for her to be out of earshot before he spoke.

"Kearney," Donn said, interrupting Collins in mid-sentence. Before she answered, he turned to the B-Deck caretaker and said, "sorry."

"No, that's all right. Good job up there," Collins said with clear sincerity.

"Thanks," Donn said and looked at Kearney. "What did you think?"

"I didn't know it was a performance, Donn. I thought this was a memorial."

"What do you mean?"

She snorted. "You know exactly what I mean. Trying to get into a fight with Margulies here. Shouldn't have done that, Donn."

"I didn't…" he started, then stopped. He stared at Kearney, who looked back at him with amused accusation. "So what if I did?" Donn winced at his own childishness.

Kearney smirked, then her eyes left Donn's to follow something happening behind him.

Donn turned to see Margulies weaving through the thinning crowd, coming towards the trio.

"Donn, Kearney, Jason," Margulies said, her voice carrying just enough recognition to cause Donn to wonder just what she knew about the three of them and their complicated relationship.

"Linna," Collins said. "A nice ceremony, wasn't it?"

"Yes." Margulies looked directly at Donn. "I will need to see you as soon as you are available."

"All right," Donn said.

"We're kind of in the middle of a conversation, Linna." Kearney placed unusual emphasis on alternating syllables, as if she were a pupil reciting iambic pentameter.

Margulies merely raised an eyebrow, deflecting the comment as casually as a horse's tail did flies. "Of course. Please, continue." She folded her arms and widened her stance.

"I was just saying how necessary this was," Kearney lied, "and what a good idea it was. Caretaker Cardenio really has the pulse of the ship, don't you think?"

Donn kept his face impassive, though behind his expression he fought to understand Kearney's attitude. Not ten seconds ago, she had been admonishing him for his tone and juvenile approach to Margulies' presence, and now she was blatantly lying to the woman on his behalf.

"He is well respected, yes," Margulies said.

"I agree," Jason chimed in. "Even on B-Deck, everyone was talking about this memorial. A very good idea, Donn."

Margulies' jaw muscles twitched as she locked eyes with Donn. "Anyway, like I said. At your earliest convenience. We need to meet."

"That sounds like he's in trouble," Kearney said, loudly. A small nearby clique of caretakers from L-Deck turned at her comment, listening.

Margulies glared at Kearney. "It's a personnel matter. Between Caretaker Cardenio and myself."

"But if he doesn't mind talking about it, then what's the problem? You don't, do you, Donn?" Kearney affected innocence as she looked at him, blinking.

"Now's not the time, K," Donn said, watching the caretakers in the half-full refectory becoming aware of their conversation.

"Yeah, this sounds more like—" Jason began, but was cut off by Margulies.

"Maybe it would be best if you all returned to your quarters or your bays."

"Why? I feel like a snack. Am I allowed to have one in my off hours?" Kearney smirked at Margulies.

Margulies kept her voice still. "Of course, but not if it disrupts the normal functioning of—"

"What disruption? I'm just gonna grab something. I feel like something from India today."

Margulies dropped her voice a half-octave. "You know very well what I mean. It's time to return to your quarters, or to your bays." She turned, aware of the crowd around her without looking, and added, "all of you."

"Kearney, maybe we should just leave," Jason said.

Donn watched the interaction, despising himself for his pettiness. Now that Collins had suggested it, he wanted Kearney to stay, if for no other reason than disobeying Collins. He knew how wretched he was being, but he also knew how he felt. And what could he do other than feel?

Kearney turned to Donn. "Should I?"

He nodded. "Yeah, I think so. I'll stay and talk to Margulies." He spoke to the other caretakers. "She's right, everyone. We're all done here." He turned back to Collins and Kearney, and managed not to sound smug. "Thanks for coming, though."

Collins nodded and said with no trace of bitterness or irony, "Thank you for arranging it." He guided Kearney towards the door, his hand on her elbow. She gave Donn one last concerned glance, and left with Collins. The others shuffled out of the refectory, Margulies' eyes everywhere but on Donn.

The instant the refectory hatch closed, Margulies turned to him. "So. What was this, then?"

"A memorial service."

"I specifically ordered you not to do this. I can't believe you didn't understand me. This was a willful act of defiance."

"Yeah. It was," Donn said. "Is that why you showed up? Like some kind of raid?"

Margulies glared at him for a moment. "I told you why I was here. I was paying respect to the dead."

"Even though you ordered me not to pay respect to the dead? You're one confused woman."

"That's all you're going to say?"

Donn shrugged, but not to annoy her. "I don't have anything else to say. You told me not to, and I did it."

"Did you think I wouldn't find out?"

Donn snorted. "I knew you would. I mean, how could you not? Made the announcement on public channels, dozens of caretakers showed up — of course you were going to find out."

Margulies snarled at him. "But you thought I wouldn't have the guts to do anything to you, is that it? You're immune? All I could do was put another reprimand on file for you? Which doesn't mean shit?"

Again, Donn shrugged. He saw the effect the gesture had on her, and spoke quickly to try and mitigate it. "I'm not trying to annoy you, Linna. This isn't personal. I just felt the nine kids deserved at least this. And a full investigation as to what happened." He hesitated, then decided to continue. "You know I looked at the video record of K-seven, don't you?"

Linna's nostrils flared. "What?"

"Oh, I sort of thought you knew. Well, just so you know I'm not trying to undermine you—"

"Yes, you are."

"No, I'm really not. Have you seen OSIRIS' video record of what was going on in K-seven prior to the camera shutdown?"

Linna crossed her arms. "Tell me what you saw."

"Fair enough. I saw Thom working on one of the computer panels in his bay. He'd somehow pried open the panel and was monkeying around in there. I don't know what he was up to, but shortly after that, the camera feed went dead. OSIRIS reported that Thom was accessing camera control. It's not hard to guess what happened. Thom got into OSIRIS' routines somehow and turned off the cameras. And he did it in such a way that no one noticed."

Linna looked suddenly defeated. "Okay, dammit, yeah. We saw the same thing. How the hell did you get access? I left orders that no one—"

"Was to enter the bay, yeah." Donn grinned without humor. "Gotta be more specific, Linna. I was able to convince OSIRIS to let me see the video. Took some doing, but..." he shrugged again.

"Goddess damn it, Donn. You deliberately went against orders you knew were intended to keep you out."

Donn scowled at her. "Look, I don't see why that matters so much. You don't want everyone in the ship to lose their minds over this, sure, but I'm already as connected as—"

"Did you see anything else?" Linna snapped.

"What? Nothing else. Just Thom working on the computer access panel."

"Just the one panel?"

"Yeah. Why, has he done this before?"

Linna shook her head. "No. Not that I've seen, at least."

"Do you think there's—"

"You need to let crew handle this. What you need to worry about is what you've done."

"What I've done? Linna, Thom murdered—"

"Shut up. That's over and done with. I ordered you not to hold this service, and you did it anyway. And you knew — you had to know — that my orders that K-seven be sealed meant I didn't want you snooping around in there. At every turn, you're demonstrating your willful disobedience."

Donn frowned. "I went against your orders, sure, but I had to find out what—"

"I said shut up. I've really had it with you. You think it's easy conducting an investigation like this? And now I've got to worry about keeping your ass in line on top of everything else?"

Donn fell silent, studying her. They stared at one another for a long moment. Donn finally said, "Listen, Linna, I disobeyed you. I know you need to punish me. I knew something like this was coming, and I guess I accept it. But the memorial was important to me, and important to the rest of the caretakers. I wasn't doing it to spite you personally. But you do what you have to do. As for me, I'm going to keep looking into this. I have to."

Margulies' voice was frighteningly calm. "Fine. Then you will be reassigned to the Freezer. One way or another, you've got to stay out of this and let me do my job. And if you can't follow orders down there, maybe you'll go into it as a corpsicle instead of an attendant."

"What? You can't do that! I'm a caretaker, damn you! You can't—"

"It's done. And you're confined to your quarters when you're not in the Freezer. Cross me on this one, Cardenio, and you'll find yourself waking up in a month from coldsleep."

Donn just stared at her, the import of her words slowly hitting home. "You're serious. I meant restrict my privileges, not this. How do you intend to do this if I simply refuse? You said it yourself: I'm disobedient. I'll disobey that, too."

"I'll bring down six or seven crew and wrestle your ass into a hibernation pod," Margulies' voice was still calm, though her nostrils were wide and horselike.

"You'd do all that? And if word got out to the other caretakers?"

"They'll stay in line. And if they don't, there's plenty of room in the Freezer for them, too."

"What about all the preborns?"

Margulies scowled. "We'll have to make do with computer monitoring. And you know how problematic that is. You saw Thom's numbers."

Now Donn felt his own incredulity fading to be replaced by anger. "You'd sacrifice the health of the preborns?"

"Bullshit. You've taken care of them to the point that OSIRIS can do the rest. But if it was to save the mission? Yes. In a second."

"They are the mission!"

For an instant, Donn thought he saw something in Margulies face he had never seen before, and which was so out of place as to momentarily stun him. For that moment, the anger left her features to be replaced by envy. He wondered at it, but so fleeting was the instant that he was scarcely sure he had seen it. She replaced her mask of anger — and Donn was now convinced that indeed it was a mask — and spoke again.

"Go back to your quarters, then report to the Freezer at eight o'clock tomorrow morning. They'll train you up on what you need to know. Do I need to bring down crew to force you back to your room?"

Donn was still shaken by what he had seen in her face. "No. I'll go."

"I'll be watching. Try anything again, and I'll do what I said. You want answers to why Agee did what he did? Stay out of my way and let me find them. You want more than a memorial for the dead preborns? You want justice for them? Then do as you're told and I'll get it." She spun on her heel and strode out of the refectory. Donn was left to marvel at his situation, and at another mystery that confronted him.

Margulies wanted what he wanted.

Chapter Six

"The Freezer?" Kearney said, her triangular face showing shock and indignation. Her shoulders, covered with a violet wrap, were barely visible at the edge of the screen.

"Yeah. I report there at eight tomorrow."

"Donn, what are—" Kearney didn't finish the thought before beginning another one. "Where does she get off doing that?"

"I dunno, K. But she did."

"And threatened to bring force," Kearney said, shaking her head. She looked down, then back up again. "All this because of the memorial?"

Donn sighed. "I don't think it was just that. She thinks I am being insubordinate."

"So? I'm insubordinate all the time. Got contraband all over my room and my body. I don't get sent to the fuckin' Freezer for it."

"Yeah, that's true. Maybe she likes you," Donn said wryly.

"Yeah. That must be it," Kearney snorted. Her tone grew soft. "Donn, come over here. Spend the night."

"I'd love to, K. But she's confined me to quarters."

"I'll come there, then."

"I thought you had a policy? People come to you."

"I do. But you're a special case, Donn. I'll be right over." The screen went dark, and Donn was left looking at his own reflection. He was amused to see himself smiling.

Kearney was at his door a few minutes later. She was wearing her standard issue coveralls, looking incongruously official. He stepped aside to let her enter. She did so swiftly, casting a glance down the corridor before stepping inside.

"Thanks for coming," Donn said. He had barely finished closing the door when she was in his arms, allowing him to hold her.

"Oh, Donn," she said into his chest. "I'm so sorry this happened to you."

He held her for a few moments, glad to be able to do so. Moreover, he knew that this was not for her — she was not one to meet problems with stereotypical feminine softness.

She was being what he needed. It's what she did. For him, for everyone.

He withdrew his arms and placed his hands on her biceps. "Thanks," he said, and her eyes showed she understood.

The more authentic Kearney returned and she smirked. "I think Yune saw me."

"Oh?"

"Yeah." She shrugged as if coming to a decision. "Fuck it. So he saw me, so what."

"Exactly. I don't see why that matters."

Kearney looked at him, her left eyebrow fractionally higher than her right. "You don't? That's 'cause you aren't a woman."

"Oh, come on, K. You really think that matters anymore? Here?"

She snorted and walked past him to his bed. She sat down on it, bouncing a little. "Especially here, Donn. We're a tiny little community, and everyone talks."

"I'd have thought you of all people wouldn't care what people say."

"I'm a free spirit, is that it? Gonna start the New Bohemian Revolution on TC-Three? Yeah, well, I'm not stupid. This little group of two hundred—"

"One hundred ninety-eight awake adults."

"Whatever. I've spent the last year building up this image, and it's served me well. I'm gonna continue it on planet."

Donn's smile faded. "What image?"

"The go-to gal. Person everyone goes to. And no," she said, smirking at him, "not because of my magic vagina, if that's what you're thinking."

"I wasn't thinking that." Donn couldn't resist a grin, even under the circumstances.

"The hell you weren't. I've always been the person other people see when they need something. Information.

Contraband. A shoulder to cry on. An ear to listen. Way before this mission I was like that. So I see no reason to stop now."

"Then why are you worried that Yune might have seen you come here?"

Kearney just smiled back. "Never mind." She paused a beat, collecting herself, and said in a different tone, "So, the Freezer, huh?"

"It won't be that bad, K. I'm just being reassigned, not spaced."

"Still. Having to leave your swimmers. How are you gonna deal with that?"

Donn shrugged with false indifference. "Sooner or later, I was going to have to turn them over to their assigned parents. So are you. I'm just doing it a little sooner, that's all. When we hit dirt on TC-Three, none of this is gonna matter, anyway. There won't be any Freezer and we'll all be working together. It's just for a month."

"Uh-huh."

A moment's silence turned into several. Donn ended it, saying, "I still don't understand what happened with Thom, though. I know he was the one who overrode OSIRIS' camera surveillance system."

"You do?"

"Yeah. I convinced OSIRIS to show me the footage from before the cameras went out. Thom had opened a wiring panel and had accessed the computer's command net."

"Damn. That's impressive. At least, I think it is. I never got into that stuff."

Donn smirked at her. "How do you get all your contraband, then?"

Kearney grinned back. "Human resources, Donn. Like I said, I'm a slut who gets what you need. And it's not like my contraband is hurting anyone. Some fabric from spare overalls, makeshift dye from food stores, homemade hootch from some of the hydroponics staff, pharmaceuticals from sickbay supply, stuff like that. Makes the trip bearable. But I don't mess with the serious stuff, like OSIRIS and his operating system. That's some serious shit."

"I know. Thom wanted to keep OSIRIS from knowing what he was doing, but he had to know that as soon as he destroyed a pod, there would be a general alarm. And he hadn't even barricaded his door. So what did disabling the cameras get him?"

Kearney's voice softened. "Don't look for logic in baby-murdering, Donn. He just snapped for some reason. You can't try to find the sense in it."

"But he took some precautions, that's my point. Just not enough of them. He didn't wake up one day and decide, 'I'm going to kill the preborns.' He had a plan, or part of one."

Kearney scooted closer to him and lay her hand on his knee, giving it a few squeezes. "You're gonna make yourself crazy with this."

Donn murmured, "'This is better for them. This is better than what they have coming.' That's what he said."

"Donn..."

"How could he think murdering them was better than the colonization effort? We were all screened carefully. We all believe in it. Right, K?"

"Yeah, of course."

Donn looked at her for a moment, then asked, "Why did you want to come on this mission? What do you think about colonizing another planet? That's not part of your 'go-to gal' image."

Kearney let go of Donn's knee and sighed with a hint of resignation in her voice, "Those are two different questions. I came along because I guess I wanted to revitalize myself. I won't say I'm running away from anything, exactly, but I wanted to be part of something ... alive and new. Especially since I'm entering my own final act."

"You—"

"No. Don't do that, Donn. I'm over fifty. Probably got fifty years left, tops. I could have just run out the clock back home, but I wanted to ... well, 'start over' is not the right way to put it. 'Begin again,' how's that?"

"Sounds fine to me. You believe in the mission, though, right?"

"Of course. Best idea Earth's had in a long time, maybe forever. Same principle as me. Earth's old, Donn. The planet itself, the people, everything. I'm not saying Earth is doomed, but it needed the same thing I did. A way to revitalize itself."

"Earth needed to have a child," Donn said.

"What?"

"Earth needed to have a child. That's what this is. A child who grew up and left the house."

"Guess that's a way to look at it."

Donn nodded. "Plus there was the war."

"Yeah. The war." Her voice carried a hint of skepticism in it.

Donn paused, then said, "You don't believe the official version of why this mission is happening?"

Kearney snickered again. "I don't believe fully in the official version of anything, Donn. You know that."

"But it does make sense. The war showed us that we're not invincible, that there is at least one alien race out here," he gestured vaguely at the walls, as if to indicate the vastness of space surrounding them, "who is capable of ending us. So we need a foothold on another world."

"Yeah. Makes sense. I'm sure that's it."

Donn chuckled once. "You don't sound convinced."

"Oh, I am. It makes sense. I'm just sure that Earth is looking to somehow exploit us once we get TC up and running."

"Exploit us? How? We'll be twelve light-years away."

"So? A-drive gets us there in less than a year. And maybe future ships will go even faster. What's to stop Earth from shipping us their prisoners? Or other undesirables once we're a self-sufficient colony?"

"So you think we're supposed to set up a prison colony? These preborns will be trained to be wardens and jailers?"

"I'm not saying that, exactly," Kearney sighed. "Just somehow, in some way, Earth will try to find a way to make the Tau Ceti colony about their interests, not ours. That's why we need to make our new home on TC-Three independent. Not a colony: a new world. Otherwise we'll be just a puppet of One Earth."

"You don't approve of One Earth?"

Kearney shrugged. "It's too young. And it was formed just because some alien assholes came to conquer us. That's not a great beginning to a government."

"Man, you're a pessimist." Donn teased.

"You bet your ass."

"That's a tough way to live, isn't it?"

"Nope. I wake up each morning surprised I'm not dead. It's a pretty good feeling."

Donn laughed. "I guess that's true."

"Now, I didn't come over here just to talk, y'know." She put her hand on his knee again.

"I figured."

"So why are you on the chair and I'm on the bed?"

Donn said, "You sure Collins won't—" he stopped himself, but it was too late. The words, and the feelings, were in the open again.

He winced inwardly as he saw the words' effect on her. Her hand froze on his knee, and she gathered herself before she answered. "Donn, we shouldn't talk about that. You know what our arrangement is, and you agreed to it. I'm not gonna commit to one person. It's not who I am. And I don't expect you to be, either."

"I know. I can't help it."

"Try," Kearney said, coldness creeping into her voice.

"Dammit, K. What do you want from me?"

"Right now? Your body against mine."

"I want more."

"You want me to say I love you? Jezeus, Donn, you know I do. I came over here to help you through this whole thing with Thom and the Freezer and all that. We talk, we have a good time, we fuck. You say you want more, but what you really mean is you want me to yourself."

"Yeah," Donn said. "I do."

"Why? Why does it have to be like that, Donn?" Her hand resumed the gentle smoothing of his knee. "I love being around you. But I also love being with others. Don't limit me, Donn. You said before that you're gonna have to give up your preborns soon. They don't belong to you, and Donn, my friend, neither do I."

"I know you don't. It's not that. Not at all."

"Not at all?"

Donn shook his head. He looked at her as if seeing her anew. She was here, now, and she wanted him. At this moment, there was no Freezer, no dead preborns, no war.

He struggled with his mind to keep that so. But a thought rose like a rock jutting out of the sea, washed by waves but unmoved by them.

You're not enough.

His tiny LEO fighter had been unable to even slow the advance of the Starfish. He hadn't detected the warning signs in Thom to prevent the murder of nine preborns. He wasn't important enough to Margulies to keep as K-8's caretaker.

And he wasn't enough to satisfy Kearney.

"Then what is it?" Kearney asked.

"Doesn't matter," Donn said, standing from the chair and setting down on the bed next to her. "You're here, I'm here, and we have the night."

Kearney smiled in surprise. "That's right, Donn. That's all that matters."

He nodded even as his mind disagreed.

———— «‹›» ————

Agnes's soft voice woke him hours later. He stirred, turning his head to see Kearney's eyes open and looking back at him.

"Dammit," she said softly, then started to extricate herself from his embrace.

He let her go and swung his feet off the bed, grunting with effort as he rose to a standing position. "Agnes, what time is it?"

"Zero seven sixteen. Your duty shift begins at zero eight hundred."

Donn looked back at Kearney and held his hand out for her. She took it and stood from the bed. Her nude body was alabaster. She looked around the room.

"In the sheet, I think," Donn said, nodding to the foot of the bed.

Kearney retrieved her clothes and shook them out while Donn selected one of his fresher overalls. The two dressed in silence.

"You going to check in on your swimmers, K?" Donn asked a few minutes later, when she was doing her best to arrange her hair in the mirror.

"Probably. I got a few in a little trouble, so I'll see how they're responding to the changes I made. Other than that, I'm mostly free today."

"Would you do me a favor, then?"

"What is it?" she asked, turning her head left and right and appraising her appearance in the mirror.

"Look in on my guys for me."

She turned. "You don't think they can go a day without you? OSIRIS or Agnes can't watch them?"

"I went in and checked on Thom's after the ... after. And his were a mess."

"That was probably because he was neglecting them, right? Not because OSIRIS screwed up."

"Even so. OSIRIS had them under observation, too. That's how I got the records. And he hadn't done anything. And I've had more arguments with Agnes over adjustments than I can remember. I'd feel better if I knew a human being I trust was watching them while I'm gone."

"How do you know I'm not gonna snap, too?" Her tone was ambiguous.

"That's not funny."

The glint in her eye vanished. "You're right. Sorry. Bad taste. I'd be happy to check in on your preborns." She sighed and stopped fussing with her hair. "Well, that's as good as that's gonna get. You don't have anything? No brush, comb, nothing?"

"Nope." Donn rubbed his close-cropped head. "Clippers. Best hair care product I have."

"Yeah. Shitload of help that does me. Oh, well. Yune will just have more clues to piece together." She turned and faced Donn, her hands on her hips. "You gonna be okay?"

"Sure," Donn said. He decided not to be flippant. "Look, Kearney, about all I was saying last night, if you need to see some other people today, then I—"

Kearney scowled. "Need to see other people? I don't need to. I want to. I'm not saying I'm gonna — maybe I will, maybe I won't — but it's not a need, Donn. And what, were you gonna give me fuckin' permission to do it?"

"Jezeus, K, just let me say it, all right? I know I don't own you, or need to give you permission to see other people or sleep with them. But just let me say it, all right? There's times a man needs to pretend certain things about the woman he's fucking. So just pretend for a little while and let me be noble. Let me have that."

Kearney stopped scowling and instead looked at him with a mixture of pity and regret. It was one of the most horrible expressions Donn had ever had thrown at him. "Fine, Donn. Say what you need to, and I'll be the woman you need me to be." Her voice was devoid of feeling.

"All I wanted to say was you do what you want to do. See other men and other women. I can't lie and tell you I like the idea, but you said it yourself — this is the arrangement."

Kearney looked up at him, and when she spoke, it was with genuine care. "Maybe it shouldn't be anymore, Donn. This is ... I don't think you can handle it. Maybe you and I should ... go our separate ways."

Donn stepped back. "What? That's not what I meant, K."

"But I think it might be what you need. You need someone you can be everything to. Someone who will surrender to you. I don't mean that in the sense of control or dominance. But you don't want someone like me. You want ... ivy. Someone who clings."

"That's not true."

Kearney sighed. "All right, Donn. All right. Maybe this isn't the best time for this. I'm sorry I brought it up, this of all mornings." She came closer and kissed him briefly. "I'll see you tonight, okay? Because I want to, not because you need me."

"Assuming I'm not a corpsicle," Donn said with weak humor.

"Yes, assuming that." She patted his flank and smiled. "Now get going. I don't want my young stud late to his first day of work at the Freezer."

"I love you, Kearney."

"Oh, Donn. I love you, too. Now go."

Chapter Seven

Donn Cardenio. I've been reassigned here." Donn spoke to the group of four cryogenic hibernation support staff members in what was labeled the "Cryogenic Hibernation Observation Room." It was a long, narrow area, with monitoring stations lining the walls. The four blue-clad Freezer staffers sat at swivel chairs in front of their monitors.

The two women and two men looked back at him dully. One of them, a woman with unkempt hair the same color of her ashen skin, said, "What was your name again?"

"Donn Cardenio. I'm sure OSIRIS has a record of the transfer."

She grunted and swiveled in her chair to face her computer monitor. Donn watched as she hunted for the appropriate key to call up OSIRIS. He wondered why the woman didn't just speak to the interface, but shrugged inwardly and let her go about her business.

As she worked, one of the other workers, a man with a close-shaven beard, said, "We've never had a transfer. I didn't even know we could. What happened?"

Donn was about to answer when he caught the image on the screen the bearded man had been watching. It did not display the cryogenic bay, nor did it have data or anything pertinent on it. Instead, Donn recognized one of the popular puzzle games OSIRIS had available to staff in their down time. The bright colors and shapes were unmistakable.

He took his eyes from the game and addressed the man. "Kind of a long story. Margulies decided I would be of more use down here." During his walk to the Freezer that morning he had rejected the idea of telling the staffers he was being punished, since that would be offensive to those who had been chosen for this duty.

"Not much to do, at least not yet," the bearded man said, turning back to his game and hitting some keys. Shapes changed color and position on the screen. Donn had played the game once or twice, but it had not appealed to him. It was simplistic and addictive.

The woman with ashen skin and hair turned back, having given up on the computer system. "I can't find it, but I'm sure it's fine." Her voice oscillated strangely, as if she were on the verge of tears. "My name is Randi. Randi Starch." She stopped, then added, "Oh, and this is Anson, and that's Shereen," Randi pointed to a woman with a wrist brace on her right hand who turned from her monitor and waved, then returned to work. "And that's Delano." She referred to the last worker, a lean man who was studying his screen intently. The man turned his head and said quietly, "Good to have you, Donn. I'm just finishing something up, so excuse me."

"Good to be here," Donn said, and he heard Anson snort. When he turned to look at the man, he saw him hard at work on whatever level in the game he had achieved. Whether he had snorted at the comment or at some game development, Donn was unsure. He turned instead to Randi. "You can't find my transfer in OSIRIS?"

"No, but like I said, I am sure it's fine. I mean, why would you be lying about this?"

"Exactly," Donn said, but the confused look on Randi's face told him her question had not been rhetorical. "Oh, well, I'm not. Do you mind if I ask OSIRIS myself?"

For an instant, Randi looked frightened, but she nodded. "No, go ahead. Maybe you can find it."

"OSIRIS, pull up my transfer order, please," Donn said.

"Oh, we don't have voice access on," Randi said, turning back to her monitor.

"I see. Well, did you want me to try on your screen?"

"No, let me turn on the voice access."

"You're going to activate OSIRIS in here?" Shereen asked.

Randi said in her close-to-tears voice, "Just for a second. So Dan can check his transfer."

Shereen sighed and fell silent.

"Okay, go ahead."

Donn paused before he spoke. He had not known precisely what to expect in the Freezer, but he had at least thought it would be comparable to his own work as a caretaker. Looking after the almost twenty-one thousand hibernating adults who would become the parents to the children he had been caring for had to be similar to his old job. Or so he had thought.

He hadn't time to reflect on the differences now. Randi was waiting.

"OSIRIS, please display my transfer order on Randi's screen."

"Done," OSIRIS said. "Have you started there yet?"

"Yes, I've been here for about ten minutes."

"Understood. Randi, please mark Donn as 'started work.'"

Donn blinked and watched as Randi carefully touched her screen on the indicated box. "There. All checked in." She turned back to Donn. "Did you need OSIRIS for anything else?"

"Uh, not that I can think of."

"Okay. OSIRIS, shut off voice access, please."

"Voice access off," OSIRIS replied.

"Why do you guys keep it turned off?" Donn asked.

"Oh, well, you know," Randi said vaguely. "Privacy, things like that. We don't really need him, so there's no reason to have him on. And it drains his attention from other ship functions."

The illogic of her response almost prompted Donn to ask further, but he resisted the impulse. "Right. Well, is there anything you want to show me about the work I'll be doing?"

"This is pretty much it," Anson said, then fell silent again, his tongue partially out of his mouth as he deftly maneuvered his shapes for his game.

Delano spun his seat and stood. "I can show you. I'm okay for now on my beds. Come on." He strode down the walkway between the chairs and opened the hatchway at the end of it. The next room contained six lockers and had a distinctly human odor.

"Yeah. You get used to it," Delano said idly. "Some of our staff is not as good about personal hygiene as they should be." He nodded his chin towards a hatchway opposite the one that led to the control room. "That's the hibernation chamber there." He looked back at Donn and sized him up. "I think I have a suit that'll fit you. You're bigger than me, but Anson's might fit." He withdrew a set of blue coveralls and handed them to Donn. "Pretty straightforward. Might be a little snug."

"Is it a clean suit, or something?"

"No. Just our standard uniform."

Donn regarded it. "But it's someone else's. Why am I putting this on?"

Delano seemed to consider that. "Like I said, it's our uniform." He stared at Donn, as if he had explained everything thoroughly.

Donn nodded. He had no particular desire to put on someone else's coveralls, especially with Delano's comment in mind, but again, he didn't want to offend the staff. He struggled into the suit, grunting as he stuffed his large frame into the garment. He managed to zip up the front over his wide chest.

"Okay. Lemme show you the place," Delano said, and opened the hatch.

Donn entered the next chamber and looked around. He was struck by how similar it appeared to his own bay. Innumerable sleeping pods were arranged in rows, columns, and trays, just like his swimmers were. The chamber was lit indifferently, neither dimly nor brightly.

He grunted. "I expected it to be cold."

"Why?"

"Hibernation, you know."

"Oh, sure. It's chemical hibernation. I guess it's technically torpor. Yeah, we lower the body temperature by about seven degrees."

"That's all?"

"That's all it takes. We go from thirty-seven to about thirty."

"Huh. I guess we shouldn't call them 'corpsicles,' then. That's probably offensive to you guys, isn't it?"

Delano half-grinned. "Nope. We call them that, too. And a lot worse."

"Do you name them?"

Delano's grin disappeared. "What?"

"Names. Do you give them names?"

"They already have names."

"No, I realize that. I meant nicknames."

Delano stared at him for a beat, then said slowly, "Why would we give them nicknames?"

"No reason. I was just curious."

"Sure. Here," Delano said, taking a small wheeled platform from a shelf near the hatchway. "Scooter. Helps us get around easily."

Donn took the scooter and examined it. "Lean forward, backward, and differential left and right?"

"You got it. Pretty easy." He took a second scooter from the shelf and mounted it. "Though Randi takes a tumble about once a week," he added, smirking.

"So you've got twenty thousand, seven hundred thirty-six down here?" Donn said, climbing aboard his own scooter and quickly familiarizing himself with the pressure controls.

"Yeah. How'd you know that?"

"I asked OSIRIS before I got here. Seemed like a good idea, to know a little about this place before starting."

"But you didn't know about chemical torpor."

Donn shrugged. "Nope. I know what I need to do my job. Do you know about embryonic metabolism and biochemistry?"

Delano looked at him for a moment, as if studying him, before replying. "I guess not. By the way, I wanted to say that the memorial service you held was touching. I think we all needed that."

Donn realized at that moment where he had recognized Delano from. He had been one of the three Freezer staff at the refectory. "Thanks. Yeah, I saw you there. Thanks for coming."

"Least I could do. Okay, let's take a ride. Get you used to the scooters." Delano rolled off down the central aisle, slowly, watching Donn.

The scooter was extremely rider-friendly; Donn quickly learned how much pressure to apply to maneuver the platform, and caught up to Delano easily.

"Okay, as you can see, these are the hibernation units. We call them 'beds' sometimes. They are completely self-contained and self-regulating. OSIRIS monitors each one of them, and relays the data to us in the control center."

Donn nodded as the two sped down the aisle. "That's a lot like the pseudowombs. So you make adjustments as necessary? If you notice one of your sleepers is in trouble?"

Delano shook his head. "Nope. OSIRIS takes care of all that. We're here mainly to verify everything is the way it should be. Turns out, taking care of corpsicles is pretty easy."

Donn watched the hibernation units pass by as he rode. He started to slow down, stopping at one of the units at random. Delano continued, then reversed course to return to him.

"Show me," Donn said, gesturing at the unit.

"Show you what?"

"The features of the pod. Or capsule, bed, whatever you call it."

Delano stared at him for a moment, then looked at the unit. "Not much to show you." He scooted closer to the sleek silver cylinder that resembled a sarcophagus. There was a small glass window that showed the sleeping face of the hibernator. Delano pointed to a row of tiny green lights near the base of the unit. "Those show the status of the unit. But they are on the big board back in the control room, too. We don't check them unit by unit. Only when the board tells us there's a problem."

"So you don't do rounds or anything?"

"No need. When we get a red light, but otherwise—"

"How often is that?" Donn said, stepping off his scooter and approaching the unit. He slid his hand over the top of the pod. Unlike his pods back in K-8, this one was cold to the touch.

"It's never happened."

Donn turned from his examination of the unit to look at Delano. "Never? Out of over twenty thousand? That's damn efficient."

Delano shrugged. "Like I said, there's not much that can go wrong."

Donn returned to the bed, feeling its contours and rounded edges. "What's the metabolic rate of one of these guys?"

"About twenty percent normal. But it fluctuates a lot."

"How so?"

"Well, the heartbeat speeds up when they take a breath, but it can be fifteen, twenty seconds between beats otherwise. Average pulse is about twelve beats a minute, but it is kind of irregular."

"So how do you monitor it, if it is irregular? What are you looking for?" Donn asked.

"I told you. We don't really. OSIRIS does."

Donn nodded absently. "How do you open this thing?" He bent down to find a seam. The unit resembled a coffin so much that he expected to be able to lift the lid and expose the sleeper. The units were laying horizontally, their occupants sleeping face-up inside.

"What do you mean? We don't open them. Why would we?"

"Suppose there's a problem, and you need to get in there to fix it. How would you?"

Delano took a breath. "You're not getting this. There aren't problems here. You're looking at twenty thousand sleeping people. They're in a state of torpor, all their functions slower. They each connect to feeding tubes, and they get low-grade electrical shocks to keep them from atrophy. OSIRIS watches them. That's all."

Donn tried to look inside, but the glass square over the sleeper's face was dark. "Do you use peepers to look inside?"

"Peepers?"

"Yeah. Penetrating sensor goggles, you know."

"We don't have that. There's no need to look inside."

Donn scowled and pulled away from the pod. "Okay, then. No offense, Delano, but what the hell do you guys actually do?"

"We're important to the mission. If we—"

Donn interrupted gently. "I know you are. I didn't mean that. I meant it literally. What takes up your days?"

Delano's indignation faded to be replaced by embarrassment. "We ... play vidgames. We watch the ship's entertainment. Sometimes have scooter races. I'm forty-four and thirty."

"You're what?"

"My record. Forty-four wins, thirty losses. Anson is ahead of me, but I'll get him."

"Good for you."

Delano snapped his chin up. "Hey, Cardenio, you mind some advice?"

"Sure."

"I'm not a moron, you know. No one gets assigned to the Freezer mid-voyage. You were the caretaker next to the room where all those babies died. Sure, you did the memorial, which was good, but now I'm thinking you are under suspicion by the crew, and you were put down here where you can't do any real damage. So maybe drop the superior attitude."

Donn looked up at Delano, who was swaying gently back and forth on his scooter. "Get one thing straight, Delano. I had nothing to do with the murders. I stopped Thom before he could kill more of them. I wasn't put down here because I am a risk."

"Yeah? Then why were you?"

"I'm an insubordinate asshole, that's why."

"Uh-huh."

Donn sighed. "Anyway, look. I'm not trying to cause trouble. If I'm acting like a shit, then I'm sorry. I just don't get how it works here, I guess."

Delano grunted. "Okay. Just don't come down here like you're something special. You're one of us now. Things'll go a lot smoother for you once you get that straight."

"I hear you." Donn continued to inspect the sleeping pod and said, "So that's it? We watch the pods, nothing happens, we go back to our quarters?"

"You got it."

"And the wakeup protocol? We're about a month out from planetfall. How does that work?"

Delano shrugged. "OSIRIS does that, too. There's a schedule back in the control room. I think it's a four-day process if I remember. But it's automated, like everything else."

"Right," Donn said. He stood next to the sleeping pod. "Well, then I guess I pulled pretty light duty. Good for me."

Delano eyed him for a moment, then finally said, "Guess so. Let's head back to the control room. Randi sometimes brings in some snacks from the refectory." He spun his scooter around and waited for Donn to mount his own and follow.

Donn took a last look at the sleeping pod and followed. Countless rows of sleeping future colonists — the people he would be turning over his preborns to in a month — flashed by in identical snow-white sleeping pods. How could these slumbering people care for his babies like he had? How could they love them? He knew from the prelaunch briefing that the twenty thousand adults had been carefully select-ed — mostly in male-female pairs, though there were a few thousand same-sex couples, singles, and communal polyg-amous units of various numbers and configurations — and represented all necessary childrearing skills and professions, but nevertheless, he was skeptical. And the Freezer crew had not done anything to allay his anxiety about the upcoming planetfall.

Donn considered Delano. The man clearly didn't care about his charges, didn't care that he and the rest of the Freezer staff were all but superfluous, and didn't feel any sense of worry at the upcoming challenges once the mission reached Tau Ceti III. He accelerated his scooter and came up alongside his guide.

"Hey, Delano, let me ask you something. Why'd you want to come on this mission?"

"Why do you ask me that?" Delano said, his eyes narrowing.

"Just curious. You said I need to understand you guys, so I'm trying to."

Delano studied him before saying, haltingly, "Well, I suppose I always wanted to do space travel. And I like people, so..." he trailed off, then shrugged slightly.

Donn waited until it was clear the bald Freezer tech was not going to elaborate further. It struck Donn at that moment that as worthless as this man was, he represented the best of the Freezer staff.

The rest of the trip back to the control room was silent.

——— ‹› ———

Donn left his post precisely when his shift ended at fifteen hundred, having met the other two technicians during the day. The Freezer crew had six members —seven with the addition of himself— and operated under a loose, barely organized shift system in which at least two staffers were present in the control room at all times while the others were off duty. Even when off-duty, though, many of them loitered in the Freezer control room. This unprecedented amount of down time at first angered Donn, but as he thought of it, he realized that due to the lax schedule he might be able to check on his swimmers after his shift.

Still clad in his blue Freezer attendant clothing, Donn made his way back to K-Deck. The Freezer was farther aft than his quarters — in fact, it was the aftmost section of *Chiron* used for habitation. Only the rear shielding protecting the ship against the effects of the Alcubierre drive, some self-contained engineering machinery, and the colonial hold were farther back.

Donn floated past the entrances to M and L decks until he reached K. He opened the access hatch and climbed "down" the ladder, feeling his weight return with gathering force. When he finished his descent, he was back to full weight (or what would be planetbound weight of 1.12 g) again.

He was near bay K-1. Banksie's inspirational quotes adorned the corridor near her bay — ones Donn normally enjoyed reading, but which he had no time for now. He entered the K-8 corridor, stepping through the hatch, and stopped when he saw Margulies standing in front of his bay entrance. She turned to face him and said with surprising gentleness, "I thought so."

"Did something happen?" Donn said, striding towards her.

"No. Everything's good. You kept your preborns in top shape."

"Did Kearney—?"

"She was here earlier. Checked in on them for you."

The left side of Donn's lip curled upward in a sardonic half-smile. "That must have been quite an encounter for you two."

"No. I wasn't here then."

"Then how … oh. Right. The cameras." Donn snorted. "Clever. And I imagine you did the same thing to me? That's how you knew I'd come here?"

Margulies matched his half-grin. "That's not how I knew."

"But you are watching me on the ship's cameras."

"Yes," Margulies said. Her voice was even, unashamed.

"So what now, Linna? You've already reassigned me to the Freezer. Do you have some new punishment for coming here to check on my preborns?"

"The Freezer isn't a punishment. It's a vital aspect of the mission, one which—"

"Cut the shit, Linna. You know what goes on down there?"

"You don't like it?"

"No, I don't. I want to be with my preborns."

"They're not yours. They don't belong to you."

Donn sighed. "Not this again. Are you going to let me in to check on them or not?"

"This isn't your assignment. You belong in the Freezer. Or in your quarters. I understand there is a lot of down time in the Freezer.

"Dammit, Linna, I can't just leave them. I care about these preborns."

"Too much," Margulies murmured, then flashed him a regretful look.

"What do you mean, 'too much?'"

Margulies licked her lips rapidly, then tucked her upper lip into her teeth for a moment. When she spoke, her voice was not her usual stentorian bellow. "We've talked about this. You are going to have to give them up. To the parents in the hibernation bay. And in a larger sense, to the colony itself. It's why I ordered you to not hold the memorial. Because you will have to let go of them."

Donn squinted. "That was the whole point, Linna. The memorial was to help us let go. Are you saying you didn't understand that?"

"No, of course not. It still shouldn't have happened."

Silence.

"What the hell's going on, Linna?" Donn finally said.

"What do you mean?"

"The way you've been acting since Thom's crack-up. You've been riding me the whole damn mission anyway, but you really got extra-bitchy during the past few days."

"'Bitchy,' huh? Never thought you were a misog, Donn."

Don chafed. "Point taken. You'd rather I said you're an asshole?"

"Watch yourself, Cardenio. I know this isn't the military, but we still have a chain of command and of respect. So clean it up."

Donn considered that. "You've given me what — ten reprimands so far?"

"Something like that."

"Are you gonna stand there and tell me that I'm not a good caretaker? You said you checked my preborns — they were all in top shape, you said."

Margulies said carefully, "You are an excellent caretaker to these preborns. One of the best we have."

Donn was momentarily taken aback. "All right," he finally said. "And I suppose I should say you run K-Deck well. Except for..." he let the thought trail off.

"What? Except for Thom? Is that what you were going to say?" Linna's nostrils flared.

"Yes, I was. But I shouldn't have..."

"No, get it out in the fucking open. You're a soldier, but you don't have the courage to accept that we are going to have losses in this mission. If not Thom, then someone else. Or something else. Alcubierre shield breakdown — some cosmic dust particle tears through the ship at superluminal speed. Internal malfunctions. Any number of things. We were always going to lose some babies. It was just a question of how, and how many. You fucking caretakers want to arrive with all of them alive and well. It was never gonna happen.

I'm not cold about losing nine of them — I'm realistic. So call me a bitch all you want."

Donn was chagrined. He hadn't meant the word to be sexist, but now that he thought about it, how couldn't it be?

She continued. "Now turn around, go back to your quarters, and report to the fucking Freezer tomorrow for your shift. And let all this go before it eats you alive. OSIRIS, lock bay K-eight. Keyed to my biometrics only."

"Locked."

Margulies glared at Donn and walked to one of the central column hatchways. She opened it and climbed the ladder. The hatch closed behind her.

Chapter Eight

Donn sat at his personal OSIRIS outlet, staring at the blank screen. Twice he had started to tell the computer to connect him to Kearney, and twice he had stopped. Part of him was indignant that there hadn't been a message waiting for him. Kearney had been at least partially correct about his need to be needed. The realization gave him no pleasure. But Kearney would never be a woman to cling to him, or to anyone. And that was in large part what had attracted him to her.

But was she independent? She had joined a mission to colonize another planet, and of all the things the colony couldn't afford, it was people who wouldn't go along with the collective good. The preflight psych tests and behavioral assessments had been very thorough. Donn remembered his conversation with one of the doctors. "We're looking for people who can take orders, who will willingly and gladly sacrifice their own needs, even their own lives and the lives of others, for the betterment of the colony." Donn had understood then why he was perfect for this assignment. Maybe he didn't always take orders well, but the rest he could do.

Why had Kearney been selected? Just because of her skills as a caretaker? She was old — significantly older than the optimum age, and certainly beyond childbearing years — why had Earth decided she would be a suitable member of humanity's first extrasolar colony?

And, dammit, why hadn't she called him?

"Fuck it. OSIRIS, connect me to Kearney."

"Kearney has a DND on her line," OSIRIS said. "Do you want an emergency override?"

"No." He sat back in his chair and closed his eyes. Too many images flooded his mind. Thom, grown grotesque in his thoughts, smashing pod after pod, tiny babies covered in wine-colored fluid bouncing to the floor; Kearney's face, looking up accusingly at him from where she lay on the bed; the nearly endless rows and columns of hibernating adults in the Freezer.

Then, the Starfish.

Earth below him, stars above, and waves of Starfish attack crafts appearing and disappearing all around him and his fellow pilots, direct-energy beams lancing out, almost invisible in the thin air, piercing the fragile shells of Earth's LEO fighters.

Later, the motel room in Florida, living alone after his hearing, watching the nations of the world bicker and argue about whose fault it had been that Earth had been unable to defend itself, then that stunning speech by Nasim Ghannam at the United Nations General Assembly in which she announced the end of hostilities between Earth and the Starfish.

There hadn't been an occupation, no alien troops on the ground, no hovering spacecraft keeping order. Just months of wanton destruction. No one had ever seen the enemy in person. Only their spacecraft, popping in and out of space and sky, appearing suddenly to rain down terror and vanishing just as quickly. No Starfish craft had been destroyed: there was no wreckage to examine, no prisoners to interrogate. Humanity did not know its enemy — did not know where they came from, what they wanted, how they could be killed. If they could be killed.

Ghannam's speech had indicated that after months of one-sided fighting, Earth diplomats had been contacted by the aliens and an accord had been reached. After the shock and relief came the questions: what did they look like? Where did they come from? What were their motivations?

If there were answers to these questions, they were being kept secret at the highest levels. All that was said, over and over, was that Earth diplomacy had succeeded. The war was over, and Earth had survived.

Donn remembered the celebrations. There were regions of the planet containing peoples who had known war for generations prior to the Starfish attack: those folk merely shrugged and began the age-old process of rebuilding so familiar to them. The softer, more privileged nations threw parades, celebrating not the diplomats but the failed warriors who had survived. It was easier to believe that military might had worn down the Starfish, and had blunted their desire to wage war, than to believe diplomacy and reason had won.

It was against this backdrop that One Earth had emerged. Slow, incremental progress toward a single planetary government had been made in the decades prior to the war, with some nations entering into commonwealths, confederations, or aggregates. But the invasion had accelerated that process immeasurably. The laborious process of unification turned into a race towards the same goal as nations saw the need to present a single, powerful front against a suddenly hostile galaxy.

For his part, Donn took part in galas thrown in his honor after the Earth Defense Force convinced him to, but all the cheers rang hollow. The backslaps landed on numb shoulders. He had done nothing but survive. And his fellow soldiers had done nothing but die.

OSIRIS interrupted his reverie. "Donn, I have a message incoming from Kearney."

He sat up. "Put it through."

Kearney's face filled the screen. "Hey, how was the Freezer?"

Donn saw she had blurred the background. That and the "do-not-disturb" she had had on her line told him all he needed to know. He swallowed away his feelings and said, "Pretty much what you'd expect. Lots of sleeping parents-to-be."

"Yeah, I'll bet. What's it, twenty thousand?"

"Something like that."

"So what do they have you doing?"

"Nothing. A whole lot of nothing. It's automated. OSIRIS runs the place."

"Really? But you do your checks, pretty much like here, right?"

He shook his head. "Nope. Just play games and sit on my ass."

"Huh. Well, I'm sorry about that. Your swimmers are doing fine, by the way. Nobody's anywhere near trouble. You must have kept them on a tight leash."

"Good. Thanks for checking."

"She seriously locked you out of your own bay?"

"That's what she said."

"This is all just a power play."

"Of course it is. I just can't figure out why."

Kearney sighed a little. "You keep trying to find deeper reasons in things. Sometimes there ain't one. You crossed her, so now she's gonna show you who's boss. No matter what it takes."

"That's funny coming from you, with your theory about Prison Planet Tau Ceti Three," Donn teased.

"I'm large, I contain multitudes," Kearney replied. "But I know Margulies is trying to throw her weight around. And that's it."

"Maybe you're right. Hey, have you got any of your hootch laying around?"

Kearney smiled. "Matter of fact, I do."

"You mind bringing some over here? I feel like getting a little drunk. Unless you are busy," he added, trying to keep accusation out of his voice.

Kearney didn't seem to notice his tone. "Well, whatcha got in trade?"

Donn raised his eyebrows. "Trade?"

"Yeah. Stuff ain't cheap."

He looked around his quarters. "I don't—"

"What's that you have on?" Kearney said, peering into her own camera.

"My Freezer overalls."

"I'll take 'em. I could use the blue fabric. You're still getting a steal, Cardenio. It's a good thing I like you."

Donn felt the beginnings of a smile form. "Okay. I'll see you soon."

———— «» ————

Kearney's alcohol was as strong as it was illegal. She diluted her own drinks with liberal amounts of reconstituted fruit juice, and Donn had set out to do the same, but as the night wore on his own beverages became stronger.

"This stuff is horrible," Donn said, taking a generous swig.

"Manalastas won't be happy with that. He takes pride in his still. It's not easy getting it to work properly under angular acceleration, he says."

Donn snorted. "Whatever."

Kearney offered Donn more from her beaker. "So, this investigation about what happened with Thom. Have you decided it's just not worth it?"

Donn sipped at his drink and made a face. "Because of Margulies? Like she'll do something worse to me?"

"Not exactly. More that there's nothing to investigate."

"I think Margulies knows something about Thom. I can't figure out what, but I know she does."

"What makes you say that?"

"Well, look. She goes apeshit over a simple memorial. She tries to lock me out of Thom's bay after the incident, but I got OSIRIS' video record anyway. That gets her even more pissed off and before you know it, I'm reassigned to the Freezer and even shut out of my own bay. Why?"

"To keep you out of the way so she can figure out what the fuck happened, maybe."

"That's what she said."

"Well, there you go, then."

Donn stared at her. "You think she's telling the truth? I don't think so. I don't trust her. I need to know why this happened."

"You are getting obsessed with finding reasons in things."

"Obsessed?" Donn looked at her with hazy eyes. "I don't think it's an obsession. I just wanna know why."

Kearney looked at her drink for a moment, then said, "So you're convinced this isn't just Margulies trying to contain you so she can do her job, or everyone being a little bit on edge from the tragedy and the upcoming landing? We have a lot happening, or about to happen, Donn."

"I dunno. Just seems like more." He grinned. "Nothing ever seems to get to you, though."

"I'm tough."

"I don't understand it," he said, swirling his drink and watching the fluid circle in his glass. "How do you get away with all this?"

"All what?"

"This. You always have something you're not supposed to have. I mean, clothes and dyes and shit like that is one thing, but alcohol? That's serious. How do you do it?"

Kearney shrugged and took a small sip. "I'm just good at it, I guess."

"But why doesn't Margulies or the other crewuns come down on you and stop you?"

"I'm well-liked, Donn."

"Oh, I see. You have connections. Are you sleeping with people in power? Don't tell me you and Mar—"

"If I were, that's none of your business."

"See, I think it is. I think it is my business."

"That's because you're drunk."

Donn pointed an unsteady finger at her. "In vino veritas."

Kearney sighed.

"It's true, then? You're sleeping with people in the crew, to keep them away? You go on your back to keep others off it?"

"Cute."

"Answer me."

Kearney's smirk vanished. "I think you've had enough. Best to drop this."

"That's a yes. Hey, remember what I said earlier. You do what you have to do to thrive and survive. Collins, anyone else in the crew — whatever they're giving you in exchange, that's your decision. Hell, it's smart. You've got one commodity that never runs out."

Kearney's voice was carefully even. "I'm going back to my parlor."

"Why? What'd I say?"

"I think you're saying what you believe, finally. I think this arrangement we have was never a good idea. You can't handle it."

"Sure I can. You and I fuck, and then you fuck some other folks. Simple."

Kearney stared at him, and even in his drunken state, he saw the hurt in her. "That's what I am to you, aren't I? A life support system for a vagina?"

"What?"

"Just a woman who fucks you." She rose from the bed and smoothed her overalls. "I know you've been under stress lately, so I've made allowances for your asshole behavior. But now you're just hurting me."

"Hey, hey," Donn said, reaching for her.

She easily deflected his grasping hand. "No, Donn. I'm an outlet to you. Someone you can go to in order to release something. Talk, tension, whatever. You think that's what I'm here for."

"Aren't you? As a friend?"

Kearney's lips formed a tight line before she spoke. "Friendship's gotta be more than that, Donn. You're not one of the preborns; I'm not here to be your caretaker." She headed for the hatch, paused with her hand just short of the button. "You need something, Donn. I don't know exactly what it is. Maybe it's what you say — you need answers. I don't have them, and as a matter of fact, I have questions of my own." Her voice cracked slightly. "But you've never asked about them, have you?" She pressed the button and the hatch opened.

Kearney stepped through and without looking back, closed the hatch behind her.

Donn stared at the closed hatch, words crowding for release in his throat. "It'll be okay," he said, not believing himself.

"OSIRIS." He weaved towards his computer screen. "Go to the art archives. Show me a full screen projection of Picasso's *Guernica.*"

The screen lit up and Donn sat down heavily in the chair. His eyes wandered over the shapes and images, coming to rest on the left hand side of the painting. He looked at the bull. He saw the screaming woman holding the dead baby.

He saw himself in the bull, and didn't know why.

Chapter Nine

With supreme effort, Donn kept himself from snapping at Randi when she greeted him in the Freezer control room. Her voice was as indistinct as her face: both threatened to disappear into the background of the quiet room. Anson had merely grunted, his eyes darting back and forth across his screen as the fast-paced game demanded his attention. Shereen was picking at something near her wrist brace. Donn glanced at Delano's station, and snorted when he found it empty.

Randi followed his gaze, then looked back at him. After a pause, she said, "Delano isn't here yet."

"So I see."

"He's probably still in his quarters," she added.

"Right."

"Sometimes he doesn't get in for, well, a half hour or so. Or more."

Donn narrowed his eyes. "Should we call him? Get him over here?"

Randi gasped slightly. "Oh, no, we don't need to do that." She half turned towards Anson. "Do you think?"

Anson shrugged a little.

Randi turned back to Donn. "No, I think we'll be fine here. If there's an emergency, we can call for him. But there hasn't been an emergency since, well, ever."

Donn felt the air pressure in the room increasing with each gentle word she spoke. It was as if his brain was being smothered in feathers. "I'm going into the hibernation bay. Do a quick check."

He saw Shereen look up from where she was picking at her wrist brace. Even Anson pivoted in his seat.

"What for?" Randi said. Her voice quivered.

"Rounds, you know. Just to check up on everything."

"We can check from here." Anson gestured at the bank of screens.

"I know that. But nothing beats good old hands-on experience. Sensors can only measure what they're designed to. And they can malfunction, too."

"You think we have a sensor malfunction?" Randi's eyes widened.

"No," Donn said, suppressing a sigh. "I don't. Look, guys, it's just how I have been doing things. I know it's almost certainly a waste of time, and I'm going to find that everything is as under control as it looks from here. But I believe a visual inspection can reveal things that biomed sensors can't."

"Like what?" Shereen said.

Donn faced her. "It's hard to put it into words. I'll know it when I see it. But especially since I'm new here, I think it's important for me to get a look with my own eyes."

Anson grunted and returned to his game. Shereen and Randi exchanged a look.

"Well, if you think it's something you need to do, Donn, then I guess go ahead." Randi spoke each word as if she had no idea what the next one was going to be.

"Thanks," Donn said, and entered the hibernation antechamber. When the hatch closed behind him, he let out a sigh. The prospect of spending the day in the Freezer control room with them was one he could not handle. He shook his head at the odor of skin and sebum in the antechamber and crossed into the main hibernation bay.

The bay was just as impressive as it had been yesterday. Twenty thousand, seven hundred and thirty-six sleeping adults. All awaiting their awakening a month hence, where they'd be greeted with a new world and, on average, twelve children each to care for.

Donn took down one of the scooters and headed deep into the bay, racing past the endless pods. The bay ran the entire circumference of the ship, and Donn slowed to a stop at the halfway point. Any further, and he'd be coming back to the other side of the control room to the opposite antechamber.

He wanted to be as far from his fellow Freezer techs as he could be.

Dismounting from the scooter, he surveyed the pods. He saw number 10,362 before him, and he leaned over it to try and peer inside. The tiny window in front of what would be the sleeping subject's face was dark.

He ran his hands all along the pod's surface, marveling again at the featurelessness of the sarcophagus. Nothing protruded — no hoses, no conduits, no cords. Everything was self-contained, built in to the foundation of the pod, monitored by OSIRIS with no need for human interference.

His fingers felt for the seam where the pod would open at the appropriate time. Delano hadn't seemed concerned at the lack of human access to the pods, but if he was going to be assigned to this place, especially once they were awakened, he wanted to know everything about how they worked.

He found a latch on the underside of the lid of the pod, and traced his fingers across a faint seam. There.

Donn pressed his face against the thick glass square, squinting to make out the inside of the pod. The bay was well-lit, but light was barely penetrating the glass. All he could see was the faintest suggestion of a face.

"Well, Sleeping Beauty, at least I can see you. But without peepers, I can't get a good look. I guess we'll meet soon enough once we hit TC-Three." He started to leave the pod.

He hesitated. His curiosity was gnawing at him. Why such secrecy with these pods? Why not make the glass transparent and just put sleeping masks on the corpsicles, if the worry was light interfering with their sleep? Or at least provide peepers to allow a Freezer tech to do a quick visual inspection? It didn't make sense to isolate the sleepers so thoroughly.

Would a quick opening of the pod hurt the occupant? The hibernation chamber was slightly chilly as it was, and if Delano had been correct yesterday, these corpsicles weren't that much colder than an ordinary human body. If Donn opened the pod, just to take a look, what would happen to the sleeper?

"OSIRIS," he said, waiting for an answer. He was about to repeat his request when he remembered that the Freezer staff kept voice recognition off. He could ride all the way back to the control room and turn it back on, or he could use one of the comm outlets in the bay to call Randi and ask her to activate it, but he was sure they would annoy him out of his plan.

He reached under the pod again and felt for the latch. He tugged on it, but could not budge the lid. He tried other manipulations — sliding, twisting, and pressing on the latch, but nothing he did opened it.

Donn got down on his hands and knees, grunting a little, and looked under the lid. The latch was a simple mechanical one, with no apparent electronic lock. He lay down on his back, and reached up to manipulate the latch again.

No matter what he did, the latch would not move.

After several minutes of attempts, he lowered his aching arms and grunted again. "What the hell is this for? A latch that won't fuckin' do anything?" Delano hadn't mentioned any special tool or key that was to be used to open the pods — was the man even aware how the pods opened? Donn was no longer merely curious — he was angry. Another mystery confronted him.

He could leave it alone. It wasn't his problem. OSIRIS was obviously able to open the pods and would do so at the proper time. Why not just give this all up and let it go? He could even go back to the control room and challenge Anson to a head-to-head game. Or join the scooter race pool and just have fun during his exile to the Freezer. Maybe Delano was right — it would be better to act like the rest of the techs instead of pretending he was somehow superior.

For that matter, why not leave the mystery of Thom's behavior alone?

He spun on his back so that his feet were against the pod. Still on his back, he pushed his feet against the lip of the pod and kicked upward, trying to force the pod open. A part of his mind screamed, warning him that he might damage the pod and hurt the occupant, but in his frustration at the latch he silenced that voice.

His kicks grew more powerful and less precise as he shouted at the latch, at the mysteries all around him, at the loss of his relationship with Kearney, at his exile to the Freezer, at Thom's murderous outburst, at the Starfish surrender on Earth.

Then he heard it.

A definite crack.

He spun back around and squinted at the latch. It now hung partially off its track, damaged by his repeated kicks. He returned to his kicking posture and delivered some more blows until the latch flew off to land several meters away.

Donn scrambled to his feet and looked around, then grinned at himself. "Nobody here but us chickens," he murmured, then put both hands under the seam and lifted.

The lid felt heavier than it looked. Donn gathered himself and lifted with a surge of strength, and the lid came off. He saw the magnetic closures on the inner surface even as the lid felt significantly lighter. He realized the lid hadn't been particularly heavy, but had been magnetically sealed in addition to mechanically locked by the strange clasp. He spent no time marveling at that as he lifted the lid and looked inside at the sleeper.

A woman lay before him, biomed sensor leads attached to her temples. She was clad in a form-fitting silver suit.

The pod had only been opened a few seconds when he heard OSIRIS' voice over the public address. "Alert. Malfunction in hibernation chamber. Hibernation Pod one-zero-three-six-two."

"It's all right, OSIRIS," Donn said, but the computer voice continued the alert. Donn swore under his breath. Still no voice access.

No doubt even the somnolent Freezer techs would react to this, and come themselves to investigate. He still had a few minutes: they'd dither before deciding what to do, and then it'd be a while before they made it to him on the far end of the hibernation ring.

He reached into the pod to touch the woman's face. She was cool, not cold. Her skin didn't dimple at all where he touched it.

"I'm not going to hurt you," he said, then snorted at his own words. It was one thing to talk to the preborns, but this was entirely different. He looked into the thin space between the woman and the edge of the pod, and saw no biomed leads or sensors.

"Must be in the suit," he murmured.

OSIRIS' repeated warnings stopped mid-sentence. Evidently someone in Freezer control had shut him up. His colleagues were beginning to act.

He looked back at the woman, not certain what he had expected to see. He stared at her, wondering what it was he was looking for. All this for what? Margulies would stuff his ass into an unused pod, or even wake up one of the sleepers early to free up space, as punishment for this. If she didn't decide to toss him off the ship altogether, probably naked.

"Now I've done it," he said to the woman. He sighed, glancing down her still body.

Her chest should have been rising and falling, just slightly. It hadn't moved. He lay his ear to her mouth, his face looking down at her chest.

About twenty seconds passed, and Donn started a mental count.

He remembered Delano's words about their metabolic rate. Twenty percent, he had said, though it fluctuated. How long could a sleeper go without breathing?

His count reached thirty.

Forty-five.

He pressed his ear closer to her mouth, straining to hear, to feel any exchange of air. His eyes locked on her chest, focusing on the valley of her sternum between her breasts.

One minute.

Was this possible? A minute without respiration? He cursed himself for his ignorance regarding hibernation. Had she taken a breath at all during his inspection? Was her breathing so shallow that he could not detect it? Was he counting too quickly?

Ninety seconds.

He got up from her mouth. She'd gone a minute and a half without breathing. He was almost sure. He lay a hand on her neck, tracing the cords until he found her carotid. He pressed down and started his count, still staring at her chest for movement.

Ten.

Twenty.

Thirty.

Nothing. He swore and repositioned his fingers, again finding what he was sure was the carotid, and checked again.

Thirty more seconds passed by, and he could not feel a pulse. And she had not moved her chest in the almost three minutes he had been watching.

Again, he let go of her and bent down to the indicator lights on the base of the unit.

All green.

He scanned the base again, hoping to find actual numbers and readouts instead of idiot lights, but just as Delano had shown him, all the pod would show was green. It gave him no precise information.

He heard echoes approaching from the same direction he had come — Anson's voice calling to him from the gently curving aisle of the hibernation chamber.

"I hope I'm wrong about you, lady," Donn said, looking one last time at the unmoving form, and closed the lid. He saw the latch lying a few feet away, and moved to retrieve it. He jammed the small metal piece into his zippered chest pocket. He briefly entertained the possibility of bluffing his way through the encounter with Anson: he could say that he had heard OSIRIS' alert and had rushed here to see if he could help. But since there had been no alerts down here in the past nine months, it would be pointless. OSIRIS obviously had a record of the pod being opened, and here he was, standing next to it. There'd be no point in denying what he had done.

In any case, what mattered here was not that he had defied procedure and forced open a sleeping pod — what mattered was that the so-called hibernating human was dead.

Anson came into view, coming down the mildly sloping aisle between the ranks of hibernation pods. "Donn?" He slowed his scooter and pulled up next to Donn. "What happened? Which one is it?"

Donn pointed. "But listen, you're not going to believe this." He reached for the lip of the lid and pulled it open.

"Shit!" Anson yelped. "What the hell are you doing? We're not supposed to open those!"

"I know. They're sealed shut. Never mind that. Come here and look at her." He stood at the woman's head.

Anson dismounted and took a step closer. He was still several feet away from the open pod, his eyes huge. "No! Close it up. Shit, what have you done. You'll hurt her!"

Donn swallowed. Had he killed her? Merely by opening the pod? "Call back to the control room, Anson. Get them to turn on OSIRIS' voice activation. Or check on pod one-zero-three-six-two from there. All her lights are green, see?" He calmed himself. OSIRIS was still reading green, so the computer showed the occupant as alive and well, despite appearances.

Anson glanced down and appeared to relax. "Good. But for God's sake, close the lid! You might be warming her up!"

"Come here before I do that, damn you. Feel her pulse. Look at her breathing."

Anson shook his head. "She shows green, so she's okay. But who knows for how long if you keep the pod open?"

Donn took three strides to Anson and grabbed him by the collar of his overalls. "For fuck's sake, just look at her! The lights show green, but look at her!" He yanked the whimpering Anson towards the woman. "Feel for a pulse and see if you can catch any breathing."

Anson stumbled toward the pod, coming up against it. He reached for the lid and slammed it down.

"No! You dumb fuck! Check her!"

Anson eyed Donn and then suddenly darted past him. "I'm calling control to get a readout. If you've hurt her..." he didn't finish but mounted his scooter and headed for the nearest com outlet.

Donn watched him go and shouted, "Tell them to turn on OSIRIS' goddam voice activation!" He again looked back at the green lights on the base of the unit.

There were only two possibilities that he could see. Either all was well, and the hibernating woman's pulse and respiration were simply too faint for him to detect, or the unit itself was experiencing a massive sensor malfunction and showed green in error.

But if that were true, what were the odds that of the over twenty thousand hibernation units, he had just happened to stumble upon the one that had gone bad?

He felt cold as he looked at the ranks and columns of hibernation pods, reaching gently upwards in both directions.

"Voice access established," OSIRIS' voice sounded in the bay. Anson was scooting back to Donn and the pod.

Donn wasted no time. "OSIRIS! Report on Hibernation Pod one-zero-three-six-two. Biomed status."

"Hibernation Pod one-zero-three-six-two compromised. Seal broken. Biomed status green."

"Vitals?"

"Green," OSIRIS repeated.

"Dammit, what are the numbers? Temperature, pressure, pulse, respiration."

"Body temperature twenty-nine point three three degrees Celsius. Blood pressure sixty-five systolic, thirty-one diastolic. Heart rate nine. Respiration four point five."

"So her heart's beating and she's breathing," Donn said, looking back at the closed pod.

"Randi reports the same thing," Anson said, coming closer to Donn but remaining more than an arm's length away. "She says this pod is doing fine. Except for the broken seal."

Donn nodded absently. "I guess I'm not good at detecting vital signs. Lemme try once more, now that I know she's alive. Maybe I'll be able to find it." He reached for the lid again.

Anson stepped forward and pressed down on the lid. "No, for God's sake! What the hell do you think you're doing? You've done enough damage as it is."

Donn fixed him with a stare. "You heard OSIRIS. She's fine."

"We're not supposed to open these!"

Donn kept his eyes locked on Anson. "OSIRIS, has the hibernator in this pod experienced a raised body temperature in the past thirty minutes?"

"All hibernation body functions have remained within tolerances. No appreciable change."

Donn cocked his head at Anson. "She's fine. Opening the pod doesn't hurt her."

"Maybe it will this time, you can't—"

"I need to know!" Donn shouted. "Maybe it's enough for you to look at a readout or listen to OSIRIS tell you everything's fine, but I need to see for myself, dammit. Let me do my fuckin' job, Anson. You can stay here and make sure nothing happens."

"We're not supposed to open them," Anson repeated, his voice a child's.

"Yeah, well, I do a lot of things I'm not supposed to. Take your hands off the lid," he said, and Anson did as he was told.

Donn opened the pod and looked down at the woman. "Hello again. I'm gonna call you 'Nefertiti,' okay? Just going to take another look, all right? Make sure you're doing okay."

"What the hell are you talking to her for?"

"Habit," Donn said, reaching for her neck again. He felt for the prominent artery and knew he had it. He pressed firmly on the bulging carotid and waited.

"Well?" Anson said a few seconds later.

"Shut up. Let me concentrate."

An agonizing minute passed. Donn finally said, his fingers still on her neck, "I still got nothing here." He tried again, letting go of her neck and finding the artery once more. "And I'm in the right place."

Another minute.

Nothing.

He stepped back. "I'm damned if I can find it. You try," he said, stepping back to give Anson access.

"I'm not supposed to—"

"For God's sake, man, do your duty! This is what you do — take care of these people! Now put your hands on her and do what you're supposed to do!"

Anson gingerly stepped forward and felt around the woman's neck. He took a long time to locate the carotid, and stood unmoving when he did, his two fingers pressed to it.

Donn reached into the pod and found the woman's right arm. It was wedged into a conforming, gel-filled recess, but he was able to seize her wrist. He tugged on her arm, trying to dislodge it from the recess to gain better access for a wrist pulse.

He winced a little at the thought that he was violating this woman, even just by holding her hand. The sensation passed quickly, but left a ghost of feeling in him, and he had to fight his reluctance to take her wrist pulse.

He found her radial artery and pressed it gently against her bone. He looked up at Anson as he counted silently.

Another thirty seconds passed.

"I don't feel anything," Anson said. "But all the lights are green."

"I don't feel anything either," Donn said, then switched to the inside of her elbow at her brachial artery.

"I guess pulse gets impossible for us to detect in hibernation," Anson said, releasing her neck.

"You guess? You've never done a pulse check?" Donn answered his own question. "'Course you haven't. Haven't opened the pods. OSIRIS does it all." Donn let go of her elbow and reached towards the woman's inner thigh.

Anson gasped. "Jezeus, what are you—?"

"Femoral artery," Donn snapped, then said to the woman, "Sorry." He pressed his fingers into her flesh and waited.

"Nothing there, either. Move." He forced Anson out of the way. "I'm gonna check for breathing again. Stay quiet."

He again lay his ear millimeters away from her nose, his eyes on her chest, looking, listening, feeling for any breaths.

By his count, it was two minutes before Anson spoke. "Anything?"

"No." Donn stood up. "Only one more thing to do."

"What?"

"OSIRIS, begin the awakening procedure for pod one-zero-three-six-two."

"Are you crazy? You can't—"

OSIRIS' voice calmly interrupted Anson's outburst. "We have not reached the awakening step in the mission. That won't occur for another twenty-one days."

Donn said, "I realize this. But I think the sleeper is in distress. It's a medical emergency."

"My biomed sensors show all green."

"I know they do. But I'm declaring an emergency here."

OSIRIS replied evenly. "You do not have that authorization."

Donn sighed. "Fine." He turned to Anson. "You do it."

"What?"

"Declare an emergency and wake her up," Donn said, thrusting his chin at Nefertiti.

"You're out of your mind. I'm not doing that."

"You saw the same thing I did, Anson. No pulse, no breathing—"

"None that we could detect. But obviously, she's fine, since all the lights are green."

"Could be a sensor malfunction."

"We've never had any."

"Always a first time. If we just sit here, staring at the little green lights while this poor woman is in trouble—"

"And what if it's nothing? If she's doing fine?"

Donn stepped slightly closer to Anson, who shrank away. "What if? So we wake her up a little early, that's all. She's scheduled to be awakened in three weeks anyway. If I'm wrong, then all that happens is someone's awake who shouldn't be yet."

Anson looked furtively at the pod, then back at Donn. Finally, he spoke. "No. I don't have enough reason to break with procedure. I'm sorry, Donn, but I am going to have to report this."

Donn glared at him. A momentary urge to strike the man rose in him, but he suppressed it. "You do whatever you fuckin' think you have to. And God help you if you're wrong."

Anson opened his mouth to speak, closed it, then opened it again. When he did speak, his voice shook. "OSIRIS, connect me to Hibernation Control."

"Anson?" Randi's voice came over the speaker. "What's going on?"

"I'm…" he stared at Donn and said, "I'll call you on the com outlet. In private."

"What? Why?" Randi's voice was anxious.

"Just … stand by. OSIRIS, close the channel." Anson said, then backed away from Donn, keeping his eyes on him. When he was a healthy distance away, he turned and headed for the com outlet.

Donn watched him go, shaking his head. "If I'm gonna become a corpsicle for this, at least let me be sure," he murmured, and returned to the hibernation pod. "OSIRIS, give me a readout of Hibernator one-zero-three-six-two's MEG scan." He looked at the complex crown of leads over Nefertiti's head. "Just narrative is fine," he added, reaching for the crown.

"Hibernator one-zero-three-six-two displays normal Delta, Theta, and Alpha patterns commensurate with hibernation. Beta wave is statistically flat. Gamma wave is also statistically flat. SMR is at normal levels commensurate with hibernation."

Donn took a breath, then reached out and gently dislodged the sensor crown from Nefertiti's head. He delicately unpeeled the leads from her forehead and scalp until the whole assembly was dangling uselessly against her still-unmoving chest.

"How about now?"

OSIRIS repeated calmly, "Hibernator one-zero-three-six-two displays normal Delta, Theta, and Alpha patterns commensurate with hibernation. Beta wave is statistically flat. Gamma wave is also statistically flat. SMR is at normal levels commensurate with hibernation."

Donn fought to keep his voice under control as he asked, "All right. Give me a pulse report, please. Every five seconds."

"Pulse is too infrequent for five-second interval report."

"Then give me beats per minute."

His fingers trembled as he reached inside the pod again and pressed down on Nefertiti's chest, trying to compress it. The flesh gave somewhat, but did not rebound instantly as he let go. He pressed again. It was like pushing on a sandbag. He continued more forcefully and rapidly, as if administering CPR. His own breath came quickly as he labored.

"Pulse eight," OSIRIS said when a minute had passed.

Donn stopped, still breathing hard. He had compressed her chest at least thirty times in the minute.

"Eight beats a minute?"

"Correct. Pulse varies over time."

Donn stared down at the woman again. He rubbed his hands together, then interlaced his fingers and squeezed them before reaching in once more. He covered the sleeping woman's mouth with one hand while he pinched shut her nostrils with the other.

"I'm sorry, but I have to know," Donn said softly, then to OSIRIS, "Switch to respiration. Breaths per minute." An agonizing minute passed again.

"Respiration twelve," OSIRIS said. "Ordinary spike. Well within expected tolerances."

Donn let go, and Nefertiti's nostrils very slowly returned to their open position. He heard Anson coming back from the com outlet.

"Why do you think she's still alive?" Donn whispered, quietly closing the lid and looking up at OSIRIS' disembodied presence all around him.

Chapter Ten

Anson looked terrified when he came back from the communications outlet, pleading with Donn to go to the ship's provost and turn himself in for the damage to the hibernation pod. The Freezer technician was trembling when he approached Donn, stayed out of arm's reach while he spoke.

Donn half-listened, feeling contempt for the man. How Anson had ever been chosen for this mission baffled him. This weak, incurious excuse for a person was going to build Earth's first extrasolar colony?

His scorn was blunted by a growing sense of camaraderie. It didn't matter why Anson and the rest of the useless Freezer techs were on board — what mattered was that they were. They were going to become his brothers and sisters. He was going to have to rely on them and they on him.

That didn't mean, however, that he would succumb to Anson's whiny requests to turn himself in.

"I'm not going anywhere," Donn said. "We need to check these pods by hand. Get OSIRIS to open each one and see for yourself. She's dead," he said, gently inclining his head towards Nefertiti, "and OSIRIS doesn't know it."

"Just ... please. Go to the provost's office."

"The hell I am. It's possible that some of these pods are still working, or that some of these sleepers are in trouble. But we'll never know from listening to OSIRIS. Get these pods open, however you can."

Anson murmured his weak disagreements, and Donn was about to seize Anson by his quivering shoulders when he saw three figures headed their way from the opposite side of the curving corridor.

Donn shook his head and chuckled without mirth. "Margulies. A little out of your jurisdiction, aren't you? Why isn't Provost Simpatica here? This isn't K-Deck."

"Shut up," Margulies said tiredly. She dismounted her scooter and approached. The other two crewmembers flanked her. "I should have guessed you wouldn't be able to just do your job." Her nostrils widened and narrowed with her breathing.

"Listen, Linna, never mind all that. We've got a major problem here that goes way past anything I've done. The sleepers are—"

"Shut up." Margulies snapped, and looked at the crewun to her right — a man Donn recognized as James Webb. "Take him."

The crewun licked his lips and said to Donn, "Caretaker Cardenio, I am relieving you of all duties and placing you under arrest."

"We don't have time for this shit. Webb," Donn said, half-turning towards the damaged pod. "She's dead in there. And there could be a whole lot more."

Webb hesitated and glanced at Margulies.

Margulies said, "He's lost his mind. OSIRIS reports all hib pods functioning normally."

"OSIRIS is wrong. Just check for yourself."

"Webb, Goddess damn it, what are you waiting for?"

Webb looked back at Donn. "Just let me get these on you, Donn. We'll check it out." Webb approached Donn with a pair of handcuffs.

"As long as you listen to her, you won't check anything out. Look, James," Donn said, lowering his voice as he spoke to Webb, "I promise I'll go quietly if you just check the pod and find nothing's wrong. I'll be happy to be wrong about this. But check it! Now!"

Again, Webb hesitated and glanced back at Margulies. "Linna, maybe we should. It won't take long. And if he's right..."

Margulies snorted and strode to the pod in question. "You want me to check? Fine. But you get those cuffs on him." She opened the lid to the hib pod.

"Come on, Donn. Please," Webb said, and Donn reluctantly offered his wrists. He watched Margulies carefully as Webb tightened the cuffs and held him by his upper arm. The other crewun, Ailee Katuradityee, took Donn's other arm as they waited.

Marguiles felt Nefertiti's neck and looked into space, her lips moving slightly. After a minute's pause, she said gently, "OSIRIS, what do you read for a pulse on Hibernator one-zero-three-six-two?"

"Heart rate ten," OSIRIS said.

Margulies looked at Donn and for a moment didn't say anything. He was startled to see a flash of apology in her expression. Then, it was gone, and her stony face returned. "I have the same thing."

Donn shouted, "What?" He took a breath, feeling both crewmembers squeeze his arms tightly. "I've disconnected her cranial sensors! OSIRIS! Report on Hibernator one-zero-three-six-two's brainwave act—"

"Belay that, OSIRIS. Caretaker Cardenio's computer authorization is hereby suspended," she shouted over him. "You will not recognize his commands."

"Damn you, Linna!" Donn twisted violently, throwing Webb off-balance. Katuradityee maintained her hold on his other arm.

"Donn, stop," Katuradityee said.

He twisted again, pulling away from her. He broke free and dodged Webb's frantic attempt to seize him. Anson had backed far away, his face milk.

Margulies took a step forward. "Stop."

All five froze. Donn stayed in his crouch, while Webb and Katuradityee hovered warily nearby. Anson stood far behind Margulies.

Margulies spoke carefully. "Now. Donn, you'll stop resisting. Something's happening to you, and we're going to get you help for it. Maybe the stress of the mission—"

"Nothing's happening to me! You couldn't have felt a pulse on her! Linna, please, just do one more thing. Check her brainwave with the leads unattached. OSIRIS gave me a report when he couldn't have. Something's really wrong here."

"Yes, there is. I think what happened to Thom must also be happening to you."

"What?"

Margulies's voice was maddeningly soothing. "It's okay, Donn. We'll get you better. Just come with us."

Donn started to object, but his voice caught in his throat. The mention of Thom's breakdown had stunned him. His certainty gave way to doubt. Could she be right? Could he have missed the pulse and respiration, and somehow not disconnected the proper leads to Nefertiti's head? Was he seeing a crisis where there was none?

Is this what had happened to Thom?

For a torturous moment, Donn wondered how he would know if he were going insane. Could a mind know such a thing? Either everything on the ship was going wrong, or he was.

Which was more likely?

In a burst of clarity, he knew. He felt his mind clear, and everything in his field of vision was sharp and bright.

He was not insane.

Everything else was.

"You're lying," he said calmly. "I don't know why, but you are. You didn't feel a pulse."

Margulies sighed. "Get him out of here," she said to Webb and Katuradityee. "Take him to the provost. I'll meet you there." The two crew members began to tug at Donn.

"Come on, Donn. Don't make more trouble for yourself," Katuradityee said as they led him away.

"You know why Thom did what he did," Donn said, his voice rising as he was forced away from Margulies and Anson. "You know everything, don't you? You know everything."

The last thing he saw before the curvature of the corridor cut off his vision was Margulies closing the lid and turning to a still-cowering Anson.

———— «» ————

The provost's office was a tiny one. Simpatica was a pleasant woman with inoffensively delicate features. Donn had dealt with her on the few occasions when Margulies had felt a mere reprimand hadn't been enough. Each talking to had been so soft and gentle he hadn't felt in the least bit intimidated.

Provost Simpatica looked up from the report on her screen. Her young, smooth face was sad, almost sorrowful. "I'm concerned, Donn. Your outburst in the hibernation chamber was—"

"Listen, none of this matters," he said. "You have to check the hib pods. Manually. I need you to do something for me. I'll be docile and surrender to anything you want. I'll even agree to forced hibernation for the rest of the trip. Whatever you want. But you've got to check them."

Simpatica sighed. "They've been checked. Nothing's wrong, Donn."

"Who checked them?"

"Liaison Officer Margulies. She was there when—"

Donn grunted. "She's lying. I don't know why."

Simpatica managed to look even more pained. "Donn, listen to yourself. You're saying the hibernators are dead, and that Officer Margulies and OSIRIS are both lying about it. You can't truly believe that."

"I know how it sounds. But what's the harm in checking again? With someone other than Margulies?"

Simpatica studied him a moment. "I get the feeling you won't accept anything that contradicts you, Donn. This isn't healthy. You need to—" she was interrupted by the opening of the hatchway. Margulies poked her head in.

"Sorry. Just letting you know that I spot-checked a few more hib pods. All normal."

Donn murmured, "Doesn't mean anything."

Simpatica sighed. "Thank you, Linna."

Margulies nodded at Donn. "You calmed down yet?"

Donn didn't answer.

"Sarah, could I speak to Donn alone?" Margulies asked.

Simpatica looked at the two, then nodded. "Of course. He's still restrained," she said, indicating the handcuffs.

Simpatica and Margulies changed positions awkwardly in the cramped office, and when the hatch had closed behind Simpatica, Donn began to shout.

"What the hell do you think—"

Margulies slashed her hand down to quiet him as she spoke. "OSIRIS, shut off voice recognition and camera monitoring in this room. I want a total computer blackout."

"Acknowledged. Keyboard input only."

Donn blinked and looked at her, his lips a tight line. "So, you're gonna beat up a guy with his hands cuffed?"

"No, you dumb fuck. Just shut up and listen."

"Why should I listen to—"

Margulies hauled off and backhanded him a stinging blow to the face. "Shut up!"

Donn recovered, already feeling the bruise forming. "Not bad." He spat once and said, "Is that why you disconnected OSIRIS? So you could smack me around and not leave a record?"

Margulies said, "You're a stupid, stubborn son of a bitch. If you had a brain as big as your ego, you'd be pretty smart. Now, again, shut up and listen."

Donn narrowed his eyes.

"Of course I was lying about the hib pod."

His eyes instantly widened. "You didn't feel a pulse?"

"No. She wasn't breathing, either. You were right. She's dead."

Donn was momentarily speechless. Despite the crisis, he felt a small part of himself triumph that at last, someone else saw the same mystery he did.

He wasn't alone in his questions.

When he regained his voice, he said, "Then uncuff me and let's check the others!"

Margulies regarded him and looked, for a moment, sincerely regretful. "No."

"What? Why not? Come on, Linna, we don't have time for—"

"Shut up," she said again, but this time she was gentle. "Right now, I don't know what's going on. But I have to believe that the one pod you happened to check isn't the only one with a corpse in it." In a low murmur, she added, "Maybe they're all dead."

"Which is exactly why we have to tell Simpatica and the captain and the whole ship. We need to—"

"That's the last thing we want to do," Margulies said. "Listen, Cardenio," she approached and squatted to meet him at his eye level. "We've got something by the tail here. It's huge. But if we go and spread the news, what do you think is going to happen?"

"What? I have no idea, but we can't keep this secret."

"We have to. At least until we get some answers."

Donn rattled his cuffs against the chair. "Linna, please. If the sleepers are all dead, then the mission is completely fucked. A quarter million children to raise? From just caretakers and crew? We can't do that."

"Not without some plan, no. And if we let this get out before we have a plan to deal with it…"

Donn swallowed and nodded. He could see her point. If caretakers knew that in a month's time when the ship reached Tau Ceti III they would not be handing off their swimmers but would continue to care for over seventeen hundred each…

"There would be panic. Some of them wouldn't be able to handle it," he said slowly.

Margulies nodded. "Right. So for right now, what we need to do is—"

Donn gasped. He knew, all at once, what had happened.

"What?" Margulies said.

"Thom. This is why he cracked up."

"What do you mean?"

"Thom managed to tap into OSIRIS, right? I saw him do it on the camera records, and you yourself said so. That is what happened, isn't it?"

Margulies hesitated a moment, then said, "I might as well tell you. Yes. Thom somehow broke into OSIRIS' command and data storage pathways."

"He was a computer specialist before coming on this mission, wasn't he?"

"That's right."

"I thought he broke into OSIRIS' security camera command pathway when he accessed the wall panel. But I'll bet he also discovered that the sleepers in hibernation were dead. Either some of them or all of them." Donn swallowed as the implications of the crisis started to override his short-lived satisfaction of finally solving the mystery. "He found that out, and that's why..." he swallowed and stopped. Anything to avoid saying those awful words.

Margulies nodded. "Yeah. I think so." She stood up. "We knew he had broken into OSIRIS and had accessed data files. But we couldn't figure out which ones. They're sealed. But that must be it."

Donn said in a strained voice, "That's what he meant. 'This is best for them.' He was talking about the fact that..." Donn stopped and gathered himself for what he knew was true. "...some of them weren't going to make it. We can't care for that many if all the sleepers are dead. So he was trying to spare them with quick deaths."

He looked up at Margulies. The two locked eyes, sharing in the awful horror of their new situation. None of the reprimands, shouting matches, or insults mattered now. He simply saw in her a fellow traveler, another human being faced with an impossible task and an unthinkable choice. He hadn't until this moment truly thought of her as anything other than an annoyance, a stuffy bureaucrat who took up oxygen and got in his way. Now, though, as he stared at her and saw she, too, was contemplating the horrific future in store for thousands of unborn babies, he saw her as his sister.

When she spoke, her voice was tinged with sorrow. "That has to be it. If he found out about the sleepers ... but he didn't have to do what he did. He should have—" she stopped.

Donn continued for her. "Should have what? Told someone? That's what I'm saying, Linna. We need a new plan, and we need it as fast as possible. Every moment we delay we're losing our chance of still being able to pull this mission off. We need as many brains on this as we can get."

Margulies shook her head slowly. "Not yet. If you're right about Thom, then if this becomes public knowledge, who knows how caretakers and crew will react? We could have dozens more incidents like Thom's, or worse. We need the plan before we go public so that caretakers and crew won't panic."

"Who else knows about this, do you think?"

"I don't think anyone does. Just you and me."

Donn nodded, then frowned. "You said before that no one was able to look at the data files Thom accessed because they were sealed?"

"That's right. OSIRIS has some deep-encrypted stuff that no one has access to. Thom must've found a way in."

Donn's frown intensified. "Why would there be sealed data files? No one can see them? Not even the captain?"

Margulies shook her head. "We were told in prelaunch training they are part of OSIRIS' operating system, and if we went in to mess with them, we'd disrupt his functions."

Donn gasped. "Maybe...Jezeus, do you think Thom didn't discover the sleepers were dead, but when he fucked around in OSIRIS he...caused the malfunction?"

Margulies took a deep breath. "Holy shit."

"We still need to find out how far that goes. It might not be as bad as we think — there may be thousands still alive. That's why you need to get Simpatica to release me."

Margulies chewed her lip in an uncharacteristic show of indecision. "I ... yeah, okay. I see that now. I'm going to call Simpatica back in," she said, reaching for the "hatch open" button. "Just go along with my play."

Donn barely had time to turn back in his seat when the hatch opened. Behind him he heard Margulies say, "Provost? I'm all done here."

Simpatica came back around to her small desk and smoothed her jumpsuit. "Well. Let's get back to—"

"If I could interrupt, Provost," Margulies said, and Donn tried not to smirk at her show of deference. He had only known Margulies as his superior: it was fascinating to watch her as an underling, even under the circumstances.

"Of course," Simpatica said.

"I've been speaking with Caretaker Cardenio here, and I think I have an idea that would work for everyone and for the mission."

Simpatica steepled her fingers and rested them under her chin. "I'm listening."

Margulies rested her hand on Donn's shoulder. "I think he needs to go back to his bay. He's clearly not cut out for Freezer duty. That was a mistake on my part to send him there."

Simpatica looked pensive. "I'm afraid I agree with you, Linna. Not to criticize your decision, but based on what happened, I think it's clear that he'd be better somewhere else."

Donn said, his voice scratchy, "I know I would be. I belong back with my swimmers." He felt Margulies' hand squeeze his shoulder.

"But what about all the reprimands and admonishments, Donn? I've been reviewing your file, and there are a lot of them." Simpatica swiped her finger along her desk viewscreen and scanned. "A lot."

Margulies said, "Yes, there are. Here's what I propose, Provost. We put him back into K-eight, but under my direct supervision."

"What do you mean, 'direct supervision?'" Simpatica asked.

"I'll be with him the whole time. He'll never be alone with the preborns."

Donn shifted in his seat and said indignantly, "Wait a second. I don't need anyone looking over my shoulder." He did not need to summon up false anger.

"If you want to get back to your bay, you'll agree to this," Margulies said, then added in a softer tone, "That's assuming you think this will work, Provost."

Simpatica paused, looking at Donn with gentle, thoughtful eyes. "Donn, I want you to become the best caretaker you can be for us. That's going to mean following our procedures and policies. They are there for good reasons." She sighed very slightly, clearly uncomfortable with dispensing discipline. "We're all going to need to pull our weight once we hit Tau Ceti Three. I need to know if you are going to be able to be a trustworthy part of the community."

"I take my job very seriously, Provost Simpatica," Donn said. "No one can dispute that."

"Oh, no one does," Simpatica said hastily. "But you've got to see that we have a certain way of doing things, and we need you to follow that way."

"I don't have much choice, if I want to get back to my preborns, do I?"

Simpatica looked unsatisfied. "I'd really prefer if you saw the need for this and agreed to it, rather than feeling we're forcing it on you." She looked past Donn at Margulies.

Margulies added, "I would, too, Donn. I don't like the idea of supervising you personally. It's not the best for any of us. But if you came around, after all the reprimands and admonishments, and now after this incident in the Freezer..."

Simpatica sighed again. "Yes. The hibernation chamber. That still concerns me."

Donn felt the situation getting out of hand. He said quickly, "Look, I'll tell you what I told Linna here. What I did down there ... I did it for attention. It was stupid, and childish, and not professional. I felt I was better than the assignment." He watched Simpatica's expression for guidance. "So I did some dumb stuff to act out. I'm not proud of it."

Simpatica nodded. "I thought something like that had happened. And you've been under a great strain. We all have, but you, walking in on Thom and the babies..." she patted her desk. "Well, I'm sure it was difficult for you."

"And maybe I was too hard on you," Margulies grumbled behind him.

Donn half-turned in astonishment.

"You wanted to do a memorial," Margulies said. "I can understand that. It's only natural."

Donn recognized her play. "I guess I should apologize for my insubordination." He turned back to Provost Simpatica. "I am truly sorry I've caused any problems," he said, keeping his voice even.

Simpatica smiled at that, and Donn knew then that the conversation was over.

"I'm glad to hear it." Simpatica looked at Margulies. "Well, Linna, if you're okay with monitoring Donn to make sure he gets back in to the swing of things, I think we should try it." She smiled sweetly at Donn. "We don't want an able-bodied member of the team sulking when we're about to make planetfall. There is a lot to be done, right?"

"Thank you, Provost. And there is a lot to be done," Donn said as Margulies unlocked his handcuffs. He rubbed his wrists in a circular motion. They hadn't hurt him, but he wanted to show Simpatica that he had been affected by the discipline.

Simpatica pressed her palms to the desktop and pushed herself up. "Then we're agreed. Linna, come back and we'll talk later about how it's going."

"Yes, Provost," Margulies said, and she stepped back to allow Donn to leave the cramped room.

When the two were well out of earshot of the provost's office, Donn said, "That seemed to work."

"Yes, I think so. Simpatica is not a deep player," Margulies said with a hint of scorn. "Whatever she says, she believes."

"Right. And thanks for your apology."

"I didn't mean it," Margulies said, reaching for the ladder to the central corridor and starting her ascent. "You're a colossal pain in the ass, and just for that, I should have kept you in the Freezer."

Donn grunted and followed her up. "Good to know."

They entered the zero-g central shaft and pushed off aft, heading back to the embryonic bay decks and the Freezer beyond.

"We need to assess how many sleepers are dead," Donn said. "But we can't examine each one. That'll take too long."

Margulies said, "Yeah. I was thinking a sampling. I'll spot check to get an idea."

"We don't want to miss anyone, though," Donn added.

"Might be inevitable. Like you said, it'll take too long to check them all, just myself. Since I have to do it without OSIRIS." He couldn't see her face, as she was ahead of him as they floated through the shaft, but he could hear the dread in her voice. "Jezeus, this is a nightmare."

"This is one more reason we need to announce this. Linna, if we used all the caretakers, Freezer techs, and crew, we'd have over a hundred a fifty people. We could check every pod in—"

Margulies twisted in mid-air, caroming gently off the rotating curving inner wall of the central shaft. She righted herself, then glared at Donn. "I already told you. We do that, we create a panic. We'd have a dozen Thoms."

"We have to. To check all the hib pods. Otherwise, we might miss some who are still alive — some who we might be able to save."

Margulies' spin continued, and she rotated back to her original orientation, facing aft. She slid a hand against the inner wall and used it to propel herself. "I told you before. Some of us were probably going to die on this mission. It's better to lose some of us than all of us."

Her voice grew faint as the distance between them widened. "You of all people should understand that, Cardenio."

Chapter Eleven

"Hello, everyone. I'm back," Donn said when he entered bay K-8." Did you all miss me?" He swung himself into the control saddle and scanned the master board. All lights remained green — he would have been shocked to see anything else. Even if Kearney and OSIRIS had been less vigilant than he, two days' absence wouldn't have been enough to put any of his swimmers in crisis.

Despite everything, he felt a deep sense of calm when he looked out at the rows upon rows of preborns. The chaos of the mission, the events of the past few days, his own personal relationship mess — all of it became unimportant and therefore powerless to affect him while he was here. All he had to do here was maintain the health and well-being of seventeen hundred and twenty-eight children.

He got up from the control saddle and walked toward the pod racks. He didn't stop at the first one — as 1-Alpha-1, Donna got too much attention — but went halfway into the bay, walking slowly, his fingers trailing gently across the canopies of the pods.

He stopped and looked at 1-Alpha-6. His eyes couldn't help but scan the local readout. Halfpint was doing just fine. Everything right down the middle. OSIRIS had him at green status.

A horrible thought struck him.

"OSIRIS! Emergency access. Pod One-Alpha-Six. Open it up. Now!"

"You do not have authorization for this command, Donn."

"What? Why not?" As soon as he had spoken, he knew the answer.

"Liaison Officer Margulies is required for authorization to administer care to—"

"God damn it. Cancel command. Get Margulies on the comm. Urgent!"

A scant few seconds later, Linna's voice sounded in the bay. "Donn? What's the matter?"

"I need you to give me command authority back in my bay."

"Why? What's happened?"

"I need to open a pod."

"What's happened?" Margulies repeated.

Donn balled his fists in frustration. For a split second, he looked at the nearest multitool niche and considered smashing his way in. Thom's wild face swam in his memory and he put the thought aside. "Just give me access. I need to check on a preborn."

"Why not use the read—"

"Because OSIRIS might be malfunctioning again, Linna. Jezeus, what if all this time, all these preborns..." he could not finish the thought.

Margulies gasped over the intercom. "Oh, Goddess ... OSIRIS, restore command capability to Caretaker Cardenio. Recognize Margulies, password six-one-one-nine-eight-zebra-six."

"Command confirmed," OSIRIS replied.

"Open the pod, dammit!" Donn shouted, and he heard the sounds of the pod's opening cycle. Pseudoamniotic fluid was being drained to minimum levels, below the threshold of the canopy. Donn grabbed a pair of disposable gloves from his kit and watched the progress bar on the readout, and when it was in the green range, he lifted the glass and regarded Halfpint, still peacefully and unawares floating in his fluid.

Donn knew Halfpint couldn't see anything, not truly. The preborn was still looking through pseudoamniotic fluid, and in any case, his eyesight was not fully developed. But when he blinked, it was such a human expression Donn could not help but chuckle in relief, and he felt the terror recede.

He reached into the pod with his gloved hands and pressed gently against Halfpint's chest. He could feel the beating heart. "Hey there, fella. I didn't mean to interrupt your sleep. Just wanted to check on you, say hello. You go back to whatever you were doing. I'll meet you properly in about a month, okay?" He went to the preborn's tiny head, on which hair was beginning to form, and cradled it gently.

Halfpint wiggled slightly, his mantis-like arms reaching out vaguely. Donn knew he should close the canopy and put Halfpint back into his pod, but he brushed the baby's right hand with his little finger.

Halfpint made a half-hearted attempt to grasp the finger.

Donn swallowed and reluctantly withdrew his hand, dripping with fluid. "I'll see you soon, buddy." He shut the canopy lid, smearing the glass, and said, "OSIRIS, resume ordinary operation on Pod One-Alpha-Six."

Margulies' voice sounded in the bay. "What's happening, Donn?"

"It's okay. He's fine. I just had the thought that if the sleepers were dead, maybe ... maybe the swimmers were, too."

"I never thought of that. Are you going to check the others?"

"I will, yeah. Have you got any results?"

"Not good ones. I've checked twenty-nine hib pods. All dead."

"Shit."

"I did a random sampling. I'll keep checking, but we have to come to grips with the idea that they're all going to be dead."

Donn closed his eyes for a few seconds and allowed himself to feel. He had never met the sleepers — they had been trained and then put into hibernation separately — but the thought that twenty thousand humans had died in their sleep was still unsettling.

He opened his eyes and flexed his fingers. An overriding thought took the place of grief at the deaths of the hibernators.

What was to become of all the preborns now?

To his chagrin, he felt a faint sense of triumph at the thought that he would not be handing them over to strangers to look after. The mission plan to decant the babies and then give them, twenty-four at a time, to each pair of thawed foster parents had always gnawed at him. He was expected to give up his children to these unknowns? Yes, he knew they had been specially selected and trained for just the task, but he had always felt resistant to the idea.

It dawned on him what Margulies had been trying to tell him. His level of attachment to the preborns was unhealthy. What kind of resentment would he have felt at the new parents? And what unhelpful actions would have resulted from that unconscious resentment?

But none of that mattered now. He chastised himself for his feelings of satisfaction that he would not be handing over the babies after all. Taking care of seventeen hundred preborns in artificial wombs was one thing. Caring for the same number of crawling, crying, hungry human babies — all the while building an extrasolar colony — was quite another.

"You still there, Donn?" Margulies asked.

"Yeah. Just trying to think this through," he said, and shut his emotions away. His military training took over, and he started a purposeful stride back to his control saddle. "Let's both do some more checks, and reconnect later. Will you be able to have a better sense in, say, two hours? I think I can do about ten percent of my pods by then."

"Two hours should get me about fifty more hibs. But I'll let you know immediately if I find any still alive. Good luck, Donn."

"You too, Linna."

——— «» ———

Half an hour later, Donn had managed to confirm the healthy status of twenty-two of his preborns. Not a single one showed any distress, and when he cross-checked the data he had by his hands-on examination with what OSIRIS recorded, everything matched up. The checks had become routine, but Donn did not allow himself to lose focus. The next baby might be the one who was in trouble. He advanced the retrieval rack to 10-Beta-1 and reached for the canopy.

"Incoming message," OSIRIS said.

Donn looked up at the ceiling. "Send it through," he said, then added, "Linna? You found one?"

A male voice answered. "No, Donn, this is Jason Collins."

"Jason?" Donn stared at the ceiling for a moment and fought off anger. "What do you want?"

Donn heard the gentle sigh from the other man. "Okay, if it's going to be like that. I didn't want to annoy you. I wanted just to check in, see how you were doing. I never got a chance to after the—"

"I'm good. Little busy right now."

"Sure. I heard about what happened. With the Freezer."

Donn stopped his examination of Quincy. "You did?"

"Yeah. Kearney told me."

Donn grunted. "I'm sure. What else are you guys up to?"

There was a moment before Collins answered. "Let's be honest, Donn. This is awkward for both of us. I don't know what kind of arrangement you got with Kearney, but as far as I'm concerned, she's just someone I spend time with."

"And fuck."

"If you want to be like that about it, then fine. Yeah, we have sex. You really want to talk about this? Because this is not why I contacted you. I'm not calling you up so you could hear us in the middle of it."

"Sorry. You're right. We're best pals." Donn shut the canopy for Pod 10-Beta-1 and advanced to the next one.

"Jezeus, Donn. I called to see how you're doing, and mention that I think something weird's going on with the mission. But all you wanna do is get all nasty that you can't have Kearney to yourself, so let's—"

"Hold on," Donn said as the next pod clicked into place. "What do you mean, something weird is going on with the mission? What's weird about it?"

"I don't think we should talk about it over the comm. I was going to ask if I could meet up with you. But if you're too messed up over the whole relationship triangle, maybe we'd—"

"No. Come to my bay. K-eight."

"You sure?"

"Yeah. I'll be in here." Donn heard the slight but unmistakable sound of the connection terminating, and continued his checks on the pods methodically, his mind on this new development.

Jason Collins was by no means a friend. Donn knew, if he ever cared to admit it, that the man was friendly and competent and had gone out of his way to be gracious about their situation. That just made him all the more detestable — did he have to be so reasonable and damn good about it all? Not to mention his boyish handsomeness and overall sense of cool competence. There was simply nothing to objectively dislike about Collins.

Donn knew that once again he was being childish. He was facing a crisis in the mission beyond anything he could have imagined even days ago. Thom's murder of the preborns now felt like a distant memory, one which should be lamented mildly and then put away, just like Margulies said. And now he stubbornly refused to grant Jason Collins an inch of respect just because he was sleeping with the same woman he was? And was probably better at it?

"Put it away," Donn growled to himself as he shut the pod canopy of 12-Beta-1 and jabbed the "advance" button.

It was a full ten seconds before he realized the machinery had finished cycling. He began on 1-Gamma-1.

———— «» ————

Donn saw the shining light of a visitor waiting for authorization to enter his bay. Agnes, as per instructions, had remained silent. He didn't know how long the light had been on.

"Open the bay," Donn said, feeling around 2-Delta-1 for a pulse. His gloved hands were coated in pseudoamniotic fluid, and the front of his coveralls shone with the residue as well.

"Donn?" Jason's deep voice called from the entry hatch.

"Here," Donn said, smiling slightly as the steady beat of YooHoo's pulse met his fingertips. He murmured, "looking good, kid. See you soon," and closed the canopy. He heard Collins' footsteps approaching and saw the man's wide-eyed expression when the canopy lid came down.

"Jezeus, what are you doing?"

"Checking on my preborns," Donn replied. He heard the curtness in his own voice.

"Like that? You're not worried about hurting them?"

Donn advanced the rack and looked at Collins. "I'm being careful."

"Something wrong with the computer?"

Pod 3-Delta-1 slid into place. "I don't know. It's hard to explain. This is the surest way to know if they are doing well." He opened the canopy. "Hey, Mozzarella. Sorry to bug you, but I won't be long." He reached in and felt for the pulse.

Collins snorted a brief laugh. "Mozzarella. I like that."

Donn felt the pulse and turned his head to face Collins. "The nickname?"

"Yeah. I do that, too. Helps me remember something about them, you know? My one guy gives me all kinds of problems. For a while, everything I sent him made him respond the other way. Increase potassium, and his pH went up, not down. I call him 'Riverside.' It means—"

"To go back the other way, yeah," Donn said, withdrawing from 3-Delta-1. "That's from the LEO squadrons." He closed the canopy and studied Collins. "You were in the LEO group?"

"No, no. My brother was, though."

Donn studied his rival for a moment. "I'm sorry."

"Yeah." Collins cleared his throat and patted the canopy. "Mozzarella, huh?"

"Yep. I was using the peepers on him one day, and he started pissing. Because of the setting I had them on, it showed up white. Like a long string of—"

Collins laughed hoarsely. "Mozzarella. I get it. Cute."

Donn reached for the "Advance" button, and saw Collins give the canopy a gentle caress before withdrawing his hand.

Pod 4-Delta-1 swung into place.

"What did you want to talk about?" Donn said, opening the canopy and looking down at Lady X, her arms folded in front of her in a pose that had earned her the name.

"Can OSIRIS hear us?"

Donn snapped his head up at that. He paused for a moment, then said, "Agnes, you and OSIRIS shut down voice recognition and recording, please. Manual input only."

"Acknowledged. Voice recognition disabled."

Donn looked at Collins expectantly while he felt for Lady X's pulse.

"Something's very wrong on this ship," Collins said. "There're too many things that don't add up."

"Like what?"

"First of all," Collins said, "realize that the stuff I'm gonna say is borderline treasonous. If Simpatica or Captain Vincent hears about it, that'll pretty much do it for me."

"Wait a second," Donn said, stopping his physical exam of Lady X. "Are you talking mutiny?"

Collins shook his head. "No, not that kind of thing. I mean I've been thinking a lot about the way this mission is set up, and I just don't get it. So much about this is wrong. Just doesn't make any sense."

"Give me an example." Donn resumed his search for Lady X's pulse.

"Take these preborns. What's the point of doing it this way? Sending a quarter million embryos, to be grown in space, to colonize a planet? Why do it that way?"

"You got the briefing. It had to do with One Earth law. If they were born on Earth, they'd be citizens of whatever country they were born in. Even as wards of the state, they couldn't be shipped off without—"

"I know, I know," Collins said. "But I gotta be honest, that just seems like legal bullshit to me. So growing them here, in space, that makes it all okay?"

"Legally, yeah, I guess. That's what they told us in the briefing."

"You don't think that's messed up?"

Donn found the pulse and closed the canopy, advanced the rack to 5-Delta-1. "I didn't understand it fully. Maybe I wasn't really in a mental state to question it, I don't know."

"What do you mean, mental state?"

Donn stopped, his hands on the canopy edge of 5-Delta-1. "I was in bad shape after the war. I just wanted, I don't know, a fresh start. A place where I'd be surrounded by life, I guess."

Collins nodded. "Sure."

"One Earth offered us a bunch of retraining opportunities. Guess it was their way of trying to make up for the way they treated us after the war. So I went into caretaker training. Found I had a knack for it. Plus, I liked it." Donn narrowed his eyes, now angry that he had opened up to this man. "Look, I don't expect someone like you to understand. Guys like me who served and lived ... we saw more than you will ever know."

Collins raised his hands to chest level, palms out. "Hey, Donn, I know. I know you were in the LEO force. Jezeus, I can't even imagine what that must have been like. I'm not judging you or why you chose to go on this mission. Hell, it's as good a reason as any. Better, really."

"Yeah. Sorry," Donn added with a grunt.

"It's fine. I just never thought this way was the best way. I think we should have just sent adults and let 'em screw their brains out and make babies the old-fashioned way."

Donn nodded. He looked at Jason for a long moment. The man had a point, but the mention of the adults brought back the reality of the situation with crushing finality. Whether or not the mission had been viable seemed immaterial now. He watched the man, weighing if he should trust him with his knowledge of the sleepers' status. "Jason, you need to know something. Something I discovered and which Linna Margulies is helping me investigate."

Collins scowled. "Margulies ... she's your K-Deck liaison?"

"Yeah." He took a breath. "The sleepers might be dead."

Collins froze. He stared unblinking at Donn for a long while, then murmured, "This mission's over."

"We still have a quarter million babies to—"

"It's over. We can try to make it work, but there's just no way. It's all over." He scowled. "You're sure? About the sleepers?"

"Only that so far, twenty-nine are dead. No, thirty. Linna's twenty-nine and my single one. She's spot-checking the rest, but so far, we're thirty for thirty."

"Why spot-checks? Why not use OSIRIS?"

"When I opened one of the hib pods and checked myself, OSIRIS gave vital signs that didn't correspond to what was really happening. The human inside was dead, but OSIRIS was still reporting her as alive."

"You're sure," Collins said, his inflection a statement. "Otherwise you wouldn't be telling me this."

"Yeah. Even with the leads detached, OSIRIS was giving off vital signs."

Collins pressed his right hand to his forehead and swept his close-cropped hair back. The tiny blond strands flattened and then sprang back up when his palm passed over them. "We can't go on. There's no way to make this viable now."

Donn shook his head. "We can't execute a flip. The A-drive will disengage automatically in under three weeks. You know that as well as I do. It's all preset."

Collins pressed his temples for a moment, then looked around him. "How're we going to take care of a quarter million babies? Fewer than two hundred of us. It's over. It's over. It's over," Collins repeated it like a mantra.

Donn watched him carefully, mindful that the nearest multitool was closer to Collins than it was to him. He slowly started to maneuver himself to be between Collins and the heavy tool. He cursed himself for blurting out the situation without preparation. Once again, he admitted with grudging respect, Margulies might have been right.

Collins' head had been slowly lowering as he repeated "it's over," but he snapped it up with a start. "OSIRIS was reporting the sleeper as alive even with the leads disconnected?"

"Yeah."

"That's why you were manually checking your swimmers. You don't think you could trust—" His eyes went wide, and Donn knew instantly what the other man was thinking.

"I need to get back to my bay," Collins said, half-turning, his eyes searching Donn's, as if looking for permission to leave.

"I understand. No one else knows yet, Jason. You, me, and Margulies. She thinks we should keep it that way until we can figure out what to do."

"All right. I'll be in touch. Personally — not through intercraft." Collins did not wait for acknowledgement, but hurried out of K-8.

Chapter Twelve

When Margulies called again, Donn had almost finished checking his own bay. He'd become adept at quickly finding a pulse on the preborn, having reduced the time per pod to around twenty or thirty seconds. He might have reduced that still further had he ceased the personal contact, however brief, he made with each swimmer. He couldn't help himself. He needed to reassure each preborn with a gentle caress.

Pod 10-Kappa-10 housed Pele, and Donn had just opened the canopy when OSIRIS altered him to a communication from Margulies.

"What did you find?" Donn asked, swiftly checking on Pele and finding a strong pulse. He had already closed the canopy and slapped the "Advance" button before she responded.

"All dead. I sampled something like a hundred and fifty. All the same."

"Jezeus," Donn said, opening 11-Kappa-10 and reaching inside. "At least you're okay, Plum," Donn said and closed the canopy.

"What's that?"

"Nothing. Just checking my preborns. Everything's good here."

"Thank Goddess for that."

"Collins came over to visit," Donn said, seeing 12-Kappa-10 slide into place. "I told him what's going on."

"Why'd you do that? Shit, Donn, we can't let this get out—"

"Relax, Linna. I know we can't, not yet. But he already had his own doubts about the mission, so it just seemed like the right thing to do."

"Where's he now?"

"Checking his own preborns. We'll have to do that, too, Linna."

"Do what?"

"Check manually every single preborn on this ship. We can't trust OSIRIS to be accurate. Just because so far, every single one of mine is okay doesn't mean that's true for every deck or every bay."

He heard Margulies sigh. "No, it doesn't."

Donn pressed his point even as the rack reset to the Lambda group. 1-Lambda-1 appeared in the cradle and Donn opened the pod. "And that'll require all the caretakers to do what I'm doing now. We've got to tell people, Linna. This can't stay a secret."

"Damn it, Donn, don't you think I know that? But have you forgotten about Thom? We could have mass hysteria on our hands."

"Thom found out about this suddenly, from a computer file. When I told Collins, he didn't snap. He was shocked, sure, and worried for his own preborns," Donn hesitated, then decided not to relay the information that Collins had said "it's all over." He had to think away his anxiety that Collins would return to his bay and methodically murder his own preborns just as Thom had tried to do.

"Donn? You still there?"

"Yeah. I was just thinking — when Thom went crazy, OSIRIS acted immediately to alert us to the malfunctions. Unlike what you found in the Freezer."

"So?"

1-Lambda-1, known as Mouse, returned to her location in the rack while Bruiser slid into the receiving slot. "So now I'm beginning to think whatever's wrong is confined to the Freezer. My swimmers are all checking out fine."

Margulies murmured, "Thank Goddess again." She added in a normal voice, "It was no picnic here. Dozens of dead bodies."

Donn stopped suddenly, his gloved hands on Bruiser's ankle. Until that moment, he hadn't considered what finding corpse after corpse would do to Linna. He was so used to her being unflappable and tough that he rarely thought of her as a person. "Are you okay?" he said to the air while feeling for Bruiser's pulse.

"There's no time for that." Her voice was iron. "How much longer on your bay? I can come help you finish it off and we can talk more about what we're going to do."

"I've got about three hundred left. Might take me an hour, maybe a little longer."

"That's fast."

"I got a system," Donn said, closing Bruiser's pod and advancing to 3-Lambda-1. "Hey, speaking of that, how'd you gain access to the hib pods so easily? I had to kick mine open."

"I brought a lever. Pried them open," Margulies growled. "I'll join you in your bay and we can finish this. Might as well have Collins in on it, since he knows."

"I'll get him. See you soon, Linna."

———— «» ————

Margulies arrived shortly thereafter, and her presence sped up the process somewhat. Donn found himself watching her for the first few checks, warning her to be gentle with the preborns. She handled them with cold efficiency, showing none of the personal touch Donn had. She was still slower than he was, but that was only due to her unfamiliarity with the shortcuts Donn had learned over the past eight hours.

Finally, Pod 12-Mu-12 was shut, and Donn looked at Margulies. "Everyone's fine. Jezeus," he added, a wash of relief cascading over him. Worry he had tamped down deep within him now faded away. Whatever else might be happening on board the ship, his little corner of it was fecund with life.

"Thanks," Margulies said, stripping off her gloves.

"For what?"

"Letting me touch your preborns. I needed that after the Freezer." Her gray eyes showed no sign of softness, but Donn understood.

"You're welcome. It's wonderful, isn't it? How warm they all are, little hands grasping, tiny little movements..."

"Yeah. It is. I envy you guys. Sometimes."

Donn's mouth opened slightly. This was a side of her he had never seen. A feeling of unease at this new aspect of his longtime adversary made him say, "Maybe we should take this to my quarters. We can clean up there," he said, looking down at his saturated garment. "I'll let Collins know."

"Good idea."

Donn sent Collins a message about the meeting, and he and Margulies walked through the gently curving corridor to his room. Margulies snorted as the pair passed Thom's graffiti.

"What?"

"Nothing," Margulies grumbled.

"You don't like this, do you?" Donn said, indicating the amateur artwork.

"No."

"It's just a little minor rebellion, Linna. People expressing themselves," Donn said, rolling his sore shoulders.

"No such thing as a minor rebellion. This isn't a playground or a middle school. It's Earth's first interstellar colonization vessel."

"You weren't in the High Guard, Linna." Donn said, looking at the frescoes of fantastical creatures.

"What does that have to do with it?"

"Our first contact with an alien species, and it was in war. Some might say that was the most significant moment in all of human history. And what did the LEO squadrons do? We stenciled little pictures on our fighters of anthropomorphic Starfish being blown up. Or wrote limericks about killing them. You must have heard of some of them. 'Twinkle, twinkle, little Starfish/How I wonder how you go squish?/ Up above the world so high/Blow your legs off 'till you die."

"No, never heard that."

"It's what we do. People. Make shit our own. Little kids own their toys once they mark them up. Or paint on walls to mark it as theirs. This is no different."

"This ship isn't a toy, and we're not kids."

"You know what I mean. We had to do that in the LEO squadrons. If we sat back and thought about how important what we were doing was, we'd have froze up. We had to make it a kind of game, a fuckin' joke."

"Didn't help."

"Watch it," Donn said, the fatigue of the past eight hours catching up to him. "Thousands and thousands of men and women died up there. What'd you do in the war?"

"That's your job," Linna said. "A soldier's job is to die when we all tell you to."

"Jezeus, Margulies. That's pretty harsh."

Linna shrugged. "Sorry, but we have to be tough. Especially now. What we've got in front of us is serious. And no damn jokes written on a wall are going to solve our problems." She stopped at the hatchway to Donn's room. "And I was a safety manager at a defense contractor plant. We made surface to air missiles."

"Didn't know that," Donn said. "Is that what you did before the war, too?"

"Sort of. I was a lawyer."

Donn had raised his palm to unlock his door, but froze mid-action at Margulies' comment. "No shit? What kind of law?"

"Workplace stuff. Occupational safety and health administration, mainly. When a worker got hurt on the job, we'd come in and see what management was doing wrong."

"That fits. Explains a lot, really." Donn reached over and pressed his palm against the lock. As the door opened, he said, "Anyway, you're right. This is serious. So let's get to—" he froze when his eyes regarded the room.

Kearney stretched from her reclining position on the bed, nude. Her eyes opened, first as slits, then grew much wider as she saw not just Donn, but Linna Margulies in the doorway. "Shit!" She scrambled for the sheets.

"Goddess, Cardenio," Margulies said accusingly.

"What the fuck are you doing here?" Kearney's eyes blazed at Margulies.

"Kearney, this isn't a good time." Donn approached the bed and found her coveralls in a crumpled heap; he handed them to her. "I'm sorry, I didn't expect to find you here."

"I was just trying to surprise you," she said. "I thought it would be a good way to make up for our little spat."

"How'd you get in?" Margulies said, crossing her arms.

Donn turned to look over his left shoulder. "I've given her palm access. A while back."

"Against regulations," Margulies murmured.

"Eat shit," Kearney said, pulling on her coveralls awkwardly, the sheet partially obscuring her body.

"Just get dressed and get out," Margulies said.

"Why? What's going on?" Kearney looked at Donn.

"It's—" he stopped, then half-turned again to Margulies. "She should stay and hear this."

"Why?" Margulies said, her arms still folded across her chest.

"She's going to find out eventually. Might as well tell her now. Besides," he looked back at the wide-eyed Kearney, "I want to tell her. She might have insight as to what to do. She knows the crew and caretaker corps pretty well."

"I'll bet," Margulies murmured.

Donn spun and advanced on an unflinching Margulies. "Knock that shit off, you hear me? You were the one saying this was serious and dirty little jokes weren't gonna help."

Margulies' smug demeanor faded. She uncrossed her arms and put them on her hips. "You're right," she grumbled. "Kearney, sorry. Uncalled for."

The apology only served to make Kearney all the more amazed. "Okay, what the hell's going on? You two better start talking."

Margulies glared at Donn, as if daring him to speak. He met her gaze and hesitated. Not out of fear, for he had almost made it his second job to defy her these past eight months, but from a slowly growing respect. It occurred to him that of all the people on the mission — Kearney included — it was Margulies who had been with him the most during the crisis.

The thought bothered him. He snorted and turned to Kearney, and the words tumbled out. "Linna and I have discovered a serious problem in the Freezer. It's looking like the sleepers are dead."

Kearney's pale complexion did not change. "What? What do mean, 'it's looking like?' Do you know for sure?"

"Yes and no. We know of … what's the total, Linna?"

Margulies only hesitated a fraction of a second. "One hundred thirty-eight."

"Plus the one I found. So one-thirty-nine. All dead."

Kearney's voice was breathy. "One hundred thirty-nine sleepers dead, out of twenty thousand?"

"No, K," Donn sat down on the bed with her. "We've only checked that many. Linna has been in there for hours, doing a sampling."

"A sampling? I don't understand. Why not just ask OSIRIS for a summary? And why didn't OSIRIS alert you to—"

"OSIRIS is malfunctioning," Margulies broke in. "At least, down in the Freezer he is. He's not giving the proper readings on the sleepers. I had to check manually."

"Christ," Kearney said, invoking the old-fashioned name without irony. "Is this connected to Thom's thing?"

Donn looked up at Margulies. He stood up, equidistant from the two women. "There's no obvious link. But then, on the other hand, what are the chances that these two things..." he trailed off, looking at a corner of the room while he thought.

"I mean, didn't he do something to OSIRIS, Donn? He accessed the camera control function, or something like that, right?"

Margulies spoke slowly. "I sent my report to the technical branch of the crew. Norman was working on it ... I've heard nothing back from him. I've been busy, myself. With you," she said, indicating Donn.

Donn heard her but did not acknowledge the reference. When he did speak, he said to the room itself, "I don't know enough about OSIRIS' workings to be able to determine if Thom's tampering could have an effect on the Freezer system. Who would know? Norman?"

Margulies said, "He's the one to ask, yes."

"Don't you know?" Kearney said with unconcealed scorn. Her comment was directed at Margulies and though it had the syntax of a question, her voice made it an accusation.

"No, I don't. I am not a computer expert," Margulies answered evenly. She turned to Donn. "I will ask Norman to look into this. In the meantime, we have some—"

Donn interrupted. "Hold up. If Thom's tampering with the camera system somehow managed to disrupt the Freezer hibernation controls, and also made OSIRIS blind to the problem, then why…" he shook his head.

"What?" Kearney prompted.

"If Thom caused the problem by tampering with the camera system, then that just leads us backwards. Why was he messing with OSIRIS in the first place? We've been saying that he snapped because he found out about the sleepers. But if he was the cause of all this, then—"

"I see what you mean," Margulies said. "Chicken-and-egg."

"Yeah. Damn it." Donn clenched his fists for a moment, then looked at Margulies. "As soon as possible, we need that answer from Norman."

Margulies nodded, and Kearney let out a long, sustained, "wow."

"What is it?" Margulies looked at Kearney in annoyance.

"Caretaker Cardenio just gave K-Deck Liaison Officer Margulies an order, and she agreed to do it."

Margulies' nostrils flared, and she inhaled noisily.

Donn interrupted before the room broke into chaos. "Knock it off, K. We've got a lot to do here."

"We do?"

"Of course we do! What do you think the odds are that any of the sleepers are alive? Linna sampled over a hundred. All dead."

"One hundred out of twenty thousand is less than one percent. Maybe it was a bank of them, or something. A section."

"I know how to do a sample, Kearney," Margulies said. "I went all over the Freezer to do my checking. It's not a single bank or section. It's systemic."

"If you say so," Kearney said.

"I do say so. Don't you realize the significance of this? If all the sleepers are dead, then—"

Donn completed Margulies' thought. "Then we'll have to become mommy and daddy to seventeen hundred kids each."

The three froze in their triangle — Margulies standing defiantly, hands on hips, chin outthrust; Kearney sitting on the bed, her hands folded demurely in her lap; Donn occupying the space between them, scanning the wall of his cabin, looking at the changing artwork his computer outlet projected on the white surface.

As if on cue, the visitor chime sounded. Donn glanced at the door and saw Collins' tall form on the door monitor. "Agnes, let him in, please."

Collins entered and surveyed the room. His eyes appeared to take it all in rapidly, stopping on Kearney. "Oh." He looked at Donn, his expression carefully neutral. "You didn't say she was in on this."

"I wasn't," Kearney said before Donn was forced to answer. "They just now told me."

"Got it." Collins looked at the others. "So what's the plan? You all realize there's no way we can make this work anymore, right?"

"What do you mean?" Margulies said.

"All the sleepers dead. No parents. The mission was already going to be a longshot as it was, and now—"

"Jason, stop," Kearney said softly. Donn felt a sharp sting of jealousy at her intimate tone, but watching how Collins immediately shut up in obedience was a balm.

"But he's right," Margulies said. "I don't see how this is going to work either. At least, not with the original mission parameters."

The words hung ominously in the air. Donn whispered, "What are you suggesting?"

"That circumstances have changed, obviously. The original plan was twenty-four children per parental pair, thirty-six in a triad, and so forth. Twelve kids per person. With twenty thousand, seven hundred thirty-six sleepers." Margulies stopped, as if she had finished.

"Of course it's changed," Donn said. "The math is just … different."

"It's impossible, Donn," Collins said, shaking his head. "Seventeen hundred kids each? Without pod support? You know there's just no way. Like I said, it was almost impossible at the numbers she just gave you. The original numbers."

Donn looked from one to the other, then finally said to Margulies. "Finish your thought. Because I think I know what you're about to say, and I need to hear you actually say it. Stop pussyfooting around and just say it." He pinned her in space with his eyes, daring her to speak the unspeakable.

Margulies took a breath, her eyes not leaving his. "We can stay with the original math. The original ratio."

Collins tilted his head. "How? We don't have the sleepers."

"No. I mean … with the caretakers and crew we have now. One ninety-seven."

Collins furrowed his brow. "I still don't see what you mean. We have one ninety-eight, actually, but we've got almost a quarter million preborns. We can't do a twelve to one ratio. That would put us at what? Thirteen-hundred each?"

Donn said in a hoarse whisper. "Yes, we can. If you follow her cold logic. One ninety seven," Donn added. "Thom is incapacitated."

"No. He's dead," Margulies said.

The words froze the air. No one spoke nor moved for a timeless interval. Donn had not wished the man dead, but having heard the news, he found he could not summon up grief.

"So one-ninety-seven," Donn said coldly. "Times twelve." He glanced quickly at Collins and then Kearney. "How many's that?"

"What? Uh, two thousand, three hundred sixty-four," Kearney whispered.

"That's how many we can save?" Collins asked.

Donn choked, "OSIRIS, number of current surviving preborns minus two thousand, three hundred sixty-four."

OSIRIS answered immediately. "Two hundred forty-six thousand, four hundred fifty-nine."

Donn turned back to Margulies, his voice iron and bowels water, "Say it that way, Linna. Say that you want to murder that many preborns."

"Donn," Linna said simply, "I'm trying to find the best way out of this. Don't make this harder than it already is. You think I like this idea?"

"I have no idea what's going on in your heart. To even consider this—"

"Donn, please, we have to work the problem," Collins said.

Whatever grudging admiration and goodwill Donn had towards Collins vanished. "You? You're thinking about this? You're a caretaker, goddammit!"

"I'm not saying anything. I'm saying we need to—"

"No," Kearney said, her voice small. The three others stopped and stared at her. Despite her quiet voice and small frame, all listened.

"We can't even consider this," she said.

Margulies' voice had a faint pleading quality. "I'm not seeing any other way. Maybe we can play with the ratio, but we're not trained parents, so I don't see how it can be that large."

"No."

Donn watched Kearney. He'd seen her animated, enraged, orgasmic, sarcastic, flippant, but he had never heard her so resolute.

"We will not cull the numbers. That's unthinkable."

"But how—"

"We will deliver all surviving preborns."

Margulies looked at Collins, but the tall man seemed unwilling to champion the grisly cause Margulies had advanced. She licked her lips and said, "I don't like it either. I hate that it's come to this. But we can't deliver them all. We will lose some. It's inevitable. You have to see that."

Kearney's voice was flat. "The decision is not ours to make."

"So we're going to let nature decide who lives and who dies? We might lose more than we need to that way. Trying to care for them all might cost us all of them. The entire colony might die out while we try to save every life."

"We will not cull the preborns in advance. Our mission is to deliver them to Tau Ceti Three. We will do that. What happens after is not in our hands." Kearney finally stood up. She was shorter than everyone else in the room, and slighter. But her posture was erect, her face firm. She looked at each person in turn. "We will not talk of this again. Put it out of your minds."

Donn stood up a little straighter and nodded. "I agree. This is not an option, Linna. Jason."

Margulies said, "It's easy to dismiss this as horrible, and make brave speeches, but we need to face the situation as it is. We don't have the resources to take care of that many kids. Not even close. You both have to see that. Try and save them all, and we will lose them all. Make a terrible, horrible decision now in order to save thousands of lives."

"Murder hundreds of thousands. That's what you're proposing," Donn yelled.

"Goddess damn it, Donn! I'm not a monster! I'm trying to save lives!"

"By killing?" Donn said.

"Yes!" She stared at Donn with an expression he could not identify, then with horror he saw what was about to happen to her an instant before it did.

Margulies broke down in tears.

She wept openly, her body bent double, wracked with sobs. Her hands were still, amazingly, on her hips even as she bent in half and shuddered.

Collins stared at her, but it was Donn who moved closer and put his hand on her broad, muscular back. He felt her shoulder muscles shudder beneath her coveralls.

"Compose yourself, Margulies," Kearney said. Donn shot an amazed look at Kearney. Her voice had been steel, cold, dispassionate. Her face still bore the same implacable mask —or was it finally her true face? Donn agreed with her, but was surprised that Kearney did not sympathize with the pain Margulies was in.

"Jezeus, K," Collins murmured. "The woman's hurting."

"Tears don't help."

Donn rubbed Margulies' back a little, and the powerful woman shuddered one last time then straightened, tossing off his comforting hand in irritation. "I'm fine. She's right. About the crying. But you're all still not seeing this." She sniffed loudly, but when she resumed speaking, her voice was as steady as ever. All that remained as evidence of her humanity were the moist tear stains on her cheeks. "I'm going to the captain on this. This can't be something we decide here in this room."

Collins nodded even as Kearney said, "No! No one needs to know about this until we're almost at TC. There's nothing that can be done anyway."

"What are you talking about?" Collins said. "No matter what we decide, everything's changed now. We need to alert the whole ship, and immediately. People need to know what's—"

"No matter what we decide?" Donn said, moving away from Margulies to face Collins. "I still can't believe ... you call yourself a caretaker?"

"I—" Collins looked at Kearney, as if for guidance. "I don't know what to think."

"Captain Vincent needs to know," Margulies said. "And I think Collins is right, finally. Donn and I have been talking about this — how and when to tell everyone."

"And risk another Thom?" Kearney said.

"We have to. We can't keep this a secret. I see that now. We should think about the best way to get the data to everyone." Margulies looked at Donn. "Ever since the memorial, people respect you. And it was your discovery of the sleepers in the first place. I think it should be you."

"Me?"

Collins said, "No offense, Donn, but shouldn't Captain Vincent be the one?"

Margulies said, "It'll be his decision, but I am going to suggest Donn be the spokesperson."

"I can't be a spokesperson to something I'm utterly against!"

"Doesn't matter. Vincent will never go for that," Collins said. "You know how he thinks of this command as his personal kingdom. He'll never turn over responsibility to anyone else."

The room descended into silence as the four looked at each other. It was Margulies who finally spoke. "We have to tell the captain. And from there, the rest of the caretakers and crew have to know what's happened. We at least agree on that. From there, it'll be the captain's call."

Donn said, "Linna, we can't just hand this decision over to—"

"Yes, we can, and we will. I'm going there now. I'd like you to accompany me."

"All of us?" Kearney said before Donn could speak.

Margulies hesitated, frowning. "I don't think we want too many people there. I was thinking just Donn and myself."

"I see," Kearney said, then fell silent.

Donn looked at his lover for a moment, then turned to Margulies. "I'm going to speak my mind. You know that."

"Yes, I do. I think you've earned that right." She turned and opened the hatch, then stepped through. Collins followed in her wake.

Donn turned to Kearney and said, "I won't let anything bad happen."

"Before you go, Donn, can I talk to you?" Kearney's voice was again uncharacteristically soft and meek.

Donn looked at the door and said to Collins and Margulies, "I'll be right there."

"Privately. And in my parlor. Not here." Kearney added.

Donn raised his eyebrows and said, "Yeah. Sure." The two left his quarters and squeezed past Collins and Margulies.

"Will this take long?" Margulies said.

"As long as it has to," Kearney replied without looking at the liaison officer. She did stop at Collins to take his hand and squeeze it. "Come see me when Donn and I are done."

Collins had the good grace to look embarrassed by Kearney's suggestion and shot Donn a disarming glance.

Until that moment, it had not occurred to him that Kearney might have wanted an intimate moment, and when the thought came, he was repulsed. He knew that she often treated sex as a balm, but now? Under these circumstances? He took a breath, preparatory to speaking to Kearney to tell her this was not the right time, but a pleading look from her kept his words in.

Chapter Thirteen

The walk to Kearney's chambers was a short one, made more so by the brisk pace she set. Once they had entered and she had cycled the door shut, Donn spoke.

"Kearney, I don't think this is the time for—"

"I didn't ask you here for sex. I have to tell you something."

Despite himself, Donn felt chagrined. He nodded silently and waited.

Kearney looked up at him. "You can't let the captain decide to cull the babies. You've got to stop it."

Donn blinked in surprise. "Of course I'll stop it. You called me over just to tell me that?"

"You don't understand how important this is. Donn," she stepped closer to him and placed her hand on his chest, "it's everything we are. Caretakers. If we allow the murder of hundreds of thousands of babies—"

Donn interrupted. "K, I know all this. You don't have to convince me. I won't let Vincent or anyone else decide to kill the preborns."

She hesitated, her eyes unblinking. "How far would you go to protect them?"

"What do you mean?"

She removed her hand from his chest and backpedaled to her elaborate bureau. Once there, she turned and performed some function to the top drawer. Donn could not see precisely what she was doing, but after a few seconds the drawer opened and she withdrew a small item. Her back still to him, she said, almost too quietly to be heard, "What would you do to protect them?"

"What's going on, K?"

She turned around holding a flechette pistol. "Would you kill?"

Donn took two quick, long strides toward her and grasped her wrists, keeping them down. "What the hell? Where did you get that?"

"Never mind that. The point is that I have it. You should take it with you to your meeting with Vincent. If he won't listen to reason, then you'll have to—"

"Shut up!" Donn whispered savagely. "You realize what you're saying? You're telling me to kill the captain?"

"If he decides to murder the preborns? Yes, that's exactly what I am saying." She looked down at her hands. "Let go, Donn."

Donn released her wrists and stepped back. Kearney was an excellent procurer, but this was much more than simple contraband. As far as he knew, the limited weaponry carried aboard the vessel was locked away in the colonial hold until planetfall, meant to deal with any surprises on Tau Ceti III once the colonization phase began. Surely OSIRIS would know where each weapon was at all times.

Donn shook his head. She was right — it didn't much matter now how she had acquired the weapon. It only mattered that she had it and was asking him to use it. "I'm not taking a gun to meet with the captain. I won't let him decide to kill the preborns, but I don't need a gun to do it."

"You can't know that. And if you convince him, and convince Margulies and Simpatica, then there's no need for the gun, and you can bring it back to me, and no one needs to know. But Donn, what if they don't listen to reason? If Margulies and Collins talk them into it?"

"You think Collins will agree to that?"

Kearney started to tremble. "I don't know, Donn. I don't know him anymore. What he said in your quarters..." She looked back into Donn's eyes, and he could see her searching them. "That's why I asked to see him afterwards."

"What? Why?"

"To end it with him. I can't be with a man who would consider killing the preborns."

Donn felt his heart surge in his chest, and cursed himself for the reaction. Right now, with all that was in front of them, why did this affect him?

"That doesn't matter now, Kearney," he lied.

"I know it doesn't, Donn." She offered the gun. "Take it. I hope you don't have to use it. But I am not going to let anyone hurt the preborns. I'd do it myself, but I don't think they will let me meet with them."

Donn nodded. If she used the gun to threaten her way in, she'd have tipped her hand. The pistol could not be used as a threat — if he took it with him, he'd only draw it to use it. "How are we going to complete this mission, K? I don't want to kill the preborns, but Collins and Margulies are right, too. Are we seriously going to take care of almost thirteen hundred infants each?"

"I don't know how we're going to do it," Kearney said, still holding the gun out for him. "Who knows what the future will bring? Maybe we'll be able to keep them all alive and thriving. Maybe we won't. But I will not choose to end their lives. I will do everything in my power to deliver them alive to our destination. That's what I was assigned to do, that's what you and all the other caretakers were assigned to do. And by Goddess, I will do my duty."

Donn stood a little straighter at the last word. Duty. It had been his duty to climb into his LEO fighter and engage the Starfish. It had been the duty of his squadron mates to die in battle, some mercifully incinerated instantly, others plunging down back to the planet, screaming in terror.

"Ours not to reason why. Ours but to do and die," Donn intoned.

Kearney nodded gravely. "Yes. Yes, it is. Take it, Donn. Do your duty. Your preborns ... all the little children waiting to be born, whom you have named and cared for and nurtured ... all of them are depending on you."

Donn reached out slowly and took the gun.

——— «» ———

With each step closer to the inner zero-g shaft, he felt the weight of the gun against his thigh. He'd hidden it in a zippered pouch, padded with some cotton wadding to hide its outline.

It gave him a slight bulge in his right leg, but neither Margulies nor Collins had commented on it, if they had even noticed.

They entered the central shaft and floated forward, towards the command and control center. Donn had only been there once during the voyage, and that was to receive his first reprimand for violating procedure in naming his swimmers. It had been on week eight, when the embryos had crossed over into fetuses, and the entire caretaker contingent was in a celebratory mood. "Fetustival," Kearney had called it, coining the term which echoed all the way up to A-Deck. Donn had celebrated along with the rest of his colleagues, and had begun naming his charges. The prim computer aspect had given him significant resistance, and in his typical stubborn manner, he'd pushed back. Soon he had found himself face to face with Linna Margulies, who had taken him to meet Captain Vincent and receive a lecture on the nature of caretaker/preborn relations.

Vincent had been almost unconcerned with the precise nature of the disobedience — he was far more upset that someone had challenged his authority in the first place. He had made it very clear that command rested with him and no one else; twice during the meeting he had pointed to his captain's insignia and forced Donn to acknowledge it. As the reprimand came to a close, Vincent spoke with Margulies privately while Donn waited outside to be escorted back to K Deck. When Margulies had emerged, she was in a foul mood. It hadn't taken Donn long to understand that she herself had been reprimanded for allowing disobedience to flourish. Kearney had gotten wind of Donn's reprimand somehow, and had introduced herself to him as "a fellow pain-in-the-ass."

Their friendship had bloomed, nourished by a playful dislike of authority and firm belief in the mission, and their romance had soon followed.

Donn glanced at Margulies, floating ahead of him in the central shaft and again regretted the months of petty rebellions he and Kearney had enacted against her. The woman had a thankless task, keeping order among the caretakers, and Donn remembered what she had said about being envious of Donn and his job.

His reverie was interrupted by the trio's arrival at the trip-C access hatch. Collins grabbed a handhold and swung his weightless body out of the way for Margulies. She approached the hatch and pressed her palm to the access plate.

Donn resisted the impulse to rest his hand on the flechette gun in his thigh pouch. As he watched Linna manipulate the access panel, with Collins floating near her, the import of what was about to happen hit him. It was very possible that in a few minutes, he would be drawing the gun on the captain.

The thought, coupled with the weightless environment, brought back memories of being in the LEO fighter in his parabolic arc, the rising sun behind him and his squadmates while the Starfish fighters blinked in and out of the sky. Lances of almost-invisible light shot out and sliced through the Earth ships, the explosions muted and quick in the thin atmosphere above the planet.

Would he be able to take another life?

He shook off the memory, only to have another one take its place. This time, he saw Thom, eyes wild, raising the multitool above his head.

He would have killed Thom. If he'd had the flechette gun then, he'd have fired it into Thom's body without hesitation. He knew that as surely as he knew he would have killed each and every Starfish if he had ever been given the chance.

But that was in the blood and thunder of battle, the immediacy of the moment. Thom he had caught murdering children, and the Starfish would have been war casualties. Even knowing that Vincent's decision could end far more lives than Thom ever could have, could he cold-bloodedly kill the captain? He knew ethically that stopping Vincent from killing thousands was far, far more justified than killing Thom would have been. But knowing that didn't help. Theory was cold comfort against the fiery reality of murder.

The flechette pistol felt heavy in his pocket, despite the zero-g environment.

The hatch to trip-C irised open, and Margulies swung her legs through and propelled herself down the tunnel, Collins following once her head was out of sight.

Donn watched the open hatchway on the spinning inner wall of the central corridor and matched its movement, latching onto a handhold and forcing himself down the ladder. Weight slowly built up as he stepped down, rung after rung, until he reached the bottom.

Margulies and Collins watched him descend, and for a moment, Donn thought he saw suspicion in their eyes. He nodded to them, trying to keep his face impassive.

Margulies nodded back and turned to another hatch labeled "Command and Control Center." Before placing her palm against the lock, she turned back to the two men. "You two ready?"

Collins nodded. Donn said, "Yes."

"All right. Let me do the initial talking. It's a little out of the ordinary for caretakers to come in here."

"This whole situation is out of the ordinary, Linna," Donn said.

Margulies made two quick fists with her hands, clenched them, then opened her fingers again. "Just let me at least start this my way, Donn."

"I'm not going to let you bulldoze him into—"

Collins interrupted. "We're all going to be heard, right?"

Donn couldn't tell if Collins was asking on his own behalf or on Donn's to placate him.

"We're all going to speak. But in the end it's going to be his decision. Agreed?" Margulies said, looking at Collins, who nodded.

She turned her face to Donn. He returned her gaze with his own, and said finally, "I hear you."

Margulies opened her mouth to speak, and then closed it and shook her head slightly. She placed her palm against the lock with a forceful, almost savage slap, and the hatch cycled open.

The center was a quietly active place, with nine workstations spread around a more streamlined-looking central workstation. Three of the workstations were unoccupied, though their computer monitors remained active, feeding data to no one. The chamber had a low buzz of noise, the combination of human operators moving about or speaking quietly to their OSIRIS outlets adding to the gentle sound of assorted computer chimes and alerts. It was a busy place, but not frantically so.

Donn recognized Captain Vincent in the central workstation, leaning forward and reading his screen. Margulies approached him, passing by two other occupied stations. The officers at those stations looked up from their work at the three-person envoy with mild curiosity, their eyes fixing upon Donn's fluid-stained coveralls. Donn knew them only vaguely, having been introduced at the launch but otherwise having no dealings with them. There were no indications on their workstations what functions they served, and the momentary glance Donn got of their computer screens did not suggest what they did in trip-C.

Captain Vincent looked away from his screen and toward the approaching trio. He smiled gently. "Linna, hello. What can I do for you?" His eyes betrayed slight surprise at seeing the two caretakers, and he lingered on Donn for a moment before returning to his liaison officer.

"Sir, there's something rather important we need to tell you. Can we go to your quarters to do so?"

Vincent's gentle smile vanished. "Of course." He leaned back and said to one of the other crewmembers, "Freeman, can you take over here for a bit?"

"Yes, sir," replied the dark-haired, female officer.

Vincent got up from his seat and gestured to the three to follow him. They left trip-C through a different hatch than they had used to enter it, and found themselves in a modest office with a secondary workstation, this one more closely resembling the ones all caretakers had in their own quarters. Donn had not been in this room before — when he had met Vincent for his discipline, it had been in the control room.

The room was decorated tastefully, with old-style wood-paneled citations and awards next to framed digital photographs of Vincent standing near assorted Earth dignitaries. Dominating the opposite wall was a huge, ancient helmsman's wheel from a sea vessel. It was polished to a high gloss and the brass fittings shone under the display lights. Donn could not help but take a few steps towards it to examine it more closely. A brass plaque was engraved with the legend, "Chiron. 2087."

"My first ship," Vincent said, then chuckled softly. "Just a little two-masted schooner. Thirty-seven meters. I used to take it out for—"

"Captain, please. This is very important," Margulies interrupted.

Vincent's pleasant mood faded. "Let me finish, Linna." He turned back to Donn, once again friendly. "I would take it out for pleasure cruising, fishing, that kind of thing. I got to be quite the sailor."

Donn nodded slightly, and Vincent paused a beat, purposefully waiting to acknowledge Margulies' urgency on his own terms. "All right, Linna," he said, then moved to his workstation seat. "What is it?"

"We've got a serious issue with the sleepers, Captain."

"What kind of issue?"

Margulies, despite her earlier command to be the spokesperson, turned to Donn, her face a study in hopelessness.

"Captain, we've examined a substantial sample of them, and they are all dead," Donn said.

"Dead?"

"Yes, sir. I found one dead, and then—"

"How did you find one dead?"

"I was reassigned to the Freezer, sir," Donn said, glancing at Margulies, "and while there, I examined one of the sleepers personally. Bypassing OSIRIS."

"Now I recognize you. Caretaker Cardenio. You did the memorial for the nine preborns. Yes, Provost Simpatica informed me about your reassignment. You say you found a dead hibernator there?"

"Yes, sir. So I told Linna, and she conducted her own investigation."

Margulies continued smoothly. "I was only able to test a representative sample, Captain. About one hundred and fifty. All were dead."

Captain Vincent did not speak for a moment, and when he did, his voice faltered. "So ... you don't know for sure all the hibernators are dead. You've checked less than one percent of them. The rest could still be alive."

"We need to find out for certain, of course, Captain." Margulies said.

"What does OSIRIS say?" Vincent said, looking down at his computer screen and manipulating some of the controls.

"That's another thing, Captain," Donn said, anxious to keep his voice heard. "OSIRIS is malfunctioning. He still reports all the sleepers as alive and in hibernation."

Vincent looked up sharply. "Then how do you know they're dead?"

"Manual inspection," Margulies said. "We know, Captain. There's no doubt."

Collins suddenly spoke up. "Donn, were all your preborns okay?"

"Yes. I just got done checking all of them. What about yours?"

Collins gave him a thumbs-up.

Vincent said to his computer, "OSIRIS, perform a systems check on yourself."

The flat computer voice said, "Understood. Systems check proceeding. Estimated time to completion is forty-nine minutes, thirty-four seconds."

Vincent looked back up at the three. "So what you're reporting, Linna, Caretaker Cardenio, and..." he paused, looking at Jason.

"Collins, sir."

"Caretaker Collins, is that several hundred of the hibernators are dead, possibly more—"

Donn interjected, "Probably all of them, sir."

Vincent continued, his voice rising at the interruption, "—and that OSIRIS has been compromised again."

"Again?" Collins said.

Vincent nodded. "Yes. First with Caretaker Agee, now this. Unless you think what Agee did caused the malfunction in the hibernation bay."

Donn looked at Margulies. "I don't know, sir."

"I'll ask Norman to check on that, too," Linna said. "But in the meantime, sir, we have a serious decision to make."

Vincent drummed his desktop for a moment. "I agree. First we need to assess the situation with the sleepers. We need to account for everyone."

"And the preborns, sir," Donn added.

"What?"

"If OSIRIS is malfunctioning with the Freezer, then he might also be malfunctioning with some of the pseudowombs. We should check each one. Manually. I've already done mine, and so has Caretaker Collins."

Vincent frowned. "I see what you mean. But the sleepers come first."

Donn gasped. "What? How can you say that? The preborns are—"

Vincent spoke over him, firmly but not harshly. "The preborns will be dependent on the sleepers in less than a month. If the sleepers are all dead, we will have to make contingency plans. If there are also many dead preborns that haven't been discovered, the sleeper crisis becomes less acute."

Donn stared at Vincent, then looked at Margulies and Collins. They were staring back at him grimly. "I can't believe that you would use that logic."

"Donn, please," Margulies said. "The captain is right. If there are dead preborns, that's tragic, but it won't mean we need to change the mission plans too much. But if the sleepers are dead, we will."

"That's ghoulish. All of you are acting like the possible death of thousands of preborns is nothing to worry about."

Vincent said firmly. "That's not at all what we're saying. Control yourself, Cardenio." He looked at Margulies. "Let's talk about the worst case. All sleepers dead."

"That's not the worst case," Donn growled.

Margulies raised her voice. "Stop it, Donn. You're not the only one worried here about the preborns, so just come down off your moral high ground and work the problem with us. Or leave."

Vincent waited until Margulies was done, and said calmly, "Again, worst case. All the hibernators are dead, and we're less than a month out from TC-Three. That's two hundred forty-eight thousand, eight hundred and twenty-three babies and only one hundred ninety-seven of us to tend to them."

"There's no chance we can do that, Captain," Collins said. "I'm just being realistic." He glanced at Donn. "Over one thousand babies each, without pod support? All of this while we build a colony, infrastructure, atmosphere conversion, bacteriological screening, everything? We knew how difficult this mission was when everything was going according to plan. Now, I don't see how it can work."

"Under the original mission parameters, that is," Margulies said.

Donn rested his hand on the pouch containing the flechette pistol.

Chapter Fourteen

Vincent stared at Margulies for a long moment. "I agree."

The room seemed to freeze, all four still, no one daring to take the next awful step.

Finally, Vincent said, even more quietly than he had answered Margulies, "OSIRIS, display original mission parameters in regard to personnel planetside assignments. Composite view."

The far wall lit up with a complex table of organization schematic in three dimensions. Donn had seen the diagram many times — it was the Master Colonization Plan, referred to all on board as merely the Plan. He spotted his own section of the diagram, under a tiny rectangle on the right labeled "I/E Sec." He had known that his colonial assignment was to act as part of the group's combination police force and army as a drone pilot. The extent of hostile alien life on Tau Ceti III was not known, and it was to be his job to keep the colony safe, both from without and within. He was slightly surprised to find his name still listed in the Internal/External Security box, given his history with authority onboard the ship.

The remainder of the caretakers and crew had been assigned to various colonization duties, ranging from construction to medical services to administration. The *Chiron* itself was to be used as a temporary base while members of the construction crew slowly converted it to planetbound habitation. Other environmental engineers were assigned to light terraforming, or "terrafriendly," duties.

Donn had seen and studied the incredible complexity of the Plan many times, but he had always done so with an air of admiration for the ambition inherent in it. Now, despite his own stubborn refusal to admit the current circumstances, he saw what Collins had been saying.

The Plan was now unworkable.

Vincent left his desk and approached the holographic Plan. "Even with the current deaths," as he spoke, he maneuvered his fingers to change Plan elements, crossing out names and letting OSIRIS reassign families and duties as he did so, "it's very tight." He continued to eliminate parents, watching as tiny linkages broke and children's designations reassigned themselves to surviving parents. Vincent stopped after a dozen parents had been eliminated and said quietly, "OSIRIS, eliminate four hundred and fifty total parents. At random."

The lines on the Plan redrew themselves, names flying across the air to new locations and assignments. OSIRIS said a few second later, "Complete. New assignments projected."

Vincent said, "Continue to eliminate parents until mission is no longer viable."

"Also, eliminate Caretaker Agee and the nine dead preborns," Donn said.

Vincent looked at him, a momentary flash of irritation visible in his eyes, then repeated Donn's command to the computer.

An agonizing few seconds passed while the four watched the Plan change almost too rapidly to follow. Parent names were dispassionately crossed out and their orphaned children reassigned to new ones, only to have to repeat the process as OSIRIS eliminated their new parents.

"No longer able to adjust Master Colonization Plan. Mission parameters cannot be met beyond this point," OSIRIS said.

"How many parents remain alive in this version?" Vincent said.

"Seventeen thousand, seven hundred seventy-four."

"What happens if you change some caretakers to parents?" Donn said.

"Negligible effect," OSIRIS intoned.

Donn continued, heedless of Vincent's mounting irritation. "And if we lose more parents? If fewer than seventeen thousand, seven hundred seventy-four parents survive?"

"I cannot complete the Master Colonization Plan under stated parameters."

Donn, with a hint of desperation in his voice, said, "Captain, that's just an arbitrary mission profile that's been fed into OSIRIS. He's just going by arithmetic."

"So are we all." Margulies said.

"What happens when you eliminate all the sleepers?" Collins said.

Vincent said, "OSIRIS, eliminate all parents."

The Plan disappeared to be replaced with angry red letters hanging in the air. "MISSION FAILURE."

Vincent said, "Keep the Plan on display. Remove all parents and leave children unassigned for now."

The Plan reappeared, but the upper right corner of the display continued to taunt "MISSION FAILURE."

Vincent's voice shook. "Now reassign all redundant colonists to parent slots."

A meager twenty-four names moved over to their new assignments. Donn saw that his name had not changed.

"Move me, too," Donn said, pointing at his own name. "We won't need police with so few of us."

Vincent said with a tight jaw. "Let's speak with one voice. Mine." Vincent moved Donn to the parent group to make their number twenty-five.

Donn pointed again at the Plan. "There. Oliver, economic analyst. We don't need that. Or this one, Manalastas, morale. They can both go to parent group."

"Did you hear me? Let me make the changes," Vincent said.

Donn ignored that. He searched the Plan for other names, deciding with what amounted to recklessness that certain colonization functions were unnecessary, calling out changes to the Plan to Vincent. The captain's objections ceased as Donn's passionate approach overcame protocol.

When they had finished, the parent group numbered forty-one names.

Donn said, "OSIRIS, assign children to new parent group."

Again, the movement of names commenced. It didn't last long. When the movement ceased, Vincent asked, "How many children assigned?"

"Four hundred ninety-two."

"Is that under original mission parameters?" Donn asked.

"Affirmative. Twelve children assigned per parent."

"What is your maximum allowable number?"

"Fourteen per parent."

"Do that, then," Donn said.

Vincent asked, "How many children now assigned?"

"Five hundred seventy-four."

Donn opened his mouth, ready to tell OSIRIS to keep upping the number. Twenty, Twenty-Five. Fifty. He did the math in his mind, seeing the number of survivors rise. But the other number, the number of unassigned children, changed so little as to seem insignificant.

The other three were watching him, and he could read in their expressions their thoughts.

"Do you see it now, Donn?" Collins said, gentle urging in his voice. "No matter what you do, you can't—"

"It doesn't matter. The numbers aren't what matters," Donn said.

"The numbers are all that matters," Margulies said. "We have less than a month until planetfall."

"Twenty-eight days," Vincent said.

Margulies continued, "And a minimum number of caretakers and crew who will have to build infrastructure. Even if we stretch them out and work them harder than the original mission profile says—"

"Which was already extremely difficult," Collins said.

"—that only leaves maybe fifty of us to care for the children full-time."

Donn rested his hand on the flechette gun. "But your answer ... what you want to do is unthinkable."

Margulies turned to Vincent. "He's referring to what Caretaker Collins and I believe is the only solution."

Vincent closed his eyes for a moment, gathering himself. When he opened them, he said quietly, "Reducing the number of preborns who make it to planetfall. Aborting them."

Collins looked away at the word, and Donn saw Margulies shift her weight from foot to foot.

"We have to call it what it is," Vincent said.

"Then why not say 'murder?'" Donn barked. "If you're going to say what it is, say that." His hand rested on the zipper clasp of his thigh pouch.

"Because it isn't that, and emotional words will just cloud the issue, Caretaker Cardenio," Vincent said. "You ran the numbers yourself. Even if we all dedicated ourselves to the care of the children, and somehow managed to get the colony up and running despite that, how many can we each take and be sure they will survive and thrive? Twenty each? Thirty?" Vincent shook his head. "To keep them all, we'd have to look over more than twelve hundred each. You know that's not possible. We'd just be watching over the slow, individual deaths of thousands of infants. Do you want that?"

"Who knows what will happen?" Donn said. "More might survive than we think. There might be indigenous help we know nothing about. Or Earth may send a relief ship when they learn of what happened here, and we'll get thousands of adult colonists to help. We don't know what lies ahead. I can't just stand here and allow the murder of a hundred thousand innocent lives."

Vincent sighed. "You know there's no alien civilization on Tau Ceti Three. Earth established that before we launched. And as for a relief ship — we can't count on that. You need to remember two things, Caretaker Cardenio. One, it may be that trying to save all of them will result in more deaths than if we make a hard decision now." His voice had been soft, but now, he scowled and his speech had a hard edge. "And two, I am the captain of this vessel and leader of this mission. The decision will be mine, and it will be final."

"Captain, that's just not true."

"Are you disputing my authority, Caretaker?"

Donn met Vincent's gaze squarely. "Whatever decision you make will need to be carried out by caretakers and crew. And if the order comes down to kill the preborns, I will not follow it. I'll do everything in my power to block you." He looked at Margulies and Collins. "All three of you."

"Donn, you ran the numbers. You can see what has to happen here," Collins said, his voice soothing.

"I won't be party to murder of innocent children."

"But you will be," Margulies said. "Trying to save them all will mean death. All you're doing is postponing the inevitable. And when those unattended children die — of malnutrition, disease, trauma, or some other cause — they'll suffer. If we abort them now, they'll do so without pain."

Vincent continued to stare at Donn. When Margulies had finished, he said, "I've had enough of this. I've indulged you and listened to your ideas. But now you're talking mutiny, Cardenio. Let me say this again. Whatever I order will be done, without question or hesitation. Can you agree to that?"

"No. I can't."

Vincent nodded, as if expecting that answer. "OSIRIS, connect me to Provost Simpatica."

Her high-pitched voice sounded in the room. "Simpatica here, Captain."

"Provost Simpatica, report to my quarters. And bring your sidearm."

Donn heard the apprehension in Simpatica's voice as she said, "Aye, Captain."

Collins put his hands up, as if pushing something invisible away. "Wait a second. Let's not escalate this."

Donn unzipped his thigh pouch even as he backed towards the hatch leading to the trip-C. "It's already there, Jason." He withdrew the flechette pistol. "I'm sorry it came to this. But I won't let you kill the preborns."

Vincent paled at the sight of the pistol. "Now calm down, Donn. There's no need for this."

"Donn, put that thing away," Margulies said. She took a step towards him, but Donn swung the barrel of the gun towards her.

"No, Linna. Stay where you are." He reached behind him with his free hand and cycled open the hatch.

"Donn, don't be a fool. Give me the gun, and we can talk about this," Linna said, moving again towards him.

"I told you to stay there, Linna. We've already talked. Talking's over. I'm going to make sure none of you do what you are planning on doing." He looked at Collins. "You are a caretaker. I can't believe you are going along with this."

"It's the only way to save the most preborns."

"By killing them?

Collins was silent, his eyes fixed on the pistol.

"And you, Linna … you said you envied us in what we did. But if you're going along with this mass murder, then you could never be one of us." When he heard the hatch open behind him, he carefully crawled through it, keeping the flechette pistol trained on the three. He closed the hatch, aware of the futility of his gesture since they could easily reopen it. He felt better, though, closing them off. He turned to the trip-C staff, who were turning to look at him, wide-eyed. "Just stay where you are," he said, and made his way quickly across the room. No one moved to stop him.

He left trip-C and hurried towards the central shaft. There was no sign of Provost Simpatica, even though he had passed her office on the way to the zero-g shaft. Either she was still in there, or had taken another route to the captain's office. It didn't matter — he was just relieved that he hadn't needed to use the flechette pistol.

He cycled open the hatch to the inner shaft and climbed up, feeling his weight decrease slightly with each rung. He reached the hatch to the zero-g shaft and pressed his palm against the lock.

To his surprise, the lock opened. He had expected the area to be sealed off to prevent his escape, but evidently, neither the captain nor Linna had thought that far ahead. He marveled at that for a moment, then decided not to question his good fortune. He entered the shaft and used the handholds on the rotating inner cylinder to launch himself aft.

He passed deck after deck, watching the letters climb in the alphabet as he flew further and further back. As he was passing E-Deck, he heard Vincent's voice echoing in the shaft.

"Caretakers and crew, this is Captain Vincent. Be advised that Caretaker Donn Cardenio has become dangerous. He is armed and in a potentially unstable mental state. If you encounter him, do not attempt to apprehend him but get to safety and report to command and control. He is in the central shaft at this time. Do not enter the central shaft, and if you are there, exit as soon as possible and hold your position. I repeat, Caretaker Donn Cardenio is armed and dangerous. Do not approach him. Provost Simpatica has begun her search. Let her and her staff conduct the arrest."

Donn glanced at one of OSIRIS' internal cameras as he floated by. That had been inevitable. Worse, it was very likely that now they had sealed off the central shaft and he would be stuck there in zero-g.

He shook his head at his own folly. That was why they had allowed him inside — to trap him. Once inside the central shaft, they could seal all the hatchways and isolate him. Then it would be a relatively easy matter for Simpatica and her two security officers to collect him.

He continued to float aft, passing H-Deck. What was the plan now? He would eventually hit M-Deck and then pass to the Freezer section, then the colonial hold, then the engineering areas, and then he'd be out of room. The central shaft held no areas for him to hide, and he did not have access to engineering. He twisted in mid-air, looking behind him at the forward decks. He couldn't see anyone following him, but there were other access points leading from deck to deck on the outer skin of the ship. Maybe Simpatica and her officers were using those, tracking his progress via OSIRIS. Or maybe they just hadn't yet entered the central shaft.

He saw J-Deck pass by, and reached out to a handhold to check his speed. His body pivoted around the railing, and his feet brushed against the rotating inner wall. He made his way further aft to the K-Deck hatchway and noted it was the Section 7-12 hatch. He stared at the hatch, wondering what his plan was.

As he hung before the hatch, he heard Vincent's voice in the air all around him.

"Donn, this is Captain Vincent." The words echoed in the cavernous central shaft. "This doesn't have to be violent. We've got you hemmed in. There's nowhere you can go, so just give yourself up to Simpatica and we can discuss all of this. I'm giving you a direct order, Cardenio."

Donn looked back to the forward decks. He still saw no one else in the shaft. The trip-C was only about a hundred and fifty meters distant — if Provost Simpatica and her security team had entered the shaft, he would be able to see them. They must be keeping their distance, hoping Vincent would be able to talk him down.

Donn felt a momentary surge of helplessness. What was he hoping to accomplish? He knew he was never going to shoot any of the crew. Beyond the idea of killing a fellow human being, he knew that for his plan to succeed he would need each and every member of the ship's company alive and well.

He had no leverage. And even if Vincent hadn't figured that out, surely Margulies would have. They were being careful, not because they were afraid he would use force to advance his position, but because they thought he had gone mad.

Just like Thom.

Had he gone mad? When Thom had discovered the dead sleepers he had snapped and started to kill the preborns.

No, he had not gone mad.

Everyone else had.

He stared at the hatchway to K-Deck, Sections 7-12. He pressed his palm against the lock and was not surprised when it failed to open, and the tiny readout above the lock displayed the legend, "HATCH SEALED."

"Emergency override." He tried again, but was met with the same message. No doubt, Vincent had cancelled his ability to command OSIRIS. Donn was only vaguely aware of the emergency procedures involving the central shaft — he wasn't sure if he could start some kind of environmental disaster and free the hatches. He raised the flechette gun and pointed it at the lock, then lowered it. The tiny darts the pistol fired had been designed specifically to not cause damage to the ship.

He was stunned when the lock readout changed.

"HATCH UNSEALED."

Before he could react to this, the hatch began to iris open. He raised the flechette pistol.

"Kearney!"

She flashed him a grim smile. "Yeah. Whoa, put that down, Donn," she said, ducking out of the way of the pistol.

He hurriedly lowered the gun and reached for the hatch edge. She started climbing down the ladder while he followed. When they reached the bottom, she went back up and slapped the hatch closed again.

"How did you—?"

"I have my ways. Now, what's your plan?"

Chapter Fifteen

Donn stared at her. "My plan? Jezeus, Kearney, I don't have a plan. Right now, Simpatica and her guys are coming to get me. They weren't using the central shaft, at least not yet. They might be coming using just the ordinary access points deck to deck."

"That'll slow them down a little, having to cycle through so many hatchways."

"Not much. Listen, Kearney — this has gotten out of hand. Vincent and Margulies were openly discussing killing the preborns. I think he's going to order it."

Her eyes widened. "He can't! He can't do that!"

Donn took her by the shoulders and squeezed. "I know, K, but I think it's coming. First he's going to get a full assessment of the Freezer situation. Find out if they're all dead or not."

"How?"

"He'll have to order a pod-by-pod check. If OSIRIS is malfunctioning, that's the only way."

Kearney nodded. "All right. Let's get away from this hatch, though. If Simpatica and her goons do decide to use the central shaft, we don't want to be here."

Donn nodded and started away from the hatch, following Kearney. "Sure, but…"

"What?"

"It won't matter. There is no place I can hide. If Vincent wants me, he's going to get me."

"Maybe not. I have a few tricks up my sleeve yet. I'll show you in my parlor."

Before they could get inside, Vincent's voice echoed off the walls of the corridor. "Donn, this is Captain Vincent again. You're just making this hard on everyone. We know you got into K-Deck. Please, don't harm anyone there. K-Deck caretakers, stay clear of Caretaker Cardenio. He's armed and dangerous. Right now he's heading to the caretaker quarters. Remain inside, and do not attempt to apprehend him. Cardenio, I order you to surrender. You are in violation of my authority, and you will give yourself up peacefully to the provost."

Donn looked around the corridor and saw a tiny camera where the wall met the ceiling. He'd never realized how many internal cameras OSIRIS had in the ship.

Kearney matched his gaze and quickly gave a middle finger gesture to the camera. "Come on," she said to Donn, tugging him along.

Vincent's voice followed them. "Donn, Mary Ellen." For a moment, Donn was not sure to whom he was referring. He'd almost forgotten Kearney's first name. Vincent continued. "You can't run. Stop, and we will not hurt you. No one wants anyone hurt here."

"Except the murder of two hundred thousand babies," Kearney muttered.

They hurried to her quarters, Vincent's voice continuing to plead with them. Once inside, Kearney slid into the computer station chair. "First thing, let's shut up the captain. Lenny, shut off this announcement."

"I can't, Kearney," OSIRIS said in his lugubrious voice. It was the current personality shard Kearney had going for her personal access to OSIRIS, much like Agnes was Donn's. Kearney liked to change personalities every few weeks, and this current one was a deep-voiced, rural accented version.

"Why not?"

"It's on the Captain's emergency broadcast channel. There's no way to shut it off. I'm sorry," he added, and really seemed to mean it. "He's telling me to access your bunkroom here. I've told him you don't want to be bothered, but he's going to make me do it. I'm sorry, Kea—" Lenny's voice stopped abruptly and Captain Vincent's face filled the screen. "All right. Enough of this. You two stay right where you are."

"How do you know he's not holding me hostage, Captain?" Kearney said, activating the computer's holographic keyboard. She pulled up side menus with her keystrokes and studied them as she spoke.

"Linna tells me you two are close, plus there's the rude gesture you made at the camera. For whatever reason, you've thrown in with Cardenio, so I—"

Donn interrupted. "Captain, don't punish her. This was all my idea. She's just trying to help me, that's all."

"I'll decide who gets disciplined later. Now, I just want you to surrender yourself peacefully."

Kearney typed madly on the keyboard, accessing parts of OSIRIS deep into its program. Donn watched her, distracted from Vincent. The captain continued to talk about peaceful surrender and dialogue, but Donn was fascinated by Kearney's skill and access with the computer.

"When Simpatica gets there," Vincent was saying, "have your weapon on the deck far from you, and—" he vanished and his voice was cut off mid-sentence.

"There. Now we can talk," Kearney said.

"How did you do that?"

"Doesn't matter right now. Simpatica is on her way, going to be here any moment. Lenny, what's the location of Provost Simpatica?"

"She's on F-Deck, bay seven."

"Good. Gives us a little time. Donn, we're going to have to confront her. It might get violent. You need to be prepared for that."

"I can't kill her, Kearney."

"She's part of the group that's going to kill the—"

"No, listen. We can't kill anyone."

Kearney took a quick breath. "I know it's not what we want, but this is what it's come to. I don't say this lightly, Donn, but right now, we have to kill to save lives."

"That's the same reasoning they are using."

"No, it's entirely different. They want to kill hundreds of thousands of innocent preborns. I'm saying we need to kill a small number of people to save those innocent children. There is no equivalence here."

"Maybe not a mathematical one, but it's still killing."

Kearney stared at him for a short time, and he could see she was searching desperately for a lever, some logical argument that would sway him.

He spoke before she found one. "Kearney, it's not just that I don't want to kill. Don't you see, we need everyone on our side if we're going to save the preborns. Every single adult means dozens, possibly hundreds of preborns who will live. If we start killing in order to secure our position, we consign more and more preborns to death."

Kearney took a deep breath. "I understand, but none of that will matter if we don't secure our position. If we can't convince everyone to follow our lead in this and let all the preborns live, it won't matter how many of us there are. All that matters now is that all the children survive to the end of the mission. To planetfall. And if that means we need to kill to accomplish that, then sadly, so be it."

Donn chewed his lip. "As it stands now, I don't know how we're going to win out. Simpatica and her people are surely armed, too, even if it's just with nonlethals. And even though Vincent specifically told the rest of the ship to stay away from me, how long do you think that'll last? If he needs to, he'll mobilize every crewmember and caretaker."

"Not all of them. The caretakers would never agree to murdering the preborns."

"Collins did."

Kearney looked pained for a moment. "Yeah, but he was being influenced by Margulies." She said the liaison officer's name with venom. "You can convince the caretakers to resist. You spoke with them during the memorial — they know you, they trust you."

"Even if that's true, which I doubt it is, how will I get to them? We're cut off in here, and you know Simpatica and her people are on their way, if they haven't already reached K-Deck."

Kearney turned her eyes upwards and said, "Lenny, where is Provost Simpatica now?"

"She's just reachin' J-Deck."

"All right. Seal off K-Deck. Lock all hatches."

"Okay, Kearney," Lenny drawled. "But OSIRIS is gonna be mad at me."

Donn scowled. "How the hell are you doing this?"

Kearney put up a finger to stall him. "Lenny, are all K-Deck caretakers in their quarters or in their bays?"

"No, Kearney. Caretaker Cardenio is in your room."

"All others, though?"

"Yeah."

Donn spoke despite Kearney's delaying finger. "What kind of access is this? How can you seal off the hatches and use the camera system?"

"I told you, I have a few tricks up my sleeve. That doesn't matter now. What matters is that we're safe, for the time being, from Vincent and Simpatica. And Margulies, for that matter. If you can swing the rest of the K-Deck caretakers to us, that's twelve."

"Eleven."

"There are twelve caretakers in K-Deck, Donn."

"One of them was Thom. Eleven. And eleven isn't very many."

"It's nine more than we have now. And it's a start. We can make it spread from there."

Donn didn't answer immediately. The full implications of what he had set in motion were just now dawning on him.

"Donn, we need to move. Fast. I can hook—"

"Just … slow down a second. I need to think about this."

"What's there to think about? We have—"

He snapped at her. "There's a lot to think of! What we're talking about is a mutiny. Taking control of the ship. Do you know how serious that is?"

"I do," she said gently.

"It doesn't end here. The whole mission, the future of the colony … everything." He looked away from Kearney, and his eyes were drawn again to the electronic reproduction of *Guernica* on the wall. There was a suggestion of walls on the outer edges of the painting — something he had seen but not noted before. He saw the figures within the painting trapped, unable to escape the horrors exercised upon them.

If he led this mutiny, he would become the person everyone went to for answers. If successful, he'd have saved the lives of thousands of children, but he'd then be responsible for ensuring they survived somehow on Tau Ceti III. Even if Earth wanted to send a relief ship, they'd have to build one first, and the journey would take almost a year even with Alcubierre drive. He'd have to ensure the survival of a quarter million babies, and the nearly two hundred adults watching over them, indefinitely.

But if he didn't, thousands of preborns would die.

"All right. I'm assuming your bag of tricks includes a way to override the system and let me speak intercraft?"

Kearney nodded. "I can access that."

"You are going to have to tell me how you did all this one day," Donn said. "But for now, give me access to K-Deck"

Kearney looked at him. "Not the whole ship?"

"No," Donn said, his voice firm. "Just K-Deck. And can you do it in a way that keeps it to just K-Deck? So Vincent and the others can't hear?"

"Yeah. Lenny, prepare to broadcast to K-Deck only. Secure channel — no one outside K-Deck can access. Understood?"

"Sure, Kearney. I can do that. Do you want it to be voices only, or do you want a picture to go with it?"

Donn thought about it. "Audio and visual."

Kearney repeated the command, and Lenny said. "All right. I'm ready when you are. Just let me know when you want to start."

Donn took a breath, then nodded to Kearney. There was no sense in prolonging this moment, and despite the access point lockout, he was certain Vincent and his people were working on a way to break into K-Deck. He had to work quickly.

Kearney told Lenny to begin the broadcast, and Donn looked into the camera pickup on the desk unit.

"K-Deck caretakers, hello. I'm sure you've heard the announcement by Captain Vincent about me. I'm not dangerous — you all know me, and you know what kind of a man I am. Paul, Netta, Alison, Mikelo, Vern, Devie, Basque, Christine, Luis — what Captain Vincent told you is not the whole story. Please, listen to what I have to say.

"There's been a discovery on board. We've found out that the sleepers in the Freezer are all dead." He hesitated over the unconfirmed nature of his announcement. But, he reasoned to himself, even if there were some sleepers still alive, the fundamental nature of what Vincent and Margulies were apt to do would not change. "I know this sounds incredible, but I assure you it is true. I saw one of the dead bodies myself, and even Liaison Officer Margulies can confirm hundreds more dead. The Freezer staff is unaware of this, due to a malfunction in OSIRIS." He looked at Kearney and gave her a subtle signal to kill the feed.

She went to the console and tapped the holographic keyboard. "Paused. What's the matter?"

"We need to tell the Freezer people, too. Can we hook them in to this?"

"We can. Lenny, are there any people in the Freezer besides ordinary staff members?"

Lenny asked in a low mutter, "Whatcha mean, Kearney?"

"I mean, in the hibernation chamber, is there anyone other than hibernation staff present?"

"You mean, besides them hibernators? Yeah, there are. Crewuns Freeman and Uplander are there, along with all the hibernation staff."

"What are they doing?" Kearney said.

"Looks like they are openin' all the hibernation pods manually, and reachin' in and feelin' around the hibernators. I dunno why. I'm sorry."

Donn said, "They're starting their survey. Even with Freezer people and the two crew, it'll take them a long time to check everyone. Even if they can check three or four a minute, that's still several days to get them all. We can't risk broadcasting this to the Freezer, not with Freeman and Uplander there. Put me back on with K-Deck."

Kearney tapped her keyboard again, and nodded to Donn.

Donn spoke again to the camera. "I'm going to have to ask all of you to trust me, trust that what I say is true. The mission as we knew it is over. With all the hibernators dead, it will fall to us to care for the preborns once we reach Tau Ceti Three." He took a deep breath, and continued. "I know this is a shock to you. It was to me, too, when I found out. But the worst part is this: Captain Vincent is considering a course of action that is so terrible, so horrible, that I simply had to act. That's why you heard him on the intercom telling all of you I was armed and dangerous. Because I admit, I did threaten the use of force to stop him in what he was proposing. When you hear what it was, I think you will understand.

"Captain Vincent is considering killing thousands of the preborns to reduce the number we have to care for once we make planetfall."

Donn wished he could see his audience, like he did during the memorial. Without knowing how the nine other caretakers were reacting, it was difficult to know how to tailor his message.

"I couldn't stand by and let that happen. So please, come to bay K-eight at the conclusion of this broadcast and meet with me. I want to speak to each of you personally and try and explain my actions. I know all of you, and you know me. You know I would not hurt you, despite what the captain said. Please, come to K-eight and let me talk."

He glanced at Kearney, who cut the feed.

Donn said, "Tell Lenny to cut off all communications, incoming and outgoing, from K-Deck."

Kearney relayed the command. "So now we go to K-eight?"

"Yes. Unless you want to stay here, and keep doing your tricks with Lenny."

"I can access him from any computer station."

"How?"

She smiled tightly. "It's too complicated to explain now, Donn. Let's just let it stand that I can, okay? I paid a lot for this kind of access. In ways I don't think you'd be comfortable with."

Donn just looked at her. It still didn't add up. How could she have command functions over OSIRIS — ones which presumably overrode the captain's? Even if she had slept with Vincent, that wouldn't explain how she could so easily make OSIRIS (or the fragment she had programmed into him) bend to her will.

But just now, that mystery was secondary to the crisis before him. He didn't know how she did what she did, but he was going to use it. "Can you lockout remote commands to the pseudowombs? Prevent Vincent from just shutting them off from trip-C?"

Kearney shook her head. "Not necessary. OSIRIS has a built in root command preventing that. No one can shut off the pods."

"How do you know that?"

Kearney licked her lips quickly. "It stands to reason, right? Why would the computer system have any sort of ability to kill the preborns? The whole purpose of the mission is—"

"I understand that, but we can't take that chance. I'm not saying there's a 'kill command,' but there is probably some kind of shutdown command in case of emergency. We need to disable that. Can you do it?"

Kearney looked uncertain. "I'll try. Lenny, I need you to prevent anyone from shutting down the pseudowombs."

Lenny's deep voice replied, "Whaddaya mean, Kearney?"

"I mean, no matter what happens, no matter what command you receive, keep the pseudowombs functioning. They are your highest priority."

"Well, a'course. I wasn't gonna shut 'em down anyway, Kearney."

"Have you been given that command?" Donn asked.

"No, but—"

Kearney cut in, "Good. Just keep the preborns' pods operational." She looked back at Donn. "That is the best I can do."

"Can the Captain override you?"

Kearney shook her head. "No."

Donn scowled. "Kearney, how the hell do you have this kind of authority with the computer?"

"Donn. We've got other issues."

Donn hesitated. "But you're sure your lockouts are unbreakable?"

"Completely. As it is now, the only way to affect the preborns would be..." she trailed off, swallowing.

"Thom's method," Donn said quietly. "Okay. That's very good. I can use that. If Vincent wants to kill the preborns, he's going to have to recruit butchers to do it with their own hands. And I don't think anyone will want to do that, no matter how much they agree with the policy." He paused to gather himself, then said, "Let's get to K-eight."

Kearney headed to the hatchway and cycled it open. Donn found his eyes turn toward *Guernica* once again. He saw in the suggestion of walls a dove, somehow forming a crack in the walls behind the rampaging wild bull.

Chapter Sixteen

Six caretakers were already waiting outside K-8 when Donn and Kearney showed up. One of them, a woman named Alison Hunsaker, spoke as soon as the pair came into view.

"Donn, what's happening? Were you serious about the sleepers? When did this all happen?"

Donn held up a hand to stall her questions. "Let's get inside. I'll explain it all there. Where are the others?"

Hunsaker looked up the sloping corridor. "Devie and Netta are on their way. Dev said she tried to contact the command and control center, but she couldn't get through."

Donn tried to cycle open the hatchway to K-8, but the signal kept flashing back as LOCKED. He looked at Kearney, who used her own palm print. The hatch cycled open.

"Inside, please, all of you," Donn said, ushering in the caretakers. He saw two other women hurrying down the corridor towards him — Devie and Netta. He waved them on and followed them into the bay, closing the hatch behind him.

"You all heard my announcement, obviously," Donn said. "The—" he got no further, as the eight other caretakers all spoke at once with a barrage of questions.

Kearney spoke up, loudly, "Hold it! One at a time. Alison?"

Hunsaker looked uneasily at the rest, but they seemed willing to have her be spokeswoman for them all. "Your message about the sleepers was a little unclear. Are you saying they are all dead, and you saw that with your own eyes?"

"I'm saying I saw one dead, and Margulies confirmed over four hundred more."

Hunsaker quickly broke in, "That doesn't mean that—"

"I know, it doesn't mean necessarily that they're all dead. But Margulies did a sampling. She didn't just check a single row or bank of them. Every single one she managed to get to was dead. So we have to assume the worst."

"But there still could be thousands still alive. We need to check them all." Hunsaker said, looking at the rest of the caretakers. They started to speak up again, but Donn raised his voice.

"Everyone, quiet, please. I think that's what's happening now. The Freezer staff and two crew are looking at them. But we have to accept the very real probability that we have no surviving parents to care for the children once they have been born. No one but ourselves."

Yune said, "You said OSIRIS was malfunctioning? Then how do you know the sleepers are dead?"

Donn turned to face him. "I saw one. I opened up a Freezer pod and checked myself. She had no pulse, no heartbeat, no respiration."

"Hibernation slows down those functions, though. Maybe you just missed—"

"No, Paul. I am certain. OSIRIS was recording a heartbeat where there wasn't one, respiration where there wasn't any. Listen, I know how hard this is to believe. I was in the same state of mind you are now when I first found out. But you have to believe me."

"Why is Captain Vincent saying you are dangerous, then? What happened, Donn?" Hunsaker asked, her voice strangely gentle.

"I went with Margulies and Jason Collins from B-Deck to inform the captain of the situation. And to prevent from occurring what looks like might happen unless we stop it." He took a deep breath. "What I said on the announcement was true. Vincent is very seriously considering killing thousands, perhaps almost two hundred thousand, of the preborns so the remaining ones can be cared for by the adults."

"But it still doesn't explain why he said you—"

"Because I went," he said, unzipping his thigh pouch and producing the flechette pistol, "with this. And threatened him with it."

He was not brandishing the weapon, but everyone except Kearney retreated from him.

"You threatened the captain?" Hunsaker said. "That does explain it. And that didn't change his mind?"

"No, I don't think so," Donn said.

Hunsaker looked at the other caretakers. Donn knew that if he could carry her, the rest of K-Deck would follow. "Alison — you know what side I am on. I'm with the preborns, and I always have been. You know that's true. I'm asking you to let that be enough."

Hunsaker nodded carefully. "I believe you." She looked at the others. "We've known Donn almost a year now, and he's been dedicated to his swimmers. So I trust his judgement."

"I do, too," Yune said softly. "I saw what he did to try and stop Thom."

The other caretakers were still watching Donn, their eyes moving from his face to his weapon. Donn carefully put away the flechette pistol and said, "I know this is a lot to take in. I almost couldn't believe all of it myself. But I swear to you it is true. All of it. The mission must continue, even though we will have to change how we accomplish it."

In the silence that followed, a soft, meek voice spoke. It was from Vern, the monastic caretaker of K-1. Donn recalled the Traditionalist artwork outside and inside his bay — Vern hung on to the old religious doctrines, which most people had abandoned after the War. His voice was gentle and calm. "I just have to ask — how? How are we supposed to complete the mission now, if all the hibernators are dead?"

Donn took a deep breath. "I'll be honest with you, Vern. With all of you. I don't have an answer for that. But here's what I do know: Captain Vincent and others are considering a plan to murder as many preborns as they deem necessary to ensure mission success. And that's not only contradictory, it's unthinkable."

"Why is it contradictory, Donn?" Vern asked. From anyone else, the question would have been a challenge, an affront. But Vern's gentle, avuncular demeanor softened the charge.

"Because the mission is the preborns," Kearney said. She glanced at Donn, who nodded slightly, and continued. "Donn's right. However we're planning on making it work on TC-Three, that's for later. Once we've secured the preborns and the ship."

"I agree that we can't let Vincent kill the preborns," Yune said, "but do we have to resort to violence? Why can't we talk to him, all tw–eleven of us?"

"I tried that," Donn said. "It didn't work."

Paul said, "No offense, Donn, but maybe you weren't enough by yourself. Now that you have an entire deck with you, Vincent might listen."

"That's not a bad thought." Hunsaker added.

Donn looked at the assembled caretakers. They were either nodding in agreement or looking hopefully at him, waiting for him to say something. He saw them all, everyone but Thom and Mikelo.

"Where's Mikelo?" Donn said.

The caretakers looked around among themselves.

"Shit," Kearney said, then called to the computer. "OSIRIS, this is Kearney."

"Yes, Caretaker Kearney?"

"Where's Caretaker Forgisto?"

"He's in his room."

"Do you have a camera on him? What's he doing?"

Hunsaker looked puzzled and turned to Donn. He forestalled her question by saying quietly, "Special access. I don't know, either." That seemed to satisfy Hunsaker, at least for the moment.

OSIRIS was answering Kearney. "He has been attempting to override your lockout on communications. He has asked me many times how to contact the captain or Provost Simpatica."

Kearney flushed with anger. "He has? Great." She looked at the others. "I'll just go over there and shut him up."

"No, K. Mikelo's no threat. He's always trying to call the captain on some idea or another, you know that," Donn said.

"Wait. You set up the communications block?" Hunsaker said, staring at Kearney. "Why? And how did you do it?"

"The why is obvious, Alison. Before we talked to all of you, we didn't know who was going to agree that the preborns cannot be harmed under any circumstances. So we couldn't have you running off to tell Vincent what we were planning together. As to how — that's more complicated. I don't think we have the time to go into it now. Just accept that I have deep access to OSIRIS."

"But—" Hunsaker said. Donn cut her off.

"Alison, I'm confused, too, as to how Kearney is doing all the shit she's doing. Right now we've got more urgent problems."

Hunsaker nodded. "You're right. So what do we do now? I still like Yune's plan of talking to Vincent, telling him we have the whole K-Deck. That should make him listen, and rethink his policy of killing the preborns."

"But we don't have K-Deck for sure," Vern said. "We don't know where Mikelo stands."

"I can make sure he's on our side," Kearney said. "I'll go to his cabin, convince him to come over here and join us."

Donn heard the belligerence in Kearney's voice. "We need him to be willing, not forced, Kearney."

"I'll be persuasive."

Donn glared at her. "You know what I mean. If we're going to speak to Vincent as a united front, then we can't have anyone with second thoughts. And anyway," he added, "I think I need you with me. If we're going to use OSIRIS to talk to Vincent, we'll need you and your deep access."

"I'll go," Vern said. "I think I can convince him. Just let me know what you decide to do with Vincent, all right?"

Donn nodded, and Vern left K-8.

"All right," Kearney said. "So we talk to Vincent, get him to reconsider?"

"That seems to be the consensus, yes."

"And if he doesn't?"

Donn took a breath. "At that point, I don't see that we have any other choice." He faced the other caretakers. "If this is unsuccessful, I will need to speak to the whole ship and let them know the truth. Vincent won't be able to stand up to that many caretakers, even if some of them agree with the plan to kill the preborns."

"Who would agree to that?" Yune said.

"Collins did," Donn said grimly. "And he's not a fool."

"I misjudged him. Very badly," Kearney murmured.

"Is everyone in agreement with that plan, in case Vincent doesn't go along?"

"Why not do that now?" Hunsaker said. "If we talk to the whole ship now, and then speak to Vincent, won't we have an even stronger bargaining position?"

"I don't think we should. I'm worried about how the ship will react to the news of the dead hibernators if we just suddenly spring it on them." He gasped slightly. "Oh, Jezeus ... that's why Mikelo is still in his quarters. He's trying to confirm what I told all of you on the broadcast."

"I think we all tried to. I mean, I did," Hunsaker said, looking at the other caretakers. "I couldn't get through to anyone, and OSIRIS didn't have any data, then you asked us all to come here."

"But if Forgisto becomes violent, crazed—"

"Why would he?" Yune said.

"That's what happened to Thom. We're pretty sure," Kearney said. "He somehow found out about the dead sleepers. He was screwing around in OSIRIS and must have found the information somehow. It was too much for him."

The other caretakers accepted the theory with wide-eyed and breathless understanding. Donn was still troubled, though. How could Thom have discovered the hibernators were dead if OSIRIS himself didn't know?

Donn shook his head. The facts could not be assembled into an answer yet. There were still nagging issues at the periphery of the crisis. He couldn't make everything coalesce into a whole. The image of *Guernica* swam in his imagination, the disparate images in the painting all shouting at one another.

He dismissed the image and said with purpose, "All right. Here's what we're going to do. Kearney, you're going to talk to OSIRIS, get me patched to Vincent. Can you do that?"

"No problem."

"Good. I'll try to talk to him, get him to see that we control K-Deck. If he doesn't cooperate, we can reach the rest of the caretakers and start a general mutiny."

"You think it's smart to let him know we can access OSIRIS like that?" Yune asked.

"There's nothing he can do about it, right, Kearney? Can he override your control?"

Kearney smirked. "Nope." Her smile went away and she said with a twinge of regret Donn knew he alone could hear, "I paid a lot for this access."

Donn nodded. "So he won't be able to cut us off from the rest of the ship. Perfect. Anyone have any objections?"

The caretakers looked at each other, and Hunsaker said, "I can't think of a better one. But what do we do about Simpatica and her agents?"

"They are locked out of K-Deck," Kearney said.

"Can they cut their way in?"

"How?" Kearney asked. "The bulkheads were designed to be pressure-proof."

"They could use the colony tools," Yune said. "There's gotta be some stuff in the colonial hold they can use."

Donn's eyes widened. He hadn't thought of that. The hold was an all-but-forgotten section of the ship where the terraforming machines and tools were kept. Donn wasn't even sure what the full inventory was.

"Isn't the hold depressurized? It's not hooked up to life support, is it?" Hunsaker asked.

"They could get in there using EVA suits," Yune said.

"Don't worry about the hold," Kearney said. "Even if they think of it, and manage to get in there, they won't find anything to help them. And even if somehow they start trying to cut through the bulkhead, it'll take them forever to do it. Let's not worry about problems that are far down the priority list."

"She's right. It's a good thought, Paul," Donn said to Yune, "and one which we may need to deal with later, but right now, let's go ahead with talking to Vincent. Kearney, get me a link."

Kearney spoke to OSIRIS to establish the communication, and as she did so, Donn realized again how enormous a task he had set for himself and his fellow caretakers. He hadn't even thought of the colonial hold and what it contained or the myriad issues of logistics and personnel he'd have to solve. Caring for a quarter million infants with under two hundred people while building an extrasolar colony—

"You're on," Kearney said.

Donn looked at the screen and saw Vincent's angry face. He spoke before the captain, trying to establish dominance.

"Captain. We need to talk."

"This has gone far enough, Donn. I don't know how you are doing all this, but you will release the locks on K-Deck and surrender to Simpatica and—"

Donn held a hand up. "Captain, please don't. I'm not going to give up until we get some things straight."

Vincent scowled. "I'm not going to bargain with you, Cardenio."

"I'm sorry, Captain, but you haven't got a choice. I don't really want to cause more trouble, but I will if I have to. I have K-Deck with me."

"What do you mean?"

Donn moved aside to let Vincent see the assembled caretakers behind him. "K-Deck is unified. They agree with me that you can't go ahead with your plan of killing the preborns."

Donn saw Vincent try to hide his alarm. "That decision hasn't been made yet. We're still assessing the situation."

"Captain, I've told the K-Deck caretakers everything. They know about the hibernators. They know what you're considering, and we all agree you can't do it. They won't go along with it."

"It's not their decision, or yours!" Vincent shouted, his face growing redder. "This is a command decision, and it's mine to make. If I decide the best option is to reduce the preborn roster, then that's what's going to happen. I don't require your consent."

"Yes, you do, Captain. I don't want to make this a confrontation. Just listen to me, and you'll see my position. I have K-Deck. They are with me. They won't carry out the order to kill the preborns. And if you don't agree to our points, I'll contact the rest of the ship and get them on my side, too. You won't have anyone to follow your orders."

"I don't need you. I'll be able to do it through OSIRIS."

Donn's lips tightened. "I don't believe you will, Captain. OSIRIS has safeguards against this." He glanced at Kearney, who nodded back. "In fact, why don't you try to order it now, and see what happens?"

He heard the gasp from several caretakers, and forced himself to resist looking at them. He heard Kearney speaking to them in a low voice. "Trust me. OSIRIS will not obey that order."

Vincent looked back, stunned. "Very well. OSIRIS, hypothetical command."

Donn heard OSIRIS' voice through the communications panel. "Ready."

Vincent continued. "I want to shut down all pseudowombs in Bays A through J." His voice shook. "Cease all life sustaining functions to those pods."

For a split second before OSIRIS answered, Donn held his breath. If OSIRIS agreed to the order, he knew all would be lost. He wasn't thinking of his own punishment, or the future of the colony. He was thinking of Blueberry, and Lunchpail, and the thousands of swimming preborns he had cared for and who would one day take their place as the founding generation of Earth's first extrasolar colony. If he was wrong, if Kearney had been wrong about OSIRIS, he would have handed Vincent the means to kill thousands.

OSIRIS answered, "Command invalid."

Donn breathed again.

Vincent narrowed his eyes. "This is Captain Vincent. I am hypothetically ordering you to shut down Bays A through J."

"Command invalid."

"Hypothetical command. Shut down all power to Decks A through J."

OSIRIS answered, "I do not read an emergency that would—"

Vincent shouted, "Dammit! Hypothetically, assume a shipwide emergency! Shut down power to Decks A through J!"

"Hypothetical emergency accepted. Decks A through J power shutdown commencing. Power to all caretaker bays remains on."

"What? I ordered a complete hypothetical shutdown of the deck!"

"Hypothetical deck shutdown accepted. Bay shutdown not possible. All bays to remain operative under all circumstances."

Donn said, "Captain, I think you can see—"

Vincent wasn't listening. "OSIRIS! I am the captain of this vessel! I have ultimate authority over all functions!"

OSIRIS answered, flatly, "Incorrect. Certain functions hardwired and cannot be superseded. Preborn bay function is paramount. There is no higher function."

Vincent was apoplectic. He glared into the camera pickup and spoke to Donn. "I don't know what kind of trick this is, but—"

"It's not a trick, Captain. OSIRIS knows what the mission truly is, and knows nothing can stop it."

"I'm in command!"

Donn matched the captain's rage with resolute calm. "Yes, sir. But there are certain things even you aren't in command of. The health and safety of the preborns is one of them. K-Deck is the other. Now that you've seen you can't carry out the order, will you listen? We have to—"

"I don't have to do anything! If I decide to reduce the numbers, then I will! I'll open the bays to space if I have to. But I will have command!"

Donn realized that he was pushing Vincent too hard. The man was no longer concerned about the colony, or what would be the proper decision to make. Now that his authority had been challenged, he could think of nothing else. The man would take any steps to assert his control, and at this point, the correctness of the decision to kill the preborns was not the issue. It was merely that he was being denied command. He had to defuse this, and find a way out for Vincent. "Captain, I am not trying to start a mutiny. We just want you to—"

"That's exactly what this is! You've done something to OSIRIS to take away my command functions, and you've convinced the rest of K-Deck to go along with your rebellion. If you don't undo whatever you've done, I'll shut off life support to your deck."

Donn glanced at Kearney, who said quietly, "I can keep it going. Don't worry."

Donn looked back at the camera. "You won't be able to, Captain. We can override OSIRIS from here."

Vincent pounded his desk in frustration. "Damn you! I don't care what it takes, Cardenio, but I will regain command. You do whatever you want, but know that I will be in command. Whatever these little computer tricks are, I'll get past them, and you and your mutineers will be dealt with."

"And the preborns? You'll kill them?"

Vincent hesitated for a moment. The comment seemed to affect him, but he said with faltering composure, "I will do what I have to do."

"So will I, Captain." Donn signaled to Kearney, who ordered OSIRIS to break communication.

"Jezeus," Hunsaker said. "He's serious. He really wants to kill all the swimmers."

Donn stared at the blank screen. "I think he wants to be in command. Now it's all about that."

"What now, Donn?" Yune asked.

"Now, I talk to the ship."

Kearney said, "The whole ship? Maybe you should just talk to the caretakers. I can arrange for that."

Donn shook his head. "No. It needs to be everyone."

"But that could make everyone panic."

"I'll keep that in mind. But everyone needs to hear this, not just caretakers. Crew does, too. You heard Vincent. He considers this a mutiny. And I think we're one step away from that. Do any of you want to be released from this?"

Kearney gasped and said, "Donn, we can't—"

Donn stopped her. "K, I can't force anyone to go along with us. This will only work if everyone agrees." He looked back at the rest of the caretakers. "You heard the stakes. You heard what Vincent is considering. I put it to you all that we can't allow that. I don't know what the future holds for the preborns," he said, sweeping the small group with his eyes, "but I know that each and every one of them deserves a chance at survival. I can't promise they will all make it. Probably some of them won't. But I agreed to become a caretaker because I wanted to help. If you agree, and if you choose hope, then stay with me."

The caretakers looked back at him, unblinking. No one spoke. Hunsaker took a small step forward.

"I'm with you, Donn."

The rest followed.

Donn nodded, then turned to Kearney. "Get ready to hook me into the shipwide com."

Chapter Seventeen

Kearney smiled grimly. "Yes, sir."

"Shouldn't we check on Vern and Forgisto first?" Yune said.

Donn exhaled. "That's a good idea. Gives me a chance to think of what I want to say."

Kearney spoke to the computer. "OSIRIS, hook me into Forgisto's cabin."

"Communication refused."

"Override."

"Acknowledged. Communication established."

Kearney looked expectantly at Donn, who said, "Vern? Mikelo? Are you there?"

The monitor display showed Mikelo and Vern both seated. They turned to the camera, Mikelo looking pale and nervous, Vern looking as placid as he always did. He said, "Yes, Donn. We're here.

"What's happening? Have you talked to Mikelo?"

"Yes, I have."

Donn remembered that Vern wouldn't say more than he needed to and that he would have to ask more specific questions. It wasn't stubbornness, but merely an economy with words.

"And? What's the result?"

Vern looked at Mikelo, who answered in his nasally whine, "I am just concerned, you know, about all that's going on. I'd prefer to speak to the captain directly to find out what our options are, what's happening, how best we can serve the preborns." Where Vern was terse, Forgisto was verbose. But he tended to say less than the austere Vern despite his prodigious verbiage.

Donn summoned up his patience. Dealing with Forgisto was tricky. He needed to be stroked. He was a competent caretaker, thorough and skilled, but had a streak of underhanded ambition in him. "I understand, Mikelo, but that's not really possible. Speaking to the captain, I mean. He's decided on a course of action we can't accept."

"I realize that," Forgisto bleated, "but I'd still like to talk to him. Maybe we can convince him not to go through with it?"

"I've already tried that."

"But maybe if I tried?"

Donn felt his patience already running out. "Mikelo, I promise you, he's adamant. The time for talking is over. We need you to come to K-eight and help us determine our next step."

"You need my help?"

Donn heard the burgeoning confidence in Forgisto's voice and fueled it. "Yes, exactly. We can't proceed without your input. We're all waiting for you here in K-eight."

"Well, I guess if you need me, I'd better come over." Forgisto rose. Vern stood up too, looking slightly amused.

Donn gestured to Kearney, who cut the feed.

"I think he needs to be watched," Kearney said.

"Who, Mikelo?" Donn said. He shook his head slightly. "No. He's always like that. Talks a lot, but there's nothing behind it. He's harmless."

"I'm gonna keep an eye on him all the same."

Donn shrugged. He knew Forgisto and the man was all talk. He might be dangerous if he weren't so timid. As it was, other matters were far more important.

"Are you ready to address the whole ship, Donn?" Kearney said.

"Almost. I want to check on the Freezer."

"Why?"

"I want to find out what they've discovered. Last time we checked, the Freezer staff and a couple of administrators were in there. They must have checked fifty or so pods by now. I want to see if they've found anyone alive." He thought for a moment, the others watching him. "Can you ask OSIRIS to locate Delano, or any of the Freezer staff who are not near to an administrator, and see if we can activate a communications panel near them? I want to be able to speak to one of them without an administrator listening in."

Kearney nodded. "I can ask OSIRIS, but even if we can do it, what's to stop the guy you talk to from telling an admin?"

"Nothing, but all I want is information. I don't care if the admin knows I am asking — I just want to speak to a Freezer tech who can talk back."

"What will this do for us, Donn?" Yune asked.

"If they've found some living hibernators, that will change what I tell the whole ship. I want to have my facts straight when I address everyone."

"What if the tech lies to you?" Kearney said.

"I'm going to have to chance that," Donn said. "I need to know what's going on down there."

Kearney looked uneasy. "Donn, I don't think this is a good plan. There's nothing you can learn from this that will change anything. Even if you do get to speak to a Freezer tech, they won't tell you anything. Or they'll lie to you to try and get some kind of advantage. Shit, they might even be waiting for your call so they can tell you they've found all the other hibs alive, and your mutiny here is unnecessary. Just to draw us out."

"They'd have announced something like that already, K, if they want to restore order. They wouldn't wait for us to call them."

Kearney shook her head. "I'm still against this. I think you should just address the whole ship with what you have now. Nothing you hear from the Freezer changes anything."

Donn narrowed his eyes, but it was Hunsaker who spoke up. "Mary Ellen, I'm sorry, but I disagree. Whatever we learn from the Freezer is valuable."

"But we can't trust them!" Kearney was growing more and more passionate.

"We can make that determination once we've heard from them," Hunsaker said calmly. "Right now, we don't know anything about the survey. If we can connect to a hibernation staffer, we might be able to find something out."

"They're just going to lie to us, use our own questions to feed us bad data."

"Even that would be something, Mary Ellen." Hunsaker looked at Donn. "I think we should contact the Freezer."

"It's a waste of time. We need to address the whole ship, now. Before we lose initiative," Kearney said.

Donn regarded her for a moment. "I could have been talking to the Freezer all this time. Please connect me, Kearney."

"Who put you in charge of all this?" Kearney asked.

Donn felt rather than heard the rest of the caretakers' shock at the sudden challenge in Kearney's voice. He kept his eyes on Kearney and met her petulant challenge with gentleness.

"You did, K, when you put the pistol in my hand and told me not to let Vincent kill the preborns." He half-turned to the rest of the caretakers. "I don't claim any authority over any of you. I'm a caretaker, same as all of us. If one of you thinks you can better reach a successful result, please, say so."

As if on cue, Vern and Mikelo entered K-8.

Mikelo looked around the silent assembly and said, "What's happening?"

Kearney scowled at him. "Nothing. We're just about to contact the Freezer to find out what's happening there."

"Why?" Mikelo said. "Should we talk about this before we do it? I don't want to do anything without a full analysis of—"

"We have talked about it, Forgisto," Kearney snapped. "Dev, can you please fill in Mikelo and Vern?" She turned back to Donn and spoke in low tones only he could hear. "I still think this is a mistake. Keep in mind that they have no reason to tell you the truth."

Donn smiled tightly at her. "I know. Thanks for keeping me honest."

Kearney grunted, and Donn knew her well enough to understand that this was as close to an apology he was going to get from her. She spoke to OSIRIS and relayed the complex command Donn had wanted.

OSIRIS indicated that hibernation technician Delano was alone deep in the Freezer, far from any administrator and close enough to a communications terminal that he should be able to respond if he wished. Donn frowned — he and Delano had not parted on the best of terms, but Donn had little choice. He told Kearney to make the connection, and a few moments later, Delano's face appeared on the monitor.

"Hello? Who's this? Donn?" His eyes widened as he recognized the caretaker. "What the hell's going on?"

"Yeah, this is Donn. Have you been conducting the survey down there?"

"Jezeus, Donn, what the fuck's going on?" He looked hurriedly to his left, then back into camera range.

"Are you alone?"

"Sort of. Freeman is about ... I dunno, two hundred meters away."

"Past the slope?"

"Yeah."

"Okay, good. I need something from you. Are you—"

"Wait, wait. Freeman said you're some kind of fugitive. We can't contact the captain; OSIRIS has blocked out all communications. What the hell's going on?"

"Have you found dead hibernators?" Donn said, ignoring his questions.

Delano paled. "Shit, yeah. I've checked fifteen pods so far. All dead. Anson said you found a dead one when you were with us?"

"Yeah. That's why you're doing your hands-on survey. OSIRIS is malfunctioning in the Freezer."

Delano nodded. "Yeah, we've confirmed that. Each one I find dead, OSIRIS says they're still alive. Even with biomeds disconnected. What's happening, Donn? Did you know this when you came to us, and that's why you checked one of the pods?"

"No, I didn't. Listen, Delano, maybe this isn't the best time to say this, but ... I'm sorry for how I acted toward you guys."

Delano looked stunned. "What?"

"I was an asshole when I was with you. Acting like I was better than all of you. But I'm not. And right now, you and your crew might be the most important people in the ship."

Delano swallowed. "Why?"

"Because what you find down there will affect the whole mission. Do you know if anyone has found a living hibernator yet?"

Delano shook his head. "No. I mean, no, no one has. We are told to alert each other if we find one, and so far, no alerts."

"How many of you are searching?"

"Seven. Five Freezer staff and two admin. We're all in different sections."

"And you've done fifteen. So altogether, you think maybe you've done one hundred or so?"

"Maybe more, if the others are going faster than I am. I'm being pretty thorough." He shuddered briefly. "I can't believe this, Donn. What if they're all dead?"

"I know, Delano. That's what I'm trying to deal with, myself."

"All this time … we've been watching dead bodies."

Donn nodded, then scowled. "What do you mean, 'all this time?'"

"I checked. They've been dead for months, maybe a year."

As Donn reeled, he heard the rest of the caretakers gasp and react in shock. He looked at them briefly, and saw their wide-eyed dismay. Only Kearney looked skeptical. Donn turned back to Delano. "Are you sure?"

"Yeah. That's why I've been going so slow. I did an autopsy on one."

Donn blinked. "I didn't know you guys were trained in that."

"We're not, normally. I was a veterinarian on Earth."

Kearney interjected. "Freeman let you cut one open?"

Delano peered into the camera and asked, "Who's that?"

"Mary Ellen Kearney. She's working with me. Delano, was Freeman with you when you performed your autopsy?"

"No. And it wasn't a full autopsy. I just did it in the pod." He grimaced, evidently remembering the experience. "She'd been dead a long time. But she had all the preservation chemicals in her."

"The hibernation cocktail?" Donn asked.

"I don't know. I wasn't able to analyze the stuff. But there was definitely emulsion in her. I think it had to have been the hib cocktail, and she just didn't survive the initial descent into torpor when she was put in."

Donn thought for a moment. "Thanks, Delano. I'm sorry you have to do this. It's gotta be hard."

"It's hell, Donn. Over and over, dead. Dead. Dead." He swallowed again. "This was my job. To look after them. And all this time ... they were dead."

"I can't imagine what you're feeling now. If I found out my swimmers were dead ... I don't know if I could handle it. You're holding up well."

"No, I'm not," Delano said. "What do we do now? If they're all dead..."

"I'll have something on that in a little bit, Delano. Keep watching and listening to the comm. And be careful around Freeman."

"Why?"

"Something's coming, and I'm not sure—" Donn saw Kearney signaling wildly out of camera range. "Hold on, Delano." He looked at Kearney, who gestured for him to come to her. He walked out of camera range and listened.

"There are five Freezer techs and only two admin down there," Kearney said.

Donn realized what she meant. "Right." He glanced back at the monitor to see Delano's anxious face still filling the screen. "But I can't tip my hand early. If Delano tells Freeman and Uplander what we intend, it won't work." He thought. "I need to just plant the seed."

Mikelo came over to them while they spoke. "Plant what seed?"

"Not now, Forgisto," Kearney snapped.

Donn went back to the camera, leaving Kearney to handle Forgisto. "Delano, like I said, keep listening to the communications panels. I will have something for you soon. And when I do ... I want you to take action accordingly."

Delano looked confused. "What?"

"Just know that any action you think is appropriate, I'll back you up. We're all in this together."

Delano's confusion intensified. "I don't know what you mean, Donn. What action?"

"You'll know. For now, that's all. I'll be in touch." Donn indicated the communication was over, and Kearney cut the feed.

"What's happening here?" Forgisto cried. "You're talking about actions and backup. You said nothing would be done without my input and a full discussion. And now you're—"

"Mikelo," Donn said with as much patience as he could muster, "Vern told you what's happening, right?"

"Yes, but—"

"And you know what the captain is planning to do?"

"Yes, but if I could just talk to him, I'm sure I could make him see that his plan is not only impossible, but immoral and wrong."

"I'm glad you agree, but we've already tried talking. We're past that," Donn said. "I'm going to talk to the whole ship now, and when that's over, the mutiny will have begun."

"Mutiny?" Mikelo whimpered.

"Yes." Donn turned to the rest of the caretakers. "It's important you know what this means. Once I address the ship, we will be in a full mutiny. We will have to take over the ship in order to prevent the murder of the preborns."

"And that will mean violence," Kearney added.

Donn raised his voice. "I do not want violence. Not only are these people our shipmates, but we will need every able bodied adult once we reach TC-Three." He looked at Kearney and continued. "Each adult we kill or incapacitate is one less adult available to care for the children. So killing a crewmember or fellow caretaker is killing the children in the future."

"This is unbelievable," Mikelo said in his high whine. "I am going to the Captain now and telling him—"

"No, you're not, Mikelo," Donn said quietly.

"You're talking about a violent mutiny! You haven't even tried to talk this out! I am sure he will listen to me." Mikelo turned to leave the bay.

"Stop," Donn said, reaching into his thigh pouch for his flechette pistol. He looked at Kearney, who spoke to OSIRIS.

"OSIRIS, seal the exit to K-eight."

"Acknowledged. Bay K-eight exit sealed."

Mikelo turned back. "You've locked us in? Am I your prisoner, Donn?"

Donn felt the situation spiraling out of control. "No. Listen, we can't have people going off on their own. We need to be unified." He turned to Mikelo. "You wouldn't have been able to leave K-Deck anyway. It's also sealed."

"Then why did you pull a gun on me?" Mikelo said.

Donn shrugged and put the pistol away. "There. It's away. I pulled the pistol on you and locked K-eight because this isn't some seminar or bull session in the Gem Diner. This is real. We need to be together on this. The ship is about to be plunged into chaos as it is. I need K-Deck to be unified. If you can't do that, Forgisto, then I'm gonna keep you under guard here."

Mikelo spluttered. "On … on whose authority?"

"Mine."

Yune said, meekly, "Donn, if he disagrees with us, maybe just let him out of K-Deck?"

"No, Paul. If he's not with us, he's with the killing of the babies. There can't be any middle ground." He looked at Forgisto. "So, what's it going to be?"

Forgisto looked shocked. "That's a false dilemma. I'm not in favor killing babies, I'm just—"

"Just?" Donn snapped. "Just what? This isn't some classroom lecture about logic or rhetoric. If you're not fully committed to us and our cause, I need to know that now, and take appropriate steps."

"Steps? Like what?" Forgisto shrank away slightly as he spoke.

"I'm not going to hurt you, Mikelo. I need you. The children need you. But if you don't … if you can't commit fully to us," Donn swept the rest of the caretakers up with his hand, "then I have to know that. I'll need to detain you so you don't interfere. And once we've taken the ship, you'll be released. I ask you again — what is it to be?"

"Donn, it's obvious you can't trust him," Kearney said. "Lock him in his quarters and be done with it."

"No, K. If Mikelo agrees to be with us, that means we have all of K-Deck. And every person counts." He turned back to Forgisto.

"I can't agree with killing the preborns," Mikelo said slowly. "And if you have spoken to Vincent as there's no room in his mind to change his decision, then I agree with you. We have to take the ship and—"

"Good." Donn looked at Kearney, who spoke volumes with her expression. She turned her gaze back to Forgisto with a scowl.

She'd watch him, Donn knew. He didn't fully trust Forgisto, either. Not that he would actively betray Donn and the others — he was not bold enough for that — but what weak resolve the man had would fold in the face of strong words from Vincent. He could be flipped. Kearney would be watching, though, so Donn could turn his back on Forgisto and concentrate on the next step.

He blinked and felt fatigue start to catch up with him. He couldn't remember the last time he had slept — had it been a full day yet? He rubbed his eyes and felt the bitter soreness of eyestrain.

"You okay, Donn?" Hunsaker asked.

Donn snapped his head back up. "Yeah. Just a little tired. I'll be fine."

Hunsaker nodded, but did not seem satisfied with that answer.

Donn turned to Kearney. "All right. Patch me into the whole ship, please, K. All sections. And can you make it so I cannot be cut off?"

"Can do. You want it one-way? Broadcast only? Or do you want to accept communications, too?"

"One-way. After I talk, we'll need camera hookups all over the ship. Can you route them through my control board?" He looked at the multiple screens in his bay and realized he hadn't checked on his individual swimmers in a long time. His own swimmers had diminished in his attention now that he had a quarter-million of them to think of. The realization made him uneasy. He felt as if his devotion was a finite quality, like a limited resource of ink or paint he was being asked to spread across more and more canvas. The wider area he tried to cover, the fainter the hue.

He half-listened to Kearney set up the communications format he had asked for. He had not thought of her as a romantic companion since this crisis began. They hadn't left their relationship in a good place, and he knew most of that had been his fault. He hadn't been willing to share her: not in the sense that he felt he possessed her body, but that he was, or ought to be, sole custodian of her happiness. There was a power to that, he knew, and he knew with awful reflection that it was a form of dominance, of control. He wanted to control something in her life. And thus, control his own.

He looked behind him to the yawning bay. Was that why caretaking held such attraction to him? The aspect of control? These seventeen hundred-plus preborns depended on him. Did he like the feeling so much that he was not willing to let go of any of them? Did he truly value their lives, or did he value their lives in the sense that he had control over them?

And this whole crisis — could he deny that some part of him liked being listened to, obeyed? Since coming back from Vincent's office, he knew he had changed. When Kearney had handed him the flechette pistol and sent him to the captain's meeting, his rebirth had begun.

"All ready, Donn. Just like you wanted it," Kearney said.

"Thanks." He took a deep breath and looked at the others. "Do me a favor — all of you, stand behind me, okay? So everyone can see you are with me."

The caretakers assembled in a rough semicircle behind him, facing the camera.

"Okay, K, put me on."

"OSIRIS, begin broadcast."

"Attention, caretakers and crew. This is Caretaker Cardenio speaking. I have an announcement you all need to hear."

He imagined his words echoing through the corridors, the bays, the central shaft, the engineering spaces, and the command and control center.

"Myself, K-Deck liaison officer Margulies, and others have discovered a shocking tragedy. We have confirmed that many hundreds and, in all probability, each one of the twenty thousand, seven hundred and six hibernating adults slated to become the parents of the children are dead. Let me say that again. We know a lot of the sleepers are dead, and it's likely they all are."

He paused, partially to let the words sink in, but also to gather his own thoughts. "Right now, the Freezer staff and two crewmembers are conducting a pod-to-pod survey of the hibernators to get an accurate count. But I can say from my own personal knowledge that the strong likelihood is that none of them are alive. I know this is incredible news, and you have a lot of questions about it, just like you have questions about the communications blackout. Probably, members of the crew have gone to you individually to try and calm you and keep order. I'm not trying to cause chaos, but I had to shut down communications so that I could speak to you all now and tell you the truth."

He took a small step closer to the camera. "Because the hibernators are dead, your captain and his crew are considering a monstrous plan. I barely have the words to tell you how very evil this idea is. Let me just say it in plain language so you can hear it for yourselves.

"The command staff and crew are planning on killing hundreds of thousands of preborns before we reach TC-Three. They say that without the hibernating parents to wake up, there is no way to care for all the children. So they must die now.

"Caretakers, I understand how this sounds. I know how hard it is to believe this. I heard it with my own ears. I was present in the discussion less than two hours ago. I promise you this is true."

He paused, resisting the urge to wipe his brow. "Caretakers — and crew, as well — I know you don't want to do this. You didn't spend nine months caring for your preborns only to have them killed. I urge you all to join with us on K-Deck," he said, stepping a bit to the side to show the rest of the caretakers, "in resisting the captain and his plan. If we all rise up as one, and refuse to carry out this mass murder, Captain Vincent and the command staff will see how committed we are and will abandon their plan to kill the babies.

"One last idea. Once you've accepted the facts I've told you, you will wonder how we will set out caring for the quarter-million babies once we reach TC-Three. I will be as honest as I can; I don't have that answer yet. Once we secure the ship and the lives of the preborns, we will set up a ... committee to design a new mission profile, one that ensures the survival of the children. Of all the children.

"Each deck, please select one representative from among the caretakers to report, via the communications network, your status. I mean ... report in to us here what's happening on your deck, and if your caretakers are with us and with the preborns. I urge you not to hurt anyone — work with your liaison officer, not against them. They are probably just as confused as you. We will need every able bodied adult once we land on TC, and crewmembers are part of the caretaker family.

"I'll wait for your reports. Caretaker Cardenio, out."

Kearney said quietly, "OSIRIS, end broadcast."

"Now what, Donn?" Yune asked.

"Now we wait."

Chapter Eighteen

Donn explained to Kearney that he wanted the ability to sift through incoming reports without being overwhelmed by them. Despite his admonishment that each deck send a single report to him, he knew he would get a flood instead. Kearney worked with OSIRIS to display the reports on the bay's monitors, while the other caretakers all agreed to handle the reports as they came in. They worked well together, volunteering to listen to decks on which they had acquaintances or friends.

As the organization developed around him, he found himself physically stepping back and allowing it to progress. He started to tremble now that the tension of addressing the entire ship had eased. Fatigue crept up on him, and he found his attention wavering. He imagined for a brief few seconds that his role in the crisis was over, and someone else would take over.

That fantasy ended when Kearney approached him. "I don't want Mikelo talking to any of the other decks, Donn. I know you think he can be trusted, but…"

Donn returned to the situation. "I agree. Stay close to him, don't let him corrupt or derail this process. I can see him deciding he would be the best spokesperson for us, and…"

Kearney nodded. "I know what you mean. I'll keep a watch on him." She started to move in his direction, but Donn stopped her with a word.

"Kearney." When she turned back to him, he continued. "I know this might be a dumb time to talk about this, but I wanted to say I'm sorry for the way I spoke to you back in your room."

Kearney looked at him quizzically. "What do you mean?"

"I said some very hurtful things, and I—"

"Donn, honey," Kearney said, quickly but tenderly. "It's okay. Lots of pressures, I understand." She flashed him a smile, and leaned in closer. "Since we're saying stuff we probably shouldn't, let me tell you how sexy you are being now, taking charge and all that. I was an idiot for ever thinking about anyone else. You're all I need or want, Donn." She smirked. "Now, go save the children. I'll make sure Mikelo doesn't fuck it up." She flew in and gave him a quick kiss on the lips, then moved closer to Forgisto.

Donn felt his fatigue ease. That was exactly what he had wanted to hear, what he had needed to hear. Yes, it was inappropriate at this time, but nonetheless, he stood up a little straighter.

"Donn, we're getting a communication from E-Deck," Devie said, looking at her monitor. "Should I take it, or do you want to?"

"Go ahead and take it yourself, Devie. All of you, just take the reports as they come in. Give OSIRIS your assessment of the deck status when you think you have it."

"Any particular format for that?" Devie asked.

"No, I think just narrate to OSIRIS. We'll be able to figure it out." Donn said. Devie was speaking to Blaugrund from E-Deck, a competent young caretaker whom Donn knew vaguely.

As he was half-listening to Devie take the call from Blaugrund, he heard Hunsaker begin talking to Caretaker Chang from C-Deck. Then Yune was on with Adelini from H, and soon Donn could not keep it all straight. Decks were reporting in. The monitors showed faces of caretakers (and in one case a liaison officer, Bora Warren) in different states of anxiety, excitement, and outright shock.

His own band of caretakers was responding with surprising calm. Donn watched with pride as his group, who had only heard the news scant minutes ago, deftly took reports and soothed the fears of those who called in. Forgisto hovered around the monitor screens, having been denied a position, and offered ignored advice to the K-Deck caretakers. Kearney was always near him, allowing him to think he was being useful, but obviously wary of any interference on his part.

Amid the din of reports and conversations, Donn heard Basque's voice call to him. "Donn! I have a problem over here!"

Donn hurried over to her. She indicated the monitor. "I was on with Kane from L-Deck. She was saying they've been having fights, and then I lost her."

The monitor showed the interior of a caretaker's quarters, presumably Kane's. No one was in the shot, but Donn could hear sounds of a scuffle in the corridor outside. The entry hatch was open, and as he watched, he saw two bodies in close combat stagger past the opening. One of them was Kane's, and the other wore the olive livery of a liaison officer.

"Who's the L.O. on L-Deck? Anyone know?" Donn called to his group.

"It's Hartoonian. Beatrix Hartoonian," Yune called back.

Donn turned and found Kearney at his elbow, Forgisto drifting over as well. "K, can you get me a rotating camera feed for L-Deck on this monitor? Five seconds per cam, and stop the rotation when I tell you?"

"Yeah. Lemme through," Kearney said, and Donn and Basque made room for her. Kearney started to issue the commands and Forgisto spoke up.

"What's happening?"

"Not sure. Trouble on L-Deck."

"What kind of trouble?"

Donn leaned on the back of Basque's chair and glanced sideways behind him to where Mikelo was standing. "Looks like a fight."

"Oh, no," Mikelo said. "We need to stop that. They can't be fighting."

Donn looked back at the monitor and closed his eyes for a moment, trying to think away his growing annoyance at Forgisto. "I know that. I'm trying to get a camera sweep of the deck to see how bad it is."

"You're all set, Donn," Kearney said. The camera stayed on the interior of Kane's quarters for a few more seconds, then the shot changed to show another personal stateroom, also empty.

"K, can you get OSIRIS to tag each shot? So we know what we're looking at?"

"OSIRIS, show camera designation."

Words appeared in the upper right corner of the image: "CAM LQ1" The image changed after five seconds, and yet another empty room appeared. The designation was CAM LQ2.

Although the delay was only five seconds, the wait seemed interminable as OSIRIS cycled first through all twelve of the caretakers' personal quarters, then started the same process on the preborn bays.

"Where is everyone?" Mikelo said.

"Probably they met in a central location to talk this out, like we did, and things got — hold it! Stop camera sweep!" Donn said.

Bay L-7 was in the shot, and even from the wide-angle view of the camera, a dozen brawling figures could clearly be seen.

"Jezeus," Basque murmured. As they watched, a petite caretaker with blood on her face was tackled by another caretaker, and the two rolled on the deck, pummeling one another.

"That's Beverly," Kearney said. "Jezeus, I didn't know she had such fight in her.

"Which one?"

"The one kicking Garcia's ass."

Donn glanced at Kearney. Dottie Garcia was another of Kearney's lovers. "You know them both? What do you think's happening?"

"Hard to say. But if I had to guess, Garcia's probably with us. Beverly ... might not be."

"We don't know what's happening from just this image," Mikelo said. "The fight might have nothing to do with your announcement. It could be personal."

Basque snorted. "Not likely. Oh, Goddess, look. Ippolito has a multitool. Look out!" Basque shouted at the screen as Ippolito brought the multitool down on the back of an unsuspecting caretaker. The victim was staggered to his knees, and Ippolito raised the tool to finish him.

Donn winced as the heavy tool smashed into the head of the Caretaker Patel. The caretaker fell to the deck.

"We've got to stop this," Donn said. "This is not what I wanted."

"Yes. Before they hurt one of the pods," Kearney added.

"How're you going to stop it?" Basque asked.

"Let me talk to them," Mikelo said. "If they hear me, I can convince them that fighting isn't the answer and we need to sit down and discuss this rationally."

Basque snorted again. "I don't think talking's going to cut it, Mikelo."

"No, he's right," Donn said. Both Basque and Kearney looked at him, astonished. He continued. "Let him try and talk them down. In the meantime, I'm going to L-Deck to deal with them personally."

"By yourself?" Kearney said.

He patted the flechette pistol in his pocket. "I've got this."

"That's not very effective if you don't plan on using it."

"They don't know that." Donn nodded at the screen.

"But by yourself? There's too many of them."

Donn watched the melee for a few seconds. "Okay. Maybe you're right. I'll take Yune and Vern with me."

Basque said, "Hunsaker. Take her in place of Vern. She's a tough. Vern's a sweetheart, but you don't need that now."

Donn nodded. "All right." He pushed off the back of Basque's chair and turned to Kearney. "I'll contact you when I am at the L-Deck hatch. Open it, then close and seal it behind us. I don't want any of Simpatica's people sneaking in."

Kearney nodded. "Got it. Be careful. Make sure none of the pods get damaged."

"I will." He turned from her and called out. "Hunsaker! Yune! I need you two with me."

As they approached, Kearney looked up at him with her wide eyes. "And while you're at it, watch out for yourself, okay? No multitools to the back of the head."

"I'll try. Keep Mikelo from making this worse." He addressed the other two caretakers. "We're headed to L-Deck. I'll tell you on the way what we're doing there. Come on." He went to the K-8 hatch and cycled it open.

He set a brisk pace once inside the K-Deck corridor, heading for the nearest K/L junction near bay K-3. "L-Deck is having some fights. Can't tell who's winning, or even who is on what side," he said over his shoulder as they trotted.

"Has anyone been hurt?" Hunsaker said, huffing along next to him.

"Yeah. It looks like Patel has been hit on the head. There might be more injuries."

"My God," Paul said.

"Our priorities are to stop the fighting, ensure the safety of the preborns and the caretakers, and secure the deck. In our favor."

"And if we can't?" Hunsaker asked.

"Can't do which part?"

"Secure the deck."

"Then we get outta there and high-tail it back here, seal L-Deck behind us. At least we'll know they aren't with us." He slowed to a stop before the hatchway labeled "L-Deck Access."

Yune said, "We're going in?"

Donn glanced at him. "Are you going to be able to do this? If you can't, then go back and get someone else." He spoke swiftly but not harshly.

"I … I don't know if I can do any fighting."

"I hope it won't come to that."

"But … we're going in with just loud voices, or…?" Yune glanced at Donn's pocket.

Donn unzipped the pocket and withdrew the flechette pistol. "This ought to be enough."

Hunsaker and Yune stared at him for a moment, then Hunasker said, "For you, sure. But we don't have anything. Are you sure this is how you want to do this?"

Donn hesitated, then handed the pistol to her, butt first. "Here. You take it."

"That's not what I meant," Hunsaker said, looking apprehensively at the pistol. "I meant, if it's chaos in there, no one's going to listen to us. We'll just be more shouting voices."

"I get you, but we need to get in there and put a stop to this. The longer we wait, the more we risk someone getting hurt. Or damage to a pod."

"The pods are in danger?" Yune's voice had lost all its mousy quality and he now sounded resolute. "Then let's go," he added, stepping towards the hatch and trying to cycle it open.

Donn smiled tightly. He hadn't meant to use the swimmers as a prod to action, but having done so, he felt no guilt.

Hunsaker gestured with the pistol. "Take your gun back, Donn."

"No, you keep it. You know how to use one?"

"A little. It's been a while, and I am not really familiar with this kind of gun," she said, looking at the weapon.

Donn nodded. "It's point and shoot. Nothing to it. Minor recoil, and they're designed to minimize damage to the ship. Darts flatten out when they hit something hard, so you can't blow a hole in the bulkhead. But they'll tear through soft flesh. So they are lethal."

"How many shots do I have?"

"Fifteen. The safety is the little latch on the back — yeah, right there," he added as Hunsaker found the switch. "Brandish that. Let them know you are armed. I hope that'll give us the psychological edge."

"And if not?"

Donn didn't answer, but turned to Yune, who was still struggling with the hatch. "It won't open, Paul. We've sealed it. Hang on, let me tell Kearney we're in position." He spoke to the air. "OSIRIS, contact Caretaker Kearney in bay K-eight. Tell her—"

"I see you, Donn," Kearney's voice sounded in the corridor. "You're ready?"

"Yeah. Open it up."

The hatch cycled open, and Donn stepped through. He knew that, tactically, Hunsaker should have been in front since she was carrying the weapon, but he needed to go in first. Immediately, he was greeted with L-Deck graffiti: "Welcome to L-Deck. Place contraband in collection slot" the handwritten words declared, with a crudely drawn arrow pointing at the deck. There was, of course, no slot. The graffiti was meant to be a harmless bit of tongue-in-cheek rebellion. Donn wondered how much pent-up hostility there really was behind the various bits of graffiti all over the ship and in the refectories. Had he unwittingly tapped into resentment that had been building on board *Chiron*?

"Donn, you're blocking me," Hunsaker said from behind him, and he hastily moved further into the corridor. The hatchway closed and locked shut behind them.

"Kearney, you still read me?" Donn said.

"I got you, Donn. Fighting has now spread out — it's not confined to L-seven. Spilled out into the corridor near seven, six, and five."

Donn glanced at the directory on the wall, written in official letters, unlike the graffiti.

"All right. We go left. Bay four, then five. We should be able to hear it when we get close. I'll try to stop whatever fight I see. Paul, you keep a watch where I'm not looking, okay? Alison, you got the pistol. Use it as you think you need to. Let's go," he said, and started trotting up the gently sloping corridor.

He heard the shouts before he could see the combatants, and he glanced behind him. Yune and Hunsaker were still with him, trotting along grimly. Donn motioned ahead and broke into a full run, Hunsaker and Yune keeping up.

The sight that came into view was of two pairs of caretakers, all four bloodied and panting, shouting nearly incoherent insults at one another. Two were facing him, and he recognized one woman: Fletcher. She had been at the memorial.

Fletcher's face was twisted into a snarl that relaxed when she saw Donn and his brace of escorts. "Donn!" she shouted, and the two caretakers with their backs to him turned quickly. Their coveralls had bloody finger marks all over them, and one of them, Andrade, had a split lip from which dark blood was oozing.

Donn slowed his run but continued his approach to the foursome. "What's going on here? We can't fight each other!"

All four began to shout at once, and Donn stepped physically between the pairs. "Enough!" he bellowed, and for a quick moment, he had their attention.

He seized the instant. "Talk. Talk to me. What's the matter?" He turned to the pair that didn't include Fletcher — he was all but certain she and her companion, Doggett, were on his side.

Andrade dabbed gingerly at her lip. "The mission can't go on. We all have to face that fact, or—"

"You want to murder them!" Fletcher shouted, and surged forward. Donn extended his arm and caught her charge, spinning her into the bulkhead.

"Stop! No more fighting! We can't tear into each other! The children will need each one of us!" He spoke while looking at Fletcher, who stared back at him, her eyes wild.

"But we have to do the captain's plan!" Andrade said. "It's the only way."

Donn turned to her while he was still pinning Fletcher to the bulkhead. "No. It's not. We can't kill over a hundred thousand babies to save the rest. That's not reality — that's mass murder."

"That's what we've been saying to them," Doggett snarled. "Any plan that involves killing preborns is unacceptable."

"Any plan that doesn't is foolish!" said Caretaker Malkowski, standing next to Andrade. He stepped forward towards the other man, and Donn felt a moment of panic. He couldn't release Fletcher, for she would renew the fight. But Malkowski and Doggett were moving closer to each other.

A loud bang, followed almost instantly by a high-pitched ringing, not unlike a gong, shattered the air. Everyone winced at the noise, then Hunsaker, holding the flechette pistol, said, "Knock it off." She lowered it and looked at the mark on the inside wall where the dart had impacted, then spoke again. "Donn's right. If we fight and hurt each other, no matter which plan we adopt, we're putting children at risk. Right now we need to be unified and think of a plan for success for all the preborns."

Donn released his grip on Fletcher. "Exactly. I know this is a chaotic time, and no one knows what to think or what to do. But one thing's clear: we have to commit to unity or we have no chance at establishing and maintaining a colony."

"We already don't, Donn," Andrade said, her voice calmer.

"We don't know that," Donn said. "All I know is that if we tear ourselves apart now, we will doom the preborns to death. All of them. So stop this fighting among ourselves, and let's join together to decide what's to be done."

The seven people, light years away from earth, speeding towards Tau Ceti III to establish Earth's first interstellar colony, stared at one another, wondering what was to come next.

"Come on. Let's all together find the rest of the L-Deck caretakers and see if we can't restore order. You all with me?"

Perhaps they would have gone with him anyway, but it seemed as if that brief sentence tipped the balance towards peace and unity. The four L-Deck caretakers stopped glaring at each other and turned to Donn.

"There was a big fight in my bay," Fletcher said. "We'd all met in L-seven to talk this out, but it got ugly."

"I know. We saw it. Was anyone hurt?"

"Patel," Doggett said. "Ippolito hurt him." He looked accusingly at Andrade and Malkowski.

"Hey, we didn't do anything. That was Ron," Andrade said.

"He was one of you, though!" Fletcher said.

"Stop," Donn said. "This isn't helping." He looked at all four. "Where's Patel now?"

"I don't know," Fletcher said. "We couldn't get him to the health bay, since all the access points are sealed."

Donn winced. "Is he still in L-seven, then?"

"Probably."

"Then let's get there. We need to get him help."

"What about Ippolito?" Hunsaker asked.

Donn turned to her. "What do you mean?"

"Where is he?"

"I think he left L-seven after the attack. But where he went, I don't know." Fletcher said.

Donn spoke to the air. "Kearney, do you have Caretaker Ippolito on any of your cameras?"

"I'll check. Gimme a sec."

Fletcher said, "If I were going to bet on it, I'd say he went to his quarters and hid out. When we saw what he'd done to Patel, there was a big rush of people over to him. I think he escaped."

"Got him," Kearney said. "He's in his room, alone. Looks like he's washing off blood."

"Is his room locked?"

"It is now. Do you want me to unlock it?"

Fletcher said, "You can override a hatch lockout? How are you doing any of this?"

Donn answered, "We've got deeper access than Vincent or anyone else does. Don't ask — I don't quite understand it myself. Kearney, check back on L-seven. Is there an injured person there?"

"No, I don't see one."

Donn murmured. "Might be out of camera pickup. If he is behind a pod rack or something."

"Or he was taken to someone's room for treatment," Hunsaker offered.

"Not with a head wound. At least, I hope not. We've got to get to L-seven and see if we can find him." He looked at the others, assessing his options. "All right. Andrade, Malkowski — will you please go with Hunsaker and Yune to L-seven and see if you can tend to Patel?"

Doggett snarled, "You're going to trust them with—"

"Yeah, I am, because I know both of them are smart and don't want to hurt anyone. Even if right now they think culling the preborns is an idea worth considering, I think I can trust them to stay peaceful until we can have a shipwide discussion about it. Isn't that right?" Donn added, turning to the two caretakers.

Andrade looked chagrined. "We didn't want to fight. It just got … out of hand."

"So I can trust you to take care of Patel?"

Andrade swallowed. "Yes. We won't fight anymore."

"Good." Donn nodded at Hunsaker, who looked back at him uneasily. He stared at her for a moment, and she gave a tiny shrug and said, "Okay. Lead the way." She and the other three caretakers moved briskly down the corridor towards L-7.

"What if they try something?" Doggett said.

"Hunsaker's armed. I don't think they will. And I want the three of us to try and end whatever other fighting is happening, then confront Ippolito and either get him to our side, or neutralize him."

"Neutralize him? How?" Fletcher asked.

"If he's not going to flip to us, we'll make some kind of holding pen on K-Deck. With control of OSIRIS, we can keep reluctant caretakers and crew locked up and talk to them. But right now I want to secure L-Deck. What's the situation? Who is with the captain, and who's with us?"

Fletcher said, "It's not really that clear cut. We got into a loud argument, and things got physical. There never was a really rational debate."

Donn scowled. Was that the case shipwide? Had he started a mass riot?

Doggett said, "Still, there were two camps. Andrade, Malkowski, Bakoo, Ippolito, and Wilkes are all against us. The rest are all with you."

"Wilkes is your liaison officer, right?"

"Yeah."

"So that means only four caretakers against us, and two of them are Andrade and Malkowski. Ippolito is holed up in his room. Where's Bakoo?" Donn said.

Doggett and Fletcher looked at each other. Fletcher finally spoke. "Her bay is L-one. She could be there or in her quarters."

"Kearney, can you locate Caretaker Bakoo?"

"Hang on," Kearney's voice came over the speaker. In the background, Donn could hear loud conversations. "Lots going on here."

"Trouble?"

"Not here, but we're fielding a lot of anxious calls for help. The sooner you can lock down L-Deck and get back here the better. OSIRIS, locate Caretaker Bakoo."

Donn faintly heard OSIRIS' response. "Caretaker Bakoo is in Caretaker Nipono's quarters."

Fletcher said, "That's next to mine. This way."

Donn glanced at Doggett, who nodded in understanding and stayed behind as Donn and Fletcher hurried the opposite direction than Hunsaker had taken her group.

They got to Nipono's room quickly, and Fletcher managed to convince whoever was monitoring the hatch from the inside to open it. The room contained five people, two of whom were seated on the bed. The liaison officer, Wilkes, was one of them —Donn recognized the uniform. The other was a stout, blonde woman who glared back at the others. She had to be Bakoo.

The other three, Donn assumed, were the caretakers who had resisted the captain and thrown in with Donn and his group. Although all five were watching the hatch as it opened, it was not difficult to see what had been transpiring. Wilkes and Bakoo were being convinced of the error in their position, though it was unclear how forceful the three caretakers had been.

Fletcher spoke, entering the room with Donn immediately behind her. "Caretaker Cardenio is with us."

Donn was momentarily chilled to see the effect his name had. Those already in the room stiffened, and expectation hung in the air. He swiftly stepped from behind Fletcher and entered the now-crowded room, "Wilkes, Bakoo," he said curtly. He then turned to the nearest caretaker, Nipono. "You haven't hurt them, have you?"

Nipono looked surprised. "No."

Bakoo said loudly, "You've kept us here against our will! Forced us to sit here and be yelled at while—"

Donn turned to her and barked, "Quiet down." Bakoo hesitated, then opened her mouth to speak again. Donn added, "If that's the worst that happens to you, count yourselves lucky. For what you were going to go along with I should have you spaced." He turned back to Fletcher. "Don't let them leave unless you get assurances of their cooperation."

Fletcher nodded.

One of the other standing caretakers, Hertzog, said, "They could say anything now, just to get us to release them. How are we going to guarantee their compliance?"

Donn looked at the four standing caretakers. "I'll trust your judgement on that. When you are satisfied about their loyalty, let them go. But don't hurt them." He looked back at Wilkes and Bakoo. "We're going to need everyone once we make planetfall."

"And if they never cooperate?" Hertzog asked.

"Then keep them confined. Once the births start happening, they'll come around. Hopefully it'll be sooner than that. If necessary, we'll have a holding pen set up for any caretakers and crew who still refuse to see the obvious." He moved to the hatch, Fletcher stepping aside for him. "I'm going to check on my other team. They were going to find Patel, see if we could get him aid."

"We left Franks and Silver with him," Hertzog said. "Franks has some medical training. But Ippolito ran off somewhere. He's the one who hurt Patel."

Donn nodded. "We have him. He's in his quarters, sealed in. He's not going anywhere."

Hertzog looked unconvinced, but Donn turned to Fletcher. "Explain the situation to them, okay? I'm going to check on Hunsaker. We'll be in touch from K-Deck."

He exited the room, and when the hatch closed behind him and he was alone in the corridor, he took a deep breath. He felt the beginning of panic swell in him. He had to keep moving, keep making decisions — if he stopped, as he was doing now, he'd start to think about what was happening and wouldn't be able to act.

He checked his bearings and started for bay L-7. "Kearney, how's everything holding together?"

"Barely. Fighting all over the ship."

"Can you figure out which decks are secure?"

"You mean, which ones are ours and which ones aren't? That's really a hard call to make. But I'd say we control G and everything aft of it. Not counting L."

"L is ours," Donn said.

"Good."

"But we have at least one wounded here. Caretaker Patel took a blow to the head. We need to get control of the ship so we can tend to the injured."

Kearney said, her voice a little strained, "If it's not life-threatening, then that will have to wait. Securing the ship and the preborns is everything."

Donn didn't answer. He reached L-7 and entered. Hunsaker, Yune, and the two other caretakers, Franks and Silver, were in a small huddle around a figure lying on the deck. Hunsaker saw Donn enter and moved towards him.

"Patel is conscious, but Franks says he has a concussion at least, maybe a skull fracture."

"Is he in danger?"

Hunsaker looked behind her, then back at Donn. She lowered her voice. "Franks isn't sure. If he's got a skull fracture, that would be bad. She said something about an edema — brain swelling. But Patel is awake, though pretty out of it. Either way, Franks wants to get him looked at by the medical scanning equipment."

"Shit. That's what I was afraid of," Donn said. Despite his low tones, Yune heard the vulgarity and broke from the huddle to them.

"He needs to be looked at, Donn."

"Hunsaker told me. But we don't have control of the ship. The farther forward we go, I think the less control we have."

Yune said, "We could go aft instead. The colonial hold has medical equipment."

"Does it have a machine to scan someone's brain?" Hunsaker asked.

"I don't know. We could check with OSIRIS for an inventory," Yune said.

Donn nodded. "That's a good idea. And we will need the arms that are there. If the rest of the ship is fighting, we might have to go deck by deck forward. That means weapons, and that means the colonial hold."

"What about Patel in the meantime?" Hunsaker asked.

Donn approached Franks and Silver, who were still hovering over the injured Patel. "I'm sorry this happened. Alison brought me up to speed on his condition."

Franks said, "I don't know what more I can do here."

"I understand. We're going to check the colonial hold for medical equipment. You need a brain scanning machine?"

"It's called a p-pet scanner. Portable positron emission tomography. And yeah, if you can get me one, that would help enormously."

"Got it. We'll look for one. Otherwise, will you just keep him here?"

"Yeah. Nothing else to do. Nate and I will watch over him," Franks said, glancing at Caretaker Silver.

"Good. We'll be in touch with your whole deck soon." Donn nodded at both then gathered Hunsaker and Yune and headed out of the bay.

Chapter Nineteen

Donn, Alison and Paul made their way to one of the central shaft hatches and paused at the foot of the ladder. "Kearney, open up D-Deck central shaft hatch one, please."

"You're going in the shaft?"

"Yeah. Do you read any crew in there?"

"No. All clear. Unsealing hatch."

The red lights turned to green, and Donn cycled the hatch open then climbed upwards, feeling his weight decline with each rung. The inner hatch opened to his command, and he jumped into the central shaft with a grunt, careful to snag a cable on his way. Hunsaker and Yune followed, and the three made their way aft, passing M-Deck until they reached one of the personnel hatches that led to the hold.

The hold was easily as vast as two of the pressurized decks — Donn remembered from his preflight briefing that it made up over fifteen percent of the entire ship. It was unpressurized, as there was no reason for anyone to enter or even think about the cargo area until the ship had landed on Tau Ceti III and the colony was under construction. Donn knew, as everyone did, that the hold contained construction equipment, power plants, foodstuffs, atmospheric reducers, terraforming supplies, raw materials, fabrication machines, and everything the fledgling colony would need to make it a going concern.

That included weapons.

Donn had paid special attention to that almost a year ago, as his colonial role would include their possible use, but during the nine month journey, he had become so engrossed in his duties with the preborns that all thoughts of the hold and his eventual job within the colony had left him.

He floated before the personnel hatch and examined it. The indicator readout showed it as sealed and the area beyond it as vacuum.

"Now what?" Hunsaker asked, reading the hatch display.

"I don't know. Is there an airlock with environment suits inside, or do we need to pressurize the hold to get in there? Or are there chambers, and we can just pressurize the ones we need?" Yune said.

"Your guess is as good as mine," Donn said, then to the air, added, "Kearney, need some help again."

"Go ahead, Donn."

"We're at the colonial hold hatch, but can't get in. Can you pressurize the—"

"You're where?" Kearney's voice was frantic.

"At the hold. What's wrong?"

"Why the fuck are you there?"

"Calm down, K. We had the idea to see if we could get a medical scanner for Patel, and weapons to help retake the ship. While you're working on access to the hold, call up an inventory of the contents to see if either of—"

"Won't work," Kearney snapped. "Get out of there and get back to K-Deck. We need to regroup."

"Hang on, K. Just call up an inventory to see if there's a p-pet scanner. One of the L-Deck caretakers needs it to diagnose Patel properly."

"There's nothing like that in there," Kearney said quickly. "I need you back in K-Deck, now."

Donn scowled. "Just take a look in OSIRIS. And look for weapons, too."

"Donn, it's a waste of time. You can't get in there, and there's no medical—"

"Dammit, K, just check!"

There was a brief pause, and Kearney came back on the line. "No. No p-pet scanners. And no weapons."

"That's wrong. I know there are weapons. I was one of the guys supposed to have one on TC." A thought came to him. "And I'll bet that's where you got the pistol, didn't you?"

At his words, Hunsaker unzipped her thigh pouch and handed him the flechette gun. He pocketed it. Kearney continued on the com, "No … doesn't matter. You can't get in there anyway. It's not pressurized."

"I know that," Donn said, growing angry. "That's what I need you to do. Pressurize the hold so we can get in there."

"I can't."

"What do you mean, you can't? You've been making OSIRIS your slave for hours now. You're telling me you don't have that kind of access?"

"Yeah, that's what I'm saying. Now get back to K-Deck."

Donn looked at Yune and Hunsaker, who were staring back at him, uncomprehending. They hadn't heard what he had in her voice.

She was lying.

"All right, K. We'll get back to K-Deck. And you and I will talk."

Bay K-8 was buzzing with activity when he reentered with Hunasker and Yune. There were more scenes active on the monitors than there were caretakers to watch them, and Donn saw Kearney rushing from one station to another and speaking hurriedly with caretakers to maintain calm.

"Why don't you two take some calls," Donn said to Hunsaker and Yune, who had already begin moving to do so. Kearney looked over at Donn and caught his eye. He gestured with his head for her to follow him deeper into the bay.

Once out of earshot, he said, "What's going on, K?"

"No change. We have control of G through M, but the—"

"That's not what I mean. I'm talking about the bullshit with the hold."

Kearney looked puzzled. "I told you. I don't have access to that level in OSIRIS."

He studied her for a moment. She put on the affectation of bewilderment well, but he still saw through it. "That's not true. You can override the captain, you can control every hatch, the entire comm system, records, security cameras and so on. You absolutely can open the colonial hold."

"No, I really can't."

"Then where did you get this from?" Donn said, unzipping his thigh pouch and withdrawing the pistol.

"Not from the hold. Look, Donn, forget the hold. We can't get in there, so we'll have to take command of the ship without any of that stuff."

"Kearney, it's time for some answers. Where did you get the gun? How do you have such access to OSIRIS?"

"Don't you trust me?"

For a split second, Donn wasn't sure of his answer.

"Yeah, I trust you, which is why I'm so confused as to why you're lying to me, K."

Kearney looked hurt. "I'm not lying. I've always been honest with you, Donn. Even when it's hurt you — like with Collins. I've tried to protect you from some of the worst truths, but I've never lied."

"I know. So why are you doing it now?"

Kearney's expression changed from hurt to anger. "If you don't trust me, maybe you'd better put me under arrest."

"Stop that. I don't want to put you under arrest. I want you to tell me the truth."

"Will any of it matter, Donn? What can I tell you about the pistol that will change your mind on what's going on out there?" she said, sweeping her hands around her to encompass the forward decks.

"I don't know. I just know you're hiding things. I need to know, K."

"You and your damn mysteries," Kearney murmured. She sighed and said, "All right. I got the gun from Vincent."

"Vincent?"

"Yeah. You were right. I have been lying to you, Donn. I wanted to keep this from you, since I saw how you weren't able to handle me and Collins."

Donn knew what she was going to say before she said it.

Her voice was quiet and timorous. "I've been sleeping with Vincent. That's how I got this pistol. I took it from his quarters. And that's how I got access to OSIRIS. I ... convinced Vincent to give me his command codes. I used them to override his and lock him out."

Donn was surprised at his own lack of emotion. He merely nodded and said, "I see. Smart."

Kearney watched him for a moment. "You're not flying in to a rage. Or calling me a slut-whore or whatever. Don't you want to?"

"No. I want to get control of the ship and secure the preborns. What you did… what you do… that's your business. Always has been. It's who you are, Kearney. I can either accept it and accept you, or I can walk away from you. But I can't change you."

"Are you going to walk away?" She looked at him, her moist eyes looking up through her lashes.

As an answer, he pulled her close and kissed her.

When the kiss ended, she broke away and started sobbing. "I don't deserve you. You're good, and I … I…"

"Shut up. You're you. I'm me." He grunted and smiled. "It's not much of a philosophy, but it's all I got."

She chuckled amid her sobs. "Real deep, Cardenio."

"Why didn't you just tell me this when I first asked?"

Kearney's weak smile vanished. "We weren't in the best of places then, Donn. Knowing about Collins sent you into a rage. What would you have done knowing I was whoring myself out to Vincent?"

"Whoring?"

She smirked bitterly. "You always wondered how I got my contraband. Now you know."

Donn nodded, scowling. "You sent me to the meeting with him with the gun. You were ready to have me kill him. Your lover."

She corrected him firmly. "Not my lover. My connection. He had what I wanted, I had what he wanted. But that's why I couldn't go myself. I didn't love him, Donn. Just like I don't love Collins." She paused and looked up at him again. "I love you."

"I love you, too, Kearney."

She stood on her toes and kissed him quickly. "But right now, we have a lot still to do. Are you okay?"

"With all you told me? Yeah, I am. Maybe later I won't be, but you're right. We have other issues now."

Kearney's hopeful expression faltered. "Oh."

"What?"

"The part about 'maybe later you won't be okay.' I was hoping — fuck, this is so stupid."

Despite himself, Donn grinned at her sudden awkwardness. "What is it?"

"I know this couldn't be a worse time to bring this up, what with the mutiny you are organizing, and the rewriting of the entire mission, but ... I was hoping that once we make planetfall and get the colony going and everything calms down..." she swallowed.

"Just say it, K."

"I was hoping we'd ... get married."

Donn stared at her. "Married? Like, old-fashioned marriage?"

"Okay, it's stupid, never mind."

"No, it's not. I just hadn't thought of it."

"I know, never mind, forget it, okay?"

Donn looked at her, then said, "Yes."

"Yes what? Yes, you'll forget it?"

"Yes, I'll marry you."

Kearney's eyes widened. "You will?"

"Sure. But right now—" he was interrupted when she threw her arms around his neck and kissed him over and over.

"Kearney, okay, stop," he said amid the flurry of kisses, laughing a little. "We've got work to do."

She pulled back, her eyes wet. "Yeah. Yeah. Okay. Goddess. Calm down." She grinned at him. "Let's get back to the issue at hand."

Donn nodded and turned back towards the control room, Kearney following. He had only taken a few steps when he suddenly turned to take her hand and walk with her together, side by side.

What he saw was so momentary he wasn't sure it had even happened. When he turned to face her, she was wearing an expression that was naked, smug contempt. Almost as soon as he saw it, he face changed into her familiar mask of snide amusement.

"What?" she said, looking at him with affected surprise.

"I ... just wanted to hold your hand. So we could go back together," he stammered.

"You okay?"

"Yeah. Just thinking of all we have to do," he said, his voice unsteady.

The lie seemed to work, for Kearney nodded and said, "Sure. Let's get to it, then." She reached and took his hand.

Her hand was oddly cold.

As soon as they reentered the control suite, Forgisto began complaining. "We have a problem in D-Deck. I've been talking to Margulies, and she says—"

"You've been talking to Margulies?" Kearney said, immediately releasing Donn's hand and hurrying to Forgisto's seat. "What the fuck for?"

"I thought we were trying to find a nonviolent way out of this," Forgisto whined. "She is willing to have a discussion, but it has to include Donn. In person. She won't negotiate with me."

"What's she doing on D-Deck?" Donn asked.

"She must have been there when we locked out the hatchways," Kearney said. "Probably trying to go deck-to-deck to assure the caretakers there."

Donn couldn't help but stare at Kearney, wondering at what had happened a few moments ago in the preborn bay. She looked at him. "You're not going to talk — what's wrong?"

"Nothing. Gimme a sec. I need to see a man about a horse." He headed for the exit hatch.

He heard Forgisto say, "He needs to what?"

Kearney said, "Take a piss."

He exited K-8 and somehow made his way to his quarters. For the first time since launch, he was aware of the gentle spinning of the ship. Once inside his room, he paused before speaking to OSIRIS, hoping that he still had access to his own bay cameras. If not, and if Kearney was monitoring access attempts, she'd wonder what he was doing. But he had to be sure of what he had seen.

"OSIRIS, call up security camera records of bay K-8. Last twenty minutes."

He sighed in relief when Agnes said in her prim tones, "About time you talked to me, Donn. I've felt ignored. Security records being displayed on your monitor." His wall lit up with the scene from his bay. The time index showed the bay as it had been twenty minutes ago — empty save for the figures of the caretakers on the very edge of the screen working in the control suite. The security cameras were meant to monitor the preborns, not the control suite.

"Fast forward times four," he said, and the time index clock advanced rapidly. Presently, he saw himself and Kearney speed into the bay to talk. They were perfectly framed in the shot. He watched their discussion, then said, "Normal speed," once the scene was close to what he wanted.

He saw her fling her arms around him, kissing him as he accepted her proposal. When the embrace ended, and his image turned towards the control suite, his back to her, he said, "freeze image."

There she was. He had not imagined it. While his back had been turned, Kearney's expression of joy had disappeared instantly to be replaced with the hard, cold visage he had seen. He told Agnes to advance at one-tenth speed, and saw without doubt that when she thought he wasn't looking, Kearney was smugly and emotionlessly in control. He replayed the scene again.

She had manipulated him, and was crowing silently in victory for a moment. Her words of love, her proposal of marriage — it had been an act.

But to what end?

What else had been a lie? The entire conversation? She had said she had been sleeping with Vincent to obtain her contraband, her pistol, and the OSIRIS overrides. It fit perfectly — how else could she explain everything about her?

It fit perfectly.

That in itself was suspect.

The story about Vincent was too neat, too exact. It had settled into his mind smoothly, its edges matching with what he already knew of her, with the persona she had so carefully constructed. But it was too easy, a too-convenient fiction.

Why would she lie about sleeping with Vincent?

She was willing to present herself to him as a whore, a slut who slept around to get what she wanted. If that was a lie, a false front, what could it be concealing?

He stared at the replay, watching a Kearney he realized he didn't know. One he had never known.

Chapter Twenty

At the entrance to K-8, Donn stopped and set his face. Whatever game Kearney was playing, he had to delve one yard below her. He entered the bay and strode to the control suite. The other caretakers were still working the screens, receiving input from other decks. Donn said, "Okay. I'm going to meet with Margulies."

"You can't be serious," Kearney said. "You do that, and she'll have Simpatica's officers all over you in seconds. She doesn't want to talk — she wants to isolate you and get you alone so she can nab you."

Donn fought to keep anger out of his voice. "I agree that it's dangerous, and might be a trap. So we're going to agree to do this here, on K-Deck, where we have numbers."

"She said it has to be in the central shaft," Forgisto muttered.

"Well, tough titty. It's here or nowhere," Donn said. "If things get rough, I've got all of you to back me up, right?' Donn said, looking at Kearney.

She looked uncertain, "Sure, but—"

"No buts. We want to take control of the ship — this might be the way to do it."

"Margulies is one of them," Kearney said. "She's a representative of the captain and his murder—"

"I don't think she truly is," Donn said. "I think I can convince her. She's always been a practical person, and—"

"She's a cast-iron bitch, is what she is. She doesn't care about the preborns. She's willing to kill thousands of them!"

"That's not true, and I'm done arguing about this." He forced himself to turn away from Kearney, lest he betray himself with a look. "Have you still got her on the line, Mikelo?"

"Yes," he said, and spoke to OSIRIS to reconnect.

Margulies' face appeared on the screen. "Donn. We need to talk."

"I agree."

The two stared at one another for a moment, then Margulies said, "I'm prepared to meet with you as a go-between to the captain."

Donn smirked. "Still the liaison officer, Linna?"

She nodded. "Yes. That's the whole idea. If you'll come through the shaft to the command and control center, I'll—"

Donn snickered. "Not a chance. You come here. Alone."

Margulies shook her head. "Not acceptable. If you come to the trip-C I will guarantee your safety."

"Linna, don't take offense, but I don't believe you."

Margulies's nostrils flared. "You think I'm lying to you?"

"No. I just think that a guarantee from Vincent isn't worth anything. I think someone's lying to you." He sighed. "Come on, Linna. Use your head. Vincent and Simpatica have told you whatever they wanted you to hear to get me there. They have no intention of letting me back here if things don't go their way. You ought to know that." Donn resisted the impulse to look at Kearney as he spoke.

Margulies looked annoyed. "I only know what they've told me."

"You've been lied to. We all have," Donn said. He saw in his peripheral vision Forgisto pivot to look at him, and he could feel Kearney's gaze on him.

Margulies scowled. "What do you mean?"

"The hibernators. You know the reports. How many have you checked?"

"Over a thousand so far. All dead," she said.

"Not just dead … they've been dead since the beginning of the voyage. And OSIRIS has been lying to us about their status."

Margulies said, "How do you know that?"

"I spoke with Delano. He did an autopsy on one. Something's going on here, Linna, and you and I are just pawns in the game. We need to figure it out."

Margulies hesitated. Donn could see in her face the doubts she must have had for days. He pressed his point.

"Linna, we've always been at each other's throats. But this is bigger than both of us. I gotta tell you … I respect you. Even when you were slapping me down and sending me to the Freezer, I respected you."

"That's why you resisted my authority every Goddess damn chance you could?"

"I resist authority when it doesn't make sense, Linna. It wasn't personal. We discovered the dead sleepers together. We can work together for the success of the mission. I know in your heart you want what's best for the preborns. We just disagree on what that is."

"Then come to trip-C and let's talk it out," Margulies said.

Donn shook his head. "I didn't say I trusted Vincent or Simpatica."

Forgisto said, "Why not do this over communications? Like you are now?"

Donn waved the comment away, but Margulies responded to it.

"We want this to be face-to-face. Not over the communications net. A net you seem to have control over."

Donn tried not to look smug. "That's true. We have control of OSIRIS. I'm sure you've had poor Norman working his ass off trying to override us. I'll bet he's told you it's impossible, so now you're calling for a meeting."

Margulies' lips tightened. "That's a lot of it, but not all of it. We have reports of fighting in many of the decks. We can't tell what's happening, but some crew have been trying to restore order. And failing. People are getting hurt, Donn."

Kearney chimed in. "How have you been getting reports?"

Margulies did not look at her, but answered. "Yelling through bulkheads. We have an idea what's going on. It needs to stop."

Donn leaned in close to the camera. "I agree, but what's even more important than that is we abandon once and for all the plan to murder the preborns. If that's not something you're prepared to discuss, then I'm sorry, Linna, but the mutiny will continue. And we will win."

Margulies shifted in her seat. "So you do understand what this means. I wondered. I guess I should have seen something like this coming. You always were insubordinate."

Donn pushed back away from the camera, his hands slapping the console. "Damn it, it's not about me and my rebellious streak. This is about the safety and well-being of hundreds of thousands of children! You want to cast this as me versus you, then you don't understand what we're doing. Shit, Linna, how can you be on the side of death?"

Margulies looked hurt momentarily. "I'm not. I'm trying to save as many preborns as I can."

"You can't say that when you're willing to murder tens of thousands of them."

Margulies glared at him for a long moment. Donn met her gaze. When she finally spoke, her voice was raspy. "This is pointless. We've been over this. We get nowhere."

Donn glanced at Kearney, who looked back impassively. He couldn't afford to let this opportunity slip by — although his position seemed strong, the mystery of Kearney's behavior and true loyalty made that strength a fiction. And there was the matter of Patel, and perhaps other caretakers who were hurt and in need of medical help. He could hardly claim to be championing the cause of life for all when he refused to end a conflict that put lives in danger.

"Not like this, we don't. You're right. We need to meet. But is has to be here. On K-Deck."

"I'm pretty sure Vincent and his staff won't like that. For the same reason you don't like coming to trip-C."

Donn shrugged. "True, but those are my terms. I think you need this meeting more than we do, so I'm betting he will agree to it."

"Can you release the communications lockout so I can talk to him, tell him your proposal?"

"Why didn't he just talk to me himself?"

Margulies grunted. "I told him I would be able to get through to you better."

Donn nodded. "I see. I appreciate that, Linna. I honestly do." He peered at her. "You don't want to kill the preborns, do you?"

"Jezeus, of course not!"

"Good. That's a start, Linna. I can work with that. We'll release the comm lockout for you. For half an hour. And only from that outlet to trip-C."

"Thanks." Margulies added, "You know he's going to try and use that access to his advantage, right? Try and get deeper into OSIRIS with it."

Donn looked at Kearney, who merely shook her head, smirking. He turned back to the screen.

"I'll bet he'll try. Don't waste the half hour. Let me know what you decide. We'll be waiting."

He shut off the connection and turned to the others. "Okay. What do we all think?"

Forgisto said, "I think talking is a good step. We need to make sure no one gets hurt, caretakers, crew, preborns, so we can have a successful mission and..." he continued, rambling meaningless jargon, until Kearney interrupted smoothly.

"I'm not against the idea of meeting with them. Like you said, here. Where we are in a position of strength."

"Right." Donn called to the other caretakers in the bay. "Everyone, tell whomever you're talking with to stand by. I need you to listen to what's about to happen, and give your opinions."

He relayed the situation to the caretakers, then listened to their thoughts. He had to cut Forgisto off several times, or the man would have eaten up the entire half-hour with his endless and worthless strings of words.

As the time was nearing its end, Donn said, "All right. We're going to meet here, in K-eight. We'll be on this side," he indicated the long section of the bay where the preborns were, "and they'll be there, near the hatch."

"Blocking the exit?" Basque asked.

"We have control of OSIRIS," Kearney said. "We can open the hatch anytime we want."

"But whomever they bring will be physically in the way," Basque said.

Donn said, "There's no way we can maneuver them deeper into the bay while we wheel around and take the entrance. Besides, there will be eleven of us here. With multitools and one pistol. I won't let them bring more than that." He looked at all of them. "I know none of you signed up for what's about to happen. I'm sorry it has come to this. You wanted to take care of preborns and help them grow into children, and create a colony to help all of humanity. And now I'm asking you to be prepared for violence."

He scanned the room, seeing the uneasy faces, the nervous postures. Yune was hefting his multitool with obvious discomfort. Vern had refused even to consider using a weapon and had said he would not engage in violence no matter what. Hunsaker stood with her legs apart, stolid and unmoving. Forgisto's face was pinched in timid disapproval. For a moment, Donn saw the faces of the LEO force again, all standing in their flight uniforms on the tarmac of Kennedy Space Center, ready to launch.

He shook off the vision. This wasn't the same. He was going to negotiate, not engage in battle. If he did his job right, there would be no fighting — in fact, the fighting would end, and everyone would be safe.

His eyes settled on Kearney. She was searching his face, and he tried to keep his expression blank. He'd listened carefully to her comments on the upcoming meeting, but she had made few. She'd been the one to suggest they place themselves closer to the swimmer pods, and everyone had agreed to that. Donn didn't know why she had wanted that, but he couldn't think of a reason against it. Otherwise, she had seemed eager for the meeting, which, more than anything else, frightened Donn.

Agnes said suddenly, "Donn, I have Linna Margulies calling again."

Donn moved to the seat in front of the monitor, the rest of the caretakers following him. They took up a position behind him without his direction. A ghost of a smile played on his lips at that gesture, and he opened communications with Margulies.

"Hello, Linna. What's the answer?"

Margulies looked haggard, as if she had aged a decade in the last half hour. "He agreed to meet with you there, but he's got his own conditions. Are you ready to hear them?"

"Go ahead."

"Okay," Linna glanced down, as if consulting notes, and said, "First, he wants to bring me, himself, Simpatica and her three officers, and the rest of his command staff. So that's Warren, Freeman, and Uplander."

"Nine people," Donn said. "That's a big group, Linna. Why does he need Simpatica and her guards?"

"It's what he wants," Linna said, her tone betraying her disagreement with the request. "I'm just telling you. And you're going to need to release the hatch lockouts so everyone can get to K-Deck."

"We'll release the hatches you need. And we'll be watching on cameras, so if he tries anything, we will know."

Margulies nodded. "He won't try anything."

"All right. Go on."

"He also wants you to release control of OSIRIS to him now."

"Not going to happen," Donn said curtly.

"Yeah, I didn't think so," Linna said, glancing back down to her notes. "And he wants you to go on comms to call for an immediate cessation of hostilities while the conference is taking place."

Donn considered that. "That may be possible. Is that all?"

"Well, he said he wants assurances that you won't hurt him or his people, that you'll agree to end the mutiny in exchange for the discussion, that you will surrender yourself and anyone involved in the planning of the uprising for disciplinary action."

Donn snorted and grinned at Linna. "You told him there was no way I'd agree to all that, right?"

"More or less."

"Well, as to the assurance that we won't hurt him or his people, I can give that as long as he is willing to do the same. So I take it then his people won't be armed?"

Now Margulies snorted. "Oh, they will, I'm sure. Simpatica and her guys will have shockers. But he assures you no one will be hurt."

Donn and Linna looked at each other, both aware of the meaninglessness of that promise.

"So, what's your response, Donn?"

"We will agree to meet here in K-eight. We'll all be here, all eleven of us. But the whole point of this is to do away with the plan to murder the preborns. If that's not something he's prepared to agree to, then we might as well call it off now."

Margulies nodded slowly. "I've been instructed to tell you that he will listen to your plan."

"You don't sound optimistic, Linna."

"I'm not. I don't see how you're going to convince him. Or me."

"We'll see."

"And the announcement to end hostilities?"

Donn nodded. "I will do that right now. As a show of good faith that I am willing to talk. Please make sure he understands that just as I can tell caretakers to stop fighting, I can also tell them to take the ship by force if needed."

"You should tell him that yourself. I'll see you down in K-Deck, Donn."

When the monitor went black, Donn turned to the group. Many of them started to speak anxiously about the large contingent Donn had agreed to allow into the bay. He stood from the chair and held up his hands to stem the fear.

"Listen, listen!" Kearney shouted, and the caretakers stopped. "Don't you see? This is perfect. We're going to have the entire command staff here, along with all the Provost officers!"

"That's the whole problem, Kearney," Yune said, the multitool in his hands shaking.

"No, it's just what we want. If they're here, that means they're not in the rest of the ship! We can take the ship easily."

"No," Donn said.

Kearney looked at him. "No? Donn, it's the perfect opportunity. While we're—"

"Not while we're negotiating. That undermines the whole process."

Kearney sighed. "Donn, I know you want to do this right, or with honor, or whatever. Normally, I'd be all in favor of that. But the lives of hundreds of thousands of preborns are at stake here. If it's a matter of lying to Vincent, sneaking around, being dishonorable — or letting those preborns be murdered, then the choice is obvious."

"That's not the choice. If we take the ship like that, we'll be fighting forever. The nine people down here, the rest of the crew, and probably a lot of caretakers will be against us for that. We need to be united when we get to Tau Ceti, or what little chance we have of success will vanish."

"We'll make it work, Donn, but if we give up this chance—"

"No, K. That's not an option. If talks break down, and things get out of hand, then we can seal the bay and deal with it. But I'm not going to set that plan in motion now."

"You've got to! It's the best—"

"No!" Donn shouted at her, and she fell silent. "Now set me up on intercraft. I'm going to make the announcement to stop fighting while the talks are going on."

"That's what they want, since they're bringing their force down here," Kearney murmured. She nevertheless complied with Donn's order, then stepped away. She looked at him coldly. "Intercraft enabled, Caretaker Cardenio."

He addressed the camera. "Caretakers and crew, this is Donn Cardenio. I am meeting with the command staff shortly to work out an agreement to end hostilities and plan the rest of the mission. A plan that will ensure the safety and health of all aboard. During these negotiations, I ask all of you who are loyal to the children, and all others, to stop your fighting. We need to be a unified ship to be a unified colony. Stop the fighting, and we will begin the process of planning for our future." He stopped, then turned to Kearney to ask her to end the transmission.

She was gone.

"OSIRIS, cease transmission, please," he said, and was mildly surprised to hear her acknowledge the order and cut the line.

"Where did she go?" Donn asked Hunsaker.

"Kearney? She said she was going to her parlor for a second. Bathroom."

Donn scowled. Everything she did was suspect, now.

"Is something wrong?" Hunsaker asked.

"What? No. That just made me think of it." He stood up and said. "Anyone who needs anything personal, better do it now. When Kearney comes back, she'll unlock the hatches to let Vincent's group in here, and we'll start."

Some of the caretakers shuffled out of the bay, heading to their quarters. Donn himself headed to Kearney's room.

When he got there, he stood outside the hatch, out of range of the camera. What was he going to say to her? That he knew she was lying, but he didn't know why or how deep the lie went? That would only serve to alert her that he was on to her.

No. In this game she was playing, she had more skill. He couldn't afford to give up what little advantage he had. He knew she was not what she appeared to be, and he would have to make the best of that.

He stared at the hatch for a moment, thinking of what he had lost, then turned and walked back to K-8.

Chapter Twenty-One

Vincent led his deputation into K-8, flanked by his command staff and Simpatica's guards. Margulies hung back, as if unwilling to attach herself too closely to him and his ideas.

Donn stood in the bay, near rack one, with the rest of the K-Deck caretakers arrayed behind him. He nodded at Vincent. "Captain."

"Donn," Vincent replied. "We've got to stop this fighting and restore order. We're less than a month away from planetfall, and only nineteen days away from deactivating the Alcubierre drive. We need to be a unified, peaceful ship when those times come."

"I agree, Captain. But there's more to it than that. We need to all make it safely to TC-Three. That includes every one of the preborns."

Vincent clenched his fists for a moment. "That's not the best plan for the survival of the highest number of fetuses. There is simply no way we will be able to care for almost a quarter-million infants without awakened hibernators."

"What is the current count on them?" Donn asked.

Freeman spoke up. "We've managed to get through about twelve hundred, in a random sampling. All dead."

"So we need to plan for the worst," Vincent said. "I'm forced to conclude that the chances are all, or almost all, of the hibernators are dead." He looked away from Donn and appealed to everyone in the bay. "That means it's down to fewer than two hundred of us to care for the infants and build a colony. It can't be done, and thinking we can save all of them will doom more than necessary to a painful death." He returned his attention to Donn. "You are the one who is killing the preborns. You're just doing it by leaving the decision to the future."

"I don't know what the future holds," Donn said. "I don't know if it's possible to care for all of them or not. No one knows that. I just know I signed on to care for the preborns and bring them alive to TC-Three, and that's what I'm going to do."

"And whatever happens to them there is not your concern?" Vincent said.

"Of course it is. I'm a caretaker. I always will be. I'll look after them for as long as they need it."

"You'll look after twelve hundred children? Or more?"

"I'm caring for over seventeen hundred now. We all are," Donn said, half-turning to indicate the rest of the caretakers.

"They're in pseudowombs being looked over by OSIRIS! A monkey could do your job."

Donn heard the effect that had on his group. He did not need to look behind him to see their faces — the low susurration of anger and indignation told him all he needed to know. "That may be, but I'm also doing your job, Captain."

Vincent glared at him, but his eyes darted to the caretakers behind Donn. Simpatica motioned to her officers, who stood ready, hands on the battery ends of their shockers.

Donn continued. "You asked me to talk to the ship, tell my people to stop fighting. I did that, and it worked. Right now, everyone's waiting to hear from me. I could replay shipwide what you just said in here, and we'll see what happens."

He let his words sink in, then said more gently, "Captain, we can go around and around in ideology until the end of time, but the facts are these. I can take control of the ship with a word. All the shockers you can dig up won't be enough to stop the caretakers and Freezer techs. They won't agree to killing the preborns, and you know it."

"More have come around than you think, Cardenio," Vincent growled. "We've got at least seventy caretakers who see what needs to be done, and we haven't even spoken to all of them yet thanks to your communications blackout."

"Don't bother lying, Captain. We've been getting regular reports from all decks. There are only a handful of people with you, and those ones I'll bet don't know the whole story.

When the caretakers rise up and refuse to murder the babies, no one will be left to carry out your plan."

"Damn it, it's not my plan! It's the only plan that has a chance for success! I'm not a baby murderer!"

Donn softened his voice even more. "I know, Captain." Now it was Donn's turn to appeal to the entire bay. "I don't think any of you are," he said, sweeping his eyes across Vincent's group. He lingered for a moment on Margulies, who continued to stand separate. Donn turned back to Vincent. "It's very simple, then. Just accept what's already happened."

"And what's that?"

"You've lost. Your ship is now ours." Donn winced. He knew it was the wrong thing to say as soon as he said it.

Vincent's face reddened in florid rage. "I am still captain of this ship, damn you! Simpatica! Take him!"

Provost Simpatica hesitated a moment. Donn could see the events unfolding with clear slowness. Margulies started forward, her face twisted in anguish, reaching out towards Simpatica to stop her or at least distract her. The provost recovered from her surprise and gestured with her head to her three officers. They started toward Donn, each one unlimbering their shocker.

Donn reached into his already unzipped thigh pouch and brought out the flechette pistol. He had barely pointed it at the closest of Simpatica's guards, when Vincent's chest burst in a pink mist at the same time the loud report of another gun sounded behind Donn.

He turned to see Kearney swiveling her own flechette pistol towards Freeman and firing. Freeman went down, a geyser of blood issuing from her neck.

"Kearney!" Donn shouted. She did not look at him but aimed and fired again, this time hitting Uplander in the abdomen.

The caretakers behind Donn scattered, some dropping their multitools and running deeper into the bay, away from the carnage. Simpatica's three officers fled as well, heading to the exit hatch. Simpatica herself stared transfixed at the bloody scene, until a round from Kearney's gun exploded her stomach.

Donn swiveled the barrel of his gun towards Kearney. "Kearney, stop! Stop!" The gun trembled in his hand as he leveled it at Kearney.

In his peripheral vision, amid the chaos of running caretakers and crew, he spotted Margulies. She scooped up Uplander's fallen shocker and charged at Kearney. She was at least fifteen meters away: she had no chance of reaching the caretaker before being cut down by her pistol. But she came on regardless.

Donn saw the moment clearly, as if it were a painting. Kearney, her face a grim rictus, taking aim at Margulies; Linna, shocker held before her like a foil, sprinting forward, hunched over but determined; several bodies on the deck-plates, bleeding; and in the background an unfocused blur of people running, trying to cycle open the exit hatch, or retreating deeper into the bay and diving behind pseudowomb pods.

It was impossible, but he thought he could see Kearney's finger tense on the trigger just prior to firing. At that moment, he didn't see the mysterious woman who claimed to love him, nor a shipmate, nor even someone necessary to bring up the children on Tau Ceti III.

He saw a killer. And he had to end this.

He fired.

Perhaps some part of him still felt for her, or perhaps his aversion to killing was stronger than he realized. The dart did not hit her head; it tore through her hip just as she fired her own pistol, hitting Margulies in the left shoulder, turning her and eliciting a yelp of pain.

Kearney crumpled to the deck, dropping the gun and clutching at her bleeding side. Incredibly, Margulies kept coming, extending the shocker and jabbing Kearney.

Kearney's body convulsed as the electricity coursed through her. Margulies dropped the shocker and groaned, reaching with her right arm to her left shoulder. Donn slid the flechette pistol into his thigh pouch and hurried to Kearney.

"Get the gun," Margulies croaked. Donn ignored that and knelt beside Kearney.

"It's over, it's over," he said to her. She looked around the bay with squinting eyes, as if trying to remember where she was. Her face was twisted into a grimace, and bright red blood pumped out of her shattered hip, darkening as it hit the deck and saturated her clothes.

"Donn?" she said.

"Yeah, I'm here." He hesitated only a fraction of a second, then pressed both hands against the gory wound. Kearney sucked in air at that but remained still.

"I had to. Had to," she wheezed.

"I know," was all he could think to say. He glanced at Margulies. She was leaning against the pod rack and breathing heavily. "Anyone else armed?" she asked, her jaw tight.

Donn shook his head. "Get medical down here."

Margulies nodded, then shook her head. "Can't. Comm lockout."

Donn looked down at Kearney. Her pale skin was now almost white, ghostly. "Kearney, we need to get you to medical. We need to release the comm lockout to do that."

"What?" Kearney searched his face, confused.

"Tell me how to get into OSIRIS," Donn said. Her blood was flowing freely out of the mess of flesh that was her abdomen. His hands were awash in her fluids.

Kearney's eyes widened at his words. "No ... no ... I can't. Mission."

Donn reached out and held her face between his hands, smearing her temples with red. "Kearney, listen. It's over. We've won," he said. "The children are all safe. You've done your job."

"Delivered?" she said, still-wide eyed.

"Yes," Donn said. "And now it's time to turn over OSIRIS to me."

"Yes ... okay. Am I dying?"

Donn swallowed at that. She had asked him the question without fear, as if she were simply confirming something she already knew. He looked at her for a long moment, and took his hands from her face and pressed them again, uselessly, into the wound.

Margulies managed to push herself off the pod and stumbled towards Freeman's body, and knelt down next to her.

Donn said to Kearney, "Not if we can get you to medical."

"I had to," Kearney said again, closing her eyes. "No choice."

"It's all right, K. Just give me OSIRIS."

Kearney continued without acknowledging him. "Some had to die to save others. Sometimes … murder is the only way."

Donn took his hands away from her body. The blood was now oozing out. He stroked her hair. "I understand. I need you to give me access to OSIRIS, Kearney."

Kearney suddenly opened her eyes and gasped. "Donn … it hurts."

"I know. We'll take care of you. I need OSIRIS."

"Not yet … not yet. When we get out of drive."

"No, K. I need it now. To unlock the hatches and the comm system and get medical help."

"OSIRIS…" Kearney said. It was half question, half request.

"Yes, Caretaker Kearney?" OSIRIS's voice was calm amid the horror.

"Have we reached Tau Ceti Three?"

"No. We are still in Alcubierre drive."

"When … when we come out of drive … execute Schedule D."

"Confirmation code?"

"Mount Moriah," Kearney whispered.

"Code accepted. Name recipient or recipients."

"Caretaker Donn Cardenio," Kearney said, looking up at Donn, her expression almost what it had been months ago: admiration and affection.

"Kearney, we can't wait for—" Donn said.

"Accepted. Estimated time for Schedule D execution, eighteen days, sixteen hours, nine minutes."

"We need it now, K."

"No, Donn. Wait. Promise … promise you'll get the preborns there. You have to get them there."

"We will, Kearney. All of us. You'll be there, too."

"No ... I won't, Donn." She closed her eyes again and fell silent.

"Kearney ... wake up. Come on." Donn reached for her neck and felt for a pulse; it was faint, and she had stopped bleeding

He felt her pulse fade until it was no more.

He stood up from the deck, and slowly turned as if in a trance towards Margulies. She was kneeling next to Freeman's unmoving body, but was no longer examining it. She had one hand on the deck and had vomited mildly.

Donn moved to her and steadied her. "How bad?"

"Freeman's dead. Haven't checked on the others. Fuck, this hurts," she growled.

"Okay. Stay here. Sit down. I'll get help."

Margulies nodded and gingerly sat on the deck, avoiding her vomit.

Donn made short work of checking on Simpatica, Vincent, and Uplander. All three were dead. He stood from Uplander's body and looked into the bay. He saw Hunsaker coming back from the pods, some of the other caretakers peering out from cover.

"Come out," he shouted. "It's over. We need help."

He directed them efficiently, portioning off a part of his mind to deal with grief later. He had done that years ago after the Starfish and he did it again now. Dead bodies were placed out of sight for the time being, to lay side by side. Yune and Basque went into their quarters and retrieved bed linens to cover the corpses. Forgisto stood in the middle of the bay, unmoving, unhelpful. Vern tended to Margulies, offering little medical help but speaking to her in low, comforting tones.

Hunsaker approached Donn during all this, and said delicately, "I know this will sound cold, Donn, but we need to get back on the communications network and check the ship."

Donn said, "You're right. I'm not sure ... shit, I'm not sure what kind of access I have. It's..." he looked around, searching for something he himself couldn't identify.

Hunsaker looked with him, mistaking his search for an assessment. "I know. It's horrible. This isn't how we wanted this. I didn't even know Mary Ellen had a gun."

"Neither did I," Donn said. "All right. You're right. Check status." He walked unsteadily towards the control suite of the bay, Hunsaker close at his side, her hand gently guiding his elbow.

He sat down heavily in the control chair. "OSIRIS, please…" he stopped, unsure what to say.

Hunsaker said quietly, "Cameras?"

"Yes … can you give me the camera feeds for trip-C?"

"You're not authorized for that, Donn," OSIRIS said.

"Mount…" Donn thought, trying to remember. "Mount Moriah," he tried.

"That code is keyed to Caretaker Kearney only."

"She's dead," Donn said simply.

"I'm sorry to hear that," OSIRIS responded coldly, "But the code is still keyed to her alone."

"Damn it, we need camera access."

"That is restricted to command crew only."

"Kearney wasn't command crew. She had access," Donn said.

"I'm not allowed to comment on that."

"The command crew is also all dead."

"Understood," OSIRIS said, then fell silent.

"What contingency plan do you have if all the command crew are dead? And Kearney's dead, too?"

"I'm able to continue monitoring the pseudowomb pods, life support systems, engineering—"

"Engineering, yeah, let's look at that. Can you transfer command to one of the engineers?"

"No, I can't."

"Then what fucking good are you?" Donn shouted.

"I'm able to continue monitoring the—"

Donn interrupted. "Just … okay, what about hatch control? Can you give me that?"

"No. You're not authori—"

"How are we supposed to do anything with all the hatches closed?"

"They're not all closed. Some hatches are released."

"What? When did this happen?"

"Thirty-four minutes ago. I was given an order to unseal specific shipwide hatches."

Hunsaker said, "We needed to unlock them to let Vincent and his group get here."

Donn nodded. "That's good. What about the communications system? Is it locked or not?"

"Intercraft communications are enabled. Do you want to broadcast?"

"No, not now. Keep it unlocked, though." Donn turned to Hunsaker. "We've got to find out who's hurt, get medical to them. And find out who on board has any kind of medical training besides the surgeon."

Hunsaker nodded. "Yeah. Set up triage places on each deck?"

"Good idea. OSIRIS, show me a schematic of which hatches are open and which are locked." Donn studied the display. "Looks like we can reach each deck, one way or another. Can you take care of the triage?" he said, rising from the chair.

Hunsaker said, "Sure, Donn. It's gonna be okay, right?"

"We'll have to make it so, Alison."

She sat in the chair and took a breath. "What should I tell the ship?"

"Tell them the truth."

"Okay." Hunsaker asked OSIRIS for intercraft, and Donn left the control suite to go back into the bay.

He approached Vern and Margulies. Vern was still soothing her and had laid her on the deck, a bloodstained pillow under her head and bed linens over her body. He looked up at Donn and said gently, "I was thinking about keeping her out of shock."

"Good thinking. We should elevate her legs, too."

Vern got up from his kneeling position and said, "I'll look for something to do that." He moved off.

Donn knelt next to Margulies and tried to smile. "How're you doing?"

"Hurts like a motherfucker."

"Yeah."

"What's ship status?"

"We're checking now. Organizing medical. Someone'll be here quickly."

"Good."

Donn reached out to pat her good shoulder. "I'm sorry, Linna."

"Not your fault. You tried."

"I had no idea she was armed, or would—"

"Is she dead?"

"Yes."

To his surprise, Margulies looked pained. "Dammit. I'm sorry. I shouldn't have shocked her."

"That's not what killed her. I did," he said.

"You had to. She was killing us all."

Donn nodded, not trusting himself to speak.

Margulies shifted a little, grimacing. "We need a memorial. Assuming we all make it out of this alive."

Chapter Twenty-Two

Donn sat at the control suite again, trying to assemble his thoughts. His mind was sluggish and stubborn, clinging to images and memories he did not want to see nor remember. The awful scene of a few scant minutes ago blended with his fight with Thom, and his memory skipped across the months and years like a stone on a pond. Kearney, lying in a pool of her blood; Thom hitting the deck with a sickening crack; his wingman's LEO fighter breaking up and exploding, flaming pieces of debris falling in a long, graceful arc back to Earth.

Donn himself holding one of the slaughtered babies, moist and warm, in his arms.

Skip. Skip. Skip.

He shook his head forcefully, as if the physical action would pry control of his mind from whatever held it in thrall and allow him to live in the moment and solve its problems.

Hunsaker hovering behind him said, "Are you okay?"

Donn gave a shrug.

"You should sleep. How long have you been up?"

"I have no idea. But I need to talk to everyone. Then we gotta organize that medical triage."

"I can do the triage. You should grab some sleep now, when you can."

"After this. Agnes, set me up for intercraft broadcast. Go."

Agnes said, "Very well, Donn. Broadcasting now."

Donn looked into the camera and sat up a bit straighter. "Shipmates, this is Caretaker Cardenio. I have an important announcement. Please stop what you're doing and listen.

"I told you about an hour ago that I would be meeting with Captain Vincent and his staff to come to an agreement. I also asked you all to stop fighting so we could come together in peace for a solution to our problems."

Donn felt his attention sagging. He summoned up what little reserves he had and spoke more forcefully.

"I am very sorry to say that the negotiations ended in bloodshed. Captain Vincent is dead, along with command staff members Freeman, Uplander, and Provost Simpatica. Caretaker Kearney is also dead." Donn paused a moment to think away some of the grief.

Hunsaker shifted her weight behind him but did not speak.

"I urge all of you to remain calm. There is no more reason to fight. Any of you who felt the captain's plan to reduce the number of preborns was correct should know that plan will not be put into effect. I also want those of you who did not support that plan — those of you who were with me and the rest of K-Deck — to welcome those caretakers and crew who had a different idea."

He imagined the faces of caretakers and crew, some angry, some desperate, some bloody, all listening and waiting for his words. He saw them not only as fellow travelers, but as future parents. "We're all brothers and sisters here. And we all need to be fathers and mothers pretty soon. There's no sense in fighting any more. The children, each and every one of them, will be birthed in a few weeks, and we need to prepare a new mission profile to accomplish our goals."

Donn paused, his mind refusing to recall what came next.

Hunsaker leaned towards him, still out of camera range, and murmured, "Medical."

Donn spoke into the camera. "I know there are some injured among you. We are setting up a medical triage through K-Deck to deploy our medical resources to best effect. Caretaker Hunsaker will be the contact person for that. When I finish here, please send your requests for aid to her."

Hunsaker murmured, "And medical personnel."

Donn nodded and added, "Also, you'll be sending her the names of anyone on your deck who has medical knowledge or training. She will explain more in a moment."

He took a breath, feeling fatigue steal his focus. He struggled through. "When we have made sure everyone's been treated medically, we can begin the process of a new mission profile. I'll let you know the details on how we're going to decide that later." He hesitated again, trying to think of an inspirational closing.

Nothing came. What could be said? Perhaps an orator would have been able to find the words to spur everyone to action, to inspire confidence and hope, but the truth was, Donn himself didn't know what the next step was, and at that moment, he had little hope.

"Here's Caretaker Hunsaker," he said, getting up from the chair and relinquishing it to her.

—— «» ——

Despite his tiredness, sleep did not come easily. He knew that the K-Deck caretakers were capable and would organize the medical triage as best they could, but when he closed his eyes, his mind recalled images he could not ignore.

He thought of Earth. He'd never been sentimental about it: when other LEO pilots had gasped upon seeing the planet from orbit for the first time, he had merely verified his altitude and told his squadron to tighten their formation. He knew his initial decision to leave was more about running away than it was about running toward, but in the months aboard *Chiron* he'd come to love the swimmers under his care. Earth had faded in his mind.

Now, though, he saw sunsets off the Florida Keys, felt the stinging heat and humidity of the American South, heard the calls of herons and robins.

He drifted to sleep, and dreamt of children. Thousands of children, arms joined in a huge ring, singing and dancing with leprechauns and dragons, himself among them, laughing. Kearney was next to him, holding his hand and smiling up at him. He smiled back, but even in his dream-world he knew she couldn't be there. The realization came suddenly, and she started bleeding from her mouth, collapsing onto the verdant lawn and staining it with wine-colored blood. A grotesque bull, white and surreal, charged the children, goring them, sending them to the grass, trampling them underfoot. The singing and laughing turned into screaming. The erstwhile mythical creatures turned savage. Dragons grew fangs, centaurs snorted and kicked, elves drew wicked swords.

The scene devolved into a chaotic mess, children and now adults whom Donn impossibly knew were mothers and fathers, dying, being dismembered, wailing to the unhearing sky. A bare light bulb dangled in the air, the all-seeing eye stared unblinking at the scene, and all color left the tableau.

Just before he awoke in shock, he recognized the scene. *Guernica.*

———— «» ————

The next four days were a blur.

Hunsaker had organized the medical triage well, creating a database of medically trained staff from reports alone (OSIRIS would not allow access to the personnel manifest that listed the cross section of skills possessed by all aboard) and assigning people to care for the injured. There had been half a dozen serious cases, including Margulies and Patel, but aside from those who had been killed in the massacre in K-8, no one else had died.

Donn had spent the time delegating tasks mainly to K-Deck caretakers, though Fletcher and some others had come into his circle of trusted allies.

On the fifth day after the massacre, two weeks before the ship was scheduled to come out off Alcubierre drive, Donn sat with Margulies in his room.

"When are you going to be able to get rid of that?" Donn said, gesturing with his chin to her sling.

"Not sure. Doc thinks this might never really heal right. Broke some bones in there, or something. I'll live. Good thing I'm right-handed."

"Yeah." He leaned back in his chair, balancing it on the back legs. He regarded the liaison officer. "So I think we need to convene some kind of panel or something to design a new mission."

"We do," Margulies nodded. "You have the people you want in mind?"

"Sort of. Hunsaker, of course."

"She's been good, running the triage and logistics."

"Yeah. Fletcher, from L-Deck."

Margulies nodded again.

"You."

Margulies snorted. "Me? Why'd you want me? I was against you, remember?"

"I know that." He leaned forward, setting the chair on all four legs. "You were just doing what you thought was best for the colony."

"That's what I've been saying. That's what the captain—" she stopped suddenly.

"I don't know about that, but I know you."

"You do, huh?"

"I think so. You said to me once that you sometimes envied us. Caretakers."

"So?"

"So now, in a few weeks, you'll be just like us."

"We all will."

Donn shrugged. "I'm trying to pay you a compliment, Linna. And I want you on the new mission profile panel. Are you gonna accept or not?"

"Yes. You need someone who thinks of practical matters."

Donn scowled. "You're saying I'm not practical?"

"I'm saying you have an idealistic streak. It gets in the way."

Donn stared at her, then said firmly, "All the preborns are being born, Linna."

"I know. You refuse to see reason on that."

"Don't start this again. We're—"

"I'm not starting anything," Margulies said, gesturing with her right hand. "I realize you won't budge."

"Don't pretend you're not relieved. You didn't want to carry that out."

Margulies sighed. "Of course I didn't. But I still think it is the best plan."

"You wouldn't have been able to do it."

Margulies sat still. Her gaze drifted down to her feet. "I honestly don't know, Donn."

"OSIRIS wouldn't have let you do it by remote. You would have had to go pod to pod, like Thom. You would have had to kill them with your bare hands."

"Jezeus, Donn, why the fuck are you telling me this?"

Donn sighed. "Sorry. Let's drop it."

The two sat in silence for a few moments, each one waiting for the other to speak. Presently, Margulies said gently, "Hey, did we ever figure out what Kearney meant? And how she had the access she did?"

"Meant by what?"

"That code she used. 'Mount' something."

"Mount Moriah."

"Yeah. What does it mean?"

"I don't know."

"You haven't looked it up?"

Donn shook his head. "With everything that's been going on, getting medical attention, securing the ship, I haven't had time." Donn turned to the computer screen. "Agnes, access the encyclopedia database. What is Mount Moriah?"

Agnes answered and displayed a map of Old Jerusalem. "Mount Moriah is an elongated ridge, maximum elevation seven hundred and seventy-seven meters at this location in Jerusalem." An arrow appeared on the map, pointing at an unremarkable ridgeline.

"That's all? There has to be more," Donn murmured. "Why would she use this as a code word? Agnes, you said Jerusalem. Give me any religious allusions to Mount Moriah."

"Mount Moriah is the biblical site of the sacrifice of Abraham. In the Muslim faith, the site of the sacrifice is Mount Marwah, though—"

"Stop," Donn said. He looked at Margulies. "She said she needed to kill to save lives. I guess that is what she meant."

"Same thing the captain said," Margulies said quietly.

"And Kearney was wrong, too," Donn said. "She shouldn't have done that. Jezeus, Linna, I fucking killed her because of it! So I guess I killed her to save you. When does it end? When do we stop killing in the name of saving lives?"

"Donn, come on. At that moment, there was no negotiation. She was shooting at us. You can't be absolute about this — about never killing anyone under any circumstances. You—"

"I can and I will. That might even be the first law of the colony. No one kills anyone else, for any reason, ever."

"You can't just decide laws by personal fiat!"

Donn shot up from his chair, knocking it over behind him. "Stop telling me what I can't do!"

Margulies regarded him for a moment, then rose painfully herself. "I can see you're not in a mood to talk about this. Let me know when and where this panel of yours is going to convene." She cycled open the hatch and said as she stepped through, "But if you're going to try and be a dictator in this new colony, you damn well better expect resistance from me."

Margulies left his room.

———— «»————

"Thank you all for coming," Donn said, looking at the assembled faces. They'd rearranged the tables in the Gem Diner into a loose oval, Donn seated at one end in a subtle indication of the "head" of the group. He stared at Margulies, who took up a position directly opposite him.

Hunsaker sat on his right, and as he looked at the people who filled the seats, he was proud that fully half of them were from K-Deck. He'd come to think of them as his own personal council.

Even as he thought that, he realized how wrong it was. He had to open his thinking to include everyone; no one could be special to him. Everyone would count, but none too much.

He cleared his throat. "As you all know, we need to craft a new mission profile to match our current conditions. So let me lay out what those conditions are." He leaned forward and placed his hands, palms down, on the table. "We have two hundred and forty-eight thousand, eight hundred and twenty-three preborns due for birthing starting in fifteen days. We will be out of Alcubierre drive and back into normal space in fourteen days. Planetfall is scheduled twenty-one days from now. Progress is continuing on hibernation medical checks. So far, I believe we have checked over two thousand of them. None are alive. We will continue to check, but I'm going to proceed as if all hibernators are dead."

He saw the effect his words had. Everyone at the tables knew the facts, but to hear them laid out, one after another, had an impact. People shifted uncomfortably in their seats, looked around at one another, made little noises. Only Margulies remained still, her eyes focused intently on Donn.

"Look, everyone," Donn said, his formal demeanor broken by Margulies' icy stare, "we've got a monumental job in front of us. We have to come up with a plan to care for the quarter-million babies while also building and maintaining a viable colony on Tau Ceti Three. And it's just us — one hundred ninety-two caretakers and crew. In fact, let's stop with that distinction. One hundred ninety-two colonists."

He spoke to the air, "OSIRIS, display colonial hold inventory." The table lit up, projected from above, with a comprehensive list of all the equipment and supplies waiting for them in the hold. "Here's what we have to work with, not counting the ship itself, of course. What I want to do now is have all of you study this list and begin brainstorming. Look at it, see what strikes you, and speak up. No idea is a bad one."

He looked across the table and saw Margulies' head snap up sharply.

He added, "Let me back up. One idea is off the table. We are caring for all the children. We're not sacrificing any of them. Is that clear?"

There were signs of assent, some demonstrative, some grudging, but Donn was only interested in one. He locked eyes with Margulies, who nodded gravely and turned her gaze to the list of equipment.

No one spoke for a long time. Everyone studied the list, then continued to pretend to. Donn resisted the impulse to speak and prod them. He was waiting to see who took initiative so he could assign persons to head up areas of the mission planning.

Hunsaker finally commented. "We should make maximum use out of the pseudowomb pods, even after birth.

That will help cut down on how much we have to directly care for the children."

Fletcher added, "But we still need to handle them personally." She looked at Donn. "Children need to be held and cared for by people, not machines."

"The first thing to do, regardless, is setting up the pressure domes," Margulies said. "Nothing else will matter if we can't breathe down there. That part of the mission profile can't change. It's still the top priority."

"Then water reclamation," added Vivana, a member of the engineering corps. "If it's harder to harvest water from the planet than we theorize, we need to get the reclamation stations working immediately."

The discussion grew robust, and Donn mostly sat back and listened, only speaking to keep the group on topic and productive, or when a discouraging comment threatened to disrupt the process. Hours later, when the discussion turned into an argument then threatened to become nasty and personal, Donn intervened.

"Stop. We've been going for four hours now, and we have some good ideas. But right now, I'm calling a thirty-minute break. Take care of personal business, get something to eat or drink, and come back here at," he checked the time, "thirteen hundred and ten."

People stood up, some wandered out of the diner, others moved to the food and drink dispensers. Donn himself got up and left the room.

He was heading for his bay. To his swimmers.

Once inside, he closed the hatch and felt immediately relaxed. He was home, with his preborns, and everything made sense again. The softly-lit bay, the blue running lights, the quiet.

He walked slowly towards the racks, smiling absently.

"Hi, everyone. I'm sorry I've been gone. A lot has happened." He slid his fingers along the curving glass canopies as he strolled deeper into the bay. "We're almost to your new home. You guys are coming out soon, and I am so excited to meet you all." He swallowed and continued. "It's gonna be hard, I know. Right now, you're all safe and warm, just floating along, not a care in the universe. I'm sorry for what's about to happen."

"You're gonna be scared, and sometimes lonely, and maybe it will be days before you see me." He stopped at Rack Seven, near the midpoint of the bay. His voice grew louder, as if it mattered that all the preborns could hear him. "But I'm gonna keep caring for all of you, and all your little brothers and sisters in the other bays. You're not forgotten. You're all loved."

"I like that." Margulies's voice echoed from the control suite.

Donn turned and saw her standing near the entrance hatch.

"What do you want, Linna?" he growled.

"I wasn't trying to eavesdrop," she said, coming towards him. "But there are some things to discuss. I didn't want to do it in the diner, since it might be off the point."

"What is it?"

"Kearney."

"What about her?" Donn turned away and placed his hands delicately on Pod 1-Alpha-7 — Dandelion.

"There are still a lot of questions about her. We need to answer them."

"Why? What does it matter now?"

Margulies continued to walk towards him. "Because it might impact the mission. I'm not looking for vengeance," Margulies said, the fist of her left hand, arm still in a sling, clenching. "But her access to OSIRIS, the fact that she gave you delayed access to her codes…"

Donn shrugged. "I don't know." He turned from 1-Alpha-7 and faced Margulies. "I thought you were supposed to be the practical one, and I was the dreamer? We've got more pressing matters in front of us."

"Not if OSIRIS is malfunctioning, we don't," Margulies said.

"What?"

"The hibernation section might not be his only fuck-up. What if he's unable to bring us out of A-drive? Or can't do planetary insertion? We're all just trusting his ability to land this thing safely on the surface, and we really have no idea if he is working."

"Yeah? And what do you want me to do about that? I'm not a pilot, neither are you."

"Vincent and his crew were," Margulies said.

"What are you saying? Kearney killed them to make sure the pilots were dead?"

"No, I'm not. All I'm saying is we still have unanswered questions. And some of the answers might affect the mission."

Donn paused, then said, "Damn you, why are you doing this? I've barely been able to keep those thoughts out of my head. Why did Kearney do what she did? Why did Thom? How did OSIRIS not catch that the hibernators were dead so long ago? Why does he keep reporting that they are still alive?"

He had been staring at Margulies while he spoke, but now his eyes unfocused and he looked at nothing. "Why did the Starfish stop? What does the painting mean?"

Margulies scowled. "What?"

Donn came back. "Nothing. But the point is, I've been keeping those questions away. Because we've got work to do. Now you bring them back up."

Margulies's stone face softened. "Sorry. I didn't know." She sighed. "I guess you're right. I said pressure domes were our number one priority, and I still believe that. These other questions will have to wait. Hell, if OSIRIS can't land this thing and instead crashes us into the sun, we won't have to worry about water reclamation, will we?" A hint of a grin played on her lips.

Despite everything, Donn felt himself smiling. "Oh, that helps."

"Sorry. Probably bad taste."

Donn shrugged. "Gallows humor. It's okay. I don't know when any of us will really laugh again."

Margulies stepped even closer. "We will, Donn. And you know as well as I do when that'll be?"

"When?"

Margulies looked at Pod 1-Alpha-7. "When this little one does for the first time."

Chapter Twenty-Three

The mission discussion continued, and the players in the room made themselves more and more evident. Margulies continued to be practical, though Donn could hear in her words and her tone how much she had come around. She wanted this to succeed. She wanted to save every child.

So did they all. There were occasional bouts of frustration with the challenge, and angry demonstrations when a plan was shown to be unworkable, but the overall attitude of everyone present was positive. Donn felt himself being caught up in the excitement when someone had an idea that got the table energized, such as when Fletcher and Hunsaker worked in tandem to develop a brilliant arrangement to care for the babies while colonists were working on infrastructure, rather than section off child care and colonial construction. "Bring Your Baby to Work Year" was the whimsical title of their program, and it galvanized the group. It was as if that single suggestion made anything else seem possible.

As the days went on, Donn divided the group up into departments, each with its own coordinator who would report to him. He chose Margulies to be his deputy, despite her desire to head up the Infrastructure department. He told her, privately, that he needed her to help him mesh all the ideas together.

The mission was taking shape. It was true that it hinged on several untested and somewhat shaky assumptions — that there would be no further malfunctions in OSIRIS; that there would be no significant birthing problems; that currently injured colonists would be able to work as efficiently as able-bodied ones; that there would be no unpleasant surprises on Tau Ceti III.

Most of all, the unspoken assumption that they all shared was that there would be no counterinsurgency. That no remnants of Vincent's viewpoint remained on board, and no colonist would work against the mission.

Donn often took a mental step back from the details of mission planning to regard the whole endeavor: something he had not done when he had merely been a caretaker. He still spent time in his bay, talking to his preborns, checking on their progress. OSIRIS still dutifully monitored their progress, and Donn still made tiny changes to their environments despite the fact that it no longer mattered. They were due to be birthed in a few days, and their development was as close to complete as was possible. Infinitesimal changes in their potassium intake or blood oxygen levels would have no effect on their futures at this point. But Donn did it anyway. It was what he knew how to do.

He was well aware that the chances were high that many of the children would die on Tau Ceti III. Something would happen. It was nearly inevitable. An accident, a disease, malnutrition — the odds stacked against the colony were enormous. But he only knew those facts with his mind. His heart knew differently.

He had asked his coordinators to present him with a preliminary draft of their section of the mission profile the night before OSIRIS was supposed to open his full access under Schedule D, whatever that was. He and Margulies had spent long hours poring over the new profile, noting weaknesses and discrepancies, making notes in OSIRIS.

Overall, the drafts were solid. In several spots, however, across all departments, there were questions only answerable either once the ship landed or when Donn was granted full access to OSIRIS. He and Margulies compiled the list of questions and waited in his room.

"OSIRIS, how long until Schedule D implementation?" Donn asked for the tenth time.

"Four minutes, sixteen seconds."

Margulies wrung her hands. "Still weird to me that OSIRIS gives you that data. Or even acknowledges there is such a thing."

Donn shrugged. "He's got weird gaps in his security. Probably because Kearney was fucking with him for so long."

"So long?"

"Yeah. She said that sleeping with Vincent was how she got a lot of her stuff, but I don't—"

"What?" Margulies gasped.

"Oh, I never told you that? Yeah," Donn said grimly. "She was sleeping with Vincent. In exchange for little favors. That's how she got the access to OSIRIS, and all the little contraband stuff she always had."

Margulies said, "She was sleeping with him?"

"Yeah."

"I never knew that. Jezeus, and I thought I knew everything. Freeman and Uplander, the floating crap game on C-Deck, the still in engineering, all that shit. Never even had a hint of Kearney and Vincent. Never even saw her in trip-C, for that matter." She looked at Donn. "I knew about you and her, and about her and Collins. Long ago."

Donn snorted. "You never said anything."

"Wasn't my business," Margulies said. "If you were okay with it, then what—"

"I wasn't okay with it."

"Sorry."

"How long now, OSIRIS?" Donn barked.

"Three minutes, twenty-one seconds."

Donn nodded, cleared his throat. "I still think the first thing is to unseal the hold. A lot of the drafts ask about the specifics of pieces of equipment outside their specs."

"I agree. If we're gonna ask stuff to do things it was never intended to, we need to take a look for ourselves. Who're you gonna take with you to inspect?"

"Yune wanted to go, so him. And Quevado from engineering."

"I'd like to tag along."

"Sure." Donn grunted. "Probably should call them," he said, turning towards the camera. "Agnes, intercraft broadcast."

"You're on,"

"Paul Yune and Louis Quevado, please report to the colonial hold personnel entrance. I'll be joining you there shortly. End broadcast, Agnes."

"Ended."

He sat in silence with Margulies for the remaining minutes, until OSIRIS' voice sounded in the room.

"Schedule D implemented. Deep access granted to Caretaker Donn Cardenio pending proper code phrase."

Donn took a breath and said with unnaturally clear pronunciation, "Mount Moriah."

"Access granted."

"Unseal the colonial hold personnel hatch and pressurize the hold for entry," Donn said, and held his breath.

"Hatch unsealed. Pressurization commencing. Entry possible in nine minutes."

He glanced at Margulies with a grim smile. "Sort of anticlimactic. Let's go." He rose from his chair and exited his room.

《》

There was a knot of people waiting for both him and Margulies at the hatch. Yune and Quevado were there, but a dozen or more other caretakers had assembled as well. Donn recognized several of them as members of the infrastructure team. No doubt they wanted to inspect something vital to their plan inside the hold.

Donn pressed his palm to the lock, but the lights remained red, though the pressure gauge read normal. "OSIRIS, open up the hold," he said.

"Give me the authorization code again, please, Donn."

Donn frowned, but said, "Mount Moriah." He glanced at a worried Margulies.

The lights changed to green and the hatch cycled open with a soft hiss. The interior of the hold was dark.

"OSIRIS, turn the lights on." As he spoke into the gloom of the hold, his voice echoed eerily back to him.

"There aren't any, Donn," came the answer.

Donn's frown deepened. "What?"

Yune spoke up. "Some of us have flashlights. We thought we would need them to inspect stuff."

The flashlights were passed forward to Donn and Margulies. He stepped through the hatchway and swung the beam around the hold.

The hold was vast, roughly a cubic hectare, but the blue-white shafts of light from his and Margulies' flashlights illuminated the chamber well enough. He stood a few feet inside the hatchway, staring.

It was empty.

Next to him, Margulies started to chuckle.

"What's so funny?" Donn growled.

Margulies didn't answer, but dropped her flashlight and leaned against the inner bulkhead, her chuckling turning into hysterical laughter.

Yune, Quevado, and the others began to file into the hold, some gasping in astonishment, others stammering half-articulated questions.

Donn took a few more steps, swinging the beam back and forth, as if equipment would suddenly appear from the shadows. The deck was clean and showed no signs that anything had ever been here. There were no partitions or smaller chambers within the hold, no restraint straps or webbing, no stenciled writing on the bulkheads. It was a featureless empty room with no apparent function.

"Everyone, shut up," he half-shouted at the others. "OSIRIS, the hold is empty. Explain."

"Colonial hold inventory is as follows: six heavy-duty fabrication plants, model numbers FB-nine-nine-one, FB-nine-nine-two, FB—"

"Dammit, OSIRIS! I'm standing in the hold, and there's nothing here! Where is all the equipment?"

"Colonization equipment is stored in the hold. I can give you a schematic of the layout so you can find—"

"There's nothing here!" Donn shouted. He calmed himself and added. "Stop. Stop. OSIRIS, give me the real colonial hold inventory. Code Mount Moriah."

OSIRIS said, "There is nothing in the colonial hold."

Donn turned to Margulies, who by now had slumped down to a sitting position, her legs splayed out in front of her. Her shoulders were shaking with laughter, tears streaming down her face. Yune was nothing but an unreadable wax-moon face. Quevado was methodically pacing the room. The other caretakers had diffused in all directions, some of them inside the empty hold, others back outside to the central shaft.

Donn knew that when those who had left reported back, there would be shipwide panic. The delicate stability he had managed to forge in the past few days would vanish. And he knew he could not bring them back to sanity. This discovery would end them.

He felt hopelessness seize him, momentarily paralyzing his voice. What was the point? Why bother to round up the departing caretakers, or broadcast a message of optimism and solidarity in the face of this cruel revelation? There were no words he could utter, no policy he could design, that could possibly rival this. It was over. Collins had been more right than he knew.

The faces of his preborn charges swam before his imagination, and their individual names and peculiarities came to him in a flash. They were due to taste life in a few days, and what could he offer them? What would he say to them?

Without logic or sense, the images of his children-to-be fortified him. He felt his legs carrying him to the hatch, and as if in a dream, he shouted through the central shaft, recalling the wayward caretakers. They obeyed, floating back to him and reentering the hold at his command.

One inside, he addressed them. He could see himself from the outside, as if he were a theatergoer in some grotesque drama.

"Keep this quiet until I—"

"Quiet?" the once-meek Yune shouted. "Why?"

"Because this will panic people. We can't have that."

Margulies sniggered, amid her now-subdued laughter, "Goddess forbid we panic, Donn. Might jeopardize the mission."

"You're not helping. We still have the preborns to think of."

"Preborns? We're all dead, Donn. We don't have the life sustaining supplies aboard for more than two months. And when that runs out, what do you propose we do? Maybe we should set up a task force on breathing vacuum." She dissolved into laughter again.

"Shut up!" he shouted. Caretakers began arguing with each other or with no one in particular, screaming obscenities to the air. They began asking OSIRIS for answers, but all he told them was all was well, that the hold was full, and planetfall was scheduled for six and a half days hence.

Donn could not keep them under control. He watched helplessly as the caretakers shouted at one another, at OSIRIS, at him; as they pounded the bulkheads and deck; as they searched wildly about the hold for nonexistent doors or panels; and as they left the hold again for the central shaft.

He blinked, and found himself back on K-Deck, walking slowly down the corridor to his bay. He hadn't remembered leaving the hold. Where was Margulies? Where was Fletcher? Hunsaker? He could hear shouting echoing through the curving corridor.

He passed through the K-Deck corridors, noting that the wall graffiti was bloodstained with handprints. He regarded the red smears with mild interest, and continued to his bay.

He sealed the hatchway behind him, and the faint sounds of chaos cut off. He was once again safe in the pseudowomb bay.

The familiar dimness, the comforting, gentle curves of the pseudowomb canopies, the green lights smiling back at him on each pod. He spoke quiet words of encouragement to the swimmers, calling them by name, remembering their individual biochemical trials.

The therapy worked. He stopped midway in the bay and took a breath. He walked back to his control suite and sat. "OSIRIS, Give me intercraft broadcast."

"Be advised I read seventeen monitor stations damaged. Deck-A, station A-nine, A-ten. Deck-B—"

"Stop. Doesn't matter. Commence broadcast."

"Broadcast commencing."

Donn spoke to the camera. "This is Donn." He stopped, unsure what to say next. He leaned forward and said with unartful passion, "Everyone, please, stop. Try to calm down. We're not going to solve anything by going mad. Look, I don't know why the hold is empty. Maybe there's a supply ship following us that we couldn't see while in Alcubierre drive," he said, the theory coming to him as he spoke. "Maybe it's ahead of us in parking orbit. The point is, we don't know what's happening. But giving in to panic won't help. I urge all of you to try and calm down. We'll figure this out and do what we can to—" he swallowed. "I know you're scared. I know this doesn't seem to make any sense. But running around and smashing stuff, or hurting yourself or others won't help. I can't promise anything. I wish I could. Just let me try and figure this out. In the meantime, please, just … sit down and don't do anything. Please." He told OSIRIS to end the broadcast.

Almost as soon as he ended his speech, Margulies entered, looking red-eyed and sheepish. "Donn," she said, her voice almost normal.

He just looked at her.

"Yeah. Sorry for what I was like back in the hold," she grumbled. "Won't happen again. I hope."

He shrugged. "It's fine."

"What the hell's happening?"

"I don't know," he said. "OSIRIS, Code Mount Moriah."

"Accepted."

"Where are all the colonial supplies? Is there a supply ship following us, or ahead of us?"

"There are no colonial supplies," OSIRIS said simply.

"There is nothing? Nothing in the hold, nothing coming behind us, or sent ahead?"

"That's right, Donn."

Margulies said, "That doesn't make any Goddess damn sense."

Donn silenced her with his hand. His mind was already reeling, and her outbursts didn't help. He couldn't formulate a thought. He knew he should ask about procedure and the future of the mission, but the words wouldn't come.

"Give me the full personnel file on Caretaker Kearney." He looked at Margulies, surprised at his own request.

The monitors stopped showing the pod data on his swimmers and displayed a dossier on Kearney, her portrait appearing in the upper left corner of the screen. She was almost unrecognizable with her black instead of vermillion hair, her expression showing no signs of her puckish spirit he had come to love. Instead, a steely-eyed and humorless woman looked back at him.

He read the information on the screen in wild, disorganized darting of eyes, catching bits of sentences and statistics. "…One Earth Government Special Agent…" "…mission success paramount…" "…authorized for deep access of onboard computer OSIRIS…" "…any and all methods of coercion..." "...small arms and close combat training..." "...psychological warfare specialist..."

Margulies had come up next to him and was looking at the screens as well. She murmured, "Jezeus, Donn, who was she?"

"A spy, I guess," Donn said evenly.

"For who?"

"No idea. But she was in control all along. Vincent certainly wasn't."

"Control for what? What was she trying to do?"

"I don't know," Donn sighed.

"So everything that's happened has been her doing?"

Donn didn't answer immediately. He stared at the words on the screen, seeing them, understanding them, but not comprehending them. He had slept with — and loved — a stranger.

"Donn?" Margulies prompted.

"No, not everything." Despite the chaos around him which threatened his sanity, a pattern was at long last revealing itself to him. "OSIRIS, give me a dossier on Caretaker Thom Agee."

The screen changed to show Thom's smiling face. The data on him was far more conventional: he was a caretaker, he was to be assigned to computer design and maintenance on Tau Ceti III, and his supplementary skills were listed. Donn pointed to one line.

"Computer metaprogramming and artificial intelligence design."

Margulies nodded. "Yeah. So?"

"OSIRIS, show me what Thom discovered when he—" Donn said, then stopped suddenly.

"I'm sorry, Donn, repeat your command, please?"

Margulies said, "What's the matter? Why'd you stop?"

"It drove him mad," Donn said, his voice shaking. "He found something out, and it drove him to murder the babies."

"It had to be all this," Margulies said. "What else could it have been?"

"Kearney? The dead hibernators? The empty hold?"

"Of course. Isn't that enough? It nearly got me."

Donn nodded slightly, then unzipped his thigh pouch. He withdrew the flechette pistol and extended it, butt first, to Margulies.

"What?" she said, looking at it.

"I'm gonna look at what he saw. Alone." He shook the gun. "Take it."

"Why?"

"In case it does to me what it did to him. Use it on me."

"You want me to shoot you?"

"No, I don't," Donn said. "But if I see what he saw and start to go mad, I don't want to be able to hurt the kids. So take it, and use it to save them."

"By shooting you." She shook her head. "That's insane."

"This whole thing is insane!" Donn shouted. "Now take the damn gun!"

Margulies took the pistol. "I'm not shooting you, Donn."

"I hope not," he said. He took a pair of earphones from a panel on the control board and said, "OSIRIS, change output to my headphones."

OSIRIS's voice sounded in his ears. "I'm here, Donn."

"Audio only. Give me what Thom discovered when he broke into your system. Code Mount Moriah."

——— «» ———

Fifteen minutes later, Donn took his headphones off and looked at Margulies. She was still holding the pistol, but was not covering him with it. "What? What did you find?"

Donn did not answer her. "OSIRIS, do a lidar sensor sweep. Report all contacts."

Margulies looked puzzled. "A sensor sweep? Of space?"

OSIRIS said calmly. "One contact. Range four hundred thousand, ninety-six point nine eight kilometers."

Margulies gasped. "What? Donn, what's going on? What contact is that?"

Donn whispered. "Starfish."

Chapter Twenty-Four

The ship was small. The five tapering projections from the round central hub shone with a macabre light on the viewscreen. Donn fought back terror, as he had those years ago in low Earth orbit, as the starfish-shaped ships had appeared and disappeared, firing and vanishing before he could fully register what he had seen.

This was the first time he had seen a Starfish ship just hang in space.

He hadn't gone to broadcast what he knew, but had instead gone to trip-C and sealed it shut behind him. Margulies had dogged his steps to the central shaft, and had floated after him, even threatening to use the flechette gun on him if he didn't tell her what was happening.

He had only one hope. It was beyond desperate. He didn't know how Margulies would react to what he had discovered, and he felt his own mind teetering on the edge of madness. His mind moved carefully, as a man balancing on a tightrope. A single thought out of place would send him falling to the gorge of insanity below him.

He was alone in trip-C.

"OSIRIS, contact the Starfish vessel." He had no idea if this was possible. But OSIRIS' answer did not shock him.

"Contact established."

He stared at the speaker grille. Would they even understand him? Earth had managed to communicate with them. Could he?

"OSIRIS, do you have a translation program or something? To their language?"

"Not necessary. The Tau Cetians can understand you and vice versa."

It had been one of the many mysteries surrounding the invading aliens: their home planet. Along with their motivations, social structure, even their appearance. Theories abounded, but aside from the pinwheeling design of their ships, no clue as to their anatomy had been found. But now Donn knew that the mystery of their home system had been known to certain people on Earth.

Despite the knowledge of the alien home star, he could not think of them as Tau Cetians. They had been "Starfish" to him, and so they remained.

If they were from Tau Ceti, then perhaps...

He felt a new plan grow in him. It fed not on logic or facts, but on the sweet taste of hope. He had read OSIRIS' true commands, and he knew the true nature of the mission. But even with that awful knowledge, hope remained alive.

"This is Caretaker Donn Cardenio. I'm ... in command of the Earth ship *Chiron*. I need to speak to whoever is in command of your ship."

There was a maddening interval, and Donn was about to repeat his transmission when an electronic voice said, "Irrelevant. We will board."

Donn said, "I'm ... I think we're here to ... join with you. Make a new society comprised of humans and Tau Cetians."

The electronic voice said, "Incorrect. Do you have the cargo?"

Donn swallowed. "I don't know what you mean," he lied.

"Twelve to the fifth power human embryos."

"Yes, but—"

"We will take the cargo."

"I'm not willing to give up the ... cargo."

"Irrelevant."

"No, it is relevant. I need to renegotiate the treaty."

"There will be no renegotiation. We will take the tribute as agreed to."

Donn pounded the control console. "Like hell you will! You try and come here to take them, and you'll die! We are armed and will fight you."

"You will lose. We will take the tribute."

"If you attempt to board this vessel, I will destroy it," Donn said. "I'll blow this whole thing up, and take as many of you with me as I can!"

"If you do not obey the treaty we will begin the conflict again."

Donn opened his mouth, but no words came out. He knew that was coming, but it had nevertheless stunned him. He had discovered the treaty buried deep in OSIRIS, just as Thom had so many days ago. He knew what had happened — the storing of the already-dead hibernators to maintain the illusion of a colonization mission, the empty hold which served the same purpose, and Kearney's assignment.

She'd been Earth's ace-in-the-hole, assigned to the mission to soothe any doubts on board, handle any unforeseen problems that came up, and deflect personnel who might guess the truth. She'd done her job well. There had been two more like her, an engineer and another caretaker. Thom's meddling had been the only glitch: for whatever reason, none of them had managed to distract him.

Donn also knew what the preborns were for. Fertilized off-planet, raised by computer with minimal human help — technology wasn't quite safe enough to make the mission fully automated. It had been necessary to staff the mission with almost two hundred people to ensure the delivery of the preborns. Preborns who were not legally citizens of any Earth nation, or of the One Earth government. Born in space, raised by OSIRIS, delivered by caretakers. No one's children.

And now, the mission was almost complete. All he had to do was step aside and allow the enigmatic Tau Cetians to come aboard and take the quarter million human babies as tribute, as had been agreed to by One Earth.

That's how the war had ended.

Some had to die so others would live.

"What is going to happen to them?" Donn said in a whisper. There was no answer from the electronic voice. "If I give them to you, what will you do to them?"

"Irrelevant. You will surrender the tribute."

"Not unless I know what you are going to do. These are human babies. I can't just give them to you."

OSIRIS broke in. "Donn, I'm reading something I can't identify on multiple internal ship cameras."

"Show me," Donn said.

The trip-C monitors lit up, each screen showing a different bay on the ship. Strange, starfish-shaped machines had appeared in pseudowomb bays. As he watched, he saw caretakers who had been tending to the birthing process react in alarm to the machines.

The Starfish started taking the babies.

The machines extended snakelike tentacles and seized the children, some out of pseudowomb pods, some out of the hands of caretakers who resisted and were casually killed by the machines. He saw caretakers who had a few hours ago been planning a new life sliced open to fall bleeding to the decks.

"Stop! For the love of God, stop!" Donn shouted into the microphone. He watched impotently as the Starfish machines disappeared with children, only to reappear and continue the process.

Calls flooded in from all over the ship, shouting, pleading for Donn to do something to stop the abductions. He watched, tears flowing down his face, whimpering to the aliens to stop.

He saw caretakers try to assault the machines, using multitools or bare hands, only to be efficiently cut down by scything blades. The decks were red with blood and pseudoamniotic fluid.

"OSIRIS, I want you to take the fusion reactor and ... how can I detonate it?"

"You can't, Donn."

"I want to ... to destroy the ship. How can I do that?"

"That's impossible."

"They're taking the children ... I can't let them ... I need to help the children. Let me end this painlessly. Tell me how to destroy the ship."

"I'm not allowed to, Donn. I have my orders."

"Code Mount Moriah," he said, his voice trembling.

"That code won't work."

"What?"

"It was anticipated that at this moment, Agent Kearney, Agent Bamrah, or Agent Novak would have a moment of weakness. I am therefore in control now. This mission will be completed."

Donn just watched. Starfish took babies and killed anyone they found resisting. A few caretakers stayed inside their quarters, listening to the carnage taking place, but Donn felt a strange sense of pride that many were rushing to defend the babies, even as they saw their comrades murdered casually and efficiently by the machines.

The machines were moving methodically through the decks, starting with A-Deck and moving aft. It was a matter of minutes before they had reached J-Deck. Donn opened the hatch to the central shaft and saw several caretakers floating there. They converged on him, tearing at his clothes, shouting, crying.

He slapped and punched them away, making for K-Deck. Some followed, most floated into the inner hull, their eyes glassy and unfocused.

Donn found the K-Deck entrance. He hurried to bay K-8, past screaming caretakers, past bloody smears on the wall, past smashed communications monitors, past the carefree graffiti near Thom's bay of dancing, smiling dragons.

He entered K-8 and closed the hatch.

A Starfish machine was already in the bay.

"I'm the caretaker of these babies," Donn said, "You're not taking them!"

He rushed at the Starfish machine, the walls of the bay turning transparent in his imagination, the starfield visible beyond. He was in his LEO fighter, he was on board *Chiron*. He was here, and he was there.

As the blades cut him open, and he felt his life swiftly emptying onto the deck, he felt no pain.

He saw only *Guernica*.

And he understood.

If you enjoyed this read

Please leave a review on Amazon, Facebook, Good Reads or Instagram.

It takes less than five minutes and it really does make a difference.

If you're not sure how to leave a review on Amazon:

1. *Go to amazon.com.*

2. *Type in Silent Manifest by Scan O'Brien and when you see it, click on it.*

3. *Scroll down to Customer Reviews. Nearby you'll see a box labeled Write a Review. Click it.*

4. *Now, if you've never written a review before on Amazon, they might ask you to create a name for yourself.*

5. *Reviews can be as simple as, "Loved the book! Can't wait for the Next!" (Please don't give the story away.)*

And that's it!

Brian Hades, publisher

About the Author

Sean O'Brien is an educator and writer from Southern California. He is married and has two children along with an ever-growing number of animals. He was named Educator of the Year by the California League of High Schools and has been a head varsity football coach, television broadcaster, and Gilbert and Sullivan singer (though not a good one). He's the author of A Muse of Fire, Wondrous Strange, Vale of Stars. and Beltrunner.

Need something new to read?

If you liked Silent Manifest, you should also consider these other EDGE-Lite titles…

Beltrunner

by Sean O'Brien

From The Best Traditions of Hard Science-Fiction.

Collier South has been belt mining his entire life. He's watched the small independents around him get swallowed up by the bigger corporations, forced out of their livelihoods by corporate creep. But he isn't about to settle or sellout. Broke and desperate, Collier has one last chance to land a strike. What he discovers instead has the power to change not only his life but the fate of the entire system. That is if he can keep his discovery out of corporate hands and survive the ensuing manhunt

About Sean O'Brien

Sean O'Brien is an educator and writer from Southern California. He was named Educator of the Year by the California League of High Schools and has been a head varsity football coach, television broadcaster, and Gilbert and Sullivan singer (though not a good one). He's the author of A Muse of Fire, Wondrous Strange, and Vale of Stars.

Milky Way Repo
Book One in The Milky Way Series

by Michael Prelee

Blue Collar Science Fiction...

Running a starship repo company isn't easy or cheap. It's just an endless string of fuel costs, legal red tape, shady associates and uncooperative dock officials from one end of the galaxy to the other. How will it all turn out? You never know. Especially when Nathan and his Starship repo agents are up against a cult and the mob.

About Michael Prelee

Michael Prelee is a writer living near Youngstown, Ohio. A graduate of Youngstown State University, he lives with his wonderful wife and two great children.

"Five star: Just finished reading this book and really enjoyed it. The book was entertaining, fast moving, and had good character understanding and development." - J. Fowler

"This is a wild ride. Fun and enjoyable." - Jenny, amazon.com

Bad Rock Beat Down
(Book Two in The Milky Way Repo Series)

by Michael Prelee

A Sci-Fi Crime in a Dirty, Corrupt Universe.

The starship repossession agents of Milky Way Repo are sent to the desolate settlement of Bad Rock to retrieve a vessel. Once there, they become entangled with a notorious thug running a smuggling operation for the Syndicate. Struggling to do the right thing while trying to complete their job, things go seriously awry with deadly consequences.

"The Milky Way Repo universe is populated by hard working men and women who are trying to make their way in a tough world. They are scrappy business owners who find themselves beset by criminals in the course of doing their jobs. How they deal with this adversity makes for entertaining stories." — Michael Prelee, author

About Michael Prelee

Michael Prelee is a graduate of Youngstown State University. He resides in Northeast Ohio with his family where he enjoys writing.

The Bathwater Conspiracy

by Janet Kellough

Nothing About This Case Makes Sense.

Brutal murders don't happen often in in the future and City

Detective Mac MacHenry is puzzled when the Department of National Security (Darmes) interferes with the investigation and autopsy of a dead girl.

It's not MacHenry's jurisdiction, but the outraged Medical Examiner asks her to dig deeper. Mac's paranoia grows as she follows a trail into the crumbling ruins of a part of town known as the Decayed Zone where she discovers a mysterious medical facility, a group of fundamentalist outcasts, and a secret that could change the world.

About Janet Kellough

Janet Kellough is a storyteller and author of The Thaddeus Lewis Mystery Series; two contemporary novels The Palace of the Moon and The Pear Shaped Woman; and the semi-non-fictional Legendary Guide to Prince Edward County.

**For more EDGE titles and information
about upcoming speculative fiction
please visit us at:**

www.edgewebsite.com

Don't forget to sign-up for our Special Offers

9 781770 531925